SANDRA'S NEW SCHOOL

'Don't women – don't you and I – know how to do each other far better than men?' said Margaret coyly. 'When you have dozens of would-be schoolgirls cooped up together, well, diddling is almost part of the curriculum, although there are fearful punishments for it. The aim is to make us real ladies: that is, seemly and obedient.'

'Plenty of spanking for disobedience, then?' said Sandra drily, but failing to hide her eagerness.

'There is much more than spanking,' said Margaret. 'But if you are a good girl, then you need never even bare your bum for spanking, let alone –'

'Let alone what?' Sandra insisted, her eyes bright.

'You'll find out.'

SANDRA'S NEW SCHOOL

Yolanda Celbridge

This book is a work of fiction.
In real life, make sure you practise safe sex.

First published in 1999 by
Nexus
Thames Wharf Studios
Rainville Road
London W6 9HA

Typeset by TW Typesetting, Plymouth, Devon

Printed and bound by
Cox & Wyman Ltd, Reading, Berks

ISBN 0 352 33454 1

Contents

1

Exhibitionist

All was peaceful. A single jet plane lazily traced its trail
across blue sky under a sun that glowed above white
cliffs and the sparkling calm of the Channel. It was one
of those afternoons when the last September heat of an
Indian summer seems a particularly glorious and
English property. Along the clifftops snaked a path
lined with hedgerows; above that, long, cropped lawns,
garlanded with rosebeds and rockeries, led to comfortable villas.

On one of the lawns, right down near the clifftop, a
woman lay motionless on the grass with a towel beneath
her. She was nude. Seen from above, her bare body was
a sliver of gold against her bright green lawn. A
butterfly weaved its jittery arc across the grass and
landed on her left buttock, as though summoned by its
twin, a tiny red and blue tattoo which nestled at the
lower part of the fleshy globe near the cleft.

The butterfly landed on the smooth, firm skin,
brushing the thick tuft of blonde hair which peeped
from the crack of thigh and bottom. The woman lay still
for a moment, smiling as the butterfly tickled her, then
with a lazy hand shooed it away, slapping her bare skin
with her palm as though warning the butterfly not to
come back. The buttock quivered slightly, and as
though to be fair, she slapped her right buttock too, but
a little harder.

1

This operation was watched by her companion, who was seated on her own towel, but wearing a light-pink sundress, pulled up to reveal pale white thighs, and shaded by a parasol. Gulls wheeled above the two women in the still blue sky.

Sandra Shanks, the nude, blonde woman whose repose had been disturbed by the butterfly, sighed happily and smoothed her thick mane back off her shoulders to ensure sunlight would caress every inch of her naked body; she spread her thighs so that the rays might penetrate each crevice, and contentedly resumed her basking. Her companion, Margaret Betts, looked enviously at Sandra's golden tan.

Her skin was alabaster white and though both women shared the same ripe figures, and the same long legs and shapely slender feet, Margaret was timid in the sunshine and satisfied for it to dapple her unstockinged legs, as she sipped her iced Pimm's. Sandra looked idly at her watch. After a surprise phone call from Manchester, Maggie, a casual school friend, had been welcome to stay overnight and await her husband Bill who would collect her to proceed to Southampton for the continental ferry.

Sandra heard the ice cubes tinkle in the drowsy air.

'I'm glad you got in contact, Maggie,' she said. 'We must get to know each other better. How long is it since school? Four years, I suppose. We're both twenty-two, aren't we?'

'I was just thinking how lucky you are to live down here on the coast,' Maggie replied. 'For me, leaving London for the north was a bit of a wrench, but you get used to it. I didn't know it was so lovely and secluded here. I imagined you were in a suburb of Brighton or somewhere.'

Sandra abruptly raised her shoulders, her large, bare breasts sweeping the grass whose blades were crushed by the big, crimson plums of her nipples.

'Sedgedean is a proper town,' she said, pretending to be cross. 'Actually, it's great: no snobbery, they take you as they find you, and pretty open-minded, if you know what I mean.'

She giggled mischievously, tucking in a stray breast.

'But you seem to be the lucky one. Your bloke is only away in the week, selling whatever it is he sells.'

'Bathroom fittings,' said Margaret. 'He's area sales manager, you know. The whole northwest.'

'My bloke can be away for months,' said Sandra. 'Bloody oil rigs supervisor. You see, they have to send divers down to clean the pipes, and first actually move the oil rig, just a few metres, with tugboats. It's something about insurance. While the oil rig is standing still it is a building, but once it's moved, it is a ship, and must have a proper captain. That's what Ray does: just sits and barks orders at the tugboats. They send him all over. Sometimes he gets home and they phone him at the airport, and he's off again, without saying hello, or . . .'

She giggled again.

'Good money, but aren't you lonely?' said Maggie, looking up at Sandra's opulent house in the heat haze and the gleaming silver Merc parked outside.

'Not if I don't want to be,' drawled Sandra, brushing a non-existent fly from her right nipple. 'I know what he gets up to in these tropical dumps. All those LFMs . . .'

She pouted, and Maggie raised an eyebrow.

'Little fucking machines,' said Sandra simply. 'But when the cat's away – or in Ray's case, the tomcat –'

'You don't mean –' Maggie began.

'What do you think?' Sandra giggled. 'Boys and girls, we're all the same. Aren't we, Maggie?'

Maggie blushed prettily and smiled, shifting her bare legs and drawing her dress down an inch.

'Can't think why you don't join me,' said Sandra. 'The sun's glorious on the bare bod. Too much tan isn't

3

good, but the English sun is just right, and I have a sun lamp for the winter. Then I go to a nudist club quite near Brighton. You're not shocked, I hope. It's actually quite sexless, if you choose –'

'We have them in the north, too, you know,' said Maggie. 'But the sun doesn't agree with my skin.'

Proudly, she flounced her mane of russet brown hair, rivalling Sandra's in its shiny thickness.

'Must be awfully uncomfortable, wearing knickers in this heat,' Sandra said. 'I usually go without.'

'I'm not wearing knickers,' Margaret replied. 'Not exactly . . .'

Sandra gave a puzzled frown.

'My dear Maggie, you can't be not exactly wearing knickers. You either are or you aren't.'

'Does Ray go with you to the nudist place?' said Margaret, carefully changing the subject.

'No, he thinks it's silly. That's why I go, to make him jealous. I do everything to make him jealous, the sod, but he never is. He even laughs at the idea of peepers watching me sunbathing nude! He jokes about them climbing through the hedge and, you know. As if it was just a laugh, and I was just some slag, and – and didn't matter.'

She drank greedily and lit a cigarette, sucking hard on the smoke.

'Some men' said Margaret gravely, 'are turned on by the idea of other blokes doing their wives. While they watch. Threesomes and that. I mean, blokes boast about having two women in bed at once, don't they? But plenty of women have had two blokes using her, like a slave.'

Sandra gave a knowing giggle, then sucked her Pimm's through a candy-striped straw and turned over to lie on her back. The strong slabs of her long thighs and her flat belly gleamed with sun oil and her breasts stood pertly upwards, despite their large size, as though reinforced by silicone, which they were decidedly not.

4

At her crotch, a ripely swelling mound was covered not in downy pubic thatch but by a veritable jungle of blonde curls that hung well below the pink, protruding lips of her quim and crawled up her belly almost to her navel. Sandra placed her fingertips on the lips of her quim and began to stroke herself gently with an impish grin on her wide, crimson lips.

'He'd love it if I shaved down there. All these LFMs have hardly anything, you know. But I tell him that all the geezers I've ever known go ape-shit over a big bush. Even then he just laughs.'

'Oh,' said Margaret. 'I shave. Bill likes it, and I think it's nice. Makes me feel sort of girlish. But yours is lovely. And the way the hairs hang down, peeping out your bum, and you have that butterfly sort of nestling there.'

Sandra touched her bare bottom and smiled impishly.

'If he wants to fuck, you know,' she said, warming to her theme, 'sometimes I make him take me down to the beach in the car, and do it in the back seat, so all the peepers can watch. That turns me on. It's called dogging. When the bugger's horny, he'll agree to anything to get it, like all blokes. I love my legs sticking up over the front seat, and him pumping away, and anybody watching. I love the thrill of being seen or discovered somehow. I even let him find condoms in my purse, once, and didn't even pretend to be embarrassed. He just laughed at that.'

'A real exhibitionist likes strangers to watch and likes doing it with strangers,' Margaret said coolly.

'Doesn't everybody? All the girls I know go dogging. Why do you think I sunbathe nude, here by the hedge? It's far enough so the neighbours can just see . . .'

'But anybody walking along the cliff path could see, through the hole in your hedge,' said Margaret.

'I know. I keep it trimmed,' replied Sandra. 'It's on my property, so only a deliberate trespasser could see

5

me. Plenty do, I'm glad to say. You'd be surprised how many guys are suddenly eager for a job of lawn-mowing, supervised by a female nudist. And if I like them, they get more, and in the open. That's the thrill: fucking a new body, a complete stranger, and knowing somebody might see.'

Sandra licked her lips and scratched her bushy mound.

'You have a lovely body,' said Margaret serenely. 'It's nice that you're proud, and like to show it. Such a lovely bottom, and big boobs. I'm jealous!'

'Why so coy? Maggie, you've great tits and a great bum and legs. You're a proper magnet! Surely you don't go without when Bill's away? Come on, girl talk.'

'No,' said Margaret sharply, and Sandra laughed, her bare breasts heaving like cherry-topped flans.

'I mean it,' said Margaret. 'Look.'

Slowly, deliberately, she raised her dress to reveal a garment made of steel-grey netting through which her shaven mound was faintly revealed. The garment hugged her pubis and buttocks and was secured by a tiny padlock.

'You said you had no panties,' said Sandra, peering.

'It is a chastity belt,' Margaret answered proudly. 'And Bill has the key.'

Sandra whistled and touched the thin mesh that tightly covered her friend's bare pubic mound.

'But that's barbaric! And your shaved pussy; doesn't it itch terribly as the bristles sprout?'

'Yes,' said Margaret.

'Why do you let him do such a thing?' Sandra gasped.

'I don't, Sandra. I beg him to do it. It was my idea, so that I would be faithful.'

'Faithful!' Sandra exclaimed, as though Margaret had mentioned some medieval torture device. 'While he's staying in those hotels with whatever tart he's picked up in the bar? Oh, I'm sorry, Margaret, I didn't mean –'

'I don't mind what he does,' replied Margaret, her eyes glittering. 'That's part of the pleasure, Sandra. 'You see, I made him get his nipple pierced, his left one. And he wears a little gold ring, like an earring, with the key to my chastity belt soldered to it. So if he's tomcatting, he can't forget me! Can't help feeling guilty. And when he comes back and unlocks me, why, we have the best sex you can imagine. I'm wet just thinking about it.'

In truth, the grey sheen of her chastity belt was dark with the moisture from her protruding red quim-lips. Sandra put a hesitant finger on the place and nodded. Margaret explained briskly that she was never, ever allowed to take the device off, not even to go to the bathroom. It was scarcely more than a G-string, but covered the bum-crack and pussy securely, and was a fine mesh coated in teflon.

'When I have to do the business, a strong shower spray is all I need afterwards.'

Margaret smiled rather smugly, and pulled her dress right up, until her bare breasts showed, the nipples pert and conical on a bosom as ripe as Sandra's and braless. But beneath her breasts, and pushing them up and out, was a tight waspie corset, the same pink as her sundress, and fiercely crafted with bone stays. Her waist was cinched very painfully, exaggerating the swell of her ample bottom.

'I wear this for my own pleasure,' she murmured. 'Bill knows it hurts, and that makes him guilty: there is nothing to tame a man like submitting to pain for him. And if he suspects I've wanted to be naughty, he gives me this.'

She swivelled to show her buttocks almost entirely bare under the thin efficiency of the chastity belt. They were covered in ugly blue bruises. Sandra gasped.

'He spanks you?' she said uncertainly.

'He belts me,' Margaret replied. 'A good forty or fifty

with a big leather studded thing on the bare bum. And then I cry, and he says he's sorry, and we fuck. It is fabulous. Actually –' she blushed, and started to rise '– talking about it makes me want to go. Drink goes right through me.'

'No need to go back to the house,' said Sandra.' You can tinkle in the rose bushes and rinse with the garden hose.'

'Oh, I think it's more than a tinkle,' said Margaret.

'The same applies.'

Sandra leaped to her feet and, breasts bouncing, led her friend across the lawn to the rose bushes. Margaret squatted like a dog and Sandra watched as the golden rain sprayed from her pussy, just like a garden sprinkler. Then she strained and Sandra burst out laughing. She lifted the hose and began to spray Margaret's bottom and pubis.

'It looks just like spaghetti!' she said.

'Wholewheat spaghetti, please,' said Margaret, laughing too as the fierce jet squirted her quim and bumhole shiny clean. Hand in hand, they resumed their reclining positions and clinked glasses, Margaret leaving her chastity belt showing, with her damp dress covering her breasts.

'Your dress is all wet, you silly,' said Sandra. 'Go on, take it off. You've got shade.'

Margaret lifted the dress over her shoulders, catching her breasts and making them wobble, and then grinned shyly. She sat there wearing only the waspie corset and her chastity belt, and Sandra shook her head in wonderment.

'A week without –' she murmured and looked again at her friend's moist gash, with the clitoris peeping demurely between the fleshy folds.

'Of course, you can always diddle,' she said, shrugging.

'Masturbation has never been so wonderful,' Margaret replied gravely. 'I do myself every day. And when Bill comes home, I tell him everything. I mean, I tell him all my fantasies of big cocks when I do myself. And he tells me nothing at all, for I won't let him!'

She spoke exultantly.

'That is such sweet pleasure – submissive pleasure, Sandra – to dream of him betraying me, fucking some slut in a hotel bedroom, his cock in another woman's pussy. The shame! Oh, Sandra, you can't imagine what a thrill it is.'

Sandra suddenly realised that she had been stroking her own naked pussy and that her lips were moist.

'I know what Ray does, but out of sight, out of mind. If I ever caught him, I'd cut his balls off!'

Margaret eyed her friend curiously.

'Would you really want to?' she whispered. 'I mean, suppose you peeped through the hedge and saw Ray here, on this very lawn, with a woman, both of them naked as we are. Why, we could be, you know, doing it, if we had one of those things, those toys you strap on. Maybe Ray would enjoy that. So would you mind watching him with someone?'

Sandra felt the moisture suddenly flow in her gash.

'I'd cut his balls off!' she repeated uncertainly, then laughed. 'But why would I peep through my own hedge?'

Sandra reached out and ran her fingers over the ridges on her friend's bare bottom, stroking the skin in awe. She felt her pussy moistening and her heart beating faster.

'And you let Bill thrash you . . .'

'Same as the chastity belt. I beg him to.'

Sandra took a long swallow of her drink.

'I'm sure I wouldn't like it,' she said, nervous and overly defiant. 'When did you discover yourself?'

'That I'm submissive, just as you are exhibitionist? When I realised that I couldn't tame Bill, or satisfy

9

myself, by playing his own game. To compete with tarts, you have to be the opposite. Isn't that what you're doing to Ray, Sandra? Trying to be a better, browner, more tempting version of these little brown fucking machines? Believe me, it doesn't work. He's done all that. Men want something different. They are so used to aggressive, promiscuous women. If a man suddenly finds his woman is totally submissive – that she doesn't even mind him fucking around – then he truly belongs to her.'

Margaret was breathing quite heavily, like Sandra. Both women looked into each other's eyes.

'Of course,' murmured Margaret, 'girl friendships are another matter.'

Sandra recommenced her stroking of Margaret's bared fesses.

'Whopping that bum of yours must be nice,' she said.

Margaret put a finger in the crack of Sandra's arse.

'You said we should get to know each other better, and that people down here were open-minded . . .'

Sandra did not resist as she worked the finger up and down. The heat seemed blistering, and with the alcohol she had drunk, it made her feel light and giddy. She was soaking wet between her thighs. She looked instinctively towards the hole in the hedge.

'Sometimes the girls from that posh school go for walks there,' she said dreamily. 'They always peek when I'm sunbathing nude. And I put on a show for them, as if I don't know they're looking.'

Her fingers clasped her wet pussy and found her clitoris stiff and throbbing, and she began to rub it.

'Girls will be girls,' she murmured.

Margaret too was rubbing her own clitty through the moist fibres of her chastity belt and began to pinch her left nipple with her other hand, so that it blossomed suddenly into hardness. She had let her parasol fall and her russet hair was bathed in light. Sandra reached out gingerly and touched the back of Margaret's hand, over her pussy, then transferred Margaret's fingers to her own throbbing clit, and began to stroke the wet folds of her friend's labia.

'I envy those schoolgirls. An all-girls school teaches you the sweetest ways of pleasure,' Margaret said.

She began to rub Sandra's clitty with two fingers, tweaking the stiff little organ and making Sandra sigh with pleasure. Sandra put one finger inside Margaret's gash, then two, and exclaimed that she was sopping wet.

'As if you didn't know,' said Margaret and placed Sandra's thumb firmly on her distended nubbin.

Sandra needed no encouragement to move her hand up and down against the wet, silky hole while Margaret worked vigorously between Sandra's parted quim-lips. Both women spread their thighs wide and let the soles of their feet touch in a diamond shape. Each woman, as she masturbated the other, had a hand caressing the nipples of her own breasts to hardness.

Their faces were red with pleasure, and Sandra felt the sun had melted into her as her belly fluttered and her stiff clit sent spasms of tickling joy up her spine that grew in a crescendo as her pussy trembled and squeezed on her friend's probing fingers. Margaret's gash was flowing with hot oil all over Sandra's wrist and both women leaned forward, gasping, and kissed full on the lips as they masturbated each other to long, pulsing orgasm.

Afterwards, they lay on their backs in the golden sun, hands clasping pussies, and Margaret said she was bound to tell Bill everything, but would not mention her name. Sandra insisted she did and that the idea made her wet.

'Bound!' she teased. 'I suppose he ties you up as well, in this submissive thing of yours.'

'Why, of course,' said Margaret seriously. 'That's part of it. It's lovely to be bound hand and foot, with leather thongs, gagged, and whipped on the bare.'

'Well!' exclaimed Sandra. 'Where on earth did you learn all this stuff?'

Margaret sighed happily with a faint blush.

'At school,' she said. 'Last year. It's a sort of finishing school for grown-up girls, called Quirke's, not far from here, and quite near that posh place, in fact. We used to go for walks past this very house!' She giggled. 'And we did peep at you sunbathing in the nude, Sandra, and once there was a man with you. It was lovely to watch you doing it, you know. Quirke's School is very select, about fifty girls. I mean, they are not girls, they are all in their twenties, but dress like girls. Miss Quirke herself, the headmistress, is about thirty, I'd guess, and very proper. It's a finishing school, really, and girls board for a week, or more, depending. It is a proper school with mistresses and classes and exams, all English – grammar, composition, and so on – and all girls. The school rules are very strict indeed and you are chastised for breaking them, and of course no males are allowed in.'

'Wow,' said Sandra.

'Don't women – don't you and I – know how to do each other far better?' said Margaret with sudden coyness. 'When you have dozens of would-be schoolgirls cooped up together, well, tickling is almost part of the curriculum, although there are fearful punishments for it. The aim is to make us real ladies: that is, seemly and obedient.'

'Plenty of spanking for disobedience, then?' said Sandra drily, but failing to hide her eagerness.

'There is much more than spanking,' said Margaret. 'But if you are a good girl, then you need never even bare your bum for spanking, let alone –'

'Let alone what?' Sandra insisted, her eyes bright.

'You'll find out, if you really want to. And, Sandra, I know you do. I'll give you Miss Quirke's card and if you write a very respectful letter, saying that you are a young lady in need of proper strict instruction, she might agree to send you a prospectus, and you can make your own mind up. It's not cheap. They count in guineas, so it is six hundred guineas a week, about 900 E's, and please mention my name.'

'That's over 600 quid,' said Sandra.

'It includes full board, tuition, and uniforms: gymslips and ankle socks and pleated skirts, nighties and cotton stockings and blouses and caps and so on. By the way, Miss Isobel Quirke is an old-fashioned disciplinarian, and you mustn't use vulgar words like quid.'

Sandra thought of all the old school stories she had read, where the girls of privileged families seemed to have such innocent fun. She looked again at Margaret and saw her as a picture of serenity and control, and suddenly longed to cover her naked body in stuffy skirts and blouses and tight shoes, and be a mischievous little girl again.

'Yes,' she said faintly. 'Don't forget to send me that prospectus, Margaret. Maybe I'll give Ray a surprise . . .'

Suddenly Margaret rose.

'By the way, Sandra,' she said coolly. 'You know when you hosed me clean? It hurt awfully, the jet of water right up my bottom, but I don't think you did it quite hard enough. Would you be good enough to hose me properly clean, with the jet on full strength now, if you please?'

Puzzled, Sandra agreed, and directed the jet straight between the blue welts of Margaret's spread buttocks, so that the little pink bud of her anus seemed actually full to overflowing and made her gasp.

'Spank me on the bare bum,' Margaret whispered.

Sandra delivered a vigorous spanking with her palm on the wet buttocks, about thirty slaps which made the already bruised buttocks redden beautifully, but made her palm sore. Then she obliged further by hosing

Margaret directly on her clitty, which was stiff again, until Margaret gasped and moaned in a second climax.

Suddenly there was the sound of a car crunching in the driveway, and Margaret said that it was Bill at last, come to pick her up for the drive to Southampton and the continental ferry. She smiled mischievously at Sandra and primly smoothed down her dress and adjusted her parasol, but stopped Sandra from covering herself. Margaret glowed with the pleasure of her orgasm.

'No,' she said, 'I want Bill to see you nude. Then I know he'll be fancying you all during our drive, and it will make me so mortified! And him so guilty and frustrated, he'll give me such a bare flogging! I can't wait. He'll belt me rigid in our hotel room tonight.'

'Well, I hope you enjoyed our little scene,' Sandra said. 'I did, even though my palm still aches from spanking that lovely, submissive bum of yours!'

'I did enjoy it, and aches go away, even though a submissive would not want them to,' Margaret replied. 'But it's easy to throw words around. You're a nudist, an exhibitionist. Are you ever really naked, to yourself? We all wonder what we really, truly are, and Quirke's School has helped me find out. Just ask yourself, my naked Miss Sandra: in our little scene, who was the submissive?'

2

The Schoolgirl's Friend

Sandra's heart beat as she arrived for interview with Miss Isobel Quirke. The parchment prospectus had duly arrived after a week's anxious waiting. A few sketches showed the school, a handsome seventeenth century building, and the extensive wooded grounds with playing fields. For six hundred and something quid, as Sandra figured it, it must be as sumptuous as the prospectus. Miss Quirke had summoned her for interview at twelve o'clock sharp, with three days' notice. There was no phone number.

Sandra had duly arrived in her silver Merc, parking with a rather showy crunch of gravel, and was welcomed by a very pleasant young woman of her own age who cast an admiring glance at the car, and chummily called her Sandra, introducing herself as Stephanie Long, a school prefect. She wore a dark blue blazer, a grey, pleated skirt and a white shirt like a boy's, with a striped tie and blue stockings, and high-heeled buckled shoes. Her hair was of medium length, ash blonde, and pressed shiny flat, curling demurely round her chin, where it swayed enticingly, as her full shapely bottom swayed in front of Sandra. The swirl of her short skirt revealed a rather flouncy white petticoat beneath and Sandra wondered if this was regulation for all the girls. Stephanie wore a riding crop at her belt, half hidden by the tail of her jacket.

She showed Sandra into a spacious hallway, decorated with portraits of stern women in academic dress. Some of them cradled canes as one might hold a posy of flowers. The ceiling was high and vaulted, its polished oak beams across white plaster, and the carpet was a dark blue, with oaken doors leading to various classrooms or offices.

Sandra herself wore a maroon suit with a rather short skirt and stockings of white silk, her shoes pink – and very stiletto – matching her frilly and rather bold thong panties. She usually went knickerless but had donned panties out of respect. In the dignified, austere surroundings, she started to feel less than formal.

They walked along a narrow corridor to a vestibule nicely adorned with flowers. On the way, two or three schoolgirls passed them, took off their round blue peaked caps and curtsied to Sandra. She smiled in surprise. The schoolgirls were of her own age, and no less ripe of figure than herself. As she glanced at their retreating bottoms, tight in their grey skirts, and the girls swaying on surprisingly high chunk heels, she wondered if that was how proper school 'gels' dressed.

'You only have to wear a cap if you are going outdoors –' said Stephanie, helpfully, '– unless – hmm!'

She kept her cap on, removing it only as they were admitted to Miss Quirke's book-lined study. This too was decorated with flowers and looked through French windows on to manicured lawns, flowerbeds and playing fields. Beyond was a coppice beside a charming ornamental lake. The floor was bare linoleum, looking curiously cheap amid such comfort. Miss Quirke sat at her heavy, walnut desk, smiled at Sandra, but did not stand up to greet her, nor did she invite her to sit down in the single armchair.

Sandra stood nervously in front of Miss Quirke with her hands clasped at her crotch. There was something in Miss Quirke's manner which made her feel guilty of something; 'up before the beak', as in the school stories. Miss Quirke's smile eased her anxiety. Her face was handsome and chiselled and her trim body looked well exercised.

She wore a sombre black jacket and skirt, with black shiny stockings and a frilly, white blouse, obviously silk, which opened at her neck to show a hint of generously swelling breasts – severely restricted by some kind of corsage, over a pencil-thin waist – with a plain gold locket on a neck chain. Her chestnut hair was short, but expensively styled, with a charming kiss-curl at her brow and a scalloped sweep that did not quite cover her nape. Sandra realised that all the 'girls' she had seen were exquisitely coiffed, and nervously fingered her own long blonde mane. Was it too, too unkempt?

At one end of the bookcase was fixed a hook, from which dangled a long, thin cane of bright yellow wood, quite fearsome, and with a splayed tip like a snake's tongue. Sandra felt herself blush; the cane seemed to stare at her. Then she remembered the quaint mention in the school prospectus that discipline was firm but fair, and was delivered if necessary, in 'traditional' manner for the proper 'turn-out' of well-behaved young ladies. The traditional manner obviously meant not just spanking, but the cane. Sandra wondered when its use became necessary, and swallowed hard.

Instinct told her to behave as though she were already at school; she kept her head bowed and looked up only when addressed by Miss Quirke, even though she was aware of the headmistress's bright eyes sizing her up, as a breeder would a colt. Miss Quirke politely called her Miss Shanks and explained that schoolgirls and staff of all ranks were addressed as 'Miss'. She said that due to 'outside commitments' many girls were unable to attend school for more than a week at a time. A girl's first week was as a 'fresher', after which she took her 'prelims' or preliminary examination. If she passed, and became a

17

junior, she could elect to stay on, or return later for a further week, and the 'moderations' exam. That would make her a senior, and eligible for prefectship. Weeks of residence and success at exams were credited even if continuous attendance was impossible. Exam failure meant a girl repeated her week.

'Some of our best girls have been freshers for months, or even years!' she said sweetly.

Apart from prefects, there was a complement of forty girls, ten to a dormitory. Normally the ranks had separate dormitories although circumstances sometimes dictated an overlap. There were four dormitory prefects and four school prefects – of which Stephanie was one – the head prefect and four mistresses. The school rules were quite simple, although they might seem arcane to an outsider, and a large part of fresher's week was devoted to learning them by example, as they were not written down.

'A proper girl, Miss Shanks, should know instinctively what is right,' said the headmistress with a smile so sweet that Sandra felt suddenly at home, amongst girls.

She smiled too when Miss Quirke said that the premises were free of males, her pert breasts swelling proudly over what had to be a corset. Perhaps a waspie like Margaret's was standard issue, or the privilege of rank.

'Here, we are girls among girls,' she continued. 'We are a strict school, Miss Shanks, but girls can learn so much when free of male influence –' her lips puckered in distaste '– and girls can learn so much from each other.'

'Oh, yes, Miss,' said Sandra, with an enthusiasm that surprised her, and Miss Quirke nodded in approval.

Her eyes turned to her cane and Sandra's followed.

'Strict means old-fashioned, Miss Shanks,' she said. 'Our lessons are primarily concerned with deportment, manners, athletic excellence, and, above all, correct use of our beloved English language, abuse of which is the enemy of good manners. Now, any breach of good manners does incur certain punishments, of which the cane is one.'

She smiled again, but now her perfect, white smile was icy, and Sandra shivered in foreboding, but also in a longing she had never known before. Miss Quirke was in perfect control, of her words, and of her girls. Suddenly, Sandra wanted to be one of those girls. She stammered as much, feeling absurdly shy – was it her hair? her panties? – and gasped in delight as Miss Quirke nodded.

'I think we may try you as a fresher, Miss Shanks. My instinct tells me you are a proper girl, fit for training. Present yourself at nine o'clock on Monday morning.'

Miss Quirke's tone suggested that she was being immensely polite, and that only the strictest discipline could make this tousled female resemble a proper girl, and that Sandra should feel terribly, terribly guilty if she let Miss Quirke down. She asked if a cheque would be OK, and Miss Quirke smiled thinly.

'No, a cheque will be satisfactory, Miss Shanks,' she said. 'Cheap American usage is not part of a lady's vocabulary. Six hundred guineas, for one week only. You are apprised of the amount in this distasteful modern currency. Should you pass your prelims, and wish to prolong your tuition, the fees are slightly higher.'

Then she looked at her watch, a thin, golden roundel with a white face on a black leather strap.

'Well!' she said brightly. 'I have a disciplinary appointment at twenty-five minutes past the hour, and before you decide to write your cheque, Miss, you may care to witness a minor punishment for unseemly behaviour.'

Sandra saw Miss Quirke nod to Stephanie, who took down the yellow cane and handed it to the headmistress, and with a flutter of excitement, Sandra murmured her agreement. She stood beside Stephanie to watch the caning. First, Miss Quirke flexed the cane, brushed it to make sure it was oiled and supple, then swished it in the air with an alarming whistle. She smiled coldly at Sandra.

'If you are not already aware, Miss Shanks, I trust you do not find it unnatural that all canings at our school are taken on the bare bottom.'

Sandra felt her heart thump and a tiny seep of moisture in her pink panties.

'N-no, Miss, it is quite natural to me. I mean, to cane on the bare bottom seems most efficient. It would be the most painful, I imagine, without knickers in the way.'

'You imagine correctly,' said Miss Quirke, flexing her cane. 'Then you have not yet known bare-bottom caning?'

'Why, no, Miss, not bare.'

Sandra would not admit she had never been caned at all.

'Well!' said Miss Quirke, with a warm smile. 'I am sure you will be a good girl, and never have to know what it feels like. A naked caning is, as you say, most painful.'

At twenty-five past the hour precisely there was a timid knock on the door and Miss Quirke bade entrance. Stephanie opened the door, and a tall, ripe-figured young woman of just over twenty years old came in, nervously looked at Sandra, and curtsied to her, to Stephanie, then to Miss Quirke. She placed herself before Miss Quirke's desk, holding her blue school cap at her crotch.

'Well, Miss Devine,' said Miss Quirke. 'You know why you are here.'

'Yes, Miss,' said the girl, her head bowed.

'And it is not for a first offence.'

'No, Miss. I'm awfully sorry. I don't know what came over me. It just slipped out.'

'Quite,' said Miss Quirke drily. 'And the purpose of the schoolgirl's friend –' she rapped the leather desktop with her cane '– is to stop such things from slipping out. Improper language, Miss, is simply – not – on. Is it?'

At each of those three words, she swished the cane in the air, harder each time, and Sandra saw Miss Devine pale.

'No, Miss.'

'No, Miss!' said the headmistress icily. 'That is what you said the last time, Miss Devine.'

Now her frown changed to a warm smile.

'Let us hope that after this, further chastisement will be unnecessary. Let me see. On our last meeting, I gave you four stripes of the cane. I now intend to give you six. I trust this is acceptable to you?'

Miss Devine was shifting nervously from foot to foot and her bottom was twitching already under the tight pleats of her skirt.

'Yes, Miss, of course,' she whispered.

'By the way, you observe we have a visitor, a prospective fresher. With your consent, I propose that she witness your punishment. Is that satisfactory?'

'Oh! Well, I – I guess so, Miss.'

There was a chilled silence in the study and Miss Devine's fingers flew to her mouth.

'I cannot believe what I have just heard,' said Miss Quirke with acid scorn. 'You – you ... Oh, I cannot bring myself to repeat the American barbarism. I can only assume you have got it from television. What are we to do with you, Miss Devine? Are you fit to complete your week?'

'Oh, Miss, please don't expel me!' cried Miss Devine.

'I await your suggestion, Miss,' said Miss Quirke, making motions as though to put away her cane.

'Please, Miss Quirke,' begged the girl, sobbing now. 'I'll take an extra stroke. Would that purge me?'

Miss Quirke pondered, or pretended to.

'Well,' she said thoughtfully. 'As I recall, only one girl has ever been expelled, and that was a prefect, for excessive zeal in a certain punishment. Some of us may think Quirke's is too soft these days.'

She looked at Stephanie, whose eyes glittered like gems.

'You will receive nine stripes of the cane, Miss Devine, on your bare buttocks,' she intoned formally. 'Now please lower your knickers, raise your skirt and assume a spread position over the chair back.'

So that was the purpose of the well-worn leather armchair! Sandra felt her belly tighten and her panties moisten quite copiously as the girl obeyed and she bent over the high chair back. It obliged her to stand on tiptoe, and she raised her skirt, draping it neatly over her spine. Then, with a sigh, she lowered her white, frilly panties to her knees, letting the garment hang there, stretched like a bridge. Finally she perched her cap backwards on her head, which she was thus obliged to hold high, and Sandra knew that this was part of the humiliating punishment.

Miss Devine wore a frilly, white lace suspender belt to match her panties, in contrast to the black school stockings. Miss Quirke judged that the straps were too close together and covered her fesses, so the girl had to fumble and unfasten the straps and tuck them up into the sussie belt and let her stocking tops droop sluttishly.

Sandra's pulse quickened as she saw the firm melons of the girl's naked fesses. They were already faintly striped with the marks of – perhaps – many beatings and Sandra found their mottled ridges exciting. She imagined herself in the same position – bare bum raised in submission, and waiting for the sting of the hard wood on her naked skin – and felt her quim-juice flow faster with a little tickle in her clitty which began to tingle and stiffen. She breathed hard. Never in a million years would she have thought that she could be excited by watching a cruel, naked beating, and even more thrilled by the awful certainty that one day soon her own bare buttocks must feel the cane.

'You agree to a bare-bottom caning of nine stripes for your misdemeanours, Miss Devine,' said Miss Quirke formally, 'witnessed as required by one prefect, and with your consent by the prospective new girl. Any noise or squirming deemed excessive will result in the stripe's repetition. You further acknowledge that you are free to discontinue punishment at any stage, and leave school, with the balance of your week's tuition being refunded to you, less a fine of twenty guineas for every stroke refused.'

'Yes, Miss,' sobbed the girl from her humiliant position. 'My bottom is bared and ready for just caning. Please, Miss, flog me without delay.'

Miss Quirke nodded in satisfaction and stood behind the bared girl, then lifted her cane. Sandra saw that her own bottom was a juicy peach and quite tight in her formal black skirt, which was also surprisingly short, allowing a good glimpse of long, muscled thighs and calves in gleaming black silk stockings. Sandra repressed the thrilling thought that Miss Quirke's own bum looked ripe for a bare-bottom caning and was quite possibly no stranger to it.

This impression was increased as the cane whistled in the air and delivered the first stripe to the girl's naked peach. The springy wood cracked with such precision across the soft, bare flesh of the central buttocks that a vivid, pink stripe was raised at once, and both buttocks trembled in furious agitation as Miss Devine involuntarily clenched her furrow tightly, relaxed it, then clenched the bum-cheeks hard again, awaiting the second stripe.

This was not long in coming; Miss Quirke's aim was sure, and the cane's lash wealed the bare flesh exactly on the bruise raised by the first. The flogged girl's whole body was jolted by the force of the stroke, which made

23

her bare fesses quivering jellies as the crack of her buttocks danced and tightened like a jerked whipcord.

Her breath came in harsh, poignant gasps, and Sandra was shocked to find herself breathing heavily in the excitement of witnessing a naked beating. Her face was flushed; she glanced sideways at Stephanie and saw she was agitated too. The crotch of Sandra's pink thong panties was sopping now with her quim-juice and she felt it trickle outside the panties and down to her stocking tops, past her own sussies. She prayed that her stockings would not get too wet and show humiliating evidence of this mischievous excitement, or Miss Quirke might misjudge her motives for coming to school and refuse her admittance! She slightly regretted having worn such a tarty short skirt.

The crack of the third stripe on the girl's bare jolted Sandra back to the matter. Three vivid welts now graced the white bum-skin, the third stripe diagonal to the first two, as though Miss Quirke was amusing herself with a game of noughts and crosses. Accordingly, the fourth stripe was parallel to the third, and the fifth on the very top of the bum, where the skin was so tender, and straight across.

This stripe made Miss Devine squeal and her bare bum squirmed so frightfully that Miss Quirke paused, panting herself, but said that the squeal meant a repetition of the fifth. The flogged girl sobbed her agreement and the stripe was given again, right in the same place, but this time she made only a tortured gasp, though her legs shot straight out behind her, before buckling so that her panties slipped to her ankles, as her entire body convulsed in shudders.

Miss Quirke ordered her to step out of the panties altogether so that her legs and buttocks could remain properly spread, and the sobbing girl obeyed. Her stockings now draped her knees and the reason for Miss Quirke's insistence on spread thighs became obvious, for the sixth and seventh strokes took the mewling student in uppercuts, right on the soft flesh where thigh met buttock.

Her squirming had Sandra gasping as her own pussy flowed with oily juice and she knew her panties and stockings too were soaked and well stained but did not care. She felt her clitty stiff and throbbing and longed to rub the tingling nubbin. One touch and she knew she would bring herself off.

She suddenly imagined Margaret, bent over like that, her luscious bum taking cruel stripes from a merciless cane, and felt frustrated that she had done nothing more than spank her friend's wet bottom. Maybe next time. But she felt dizzily uncertain. Did she want to wield the cane on the helpless bare bum of a girl, or be that girl herself?

Stephanie was gazing with as much lustful excitement as Sandra, and there was a dark, wet stain on her stockings. Underneath her knickers, her trembling fingers played with her riding crop.

Of course. Stephanie was a prefect and carried the means of beating other girls. All must learn to be submissives, like Margaret, but for some, a prefectship would allow the expression of their dominant instincts. All girls together, all talents made to blossom.

There was a deathly silence as Miss Quirke paused to wipe her brow, oddly lifting the hem of her black skirt to briefly reveal her own white frilly petticoat and her sussies and frilly stocking tops, which bore shiny patches of moisture. She too was excited, Sandra knew. Miss Devine was left squirming and clenching her bare bum for the last fearful stripes, but Miss Quirke waited and waited until she had calmed herself and her breathing was even.

Then she lifted the cane very high and dealt two strokes in lightning succession – vip! vip! – that made Sandra shudder in sympathy even as her quim gushed with juices and she felt her panties and stockings soaked in the liquid from her throbbing, swollen gash-lips. Her clitty stood stiff and tingled as though electric.

The flogged girl's body shuddered violently at these two cruellest stripes, and she let out a long wail, and suddenly there was a hissing noise: a golden stream flowed from her bare gash and down her stockinged legs, on to the linoleum floor, whose purpose was at last clear to Sandra.

Surprisingly, this lack of control was in no way considered an imperfection. Miss Quirke simply rang a bell and shortly afterwards another girl arrived – the same age as Sandra, Devine and Stephanie – dressed in a charming frilly French maid's uniform, with seamed fishnet stockings, white bonnet and apron, a short black tutu which made no attempt to conceal her sussies and straps, and a white lace bonnet. She carried sponges and mops and gravely wiped Miss Devine's bottom and legs before kneeling on the floor, her own pantied bum high and revealing the thong tight in the cleft of her buttocks. With a swaying of her own well-punished fesses, she mopped the floor of the newly striped girl's evacuation.

Miss Quirke congratulated Miss Devine on her good comportment and the girl curtsied before departing with her cap in her hand once more. Sandra was hopping as her clit throbbed; she longed for relief.

It was time for her to hand over her cheque. Trembling with excitement, Sandra bent down over a small writing table by the far wall, repressing the foolish suspicion that it was deliberately low so that a girl using it would show her panties and bum with her skirt riding up. She deliberately arched her back – if that was the intention – so that Miss Quirke and the prefect could plainly see her soaking gash-lips around the drenched thong of her panties and her sopping wet stockings. Stephanie curtsied to Miss Quirke and handed her the cheque which Miss Quirke laid on her desk without inspection.

Then she shook hands with Sandra – 'Miss Shanks' – and said she hoped she would profit from her tuition at Quirke's. Stephanie led Sandra back to the gravel where her car was parked and told her not to be late on Monday morning.

'Oh! I can't wait!' cried Sandra, and got clumsily into the driver's seat, her skirt riding up to her pussy, and her wet panties leaving the prefect in no doubt of her excitement at witnessing a bare-bum caning.

Stephanie smiled knowingly and waved goodbye, then sauntered back into the school building, fingers on her riding crop.

Sandra gunned the engine of the Merc, but her clitty throbbed so furiously, and her breath was so harsh, that she felt altogether too dizzy to drive. There was no one around. She lifted her skirt right up and thrust her hand into her panties. Her luxuriant bush was a swamp of love-juice, and she pushed three fingers deep into her gash, poking herself furiously while her thumb squashed and tweaked her stiff nubbin.

It took only a few moments of fervent frottage until she brought herself to a gasping, sobbing orgasm, and as her breathing calmed, she became aware that her face was in shadow. Stephanie was standing over her and had observed her masturbating! She wore a sardonic and lopsided grin.

'I think you'll do well at Quirke's, Miss Shanks,' she said. 'You seem to be one of us. Gels together . . .'

She smiled half cruelly, half lustfully.

'Just remember that in future you address me as "Miss", and curtsy to a prefect. Didn't you forget to ask something in your excitement at seeing the gel striped?'

Sandra stared at her, panting helplessly.

'Miss Devine was guilty of uttering the B word,' whispered Stephanie dramatically. Sandra frowned.

'The B word?' she said.

'Boyfriend,' hissed the blue-stockinged school prefect.

3

Smarting Wet

The Indian summer was over by the weekend and on the Sunday, which was Sandra's first day at Quirke's, the sky was grey with a steady drizzle. Sandra locked the house, set the answering machine, checked that everything was sorted, then set off to her new school. The week's tuition began the following morning: Sunday evening was a settling-in period and was free of charge.

Her instructions were quite clear, if puzzling. She was to arrive at the school at four o'clock precisely, but not in her own transport, and not even taking a taxi to the front door. Miss Quirke would consider this 'showy'. She was to wear unassuming clothes, casual but correct: a skirt, of course, and jacket and raincoat if necessary, without jewellery, nail polish or adornment of any kind. Thus Sandra wore a beige cashmere polo-neck which showed her bra-less breasts to most sensuous effect, a woollen, pocketed skirt in sensible brown and black tartan, and a tan burberry. She went knickerless – quite normal for her – with plain, black stockings and sussies, and plain slingbacks, not too high.

School was to be approached on foot by the 'bridle path'. The necessary landmark was what Miss Quirke primly referred to as a 'public house', the only structure on that stretch of coast road. The path was about fifty metres ahead. Sandra took a taxi and told the driver to stop at a large, garish building which had once been white but was now faded, with a neon sign announcing it as THE FEATHERS. The taxi driver said it used to be called the 'Whip and Saddle' in allusion to fox-hunting, but now it was dancing, striptease, 'and all sorts of stuff' going on well beyond the legal 2 a.m. closing. The huge car park was now deserted; until October, they had open-air raves.

Sandra got out and stood in the drizzle and began to unfurl her umbrella. The Feathers was open and brightly lit. She looked at her watch and saw that it was not even three o'clock. She marched in, sat at the empty bar and ordered a double gin and tonic. She had not even a suitcase: all necessary 'kit' would be issued at school.

She put her gold lighter and a pack of Marlboro Lights on the bar, sipped her drink and lit a cigarette, gulping her smoke hungrily, as it would be her last for a while. The lounge was a melange of avian and hunting paraphernalia: cages, perches, and riding crops adorned the walls, along with saddles and harnesses, dogs' muzzles, coiled horsewhips, and a variety of boots and spurs, some of which had fearsome spike heels and toes, and were not at all like a hunter's. There were old things of gleaming polished metal: leg-irons and man-traps, scold's bridles and other items of rural life only used for birds or fox-hunting.

The lady behind the bar was obviously the owner – a handsome woman slightly older than Sandra – and was well bejewelled. She smiled encouragingly as Sandra smoked, accepted one for herself and tossed her dazzling blonde mane as though to defiantly show the jet-black roots. She said it was quiet now but she did fantastic trade in the evening; got the place cheap, because of the strict drink-driving laws. But the law was a boon, because it was much easier to get an entertainment licence, and you got a taxi crowd with real money to spend, not boy-racers on the pull. Yes, a very interesting crowd, especially on Saturdays.

She had a really good body, well shown by a tight, black dress, low-cut with plenty of breast on display, and high to show firm, long legs in shiny tights, or were they proper stockings? Her smile was thin, but pleasant; her eyes heavily made-up, but hooded, with quiet confidence, like a detective's, and Sandra felt suddenly awkward, as though she and everybody else must guess her destination. The woman invited Sandra to call her Angela, implying future acquaintance, then drifted benignly away. Excited, Sandra opened her prospectus again.

Upon arrival at the school, all purses, cash, credit cards and the like were to be handed to the purser for safe keeping. All alcohol and tobacco were of course strictly forbidden. Every pupil got daily pocket money, included in her fees, for use at the school tuck shop. Tuck shop! Sandra smiled as she imagined the eager young 'gels' of her childhood reading jostling for sherbet and lollipops, even though Miss Quirke's prospectus assured that school meals were 'wholesome and sustaining'.

The tuck shop seemed part of that dreamed-of English boarding school life no one these days had ever experienced – if, she wondered, anybody ever really had. Caning was now a thing of the past in other schools if not at Quirke's. Sandra wondered if people weren't more balanced in those days. A beating on the bum – vip! vip! like Miss Devine – and you were cleansed. Especially if your bum was bare.

Suddenly Angela was looking at her and at her prospectus. She asked if Sandra would like a refill, and she agreed, putting the prospectus away. But the peroxided woman must have seen it! Nervously, Sandra lit another cigarette while Angela watched her smoke.

'I tried quitting once,' she said lazily. 'But it's hard! Imagine going a week without a smoke, or longer.'

She smiled and gazed right at Sandra, who tried to hide her blush with a plume of smoke. Angela knew! Hurriedly, Sandra finished her drink – two doubles were quite enough for her, anyway – opened her umbrella, and headed out into the thickening drizzle towards the bridle path.

This was a narrow opening in a thick hedge, and to Sandra's dismay it was hardly a path at all, just a wide rut in a matted jungle of briars and hawthorn, churned to porridge by the steady rain. Cursing, she resigned herself to getting her shoes muddy and began to trudge up towards the school, which she saw dimly silhouetted in the distance. It was a quarter to four. Plenty of time.

But despite her careful tread, three times Sandra stumbled, and once actually fell in a concealed deep puddle, so that she was almost in tears and terrified of her lateness when she reached the tip of the path and, at last, a gravelled track leading to the side door of the school, the only door pupils were allowed to use.

Her stockings were covered in mud and ripped quite seriously in four places, showing bare thigh and ankle, and there was a muddy patch where she had fallen on her bum. One of the stocking rips was right at her crotch and when her skirt rode up, a cascade of pube-hair was visible. She reached automatically for a cigarette, then looked at her watch. It was two minutes to four and there was no time. Biting her lip, she lifted her burberry and skirt and wedged her lighter and cigarettes inside the top of her left stocking, snug against her sussie strap.

'Darn the rules,' she whispered as she strode forward and rang the bell at exactly five seconds to four o'clock.

The door opened immediately and she was faced with the prefect, Stephanie Long, who looked serious. She wore a whistle round her neck, like a referee, and carried her riding crop in her hand.

'You're late, Miss Shanks,' she said blandly and

pointed to the clock which showed half a minute past four.

Sandra smiled and shrugged and gestured to her own watch, which Stephanie ignored.

'Late,' she said. 'And your clothing is dirty. Come in, Miss Shanks. You'll be showered, then issued with your kit before tea.'

Sandra stepped in out of the rain and looked at the small, drab vestibule, quite unlike the serene luxury of Miss Quirke's quarters. It smelled of polish and disinfectant and girlish sweat.

'Thanks awfully, Stephanie,' she blurted.

Stephanie Long slapped her face, not hard, but enough to shock Sandra. Then she smiled thinly.

'Just remember, you address me as Miss Long from now on,' she said. 'I'll overlook your fault because you are only a new fledge, but you are late and dirty, and I can't overlook that.'

With her riding crop, she lifted the hem of Sandra's skirt, and her eyes gleamed as she saw the thick curls of her knickerless mink matted above the ripped stocking. She held the skirt up a few moments before letting it fall. Sandra looked with pleading eyes but saw only icy scorn.

'It will have to go in the discipline book,' Stephanie said.

'But, Miss. The muddy bridle path!' Sandra blurted indignantly, but now it was the prefect who shrugged.

'Can't be helped, fledge,' she said with a rather unpleasant smile. 'There'll be a punishment, of course, probably only a spanking. I'll have your dorm prefect attend to the matter before lights-out. Now, follow me.'

Glumly, Sandra obeyed and was led through silent corridors into a large, oak-panelled hall with a raised dais. Below the dais stood a lectern which supported a huge book opened in the middle.

'The assembly hall,' said Stephanie and ordered

Sandra to wait while she entered her name in the discipline book.

She went to the lectern, uncapped her fountain pen and stood with it poised over the parchment pages.

'Perhaps you'd like to see your first entry,' she said rather nastily. 'I've no doubt there will be plenty.'

Sandra approached and looked at the roster of chastisements, all in impeccable italic handwriting, which read like some horrible Newgate Calendar:

Audrey Larch – smoking, public nine stripes.
Susan Fanshawe – hands in pockets, public spanking (50).
Jennifer Reid – jacket unbuttoned, private spanking (80).
Audrey Larch – jacket unbuttoned, tie loose, and both hands in pockets, public six stripes, two hours in cage.
Cerise Purley – bad table manners, dorm four stripes.
Zena Lambton – dumb insolence, private spanking (100) and public seven stripes, two hours perched.
Tara Devine – foul language, private six stripes.
Audrey Larch – gross immorality: dorm six stripes, public twenty-four stripes after breakfast, three hours in hoop, three hours in cage, and three hours perched.

'So now,' said Stephanie Long, changing Tara's 'six' to 'nine', 'we'll just put "Sandra Shanks – sluttish appearance and unpunctuality, dorm spanking". I'll apprise Miss Boulter, your dorm prefect, of her duty.'

Her pen was still poised and Sandra saw a flicker in her eyes, of sympathy, she hoped. She wondered what an awful miscreant Audrey Larch must be to merit so many dreadful-sounding punishments. Yet the fact of frequent and severe punishments seemed as normal to Sandra as the school building itself.

'Unless,' Stephanie said slowly, 'you'd like to get it

over with quickly. I do have a few minutes. I have to take you to shower, then to purser's for your kit, but I dare say I could attend to the matter myself. And – it is rather naughty of me – you would start with a clean slate. Miss Quirke inspects the discipline book every day, of course, as may any girl.'

'Would you really?' cried Sandra. 'Thanks awfully, Miss. It's just that, well, I've never been spanked properly before. Only in play, you understand. I'm a bit fearful how I'd stand up under a real spanking.'

They continued towards the washroom and Miss Long laughed scornfully.

'A spanking isn't much,' she said. 'It's after a public caning that you can't stand up. What Tara Devine took was just a parrot-peck.'

She showed Sandra into a cavernous chamber with wash basins, toilets and shower nozzles. She took a big, fluffy bath towel from a locker and then told her casually to strip. Sandra looked round uncertainly, for the whole ablution area was public and there were no partitions between the shower cubicles, not even the toilets, which were nothing other than buttock-shaped indentations on a long, communal trough with water gurgling unceasingly into a sink hole. Miss Long showed no sign of leaving her in privacy. Instead she turned on a hissing cold shower.

'Well, hurry up, Miss,' she snapped. 'Strip. Your clothing will be laundered and kept for your departure.'

Sandra gulped and numbly pulled her cashmere sweater over her head, feeling the cold rush of the shower on her suddenly bared breasts. When the sweater came off, and her breasts wobbled, Miss Long's eyes were fixed right on her wide nipples, which, to Sandra's embarrassment, began to noticeably stiffen as though excited by her enforced nudity. She cursed the damning evidence of cigarettes and lighter concealed in her stocking top.

There was nothing to be done. Under the prefect's eagle gaze – Miss Long was flexing her crop, now, as though she suspected – Sandra stepped out of her skirt, turning her back as though to delay the moment of truth.

'No knickers, eh?' said Miss Long. 'Well, I can see why. Quite a croup you've got, and a little butterfly feeding at your nest-hairs. I'll enjoy spanking her, especially when she's nice and wet, and you smart more.'

As slowly as she could, Sandra undid her garter straps and slowly peeled off her stockings until she was nude. Then, head lowered, and her smoking materials folded in her stockings, she tried to place her clothing in the laundry basket with the evidence unnoticed. Miss Long pounced.

'What have we here?' she crowed. 'You thought you'd get this into school, you dirty little fledge?'

She unwrapped and inspected the unlawful package.

'Cigarettes! I suppose you thought you'd sell them for tuck money? Or smoke them yourself? Wait till Miss Quirke sees this! I'm afraid it must be the discipline book. An offence of this magnitude means stripes, and in public. Now, under the shower, you mucky bird.'

'Please, Miss, may I use the toilet?' Sandra stammered.

'Well, what are you waiting for?'

'I mean, I want to do . . .'

'You want to poo? Go ahead and stop wasting time. As soon as you've showered, your wet bum will feel my palm.'

Scarlet with shame, Sandra squatted on one of the seats and waited for her evacuation under the cruel glinting eye of her new tormentor. Were all the prefects this bad? She sighed as her poo came and, when she could no longer delay – there was no toilet paper – dived suddenly under the hissing icy shower, gasping at the sudden cleansing.

Stephanie kept her under the shower for five minutes, and, shuddering with cold, she emerged for only a perfunctory towelling which omitted her bottom. Fesses wet and bare, she was bent over the prefect's stockinged knee. Stephanie had pulled her skirt right up to show her panties and stocking tops, and held Sandra's neck down with one hand while the other cracked harshly on her bare wet bottom. The fiery sting of the first spank took her unawares, and she squealed and wriggled violently.

'Oh!' she cried. 'Miss, it seems awfully hard. I mean, a first spanking, absolutely bare.'

Stephanie snapped that a Quirke's 'gel' took every punishment on the bare, as did knickerless sluts, and always in silence. Sandra felt her face crimson with shame as the spanking continued with a hard, regular beat that had her naked bottom scalded in pain, and despite all the clenching of her fesses, nothing could fend off the agonising crack of hard palm on wet buttocks. Sandra gritted her teeth and was proud that she could take a bare spanking in silence, even as her eyes welled with tears.

Crack! Crack! the spanking echoed through the bath chamber, and Sandra imagined the whole school could hear, or, for all she knew, had come to watch. Suddenly she felt excited at this fancy. She had seen in the discipline book that stripes were given in public and suspected that her importation of cigarettes would earn her just such a striping, her knickers down and bum bared to take the cane, squirming, before the eager eyes of the whole school.

She gasped, not in pain at the relentless bare spanking, but because she felt wetness in her slit. She screwed her eyes tight, but could not banish the thought of herself, bent over in shame, and bum naked, for stripes from the cane. From cruel, ice-cold Miss Quirke's cane.

The juices flowed from her sopping quim, staining Stephanie's stockings, and, without interrupting her spanking – by now on the fiftieth or sixtieth slap – the prefect cried out that she was a disgusting little slut and, as though to confirm her suspicions, thrust her fingers right inside Sandra's soaking gash, her thumb brushing the swollen clitty.

'So, spanking excites you, does it, new fledge?' she gasped. 'You revolt me.'

Sandra heard noises as some girls entered the washroom, then laughter as they saw her wriggling bum.

'My, doesn't she squirm! Give it hard, Miss!'

'Don't interrupt, you sluts!' snapped Stephanie. 'Do your business and get out.'

Sandra heard the hissing of their evacuations and then the giggles faded down the corridor. The knowledge that her shame was observed excited her dreadfully; her clitty throbbed, her quim flowed copiously and her moans were no longer of pain, but of her longing to come. She began to writhe so that her clit rubbed against the prefect's wet blue stockings, and, as she did so, realised that Stephanie had her hand beneath her own knickers on her own fount. She was frotting herself as she spanked Sandra.

The prefect's gasps were as loud as Sandra's now as both women masturbated at the awful rhythm of the wet slapping. Sandra's fesses wriggled and squirmed, the pain of the spanking now melting into a golden glow that was more than mere pain and approached the gates of pure pleasure. She cried out as her belly fluttered then shook in a tumultuous spasm that seemed to fill her entire body with glowing light. Dimly she was aware of the prefect's groans too, rising to sharp, staccato howls as Stephanie Long's furiously masturbating fingers made her gash soak her own panties in the liquid fruit of her ecstasy.

Sandra was released and the prefect panted that she

should shower again, for she was a truly dirty fledge. Sandra glowed with the happiness of her orgasm and the knowledge that she had bravely taken her first bare-bottom spanking. On impulse, she knelt and licked Stephanie's shoes and murmured, 'Thank you, Miss.'

Stephanie let her kiss her shoes, then the stockinged ankles, right up to the thighs which were wet with the two girls' love juices. At that intimacy, she called a halt, and as Sandra stepped again under the shower, she reached for the packet of Marlboro Lights and casually lit one with Sandra's gold lighter. She sucked thirstily on the blue smoke as Sandra finished showering and wrapped herself in the bathrobe.

'Miss,' Sandra blurted, livid with indignation. 'I am to be striped for having cigarettes, yet you . . .'

'No witnesses, my young fledge,' the prefect said, grinning. 'If anyone comes, why, it is you I caught smoking. That is the first rule of school life, you know. It's not the crime you're punished for, it's the getting caught . . .'

Shivering in her bathrobe, Sandra watched Stephanie Long solemnly enter her name in the punishment book: illicit possession of smoking materials. The space for her punishment was left blank. As Stephanie explained, the headmistress must decide its severity.

'It may be private, if you're lucky,' she said, 'but I'd be ready for a public striping. Miss Quirke likes to make an example where this sort of thing is concerned.'

Sandra hid her fury at the prefect's hypocrisy and hid too her excitement at her new and awful discovery; she wanted to be flogged publicly, wanted eager girls to drink in the pain and squirming of her naked buttocks, helpless as they reddened under stripes. She thought of her nude sunbathing and how Margaret had called her an exhibitionist. Yes, she thought, at the purser's office, I am! That's why I'm here. Quirke's will make me reveal what I truly am, a submissive exhibitionist.

The visit to the purser's was a simple matter of accepting a large bag of clothing which she then carried to her dormitory, led by the school prefect Miss Long, who turned her over to the dorm prefect Miss Boulter.

The dormitory was a sparsely furnished, simple room; bare, polished floorboards, white walls and a curious device like a clothes-horse sitting in the centre with straps like handcuffs at each foot. Each bed was like an army cot and had a small side table, but no lamp; the only light was a single bulb in the spotless, white ceiling.

Before Miss Long's departure, Sandra was obliged to remove and return her bathrobe, and did so under the casual eye of her dorm prefect. She stood there naked and hurried to unpack her new kit and dress as quickly as possible. She felt Miss Boulter's wide, confident eyes survey the hairy, golden bush at her pussy, her ripe peach blushed with spank-marks, and even, she realised, her still-swollen quim-lips shining with the juices of her recent excitement. And she repressed a sly and mischievous smile with the knowledge that another female in authority was eyeing her nude body with obvious desire.

The dorm prefect stood with a hand on her hip, swinging her black leather riding crop. Sandra imagined the hard fibreglass underneath the warm leather weaving. Miss Boulter was stunning: pretty as an English rose with a peaches-and-cream complexion, soft, brown eyes and full lips, but with a body hard as an athlete's and the arrogant, devastating grace of a supermodel.

She was as tall as Sandra with full, ripe curves of breast and croup and a waist that must be cinched in a corset. Her skirt and blouse were almost insolently tight, showing the ripe peach and the huge melons of her titties, the nipples big as plums and clearly bra-less. Her hair was black, brightly shining as though slicked down with lacquer, and bobbed in the mannish 1920s fashion.

She stood very tall in her dizzy heels, massive chunks of at least seven inches, and studded straps round her blue stockinged ankles. Prefects wore blue stockings, not black, though Sandra remembered that Miss Quirke herself wore black stockings like one of the girls. The shoes reminded Sandra of some of the kinky footwear she had seen in the lounge of the Feathers. Sandra imagined what Ray would say: 'thighs like nutcrackers', or something. Miss Boulter stroked her riding crop and watched nonchalantly as Sandra unpacked her things, her breasts wobbling in the excitement every girl feels at new clothing.

She had a selection of dark skirts and white blouses; a couple of long, ankle-length black dresses, strapless and low cut; boots and wellies for outside; and drab, blue-denim coveralls. There were frilly panties and sussies, lovely frothy petticoats, scarves and gloves, a little purse and shoes of quite daring height, some slingbacks, and some, to Sandra's delighted surprise, 'kiss me deadly'. Miss Boulter told her to hurry and dress for tea, without giving her any clue as to what was appropriate, and she decided a demure look would be best.

'I see you've been spanked already,' she said as Sandra rolled up her new black stockings and fumbled with her garter straps.

'I was half a minute late, Miss, and muddy from the bridle path,' she explained shyly.

Boulter laughed and slapped Sandra's stockinged thigh with her crop which stung quite hard.

'Every new fledge gets dirty on the path and every one is late! The clock's deliberately fast, you know! What a lark! How many did Longy spank you?'

'Well over fifty, Miss,' said Sandra, fastening her white scalloped bra which seemed rather too small for her.

In fact all her clothing seemed a size too small. The skirt was very tight across her bum, even though she had given detailed measurements on her application form as instructed, and every garment was sewn with a pretty little name-tag. The blouse was very tight as well and bunched her breasts up. When she tied her plain blue tie, it jutted quite dramatically over the swell of her tightened breasts. Her petticoat peeped deliciously beneath her pleated skirt.

'Fifty's not much,' said Miss Boulter. 'You've a juicy bum, gel, and she'll taste my crop, hard and often. I'd do it now, only you're due a striping tomorrow, for bringing fags in, and Miss Quirke would recognise my handiwork.'

She suddenly thrashed Sandra's pillow with her crop, alarmingly hard. Then she gestured to the clothes-horse in the centre of the dorm and Sandra realised with awe that it was a flogging horse.

'Strapped naked to the eagle,' said Miss Boulter, 'and twice two dozen welts on that bare bum of yours. Course, I only put six in the dissy book, 'cause that's the max for a dormy tickling. But here I'm boss. And there's more.'

She took Sandra across to her own bed beside the dorm entrance. It was considerably softer and wider than the girls' cots and a had a proper wardrobe. She opened this, and Sandra gasped as she saw, alongside an array of glittering frocks and evening robes, a row of harsh leather domina's costumes in rubber and leather; a selection of tawses and whips; and a broad bat of holed wood, about four feet long. She caught sight of something else before Miss Boulter closed the armoire and lovingly stroked the polished wooden bat.

'A proper paddle,' she said. 'Smarts like heck, and doesn't leave the marks of caning. Imagine yourself strapped to the horse, fledge, naked and gagged, and taking a whole night's paddling! Two hundred whops and nothing but a little red on your bare, no telltale stripes and nothing but your tears to give you away. Oh, it's such sport!'

She looked at her watch and said it was nearly time for tea. Sandra was fully dressed in her crisp new uniform and relished its tightness: every strap and thong reminded her of her body and its vulnerability.

'If I can't whop you tonight,' said Miss Boulter thoughtfully, 'I'll have to find somebody else. Miss Larch will do, she's always up to mischief. In fact I fancy you're one of her sort.'

She kicked over the mattress of the bed next to Sandra's and the bedclothes fell in a heap on the floor.

'Untidy bed,' she said with relish. 'See? I'm queen here. A hospital corner not properly folded, a speck of dust on your bed-table, a pair of shoes not straight, a smutted hankie peeping from your pillow, if you're caught diddling your clit, or another girl's, any of that, and bare bums will smart under my crop. What a pity the present Miss Quirke won't sentence tarring and feathering! But Miss Larch's unmade bed earns a good caning before I paddle her. How her cheeky bare arse will dance tonight! As you watch her squirm, Miss, snug in my bed.'

She awaited Sandra's reaction. Sandra merely blinked.

'Yes, that's prefect's privilege, you know. You have a problem?' murmured Miss Boulter, licking the tip of her crop with a wide, pink tongue.

Sandra suddenly felt her belly flutter and a seep of moisture in her new panties.

'N-no, Miss,' she whispered and looked Miss Boulter straight in the eye, while taking in the ripe curves of her titties and buttocks and long, muscled thighs which all seemed to wish freedom from the tight constraint of blouse and stocking, then imagining her nude. 'No problem at all . . .'

Suddenly the door opened and in came a fresh-faced schoolgirl, tall and full-breasted like Sandra, but with a curious resemblance to the headmistress. Her tie was loose and her appearance dishevelled. She curtsied to Miss Boulter, and blurted that she had instructions from Miss Quirke. The new fledge Miss Shanks was to receive twelve stripes at morning assembly for her most grievous offence.

Suddenly, casually, Miss Boulter slapped her twice on the face, once on each cheek, with the back of her hand. The girl grimaced but said nothing, then looked glum as the prefect told her to expect 'what for' after lights-out for her disgusting bed and her sluttish appearance. The girl appeared resigned to yet another unfair chastisement. She sighed and curtsied again, but her lips creased in a mischievous and defiant smile. So this was the infamous Audrey Larch! Sandra smiled back at her and together they walked behind Miss Boulter to the refectory for Sandra's first tea. Sandra was pensive, despite the feeling she had a new friend.

Tomorrow she would receive twelve stripes of the cane on her bare bottom in front of the whole assembly of Quirke's School! She clamped her lips and breathed heavily through her nose. Her quim was wet at the very thought and she feared her new stockings would shine with her oil. And tonight she was to submit to prefect's privilege and share Miss Boulter's bed.

She remembered the dark shape she had glimpsed, half-concealed yet unmistakable, in the dorm prefect's armoire. It was a massive, double strap-on dildo.

4

Buttered Buns

Before being allowed to enter the refectory, the girls had to line up and answer their names to the school prefect on duty, Miss Gordon. When she appeared there was an instant hush and Sandra felt a thrill of pride as she called 'present'. Eventually the complement of girls filed meekly into the compact dining hall and took their places at the six tables which stood beneath the high table. Audrey Larch showed Sandra to her place at Miss Boulter's table and the girls stood at attention while the headmistress and Matron entered, followed by the mistresses, Misses Crisp, Tate, Pottinger and Swain. All were pretty and in their late twenties, Sandra guessed, and demurely dressed, like Miss Quirke herself, except for their royal blue stockings. Three extra places at high table were unoccupied.

At a signal from Miss Gordon, the girls sat down on plain wooden benches and a group of maids – in the frilly outfit Sandra had observed at Tara Devine's caning – brought the table heads hearty plates of steak and chips. Then, as the prefects tucked in, they began to serve each table from a huge tureen of soup which smelled foully of cabbage. The tables were garnished with jugs of drinking water and a plate of thinly sliced bread – stale, and some actually mouldy – with a tub of margarine from which the girls must help themselves. Sandra received her plate of soup: it was stone cold, a watery broth with a few shreds of cabbage and a piece of fat of unidentifiable origin.

'Is that all?' she whispered aghast to Audrey.

'You poor thing, you missed the tuck shop,' said Audrey, her mouth full of stale crumbs. 'Don't worry, I've half a Mars bar left and you're welcome to it.'

Despite the miserable fare, Sandra saw that the girls were careful not to take enough bread or margarine as to seem greedy. She attracted quite a lot of respectful attention as word had gone round that she was to get twelve stripes the next morning, and the other girls were actually polite to the new fresher, surreptitiously serving her with extra margarine or even a piece of fat from their own soup. Few girls looked enthralled by the food, but despite the satisfactions of the tuck shop, all ate ravenously. Audrey explained that the shop was only open for thirty minutes a day and not everybody got into it; there was a system of buying places in the queue. She told Sandra that the three extra places were always laid in case the school governors showed up, one of them serving also as head prefect, although she was hardly ever in residence.

After about five minutes, there was a commotion at another table, where a girl had apparently been greedy and helped herself too liberally to the rancid margarine. Her table prefect pushed aside her emptied plate and rapped on the table with her cane. The girl rose and was promptly approached by Miss Gordon, who brandished her own, rather longer cane of yellow wood with a nasty snake-tongue tip. She conferred with the table prefect and then called for silence.

'Miss Tolliver seems to want more than is good for her!' she cried. 'She shall have what is good for her: four stripes for bad table manners.'

The unfortunate Tolliver was collared and made to kneel on the floor. One of the frilly maids wheeled up a giant tureen of soup and positioned it in front of the kneeling miscreant, then Miss Tolliver was obliged to raise her bum high in the air, so that her face was an inch from the rim of the greasy soup cauldron. Miss Gordon lifted her skirt and arranged it neatly on her back, then pulled down her white, frilly panties to her knees. Miss Tolliver's bare bottom was shivering quite noticeably.

'You want margarine?' cried Miss Gordon and, scooping the contents of the margarine dish in her hand, parted Tolliver's thighs and wadded the greasy stuff right into her gash until the girl's slit was filled completely.

Then she sliced the protruding oily knob and wiped it all over Tolliver's bum and thighs until they glistened.

There was a hush as Miss Gordon took her by the scruff of the neck and pushed the girl's head into the soup tureen until it was completely submerged. The prefect then rose and Miss Tolliver kept her head in the liquid, holding the tureen with both hands. Miss Gordon raised her cane and laid a vicious stripe across her bare, oily buttocks, and her bum twitched as a livid pink weal appeared. The girls set up a slow handclap.

Miss Tolliver took the second stripe after eight or nine seconds and now the surface of the liquid churned and a few bubbles appeared. After another five or so seconds, the third stripe lashed the girl's bare bum, making her whole body jerk and the soup tureen lift slightly, but still she kept her head in place. The stripes made a liquid slapping sound as the cane whipped the oily, bare skin.

The bubbling liquid and her bare bum-twitching were more agitated now as she waited for the fourth and final stripe, which Miss Gordon took her time in delivering. It was a good dozen seconds before she lashed the girl's naked buttocks for the final stripe, then grasped her hair and pulled her head up again, so that she gasped frantically at the air.

46

There was a cheer and the slow handclap turned to a round of applause until Miss Gordon stilled it with a wave of her cane. Miss Tolliver was led back to her table, with her knickers still at her knees and obliged to squat, kneeling, on the hard bench to finish her meal; in addition, her wrists were cuffed behind her back with a leather thong, so that she was obliged to finish her paltry meal eating like a puppy with the glowing red welts of her bare bottom plain for all to see. The places where the cane's snake-tongue had marked her had turned to the most horrible purple weals.

To Sandra's disgust and astonishment, Miss Tolliver was still sticky with the smeared margarine and her table companions were curtly informed that if they wanted any, they knew where to get it; there was a scramble as fingers and even tongues cleansed Tolliver's bare fesses, arse-crack and quim of every scrap of the grease.

'Greedy cow!' said one of Sandra's neighbours. 'She got what she deserved.' The others murmured in agreement.

After tea, the girls had ten minutes for 'ablutions' in the WC before going to the classrooms for 'prep' or homework. Sandra was surprised at how quickly she overcame her modesty at doing her business in public. In the very same bathroom where Miss Long had spanked her, she was happy to squat beside Audrey Larch in a row of girls with their knickers at their ankles. As her copious evacuation joined those of the other girls in the never-ceasing flush, Audrey slipped her a square of confectionery, the promised half Mars bar, and Sandra wolfed it at once.

'In one end and out the other,' said Audrey and Sandra laughed with her.

The scrap of chocolate put her in a good mood and at first she did not mind the two whole hours of prep, with only a five-minute bathroom break between each hour. One girl begged to be excused to pee, after forty-five minutes; permission was granted, but she took two stripes on the bare for indiscipline. Of course, Sandra had no work set, so was given an English grammar to study with an exercise book and fountain pen.

It seemed that freshers had a week to produce an essay of 2,000 words on the subject 'The Virtue of Being a Lady', and after a boring half hour reading the grammar, Sandra started on her essay. The time passed rapidly; she took advantage, like all the others, of the five-minute break for communal peeing, and there were two moments of liveliness where Miss Gordon awarded a girl two stripes for 'yawning' and another girl, three stripes for 'fidgeting'. Like the first, both these girls were required to bend over and bare their bottoms in front of the classroom, and took their very hard stripes in complete silence. The first girl's bottom was pale white; she trembled and her two stripes were livid. But the other had a bum well hardened with stripes and took her punishment quite casually.

There was something compelling, comforting even, in the stateliness of punishment: the lowering of knickers, the tidying of stockings and sussies, and the skirt neatly placed on the girl's back, before the formal announcement of agreed punishment and then the graceful fluid swish of the cane as it was applied to the miscreant's bare buttocks. Sandra's quim moistened as she watched.

Apart from these interruptions, there was hush, broken only by the scratching of nib on paper. Little notes were passed round unseen by Miss Gordon. Sandra wrote that it was super for a lady to find herself a schoolgirl, to live by iron routine, and not to have to think, except perhaps about English grammar and breaking the unwritten rules.

After a cup of cocoa and a stale currant bun, taken in the refectory standing up by the counter – the cocoa jugs again administered by the frilly maids – it was time for bed. Sandra accompanied Audrey to the freshers' dormitory and they changed into their nighties.

'I shan't get much sleep tonight,' said Audrey with resignation, 'but then, I rarely do. There is always a reason to whop my poor bum. You shouldn't expect much sleep either, Sandra, if you know what I mean.'

Miss Boulter, dangling her cane, eyed the pair from the other end of the dorm.

'I do know what you mean,' said Sandra, aware of the prefect's eyes on her breasts swinging bare from her unhooked bra.

She turned her back automatically to roll down her panties, smiling as she did so, for such modesty was both unaccustomed and, in Miss Boulter's dorm, useless. The other girls stripped quite unconcernedly and even stood in clusters chattering in the nude without any warning from Miss Boulter, and indeed to her obvious satisfaction.

'We all have to submit,' said Audrey carefully. 'So now is the time to ask for your money back, and withdraw, if you've any doubts. Boulter can be quite nice if she likes you, and – and quite horrid, if she likes you a lot.'

Sandra replied that she had no intention of withdrawing, nor asking for her money back 'like a cissy'.

'I know perfectly well what "all girls together" means,' she said firmly. 'Why else am I here?'

The question was for herself as much as for Audrey.

'You're lesbian?' Audrey said casually.

'No, I'm not. But I'm curious, as only women can be, I suppose. Women like each other and like to be girls again and get away from bloody men. You know.'

'Yes,' said Audrey, nodding, 'but Boulter is lesbian, one hundred per cent bull dyke, but thankfully, very pretty too.'

Audrey blushed!

'I saw inside her wardrobe,' Sandra said. 'I'm not afraid – just very curious.'

'I can't help noticing,' said Audrey, 'that your bum's very brown. You've a lovely all-over tan, like a nudist.'

Sandra smiled and said she was and had been labelled an exhibitionist; she hinted at the delights of dogging.

'Well, to get on the right side of Boulter,' said Audrey, 'don't be too showy. That's a very bad word here at Quirke's and Boulter is a Quirkean down to her G-string! Be a bit shy. She's the show-off! Do you like being bummed? I mean, have you had anal sex?'

'Only from a bloke,' said Sandra. 'Not with one of those things. Boulter's toys looked awfully big, much bigger than any bloke's cock'

'Yes,' sighed Audrey, 'they are.'

Suddenly Miss Boulter bellowed 'Dorm stand!' and every girl, whether nude, nightied or halfway between, stood rigidly at attention, then curtsied together as Miss Quirke entered the dorm. She nodded and the girls relaxed. Miss Quirke, accompanied by Boulter, made straight for Sandra and Audrey, both by now in their frilly, white nighties.

'Well, Miss Shanks,' she said brightly, 'are we settling in satisfactorily?'

'I think so, thank you, Miss,' said Sandra and found herself curtsying again.

Miss Quirke tapped the end of her cane.

'I believe we have a rendezvous at assembly,' she said with a broad smile. 'Twelve stripes, wasn't it?'

'Yes, Miss,' said Sandra, blushing deeply. 'I'm truly sorry for my offence.'

'You shall be, Miss Shanks. But I'm sure you'll bear up like a brave girl. As for this neighbour of yours –' she sighed deeply as she inspected Audrey's rumpled nightie '– she's due six stripes just now, isn't she, Miss Boulter?'

'Yes, Miss,' said Boulter. 'Untidy bed, and –'

'You needn't continue,' said Miss Quirke with another deep sigh. 'Best get it over with and I shall observe. As for you, Miss Shanks, it will be another example for you. Miss Larch knows the drill all too well.'

Audrey made a face beind her back, then shuffled to the caning-frame, or the 'eagle', in the centre of the dorm, threw up her nightie with a regal flourish and assumed position, waiting for Boulter to strap her down. Sandra gasped at her first sight of Audrey's naked buttocks: they were tanned like a hide, criss-crossed and etched deeply with the marks of numerous stripings. Boulter swiftly locked her on the frame, strapping her wrists and ankles very tightly in the leather cuffs.

'The willow, I think, Miss Boulter,' said the headmistress and Miss Boulter dutifully fetched the desired cane from her armoire, a sturdy four-footer of shiny, tan wood.

The prefect stood behind Audrey's raised bare, the cane lifted high and waiting to strike. Her eyes gleamed, her sumptuous body poised with a panther's grace and her lips parted in a thin smile. Sandra could not prevent her pussy from moistening at another girl's bare-bum caning.

'Have you anything to say before punishment commences, Miss Larch?' said Miss Quirke formally.

'Only that I promise to be good in future, Miss, and work hard to pass my prelims . . .'

Miss Quirke smiled.

'If only Miss Boulter would stop picking on me unfairly all the time!'

There was a stunned silence.

'Well!' Miss Quirke exclaimed, her face flushing. 'The wretched girl! Miss Boulter, you may give her an extra three stripes for that insolence. Your sentence, Miss Larch, is now nine stripes. Do you agree?'

'Huh! That won't satisfy her, Miss!'

'I cannot believe – Now you shall receive twelve stripes, Miss Larch. Do you agree to that?'

'Why, yes, Miss,' said Audrey with surprising meekness.

The caning began.

'Mm!' said Audrey after the first savage stripe across the bare flans of her bum, and she was warned against 'squeaking'.

At the second stripe, she gasped and her arse-crack began to clench. At the third, her knees began to tremble and, after the fourth, her legs jerked straight and her naked buttocks twitched violently at each lash of the prefect's cane. Her panting filled the dorm.

Sandra watched with ever-growing liquid in her quim. Some of the girls wore panties under their nighties, but Sandra was nude and the white cotton stained fast and clearly. There was no denying her excitement, nor that of the other girls, as the cane lashed Audrey's naked bottom with unerring and relentless precision. Miss Quirke counted, as Audrey's fesses reddened and were streaked with the purple of harsh new welts, and her breath became heavy.

'Five, six – mmm! repeat that, for squeaking – seven, eight – repeat, for shuddering – Oh! yes! – nine, ten . . .'

Audrey had taken fourteen strokes of the vicious willow and her whole body was jerking and trembling when she was finally allowed to sink for a moment on to the eagle, exhausted by her pain. But when Boulter unstrapped her, she stood up fresh as a daisy, curtsied to the prefect and to Miss Quirke, and walked jauntily to her bed, showily rubbing her wealed bottom under her nightie.

Miss Quirke professed herself pleased at Audrey's endurance, but neither her, nor Boulter's, face agreed.

A handsome, shapely girl sniggered audibly at Audrey as she got into bed; Sandra recognised her as

Julie Down, who was of their dinner table and the one who clapped loudest at Miss Tolliver's punishment. Miss Quirke left swiftly, and the main light was turned off, leaving the dorm in the blue glow of a night light. To Sandra's surprise, Audrey sat up in bed and took her nightie off, then lay humming softly, nude, with her eyes open.

Miss Boulter retreated behind a curtain which she drew around her bed. After a few minutes she emerged and crooked a finger at Audrey, but leered at Sandra.

'You didn't think you were going to get off that lightly, did you?' she said to Audrey, who meekly agreed.

The nude girl was ordered once more to bend over the eagle, this time unstrapped. Miss Boulter held a long, vicious tawse whose tongues gleamed darkly in the ghostly blue light. She was costumed in a one-piece corselet, like a swimsuit, only made of shiny, black rubber, with holes to reveal the big pink plums of her already swollen nipples, and a slit at her crotch, from which the engorged lips of her cunt protruded menacingly. The rubber garment had sussie straps fastened to fishnet stockings which were visible briefly before plunging into black leather thigh-boots with massive, pointed heels, a good seven inches.

'As for you, Miss,' she said to Sandra, gesturing at a pile of clothing on her own bed, 'hurry up and get into your proper kit.'

Sandra obeyed, shivering in delicious apprehension. Eager eyes watched as she unfolded her 'kit' and her jaw dropped. She looked in amazement at Boulter, who was teasing the crack of Audrey's bare buttocks with her tawse.

'Put them on,' Boulter rasped, 'femme.'

Sandra did so. White stockings and sussie, pink teetering stilettos, a pink chiffon tutu and skin-tight pink blouse with an uphold, wispy-cupped bra which thrust her teats together and high, but left the nipples bare – and hardening in excitement – under the gauze blouse. Her panties were a mere G-string in gaudy pink with a lush frilly edge, and way too tight, so that the thong bit cruelly deep between her cunt-lips. There were two pink clasps to braid her hair in twin ringlets and a tube of shocking pink lipstick. Boulter beckoned her new girl and Sandra obeyed the summons, unsteady on her high heels, yet with her quim-juice seeping and nipples now hard.

Boulter nodded her approval.

'A right girly,' she said.

Then, without warning, she slapped Sandra hard on the cheek, rocking her almost off balance. The slap stung, and Sandra's hand flew to her livid cheek, her eyes flashing in anger, yet already knowing better than to question her treatment. Boulter added a second slap to her other cheek; Julie Down said 'Hurrah!', the other girls quietly applauded and Sandra's gash flowed wet.

'Kneel before me and lick my boots. Do you think me cruel, femme?' said Boulter.

'You love being cruel,' said Sandra as she obeyed. She licked the leather tips and the heels for a minute each.

'I shall make you love it too,' said the prefect. 'I can't stripe your pretty girly's arse, because it must remain blank for Miss Q tomorrow. But you'll be whopped nonetheless, like your slut friend Audrey Larch. First, I'll perch you.'

The girls, led by Julie Down, cheered again. Sandra was made to balance herself on top of the whipping frame, squatting most uncomfortably so that her fesses stuck out and her quim pressed against Audrey's naked back. She tried to raise herself as much as possible, but knew that soon she would have to rest her weight on Audrey, especially as she was jerked forward suddenly at a fierce spank on her bare bum. She gasped and looked round. Boulter had donned a pair of rubber gauntlets which extended to her biceps.

54

The spank had been agony, far worse than Sandra's spanking by Miss Long and Boulter showed her why. She stroked Sandra's slapped buttocks with the palm and explained that spanking caused the spanker some discomfort after thirty or so slaps, therefore her gloves had clustered ball-bearings sewn into the palm, both to cushion the impact for the spanker and increase the victim's pain.

'You make a pretty pair of birds,' she said, licking her lips, 'and I'm going to give you a good one hundred between you, with palm for Miss Shanks and tawse to Miss Larch.'

Sandra's spanking would continue until she could take no more and then the balance of the one hundred whacks would be applied to Audrey's bare with the tawse. Sandra gritted her teeth and took the second and third spanks which smarted abominably on her bare flesh. The clenching of her buttocks made the intrusive thong of her G-string chafe even more uncomfortably in her crack.

Miss Boulter denied her the relief of counting the spanks, so Sandra had to keep track herself. The pain was awful; each slap of the steel-lined gauntlet sent shudders through her spine and she felt her bare bum flaming in pain as the crack of her arse clenched in a private twitching rhythm quite distinct from the spanking which Boulter made cruelly irregular. Twenty, thirty . . . Her eyes were moist with tears and she could not hold her perch, but sank sobbing on to Audrey whose back quivered as she took Sandra's weight.

Then Sandra realised that each spank was making her torso slide up and down Audrey's spine. Her quim was dripping with fluid as she was spanked and the flutter in her belly gave away her excitement at her dreadful submission as girls' laughter rang in her ears.

The tips of her teats tingled and rubbed against Audrey's goose-pimpled flesh, as though Audrey was rocking with the rhythm of the spanks, rubbing Sandra's stiffened clit against her hard backbone. Sandra's belly heaved, as the painful spanking grew harder and her quim dripped faster at the pressure on her clitty. It must surely be more than one hundred! In her confusion and agony, suddenly she gave way and felt herself loosen; a hot stream of piss cascaded over Audrey's bare back and buttocks and down her legs. Miss Boulter paused.

'Seems you can't take it, or hold it. Forty-three spanks, Miss. Not much good, even for a new fledge. You'll make it up, as your slut friend cleans your filth from the floor.'

Sobbing, Sandra descended and despite herself, curtsied before her tormentor and said in a quavering voice that she was ready to submit. Miss Boulter now ordered her to be 'spanked round the dorm'. She was to lay her thighs across each girl's bed in turn and take a spanking of ten from the girl's sitting position. Sandra tremulously approached the first bed, where Julie Down awaited her. Audrey was on all fours, licking the floor clean of Sandra's pee.

Fiercely, Julie grasped Sandra's neck and pulled her across the bed, calling her names. The pink tutu flew up of its own accord, revealing Sandra's scarlet, bare fesses, to which Julie proceeded to add – unfairly – a further dozen spanks with her palm, desisting only when the next girl begged for her turn. Sandra wriggled as the awful hot spanks seared her already smarting bare bottom. Julie dismissed her by calling her a pathetic femme, and pulling the thong of her G-string so that it twanged painfully against her bumhole.

Sandra passed from bed to bed, her naked bottom by now a scalded mass of pain, but she looked with moist eyes at the tawsing of Audrey Larch. Boulter was counting down the strokes of the vicious tawse-flaps. Audrey was due fifty-seven, and Boulter had only reached 40. The tawse made a dreadful, dull, slapping sound that drowned the cracks of Sandra's hand-spankings. The spread buttocks of the tawsed girl were a livid mass of purple and black and the hungry tongues of the tawse seemed to clasp the ridges of her bare flesh, seeking out every morsel of agony.

Yet there was a balletic quality to Audrey's very real squirming, as though she was practising an art at which she excelled and expected to excel for a long time to come. From time to time, the prefect would say, quite politely, 'All right, Miss Larch?' and Audrey would reply 'Yes thank you, Miss Boulter,' as though they were taking tea.

Sandra managed to distract herself from the pain of her own spanking by watching Audrey's flogging and the gyrations of her bare buttocks, and gradually found that her clit was throbbing again, and that her quim was leaving a wet patch on the blankets of the beds over which her thighs were spread.

The pain in her croup actually reached a plateau, became not dulled, but somehow welcome and part of her, so that she sighed in genuine disappointment when the last girl had spanked her ten. Sandra's bottom was aflame, her clitty throbbed and tingled and she was itching to come. Oblivious to the stream of cunt-juice marring her white stockings, she approached Miss Boulter once more and meekly begged to be of service. Miss Boulter touched her spanked buttocks suggestively and parted them as though inviting anal sex, at the same time licking her lips. But after counting twenty, she suddenly placed the tawse in Sandra's hand.

'You take over, girly,' she said. 'Your slut friend has a further nineteen coming and make them hard.'

Sandra's cunt dripped at her painful submission to spanking, yet now she was herself holding the lash in dominance, quite at odds with her girly clothing and her submissive role towards Miss Boulter. She looked down

57

at Audrey Larch's naked bottom, wealed and bruised so abominably and shuddering from stripes taken and stripes awaited. Her cunt-juice flowed more heavily than ever.

She lifted the tawse and whopped Audrey across the middle buttocks, leaving livid stripes. She repeated the stroke harder, then again, harder still, and was rewarded with the graceful squirming of the bare flogged nates, the twitches of agony and Audrey's little moans and yelps as the tongues scored her flesh. Audrey's thighs themselves glistened with softly trickling cunt-oil.

In the dim, blue light, Audrey's physical resemblance to Miss Quirke herself was striking. Sandra closed her eyes for a moment and her tawsing grew harder. Then she looked again at the bare croup beneath her and gasped as though seeing welts for the first time. She flogged her friend's twitching bare bum without mercy. The buttocks swirled and danced in front of her eyes and she dimly heard Miss Boulter cry 'Done!' just after her nineteenth tawse-stroke.

Audrey herself murmured that she was not done and could she please have some more? The girls clapped; astonished, Sandra laid two more strokes across the bare buttocks which took her whipping so insolently and Audrey clutched the whipping-frame and ground her loins against it. The juices streamed from her cunt in a torrent and she yelped harshly five or six times. By whipping alone, Audrey Larch had been made to come.

From victim, Sandra had so easily become Audrey's tormentor. Yet Audrey had wanted her beating. Margaret's words echoed: 'Who was the submissive?'

Miss Boulter gestured towards her bed and Sandra's clitty tingled in the delicious knowledge that she was going to find out.

5

Femme

The dorm was unnaturally quiet: not a breath stirred the air. Watched by mischievous eyes, Sandra parted the curtain of Miss Boulter's bed and stepped inside. Her movements were awkward because of the smarting bum.

'Kneel down on the bed, femme, with your head down, bum up and facing the wall and your cheeks well apart,' said Boulter curtly.

'Are you going to spank me again, Miss?' said Sandra.

'No. You're to be striped tomorrow and you're marked enough,' the prefect replied. 'On the bum, anyway.'

Sandra obeyed, nestling her bottom at Boulter's pillow, which was cotton, unlike the dark-blue sheets and coverlet, which were of thin latex and cool on her face. The door of the armoire opened, then there was the silky slither of rubber and the clink of buckles. Miss Boulter was now inserting one prong of the massive black dildo into the slit of her rubber corselet and between her wet cunt-lips, and she grunted with satisfaction as it slid up her gash to its full length. The rubber was flexible and Boulter buckled the strap around her waist and over her latex costume. Now she stood up and adjusted the outer prong, so she looked like a male with a monstrous erection.

'I didn't order you to look, femme,' snapped Boulter,

but did not seem displeased at the awe in Sandra's eyes. 'I like a girly who obeys orders and I like to watch her squirm and suffer. Don't expect kisses and cuddles as from some slobbering male. Just squeal if it hurts, and squeal even if it doesn't.'

Roughly, she placed her fingers on Sandra's gash and got two inside, then began to poke harshly in and out, while squeezing the already wet cunt-lips till fresh spurts of love-oil dripped out. Sandra moaned as her juice flowed. When she was wet to the prefect's satisfaction, Boulter soaked her prick with Sandra's oil, as if for penetration. The dildo prick was a huge gnarled organ of black rubber made in the rough shape of a cock, with a helmet and balls, but generously knobbled with sharp little nodules and with a little stiff plug for clitoral stimulation.

Sandra relaxed her buttocks, spreading her gash and her bumhole too, in readiness for Boulter's penetration. But Miss Boulter lay down on the bed herself, head to the wall, and slid like an eel up the latex cover until her face was underneath Sandra's bum, and the hideous latex prong quivering before Sandra's eyes, all shiny with her own cunt-juice. She pulled down Sandra's G-string to her knees.

'Queen me, slut,' said Miss Boulter. 'Sit on my face with all your bum's weight; I want to drink your juices. And while I'm tonguing you, suck on my prick, making sure you take it right to the back of the throat and push so that my end gives me a good fucking in the cunt.'

The flexible dildo was positioned so that this operation was indeed possible. Sandra leaned forward and gingerly took the rubber cock in her mouth, finding that if she tightened her lips and thrust, the other prong would move inside the lesbian's gaping slit.

Emboldened, Sandra took the whole shaft of the cock in her mouth and began to suck vigorously, licking her own juices and bobbing her head rhythmically to push the dildo well into Boulter's cunt. At the same time she lowered her buttocks on to the prefect's face, gently at first, but on feeling a stiff, hot tongue penetrate the folds of her gash, she obeyed her orders and sank her weight on to the woman's face, squashing her mouth and nose in her anal cleft.

Miss Boulter's tongue found her engorged, throbbing clitty and began to pummel it with sharp strokes, making Sandra's own sucking of the false penis more intense. Sandra grimaced at the alien taste of rubber. Every time she poked the organ to the back of her mouth, Miss Boulter jerked as the clit-plug connected with her own nubbin and the black prong sank deeper into her glistening, wet slit.

Sandra cupped the lesbian's taut buttocks as she sucked the hard, black cock. Once, she extended a finger to tickle Miss Boulter's prominent clitty, which was like a big, pink peanut sticking up between her cunt-flaps, but Boulter slapped her bare bum and replaced the probing finger with her own beside the dildo's plug and, drinking the juices of Sandra's cunt, vigorously masturbated.

Sandra squirmed her arse-globes as though she wanted to crush the lesbian's face. Miss Boulter grunted in pleasure and her cunt-oil became a flood. Suddenly her legs jerked up and the leather thigh-boots were around Sandra's neck, pressing her on to the latex cock, and pinioning her face to the lesbian's squirming belly. Sandra felt the little movements of Boulter's throat as she swallowed Sandra's own copious gash-juices, while chewing the lips of her cunt.

She was trapped in this embrace, and Miss Boulter held her head strongly until the prefect's belly fluttered and she heaved in a spasm, yelping softly. Sandra sucked and pushed on the latex dildo and her own cunt flowed at the flickering of Boulter's powerful tongue until she too began to squeal (as ordered) and gave herself up to orgasm.

Gasping, the two females disengaged. As Miss Boulter had promised, there was no 'slobbering' in her brand of lesbic caress. In a businesslike manner, she opened her armoire and took out some further equipment. She had a rubber pixy hood, which she slipped over her head, so that only her eyes and nose were visible. Then she ordered Sandra to turn over, lie on her back and lift her legs straight in the air. She obeyed and Boulter pulled off the wet G-string altogether, wadded it and stuffed it into Sandra's mouth.

She positioned herself to lean on Sandra's stockings until her legs were bent right over and her shoes were wedged on the bed-frame. Still with her weight on Sandra, Miss Boulter took two long ropes of black rubber, like her dildo, and swiftly knotted them so that Sandra's ankles were tightly fastened above her head to the top of the bed. She spread Sandra's arms and tied each wrist to a corner. Sandra lay trussed and helpless, her gash and buttocks open.

'Comfortable?' snapped Boulter, her voice muffled by the rubber hood like a hangman's. 'You may nod yes or no.'

Sandra nodded no. Boulter chuckled.

'Ever taken it in the bumhole?' she said.

Now Sandra nodded yes.

'From a man's cock?'

Yes, again.

'Not from a dildo?'

No.

Boulter chuckled longer.

'You'll be tight. It will hurt horribly at first,' she said. 'Squeal all you like, girly. You've probably had it doggy fashion but I like the missionary position for bumming a girl, because I can see her face twisted in pain. I like to hurt a submissive femme, and hooded for fear.'

She tickled Sandra's anus bud with the tip of the

dildo, now gleaming with Sandra's cunt-juice and saliva. Then she put two fingers in Sandra's gash and finger-fucked her energetically until Sandra moaned and began to writhe in pleasure, but studiously avoided touching Sandra's stiff clitty-nubbin.

'You've come once, bitch, but you shan't come again,' Boulter said. 'You want to, don't you? Like slut Larch. A good whipping makes girlies want to come. I'll take you in cunt first and make you long for it even more, but you're tied tight and can't touch that fragrant clit.'

Miss Boulter paused, and to Sandra's astonished gaze, rolled a rubber condom on top of the already moistened dildo. Then with one easy motion she sank the prong into Sandra's soaking gash and began to fuck her, carefully avoiding any stimulation of the clit. Sandra moaned nonetheless; the lesbian's fucking was practised and hard, like a man's, her belly slamming against Sandra's thighs and buttocks at each savage poke of the giant dildo.

'My, how I'd like to see you tarred and feathered. Such a pity Miss J got sacked! You may take that as a compliment, my submissive little femme.'

Sandra's groans gave no indication as to whether or not she appreciated the compliment. Abruptly, Miss Boulter stopped fucking and withdrew, then unrolled the condom from the dildo and stuffed it into Sandra's mouth along with her knickers gag. Another condom replaced it and the fucking continued, and this was repeated four times, until Sandra's cheeks were swelled to bursting with her own wet panties and a mouthful of rubber soaked in her own juices.

After a quarter of an hour's vigorous thrusting, Miss Boulter seemed not the least tired, but Sandra's quim ached and she gasped for the relief of orgasm. Boulter withdrew again and unrolled the current rubber sheath, adding it to the wad in Sandra's mouth; then suddenly turned and presented her bum and open anal pucker to Sandra.

'Put the rubbers into my bumhole, femme,' she ordered.

Sandra did as she was told, thrusting each rubber with her tongue into the widened arse-bud of the lesbian, and when she had got the thin film into the bumhole to a tongue's depth, the hole suddenly tightened and seemed to suck the rubber inside, aided by a gloved finger which pushed it right in. This was done with all of the wet rubbers until Miss Boulter expressed satisfaction at a bum well filled. Replacing Sandra's knicker gag, she reassumed her position as though for further cunt-fucking.

But with a sudden thrust of her haunches, the lubricated dildo penetrated Sandra's anus to a depth of perhaps two inches. Tears leapt to Sandra's eyes and she squealed behind her knickers gag. Boulter ordered her to relax her sphincter and let the shaft in fully.

'You've done it before, bitch, for a man's cock,' she murmured, then gave Sandra two hard slaps to the face.

Groaning, Sandra parted her buttocks to the full and the dildo slipped in another inch under the weight of the lesbian's stiffened, straining loins.

'Better,' said Miss Boulter and began to fuck hard in the anus until Sandra released a long, wailing gasp of agony and her anal passage gave up its struggle. The dildo shaft plunged in right to her root so that the two girls' bellies touched. Boulter grunted in satisfaction and her haunches began to arse-fuck Sandra very fast and hard.

'Mmm! Mmm! Mmm!' Sandra squealed, her buttocks writhing helplessly under the onslaught in her bumhole.

Boulter laughed and raised her torso to upright, still continuing her relentless bumming. Now her hand went to the stiff clitty extruded from her gash-lips and she began to masturbate as she buggered Sandra.

'Wish you could wank too, eh, femme?' she gasped as she flicked the raw, stiff nubbin. 'Wanking's the best pleasure, but if you're found doing it, your bum will be whopped purple. School rules! The only crime is getting caught.'

Sandra's loins began to adjust to the rhythm of her buggery, thrusting to each stroke of the dildo, her now eased sphincter making little sucking, clutching motions as though to prevent the shaft from escaping. At each thrust, she gasped and mewed like a kitten as her arse was pierced.

'Hurt like buggery?' laughed Miss Boulter, voice hoarse behind her pixy hood.

Sandra nodded yes.

'Want it to stop?'

Sandra nodded no.

Boulter touched her own clit again, took it between gloved thumb and forefinger, squeezed hard on the obtruded pink nubbin and squealed in a shuddering, sweating orgasm.

As her gasps subsided, she resumed the machine-like force of her buggery and began to flick her clitty again with her forefinger. She sighed in deep pleasure as Sandra squirmed, her eyes begging for the relief of coming.

'Squeal, girly!' the prefect ordered.

Obediently, Sandra squealed.

'You have a good, tight arsehole,' said Boulter as she buggered. 'You should do well in the boxing ring,' she said, as if the fact and the idea were connected. 'Miss Down's name is forward and I'll add yours.'

Sandra had no means of saying thank you, so squealed extra-loud instead at a particularly savage thrust of the dildo right at her anal root. This pleased Miss Boulter and she said so.

'And if you want to please me more, femme, you can bring me things from the tuck shop. Half your pocket money should go to your nice dorm prefect. That's the way . . .'

Sandra shook her head violently in refusal and Miss Boulter laughed. Suddenly her thighs opened and she peed copiously all over Sandra's face and blouse, the steaming, golden liquid making a puddle on the rubber sheet. She slapped Sandra's wet face, then again, and again, and after nearly an hour of ceaseless anal penetration, punctuated by more fierce slaps to the face, the cheeks of Sandra's face glowed as red as those of her bruised bottom. During her buggery, Miss Boulter had masturbated to orgasm four more times, and Sandra had peed twice in her shame.

Miss Boulter untied her but kept the rubber cords on her and obliged her to return to her own bed on all fours, propelled by kicks to her sore, inflamed anus from Boulter's boot-points. Audrey pretended to sleep as Miss Boulter ordered Sandra to lie on her back like a starfish, and now refastened her wrists and ankles to her own bed.

With a lynx's grace, she leapt on to Sandra's pillow and squatted on her face, then evacuated all the rubbers which had been wet from Sandra's cunt right over her own face. As they clung there, Boulter fitted a second, harsher pixy hood over Sandra's head, covering all of her face except for a breathing slit at her nose. In darkness, Sandra heard Miss Boulter call that Sandra was dorm femme for tonight but that her clitty was not to be touched.

Throughout the night, Sandra moaned and writhed in her bonds as girl after girl slunk to her bed and positioned herself on top of her, equipped with Boulter's – or her own – dildo, to take her in the cunt or anus, or just tongue her gash-folds and taste her juices. It was much later that she felt a soft, naked body creep between her sheets and enfold both of them in the blankets before removing Sandra's hood and her gagging rubbers and knickers.

'I hope I didn't bugger you too hard,' said Audrey. 'Gosh, your cunt did taste nice! I had to do it; everybody does. Well it's over, Sandra, and you're one of us now.'

'Oh, Audrey,' Sandra moaned, 'it was like my darkest fantasies, you know? To be spanked raw, on my bare bum, then buggered and fucked by cock after cock. I forgot that girls were doing it to me. I just know it was lovely to be tied and helpless alone in the dark, dressed like a girly and fucked so much. I wanted to come! I nearly did with one girl, though she didn't touch my clit. She sucked and bit so hard, at my bumhole as well as my pussy, and swallowed all my juice.'

'That would be Julie,' said Audrey. 'She's a cunt-lapper! Being hooded isn't so bad, for then you don't see the Bolt beside your face, wanking as you're bum-fucked. She likes to wank as another girl squirms with the dildo in her arse. As for coming, that's easily attended to.'

She reached three fingers into Sandra's sopping gash, with her thumb pressed firmly on the distended clit nubbin.

'You don't mind if I use your panties and rubbers, you know, for my own wank?'

Audrey rubbed her clitty with Sandra's wet G-string and with her free hand masturbated Sandra vigorously. Sandra yelped and gasped in relief; both girls came at once.

'You see why we always fail our exams,' said Audrey. 'None of us gets much sleep, me least of all. Even the Bolt has never passed an exam.'

'Then how is she a prefect?' asked Sandra.

'She has a hold over Miss Quirke,' said Audrey.

'I wonder who has a hold over Miss Boulter?' Sandra murmured.

Sandra's heart thumped wildly as Miss Quirke called her name, for the second time, at morning assembly.

The first was for roll call and Sandra had answered 'Present, Miss' very proudly. Now she was not required to answer but simply to stand and approach the rostrum, where the headmistress presided over her girls and kept her whipping tools. Sandra stepped up to the small dais and curtsied.

It was but an hour since the dorm was roused by Boulter's whistle and the girls had doffed their nighties to scamper nude and be first to the ice-cold showers. There was no word of the events of the night before, not even from the immaculately uniformed Boulter as she supervised the squealing, wet girls.

Breakfast had been a paltry affair of weak tea and stale bread and marge, but Sandra had been too nervous to think of food. As they squatted afterwards at their evacuations in the thronged WC, Audrey did her best to cheer her up, saying that a striped girl got a penny extra pocket money and at mid-morning break she could look forward to the tuck shop.

'A penny?' said Sandra, but there was no time for further questions.

The girls filed into assembly and their names were called, then Miss Quirke detailed the day's business, slight changes in sporting or classroom times, details of the impending boxing tournament, and suchlike. Then it was time for decreed punishments and it became obvious that Sandra's, the most serious, was to be last.

'Maureen Stopes. Four stripes for untidiness.'

'Tara Devine.' Again! 'Three stripes for rumpled stockings.'

'Susan Potts. Three stripes for general unruliness.'

'Audrey Larch –' of course there would be Audrey '– four stripes for yawning at breakfast.'

One by one, the girls approached the dais, curtsied and assumed position. 'Assuming position' included the entire operation of bending over, touching toes and lowering knickers so that no further instruction was

68

needed. There were even painted marks on the floor where the miscreant should position her feet.

Miss Quirke formally repeated the girl's sentence and asked her if she was in agreement, and each girl replied, 'Yes, Miss,' from her bent-over position. Then a short, springy cane applied the decreed stripes to her bare bottom. The cane was slightly less than three feet long and quite thin, and it made a loud vip! vip! sound as it striped the girls' naked buttocks, but the impression was given that public stripes were intended to shame as much as hurt.

Audrey grinned cheerfully at Sandra as she mounted and assumed position and she even winked as the cane descended on her well-striped bum with somewhat more than the usual force. She took her four without blinking and walked jauntily back to her seat, luridly rubbing her bottom.

And then it was Sandra's turn.

'Sandra Shanks. Twelve stripes for illicit possession of tobacco.'

Skirts rustled and there were awed whispers. Twelve stripes was obviously an extreme sentence for morning assembly.

And now Sandra prepared to assume position, her knickers down, her bum bared for the whippy, little cane and feet obediently in the worn white marks where so many girls had submitted before her.

A hint of something not quite right came when Miss Quirke ordered Sandra to remain standing for a moment, while two prefects, Long and Bustard, carried a little leather stool to the rostrum and placed it on a rubber mat which Miss Gordon unrolled. It had an indentation like a soup plate in its centre, and Miss Gordon put it in position beneath the stool's cushion.

Then Sandra was ordered to assume 'submissive' position, not touching toes, but with her bum bent over the leather cushion of the stool, her ankles at each splayed foot, and her hands clutching the well-worn grooves at either side. Trembling, Sandra lowered her knickers and raised her skirt and frilly petticoat neatly over her back, where Miss Gordon pinned them to her blouse so that her croup was well bared. Her sussie belt was unfastened and hung round her neck so that nothing marred the nudity of her buttocks. Her stockings drooped like a slut's.

Miss Quirke ceremonially opened the drawer of her desk and put away the whippy cane. Sandra twisted her neck and looked. There was a collective gasp as Miss Quirke withdrew from her drawer a package wrapped in oilcloth. She put the oilcloth on the top of her desk and unfolded it to reveal quite a different instrument from the whippy, little cane. Now there was silence in the assembly hall.

She presented to Sandra's wide eyes a quirt of four leather thongs about two-and-a-half feet in length. She formally explained to Sandra and the assembly that the leather binding enclosed springy, steel cords, so that the device was like a braided riding crop only more flexible and more suitable for a longer flogging. That the 'quirt of four' was more painful than a single cane or crop was self-evident. The heinousness of Sandra's offence required that an example must be made of her and the twelve stripes would be delivered on the bare, without adjustment.

'Adjustment' in Quirke's parlance, meant leniency: in other words Sandra's stripes were to be just as hard in a 'twelver' with the quirt of four as with an ordinary cane or crop for a shorter punishment.

'Are you in agreement with your sentence, Miss Shanks?'

Sandra whispered hoarsely that she was in agreement. At once, a fresh rubber plug was unwrapped from cellophane and pushed between her teeth for her to bite on.

'The punishment will last exactly fifty-five seconds,' Miss Quirke intoned, 'with stripes delivered at five-second intervals. The punishment shall now begin.'

There was no warning whistle of the lash. Suddenly Sandra seemed to jump out of her skin as the four braided steel thongs cracked agonisingly across her bare bottom, seeming to scald every inch of her croup at once. Her buttocks automatically clenched.

'One,' said Miss Quirke.

Sandra gasped, fighting back the rising of her gorge, her lips moving to count the seconds. Three, four . . .

The second stripe took her slightly higher, searing her upper buttocks, and her bum-crack clenched repeatedly, now joined by the whole expanse of her quivering, naked peach. Again, the awful counting, then –

'Mmm! Mmm!' Sandra squealed, biting heavily into her rubber mouthpiece. Her fesses were a lake of molten pain, squirming and wriggling without any pretence of dignity.

'Three,' said Miss Quirke.

At the fourth, Sandra clutched her flogging-stool as the white-hot pain of the four thongs made her legs jerk straight behind her, the backs of her knees straining white as the hard stripes marked her bare bum. Her jaw ached and she bit so hard into her rubber mouthpiece that her teeth were embedded.

By the fifth, her tears flowed freely and her whole body shuddered at the stripes of the hideous quirt. She counted the seconds. The sixth lash knocked her breathless and her welted buttocks wriggled grotesquely.

'Oh! No! No! Ahh . . .' Sandra sobbed.

The five-second wait between stripes seemed an eternity. Yet her belly fluttered with more than the pain of a naked flogging: Sandra's quim began to drip copiously as her whipping continued. She deliberately thrust her bare bum high and quivered it on purpose, as though to invite the quirt's lashes and show off her submission.

71

'Mmm! Mmm! Mmm . . .' she cried at the seventh, and did not cease this wailing moan throughout the rest of the set, as though she was too far gone in agony to fear a stripe's repetition for 'squealing'.

Her cunt continued to flow with the copious juices of her awful excitement under the lash and her bare buttocks quivered relentlessly like eels, wriggling and squirming as though to escape the deadly pain by burrowing into the cushion of the flogging stool itself. But the stool kept Sandra's bare nates presented tight and high for her decreed pain.

'Nine! Ten!'

The quirt's thongs continued their pitiless, slithering crack on her naked fesses at the five-second intervals like a metronome. Sandra's eyes were blurred with tears, but her belly heaved with the constant oozing of her love-oil from the engorged cunt-lips. Her teeth finally snapped through the rubber mouthpiece at the eleventh stripe, and after the twelfth, she collapsed on the stool, opening her mouth in a scream, and letting her tears flow freely.

'Exactly fifty-five seconds,' said Miss Quirke with satisfaction.

Sandra was left until her sobs had died away and then Miss Gordon and Miss Bustard unpinned her skirt and petticoat, wiped her face and helped her to her feet. Sandra mustered her dignity, pulled up her knickers and took her time making sure her sussies and stockings were proper. Then she curtsied to Miss Quirke.

'Th-thank you for my punishment, Miss,' she blurted.

She put a hand to her knickers and felt them wet through her frilly petticoat. But there was something more than love-oil. Looking down, she gasped. The bowl of the rubber matting beneath her stool was brimming with golden liquid. As she was flogged – it must have been after the tenth stroke, she told Audrey later – she had peed herself. And Audrey assured her that under the quirt of four, most girls peed at the fourth or fifth . . .

Sandra walked shakily back to her seat and when the assembly was dismissed, the other girls made way for her to go straight to the WC. Coolly, Sandra stripped naked and turned on the shower. An awed throng gathered to watch as she twisted to inspect her flogging.

Her seared bare bottom was a mass of weals, patched with red welts and deep ridges of purple. Sandra gasped and her quim-lips trembled, as did her clitty when her fingers unconsciously crept to that stiffened little nubbin. In full view of all the admiring females, the whipped schoolgirl masturbated to a loud, quivering orgasm.

For the rest of the day, Sandra swanned. She did not hesitate to yawn during the boredom of English class, an offence for which lesser girls were promptly caned with two or three stripes on bare. A measly two or three, and with a feeble little yew-cane!

Her only disappointment came at the tuck shop, where for that day she was given pride of place in the jostling queue. The dorm prefects dispensed pocket money at break time, and Sandra received elevenpence in curious old money which she scarcely understood, except that it was not very much.

Miss Boulter told her that the normal pocket money was tenpence and she should be grateful her striping had earned her an extra penny. But when Sandra got to the tiny cubicle of the tuck shop and looked at the sparse rows of chocolate bars, toffee sweets and suchlike, she found that the lowest price for anything – a quarter pound of horrid liquorice allsorts – was ninepence. Audrey offered to 'split' and they bought a shilling of toffees, which left her with fivepence.

That night she slept well, lulled by the sound of Miss Boulter's embrace of another luckless fresher. She

73

thought it might be Julie Down, who Audrey said – after her own, apparently customary, ritual of six decreed stripes – needed taking down a peg or two.

The next day, Sandra got her tenpence and arrived at the front of the tuck shop queue with her treasure of one shilling and threepence. However, it seemed that her pride of position lasted only for the day of her actual striping and there were angry grumbles. Miss Long was at the back of the line, and suddenly Julie Down punched Sandra's breasts and pulled her hair, telling her she was a soppy wet and should go to the back of the queue. Sandra responded by pulling Julie's own hair and pinching her bum and a full-scale tussle was prevented only by the arrival of an angry Miss Long.

White with rage, but with a cruel smile nonetheless, she scribbled a note and handed it to Sandra.

'Miss Crisp is present in her study,' she said. 'Both of you report to her at once.'

'Does that mean we won't get any tuck?' asked Sandra in an aggrieved voice.

'It means you'll get a little more than tuck, Miss Shanks,' said the prefect, with a smile.

6

Crisp Chastisement

'Well!' said Miss Crisp. 'Two girls for the cane at once.
You must both have been very naughty. Do make
yourself comfortable. I'll make myself comfortable too,
if you don't mind. Two sessions will be hot work, so I'll
take my cardie off.'

Sunlight streamed through the mullioned windows of
the mistress's study, the bright, autumn day outside
belying the awful fate which awaited Sandra and her
sullen companion. Miss Crisp gestured to the leather
sofa and Sandra and Julie placed themselves on it,
keeping to opposite ends, while the mistress removed
her trim, grey cardigan, revealing a blouse of rather
startling tightness for a schoolmistress, and noticeably
stretched over breasts scarcely restrained by their clearly
visible black bra.

Her blouse was open to the second button. Apart
from that, her costume was suitably demure: a black
skirt, blue stockings, and silver-buckled shoes quite high
but with chunk instead of pointed heels. Her stockings
were seamed at the back and the mesh wide, almost a
fishnet. Her glossy chestnut mane was pinned back in a
sweeping ponytail, and Sandra thought it really was like
a pony's tail, as the mistress stared at the pair of
miscreants, grinning slightly over her round rimless
glasses. Sandra estimated her age at slightly less than
Miss Quirke's, as somewhere in her late twenties.

Miss Crisp sat in an armchair and crossed her long, shiny stockings in a fluid motion that signalled easy habits of dominance. Her skirt swirled briefly and Sandra thought she saw a flash of red knicker. Surely not daring panties in such a stern schoolmistress? Then she patted her skirt down and smiled brightly at the girls.

'It seems you are both to receive six stripes,' she said with a slight whistle of surprise, then raised her eyebrows as though she had asked a question.

'Yes, Miss,' said Sandra and Julie in unison, after which they glared at each other.

'Fighting in the corridor, in the tuck shop queue!' said Miss Crisp sternly. 'Most unseemly! Miss Long, of course, cannot leave the girls unsupervised, so here you are. Private stripes should be witnessed, but for a double striping, the practice is for each of you to bear the other's witness.'

She sighed.

'We are so short of staff! However, you must be made aware, young ladies, that fighting is for the boxing ring, where it is conducted with decorum and discipline according to ladylike rules. I see you have both asked for the privilege of training, even though it is not normally accorded to mere freshers. I fear this episode will not help your chances of recommendation by the panel, of which I am senior member.'

Sandra looked more closely at the mistress's body, and sure enough saw lithe muscle beneath the womanly curves. The tight blouse showed a belly that was hard as steel, and a waist like a tube of narrow muscle, swelling into ripe thighs and a taut bum that strained against her demure skirt. Even the teats had strength behind their melons.

'It is a pity,' Miss Crisp continued, 'because you both have the build of fighters.'

The girls glowered at each other. Julie Down was of

Sandra's height, but rangier and perhaps trimmer of figure. Her breasts were slightly smaller, pert and jutting up, so Sandra pouted and thrust her own bosom out as far as she could, aware of her enemy's jealous glance, and of Miss Crisp's interested one.

'I won't ask how this disgraceful fracas started,' she began, and the two girls reacted at once.

'She butted in, Miss!'

'She pulled my hair, Miss!'

'She tweaked my stocking-top, Miss!'

'Miss, she pinched my bottom!'

'Enough!' cried Miss Crisp in a regal fury. 'After I stripe you, you shall both wish a pinch was all you got!'

Suddenly, she sighed, calming herself, then smiled again, and rose to open a large, wooden cupboard. Both Sandra and Julie looked and saw inside an impressive array of canes. Miss Crisp noted their awed gaze with approval.

'Yes,' she said, 'I am very proud of my collection. I have ash, willow, birch, hickory and rattan. Some of them are gifts from grateful Old Quirkeans whose bottoms still, I fancy, bear my stripes. Now, I wonder what should suit your naughty little bums, girls?'

Sandra and Julie looked at each other in some puzzlement at Miss Crisp's coy vulgarity. The school-mistress was stroking the polished wooden canes with affection.

'There is the question of who shall go first,' she said.

To be beaten first would mean getting it over with and being able to gloat at the rival's discomfort. On the other hand, the girl beaten second would have to meet, or surpass, the first girl's endurance. After slight hesitation, both girls volunteered to go first. Miss Crisp pursed her lips and looked each girl up and down.

'How very well-mannered,' she said acidly. 'It is a pity that forgetting your manners brought you here. Let's see. Oh, I'll take you, first, Miss Down.'

Both girls nodded nervously, still eyeing the instruments of punishment. Miss Crisp, as though playing up to their growing unease, began to stroke the woods thoughtfully like the bodies of lovers.

'The hickory,' she said, 'is very painful indeed. I remember giving Gloria Harness nine stripes and she could not sit down for two whole days, and had to sleep on her tummy, poor thing. Willow and ash are useful for close work, in the soft, little crevices by the thighs and under the seat. The rattan ... A fearsome and joyful tool of beauty indeed, and I am not sure whether hickory or rattan is more painful. In times gone by, my own bum has tasted both.'

She came to a bushy birch and riffled her fingers between the fronds, her face blushing ever so slightly.

'The crackle of Mistress Birch,' she murmured. 'Such a creature of beauty across the naked buttocks of a miscreant girl. However you have not been sentenced to the birch. So which cane shall it be? Willow? Ash? Hickory? Rattan? I leave the choice to you, ladies.'

Julie and Sandra looked at each other uncertainly, then both suddenly shrilled at once:

'The rattan, Miss!'

Miss Crisp clapped her hands in soft glee and congratulated them on their bravery.

'On reflection,' she said, 'I think I shall take those undoubtedly tough bums of yours with the hickory. Well now, let's get on with it. Miss Down, if you will please take position, touch your toes with your legs well spread and knickers to your calves, please. Or would you rather lean over the back of the chair?'

Julie answered haughtily that she could take it bending over and touching toes. She swiftly rose and took position, reaching behind her with one hand to raise her skirt over her back. Her garter belt and suspenders strained as she bent. Then she hooked a thumb in the frilly waistband of her white panties and rolled the garment slowly over her bottom, down the shiny, black stockings to her calves, so that the knickers hung taut. Her arse-globes were bare and stretched wide for the cane and Sandra could see the tiny bud of her arsehole, all brown and crinkly like a little prune, and the hairs that signalled the fleshy beginnings of her cunt-lips. The bare skin of the buttocks bore the blotches left by old stripes.

Sandra clasped her own arms around her knees and made sure she sat up straight. She was looking directly at her rival's bare bum from a few feet away, with Miss Crisp taking her own position on the other side.

'By the way,' Miss Crisp said pleasantly. 'You both know the drill. Any undue squealing or girly squirming and the stripe is repeated. I don't mind a few grunts and groans, though, and I can't expect your bums not to clench, since it's always on the bare at this school, I'm glad to say, and I'm afraid I cane pretty hard. But you're big girls and you've been striped before. How I loved your first striping Sandra; twelve fierce ones, and well taken! Some girls are soppy and have to be tied or gagged, but I don't think you are that type. Are we all agreed?'

Both girls nodded yes and agreed they were not that type. Miss Crisp lifted her caning arm to its fullest extent above her shoulder, straining her blouse and bra so that it seemed her squashed right breast might actually pop out of its fastening cup. Above her quivered the four-foot length of the gnarled hickory, reaching almost to the ceiling and a good inch thick. Her arm jerked; there was a blur, a vicious whistling and, suddenly, a loud crack.

The mottled pale pink of Julie's naked bottom was suddenly striped a savage red right across the middle of the fesses. Her bum jerked and her furrow clenched, and she wobbled slightly, but her only reaction was a long gasp of pain and surprise which was repeated. After a

79

few seconds, the second stripe turned her gasp to a rapid and harsh panting, for the stripe took her almost exactly on the first, but shifted slightly aslant.

'Smarting much?' said Miss Crisp.

'Oh! Oh! Gosh! Yes, Miss,' Julie replied. 'Mmm!'

'I told you I cane tightly,' said Miss Crisp, and without warning, cracked the cane a third time across Julie's quivering bare fesses, this time in a slash that slanted from top to bottom of the bum-skin, across the first two welts.

Julie let out a long, slow moan, gasping and evidently trying to stifle a sob. Her bottom was quivering and clenching quite violently and her long legs shuddered as she clutched her toes for support. Sandra sat bolt upright, her own breath harsh, and felt, despite herself, the hot moisture of her excitement seeping into her panties.

'Well, that's the half,' said Miss Crisp. 'I think I'll take you a little more to the underneath now, Miss. You might find it hurts considerably more, if I can aim properly with this beast.'

'Whatever you say, Miss,' Julie sobbed, then with the implacable whistle and crack of an expert canestroke, the hickory took her right underneath the seat inside her furrow, and nearly at the hairy swelling of her slit.

Miss Crisp dealt the fifth almost at once afterwards, and this time the cane snaked right beneath her furrow. Sandra was sure the tip connected with the anus pucker itself, for Julie shrieked and her bare welted bum shuddered convulsively like a trapped animal.

'Oh! Miss! Oh! That was tight! Oh gosh! Oooh . . .' she wailed.

She swallowed and panted, struggling for breath, and Sandra saw to her delight that the fleshy lips of Julie's visible quim were swollen and that her inner thighs gleamed with droplets of moisture from her wet cunt. Sandra's own cunt and clit were tingling now and she was quite helpless to prevent her flow of love-oil from sopping her panties. She clutched her thighs together, drawing the knicker cloth tight into the fold of her gash, as though to stem her tide, but it was useless.

She felt the tight cloth loosen as it was drenched in her cunt-fluid. Her clit was throbbing and she could not prevent herself from rubbing her thighs tightly together to send little shivers of ecstasy through the stiff nubbin and quivers up her spine. Her stockings made a squishy sound as she rubbed herself clumsily. She hoped Miss Crisp did not notice.

The schoolmistress lifted her skirt quite casually and wiped her brow with a hankie which she removed from her own stocking-top. Sandra saw the knickers. They were red, with little, frilly edges and there was a dark patch at the bulging crotch. Julie was still whimpering.

'Oh, dear,' said Miss Crisp, replacing her hankie and smoothing her skirt. 'I am afraid that counts as a squeal, Miss Down. Did it hurt awfully? I'm afraid you'll have to take the fifth stripe over again.'

'Oh, oh Miss. I've never been striped so hard!' Julie managed to gasp, though surprisingly firm and in control. 'It smarts so. I wouldn't have thought I could stand it.'

'But you can, Miss, and I'm glad,' said Miss Crisp. 'Your bum's well wealed now and you'll admire yourself in the mirror. Bottom up for two more.'

Julie's whole body was trembling. The repeated fifth stripe took her unexpectedly on her outer haunch, at the edge of the right fesse, and laid a savage weal. Julie's bum twitched and jerked in maddened pain and she moaned in a long drawn-out agony that nevertheless did not make a squeal. Her bum-cheeks were clenching uncontrollably as Miss Crisp dealt the final stroke to the other haunch, where it raised a welt of equal beauty.

Sandra rocked back and forth on the sofa, feeling the soaking of her cunt and gasping almost as much as the whipped girl. She could not believe it. She was dreading the moment of lowering her own panties for the cane, yet deep inside, she was longing for the smarting welt of the first stripe on her own bare bottom. The thought of her bare flogging made her cunt gush copiously.

Groaning, Julie remained in position as Miss Crisp deftly pulled her panties up and allowed her hand to stroke the gusset and brush the tops of Julie's stockings. All were moist with her quim-juice.

Without a word, Sandra rose and, trembling, curtsied to the schoolmistress. Julie was permitted to visit the adjoining bathroom, and Sandra heard her gasp of relief as a noisy jet of pee clanged against the metal bowl. Then there was a silence and a further gasp, which was more of a squeal and was repeated five or six times. When Julie returned, her face smug and flushed, she was allowed to remain standing.

Sandra bent over and touched her toes, legs spread wide, feeling her sopping knickers cling wetly to her bum-cheeks. She reached back and uplifted her skirt, and heard a gasp from Miss Crisp, then felt the schoolmistress's hand grasping the elastic of her panties. Her cunt-juice was so copious that the knickers were completely soaked. Miss Crisp roughly pulled the panties down to her ankles.

'Step out of your panties altogether, Miss Shanks,' she said drily.

Trembling, Sandra kicked off her sodden knickers and resumed position, her wet bum now fully cane-bare. Miss Crisp told her to remain spread, but to look up. Sandra saw the evidence of her excitement dangled in front of her and felt a few drips of her quim-oil on her forehead.

'You have been masturbating, Miss Shanks,' accused the furious schoolmistress, while Julie smirked behind her.

Sandra opened her mouth to defend herself, but found her head suddenly encased in her own wet panties, which Miss Crisp fastened in a tiny knot around her neck so that the soaking, quim-stained cloth was pressed to her mouth and nose and her eyes peered through her own thigh-hole.

'Wicked misses get bagged,' snapped Miss Crisp. 'And for your filthiness, Miss Shanks, you'll take a second set of stripes after my six, from Miss Down. I'll let her use the willow. It's nice and whippy, so she can get to those crevices you seem so fond of tickling. I take it –' her voice dripped with scorn '– you are lady enough to agree?'

'I submit, Miss,' Sandra blurted. 'I agree to twelve.'

Miss Crisp nodded.

'I imagine your bum is still bruised from your very first public striping, Miss. I am impressed that you took the twelver without more than wetting yourself. It must have seemed too much to bear. But girls wet themselves under caning more often than is generally admitted. I – and Miss Quirke – agree that this reaction is normal. The question is, can your bum take another dozen weals so soon? Without the comfort of being restrained, in bondage, I mean.'

'Y-yes, Miss,' Sandra murmured. 'May I please be restrained? I don't think I could take a full dozen otherwise.'

Her pussy was soaking with juice.

'It will mean riding the rail, Miss Shanks.'

'Whatever you say, Miss,' said Sandra, her voice trembling and muffled by her sopping panties.

Miss Boulter was fond of threatening naughty femmes with the rail.

Miss Crisp duly produced the rail, a simple clothes-horse and not at all awesome. It was a basic frame consisting of two triangles of wood, at waist height, with one apex widening into a chin-rest. The triangles were connected by bars at floor level and by a single bar at the top. This was the rail. The floor bars had buckled leather straps to restrain feet and wrists, while the rail itself was not a round pole but a sharp diamond shape. Miss Crisp invited Sandra to 'hop on'.

Gingerly, and holding her skirt up, Sandra straddled the crossbar rail and placed her feet, at Miss Crisp's direction, in the thick restraining straps which were mounted on a little groove and could be moved along the bar to suit the length of the subject's legs. Her belly was squashed against the sharp ridge of the rail and her feet were buckled firmly so that they could not move or even wriggle. Miss Crisp slid the buckles along the bar until Sandra's legs were stretched to the full and her whole weight was pressed on the rail itself.

The rail had a fearsome reputation. In addition to the sharp poking of her belly and breasts, the full stretching of Sandra's legs meant that the whole weight of her buttocks and torso was taken by her quim, whose lips were parted by the hard edge of the rail. The tighter the constriction of her feet, the more dreadful the bite of the diamond edge inside the gash-lips. She gasped as the sharp wood nestled against her clitty itself, the cruel impact making her tingly and wet.

Then her wrists were bound and her arms stretched out in the same way, increasing the rail's pressure between her cunt-lips. The pain was already quite enough, and was increased by the titters of glee from Julie, and Miss Crisp herself, as they observed her naked bum wriggling in a vain attempt to ease her discomfort. As small relief, her chin rested on the cup at the top of the triangle, forcing her neck uncomfortably and grotesquely back. Sandra began to gasp as her face contorted in her dismay.

'You asked to be bound, Miss Shanks, so there is no need to complain,' said Miss Crisp placidly. 'I'll give you your stripes now, but if you agree, I think I'll use rattan. Your peach is so nice and big and firm, and I feel the rattan will somehow do her more justice.'

She paused to stroke Sandra's bare, spread arse-globes with cool fingers, and Sandra felt the nails tangling in her thick, pubic forest and pulling on her mink-hairs.

'Such a thick bush,' said Miss Crisp rather dreamily. 'And the darling little butterfly seems to be feeding off its hairs. But they are disgracefully wet, Miss Shanks. You were masturbating at another girl's discomfort and that is most wicked. Therefore, it's the rattan for your bum. I've decided that it is the most painful, after all.'

She replaced the hickory and drew down the rattan. It was just as long, but much whippier, and gleaming smooth and polished with very slight striations like a snakeskin. Sandra shuddered as the cane swished the air, sending a cold rush over her wet pubis and gash.

'Why, some girls – proper submissive girls – crave the rattan, or the birch,' said Miss Crisp thoughtfully.

'Whatever you say, Miss,' Sandra stammered.

She gritted her teeth and did not cry out as the first stripe of the rattan lashed her naked buttocks, even though the force of the stroke jolted her chin against the cup and made her ankles tear at their restraining straps. She inhaled sharply, swallowed, and gulped air, the wet panties sticking to her lips and nose. There was a burning pain right at the centre of her bum-cheeks and the second stripe was laid in exactly the same place, with not a hair's breadth of difference.

It was as though a red-hot sword was pressed to her bare flesh and held there. Tears sprang to her eyes and her fesses clenched madly, as shivers wracked her whole trussed body. At each of her squirmings, the agonising sharp wood of the rail itself bit deep into her gash like some gnawing beaver.

'Oh! Oh!' she sobbed, as quietly as possible.

'Tight, eh?' mused Miss Crisp. 'You won't want to wriggle much, with the rail in your fount, Miss. Or rather, you will wriggle, but it will hurt you rather awfully.'

Abruptly, the third stripe took Sandra right at the haunch on the side of her left buttock, and she shuddered convulsively at the frightful pain on the soft skin.

'Oh! Ooo!' she squealed, her gorge rising as tears scalded her eyes. 'Oh, oh, I – Oh, Miss! Please!'

'Well, you'll take that stripe again, you cissy!' cried Miss Crisp and promptly dealt another to exactly the same weal on her bruised left haunch.

Sandra managed not to cry out but shook her head violently in its restraining cup as her legs stiffened and her bare bum clenched and wriggled. Her clitty was aroused by gnawing of the rail deep up her gash. And to her shameful delight she felt the wooden rail moisten; her cunt was juicing copiously, like a crushed submissive femme's.

7

Sparring Partners

'That's better,' murmured Miss Crisp. 'Now for the fourth.'

There was an awful pause, then a sudden 'vip' as the cane whistled, and the hard though jellied impact as it took Sandra right on the underside of her fesses, the tip brushing her thigh. She squealed in dismay and shock.

'Oh! Oh! I'm sorry, Miss,' she gasped in her agony.

'So you should be, Miss Shanks. That stripe again, too, I'm afraid. But your bum's beginning to look nice.'

The repeated fourth stripe now took her at the slant, cracking on to the squirming buttocks and leaving a stripe from top to bottom of the naked fesses. Her body jerked helplessly in a convulsion of pure agony, trying to escape the pain and the cruel restraint of the leather straps. Sandra managed to stifle her scream, but her throat tightened and she gasped for breath, gagging on her wet panties, her nose filling with the curious scent of her own pussy-juice which, despite the smarting of her cane-seared arse, she found wickedly intoxicating.

The fifth stripe was also aslant, and Sandra's arse was now a glowing pan of white-hot agony. She could no longer place the direction of the strokes and for the sixth stripe the rattan cane returned to the soft underflesh of the buttocks, again wealing on the thigh-top.

She jerked helplessly on the sharp rail, the agony of her gash's impalement turning to a kind of defiant satisfaction, as she felt her nubbin stiffen and tingle under this cruellest of stimulations. As though to show her defiance, she did indeed ride the rail, wealed arse squirming high and bare as her pussy was sawed by the blade of the crossbar and her clitty stiffened and throbbed at the deliciously cruel unfairness of her punishment.

'Well,' said Miss Crisp, 'six decreed and six taken.'

'I took eight, Miss,' Sandra blurted, her voice muffled by the hood of her soaked knickers. 'Two extra –'

'That's impudence, Miss,' snapped Miss Crisp. 'It will say six in the discipline book and the six decreed have been taken. There are no extra stripes at Quirke's, only stripes repeated. My, my, surely you don't think that the discipline book contains the whole truth.'

'I suppose I've earned further stripes for impudence,' gasped Sandra bitterly.

'Technically, yes. We shall see how you take the six you have been awarded from Miss Down for insulting her. That punishment too must be noted and must stand, but if she has occasion to repeat a stripe . . .'

Miss Crisp's words dangled ominously. It was clear that Sandra was to be flogged until one, or both, of her two enemies tired of her humiliation. Sandra began to sob loudly as she heard Julie giggle and her blouse rustle as she lifted the willow. The thin, whippy wood made a loud whistle as it lashed the air before cracking with searing force on the very furrow of Sandra's bruised arse-globes, landing squarely on her pucker, the tip licking the swollen lips of her gushing quim.

'Oh! Ouch! Oh! Oh!' she gasped, her eyes streaming at the harshness of that sly stroke, yet her belly shivered and her clit tingled more insistently at the giddy knowledge of her total helpless submission.

'I think that merits a repeat, Miss,' said Julie with false humility, and Miss Crisp solemnly agreed.

Again, she wealed Sandra right in the crack of her

buttocks, this time catching her well on the cunt-lips as well as bumhole. Sandra shrieked and her bum squirmed helplessly as she strained against her leather thongs.

'And that,' murmured Miss Crisp, moving to within inches of Sandra's knicker hood and squatting, skirts oddly up around her waist, to gaze at Sandra's pain-blurred eyes.

Sandra's arse was raised higher than her head, so that the mistress had a view of both the contorted face and the hillocks of bare wealed bum-flesh. In her squatting position, Miss Crisp was partly blocked from Julie's view by Sandra's body.

The third stripe – officially, still the first – of Sandra's new beating took her more traditionally, but it still smarted like fire.

'Bearing up all right?' said Julie, with something like concern in her voice, as if she did not wish to take the cruel teasing too far.

'Yes, thank you, Julie,' Sandra gasped. 'You really lay some stingers. Very clever, those stripes right in my crack. Oh! how it smarts! Much worse than the rattan.'

'Enough chitchat,' snapped Miss Crisp and told Julie to get on with the beating before Miss Shanks recovered.

Julie rewarded Sandra's compliment with two fierce stingers right to the already wealed flanks and this made Sandra leap in her bonds and cry out at the second stripe, which Miss Crisp ordered to be repeated. Julie dutifully lashed Sandra's bare haunch on the same welt and was rewarded with a further cry, and furious sobbing from her bared, squirming victim. She paused doubtfully.

'Harder, Miss, and faster, please,' said Miss Crisp. 'Do you want another taste of hickory? Do you think I didn't hear what you were up to in the bathroom! Those little yelps, Miss Down. I know full well you were diddling.'

Sandra looked up and saw Julie blush, then the cane came down on her naked buttocks again and another lance of white-hot pain was added to her bum's glowing burden.

'Harder! Harder! Repeat!' said Miss Crisp.

The stripes came thick and fast now, with every other stripe repeated until Sandra lost count at a dozen from Julie's caning alone. Through blurred eyes, and her buttocks now dancing in the fiery smarting of her endlessly continued thrashing, she stared at the mistress squatting to scrutinise her victim.

Miss Crisp's skirts were well up, her thighs spread, and her hands – both of them – were busy inside her red panties stained dark with juice. As she watched Sandra's naked agony, and the oily secretion flowing from her wet, speared cunt, Miss Crisp was masturbating herself.

'Julie! Look!' Sandra gasped.

Julie's cane was in mid-air and she made sure she delivered a stinging welt to the fleshy top of Sandra's bum before pausing to observe Miss Crisp. Beneath the bulging wet crotch of her panties, a little pool of love-oil shone on the office linoleum floor. Then Julie frowned.

'A hypocrite . . .' she said indignantly.

'What of it, Miss?' blustered the mistress. 'You know, it is not the crime, it's the getting caught –'

'We've caught you, Miss,' said Julie drily. 'Sandra was flogged for masturbating – so you say – as she watched me caned and now you pleasure yourself at her flogging.'

'It is your word against mine, young lady,' retorted Miss Crisp, rising to her feet.

'But it still would make a bit of a stink,' said Sandra, recovering slightly at this respite.

Julie swished the cane, not at Sandra, but in the air towards a suddenly uncertain Miss Crisp.

'I feel we've been shamefully used,' she said brusquely. 'Not just me, but this fledge too. This Sandra.'

There was a bell in the distance and Miss Crisp said they had better hurry and not miss luncheon.

'Sod luncheon!' cried Julie. 'Miss Crisp, you will please release Sandra.'

'What? How dare you –'

Suddenly, Julie lifted her arm high and dealt the woman a resounding slap across her face leaving a livid imprint on her cheek. Miss Crisp staggered back in astonishment, clutching her face, and the first slap was followed by a second, on her other cheek, which dislodged her spectacles. Miss Crisp wailed and sank to her knees, groping for the glasses, but Julie positioned her heel above them.

'Do as I say, bitch,' she said very quietly.

Miss Crisp unbuckled Sandra's thongs, and Sandra rose, swiftly 'unbagging' herself and replacing her knickers in their rightful place. She gasped her thanks to Julie.

'I'm sorry I flogged you so hard Sandra, really I am,' Julie said. 'And for your first dorm night. The question is, what are we to do to teach this hypocrite a lesson?'

She stayed Miss Crisp's hand with a flick of the cane to her wrist, as she was about to pull the bell-rope.

'You'll be expelled!' she hissed.

Julie put a foot on her neck and prevented her rising. Then she lifted Miss Crisp's skirt and, with the cane, drew down her wet panties to show the glazed, shiny orbs of her bare bum.

'What if Miss Quirke saw your knickers?' she asked impishly. 'A mistress all wet from diddling herself as she administered chastisement? What would she think?'

Miss Crisp began to stammer apologies. Julie laid three rapid stripes on her bare buttocks with her cane.

'Oh! Oh! Ouch! You bitch whore!' squealed Miss Crisp.

Julie delivered three more strokes, over in a few seconds, which gave livid welts all at the centre of the fesses, leaving the bare bum striped as though from a formal caning. Then she told the sobbing mistress to stop snivelling.

'Let us form a committee of discipline,' she said. 'I propose that the punishment should fit the crime and that the subject be given a taste of her own medicine.'

'Seconded,' said Sandra.

'Carried nem con,' said Julie gravely.

'But you can't –' Miss Crisp began, only to be silenced by an application of Julie's toecap to her arsebud.

'The committee has decided,' said Julie. 'It remains to discuss precisely what we have decided.'

Sandra promptly suggested that the bullying Miss Crisp should be tied up while they deliberated. And when the mistress raised a last, feeble objection, it was Sandra's hand that slapped her reddened cheeks with three hard blows. Miss Crisp's sobs had turned to a sullen, hopeless snuffling and she did not even bother to try and cover her inflamed bare bottom with her skirt.

It was a moment's work to strip her of blouse and skirt, and the two girls surveyed her, knickerless now, but still in stockings, bra and suspenders. Modestly, Miss Crisp stood holding her hands at her crotch, but unable to conceal the lush tangle of her wet, pubic forest. Her blue stockings were matched by blue sussies, and Julie commented that she needed a lesson in colour co-ordination.

'Red knickers, with black bra and blue nets,' she said thoughtfully. 'We could thrash her bum, first red, then black and blue.'

Miss Crisp let out a howl of anguish and Sandra coolly kicked her in the gash.

'Or give her a lesson in boxing,' she added.

'Why not both!' the two girls exclaimed together.

With the door securely locked, it was decided that a boxing lesson should come first, while the girls made their choice of cane for Miss Crisp's arse. Julie explained to Sandra that female boxing as practised at Quirke's did not exactly conform to the Marquess of Queensberry's rules. First, it was bare-fisted: no cissy gloves. Second, it was not restricted to punching, but points were awarded for slapping, especially to the breasts or cunt. The only restriction was that the head might not be punched, but only slapped, as damaged teeth were considered unladylike.

Miss Crisp, realising she could not avoid her fate, grinned slyly and began to limber her boxing muscles. Julie opened a window. The mistress's grin turned to a wail when the two uniformed girls seized the nearly naked woman and thrust her arms through the bars which were positioned on the outside of the glass pane, where Sandra deftly handcuffed her using the same thongs which had bound her to the rail. Miss Crisp wriggled and kicked, but helplessly and in vain. Her arms were trapped by the window bars and her squirming body had no defence.

'It is not a fair fight!' she cried.

'This is a lesson, Miss, not a contest,' said Julie, unhooking Miss Crisp's bra so that the big, pale teats flopped out, their nipples as erect as hard, new plums.

While Sandra bunched the mistress's sopping wet panties and wadded them in her mouth to gag her, Julie fastened the bra around the back of her neck to keep the gag in place and tied it tightly in a reef knot.

Sandra held the woman's flailing ankles together and bound them with the other thong. Julie began a fierce breast-slapping, while Sandra punched Miss Crisp directly in her chestnut forest. She felt the soft hillock of the pubis give behind her fist and her knuckles thud on the pubic bone. Then she aimed her punches lower and struck directly on Miss Crisp's fleshy cunt-lips, and on the clitty itself, still erect and hard from masturbation.

In fact, the more blows Miss Crisp's writhing body took, and the more her teats, thighs and cunt were bruised by the uniformed schoolgirls, the more her cunt-lips swelled and released copious trickles of juice which made her stockinged thighs streaked and shiny.

Julie's tit-slapping became fiercer and fiercer, and she began to take the nipples and pinch them very hard, drawing the skin out like a balloon before slapping. Sandra went to work on the mistress's taut belly whose slabs of muscle seemed hard as iron under her punches. Julie tired of mere slapping and, as Sandra returned to a vigorous drubbing of the mistress's flowing cunt, Julie began to pummel the teats with her fists, striking right to the nipples until they were deeply bruised with vivid blue blotches.

Both girls were sweating and, with only a glance, they paused to strip off blouses and skirts. Now, the nude, gagged woman was faced with two angry schoolgirls clad only in bra, panties, sussies and stockings.

Sandra seized the willow cane and motioned Julie aside, and while Julie resumed the pummelling of Miss Crisp's tender clitty and quim, Sandra proceeded to deliver a vigorous caning across the already bruised and swollen teats. She aimed right at the nipples, catching each bud with the willow's tip, and Miss Crisp's sobs were frantic behind her gagging knickers.

After several minutes of this energetic, if one-sided, sparring, the committee decided it was time for the next part of the lesson. The wailing Miss Crisp offered no resistance as her limp body was unfettered, draped over the rail and bound to it just as painfully as she had bound Sandra, with the variation that her wrists were strapped behind her back and her arms forced well up. Her chin rested in the cup, drooled on by her spittle, and there was a strange, misty gleam in her eyes as she seemed to thrust her pale, bare fesses up for punishment.

'Shall we use the hickory or the rattan?' said Sandra. 'The willow's too light for real bum-work, I think.'

Miss Crisp shook her head violently and moaned.

'Perhaps both,' said Julie. 'We can see which makes her squirm more.'

Again, Miss Crisp shook her head from side to side as though she were in a position to disagree.

'Be quiet,' said Julie, 'or it'll be the birch instead.'

At this, Miss Crisp nodded her head eagerly in assent.

'Mmm . . . mmm . . .' she groaned, her eyes bright and nostrils flaring. 'Bbbbbch . . .'

The girls raised their eyebrows and smiled. Julie fetched the bristling sheaf of birch rods, while Sandra, on impulse, upended the triangular frame so that Miss Crisp's chin was now on the carpet and her back vertical, with her legs and bum splayed in a v-shape at waist height. Julie approved this decision, as it would make their task much easier and present a far wider expanse of bare skin to work on.

She stroked the bushy twigs of chastisement.

'It is a monster,' she said. 'Why, there must be a good thirty rods in this.'

'Then she deserves at least thirty stripes with it,' said Sandra gravely, 'or until the birch is denuded. Fancy keeping such a thing.'

'Fancy wanting such a thing, on the bare,' said Julie.

Sandra swallowed, her panties sopping wet.

'I could take the birch on my bare,' she said.

As if to expel this worrying notion, she asked to go first, and delivered a fierce stripe – stripes, really – to Miss Crisp's naked buttocks with a magnificent twang and crackle of the dry scented wood. At once, the bare bum flamed in a blush and Miss Crisp groaned and clenched the crack of her arse, though whether her moan and sighing were of satisfaction or of pain was difficult to tell. Sandra said she thought it wise to continue applying the rods until Miss Crisp's reaction was unmistakably of pain.

She birched the bare flesh steadily and remorselessly, working on every inch of the buttocks from the top to the soft underside and, on Julie's insistence, making sure the thighs were striped right to the stocking tops. The birch made a lovely, dry crackling sound, businesslike yet friendly, as though caressing rather than punishing the squirming, bare bottom, and Sandra no longer tried to conceal her soaking knickers.

She looked across at Julie, who had her panties lowered and, with her eyelids heavy, was enthusiastically masturbating her clitty, by now stiff and pink and quite distended through the lips of her close-cropped cunt.

Each stroke of the birch caused her victim to writhe and prod her own cunt against the sharp rail which impaled her. Sandra's fingers slid down her belly to her bush, through the wet forest under her panties, till she came to her own throbbing clit, and with just one spine-jarring touch she knew she would come very soon.

Gasping, she handed the birch to Julie, and stood beside her as she resumed the work on the mistress's bum-skin which was now mottled red and streaked with purple with a lovely pattern of crests and ridges and deep craters where the birch tips had caught her.

Julie paid especial attention to the flanks, and the underside of the bum and, as Sandra watched in awe, she felt Julie's hand replace her own beneath her soaking panties. She responded, and as the shamed and birched mistress squirmed in pain of her own choosing, the two schoolgirls masturbated deftly and joyfully to a simultaneous orgasm of mingled coos and squeals.

The birch strokes grew erratic, but no less fierce, as Julie gasped under the continued tickling of Sandra's fingers on her clitty and Miss Crisp's hips began to buck madly, thrusting her own vulva against the hard rail. She squirmed and jolted on the device until her wails too reached a squeal and a torrent of unstemmed love-oil flowed from her dripping cunt. Suddenly, there was a crack. Her throes of orgasm had splintered the rail in two.

Now, Julie and Sandra carried the gagged mistress to the armchair, where they draped her unceremoniously over the back with her bruised, welted bum and thighs spread wide to reveal her dripping gash.

'The bitch can certainly take it,' Julie drawled. 'I wonder if I could.'

Sandra blushed slightly. Then she seized the rods and birched Miss Crisp on the cunt-lips themselves, gently at first, then harder and harder as the torrent of love-juice flowed ever more copiously from the flogged woman's cunt. Julie began to masturbate again, while kneeling at Sandra's panties and tonguing her stiff clit through the cloth. Sandra paused and rolled her knickers down, letting Julie lick her naked cunt once more, but now amicably.

Julie gamahuched her with an eager tongue, poking her lips and nose right between Sandra's parted thighs and swallowing all the love juice that flowed from her engorged gash. Sandra's aim faltered. As she was tongued from below, she looked at the bruised crimson gash she had flogged and bent as if to kiss it better.

She got her tongue between Miss Crisp's big, fleshy cunt-lips and began her own vigorous tonguing, at the same time snapping her forefinger and thumb against the stiffened clitty. The nubbin was big enough for her to grasp and squeeze, which she did, accompanied by Miss Crisp's frantic moans of pleasure.

'Oh!' Julie exclaimed. 'I've got to pee again.'

She withdrew her tongue from Sandra's gash and deftly undid Miss Crisp's pony-tail. The lush mane of chestnut hair spread like a wreath of flowers around her head. Julie leapt nimbly on to the arms of the chair and, with an impish grin, postioned her quim right above the mistress's gaping cunt and bumhole.

A hearty jet of golden, hot piss spurted from her cunt,

right into Miss Crisp's own gash, and it bubbled and overflowed all down her buttocks and leg. Julie shifted slightly and it flowed on her back as well, forming a steaming pool by her gagged lips.

Giggling, Sandra followed suit, sighing with relief as her pent-up bladder emptied itself and her golden stream of pee joined Julie's both on the linoleum floor and in Miss Crisp's mane, which was now a soaking swamp of fragrant schoolgirl evacuations.

While Sandra carefully wiped her cunt clean, Julie rummaged in the cupboard and triumphantly brandished her booty.

'I knew a witch would have them!' she cried.

They were two broomsticks, a good two inches' thickness of unpolished wood. Julie oiled them with the juice from Miss Crisp's own cunt and raised them high over her twin nether holes. The gash gaped wide enough for easy entry, but Sandra poked a finger in the tight little anus bud to enlarge and relax it, and she held its rim stretched wide with her fingernails.

Julie plunged the shafts to the hilt in both cunt and anus, and promptly began a vigorous, wooden fucking, while she recommenced masturbating her own clit. Holding the shafts in one hand, she plunged hard and fast into the clammy, wet holes as though drilling for precious metal.

Sandra released Miss Crisp from her knicker-gag and took her by the piss-sodden hair to direct her mouth towards her own cunt. The mistress needed neither instruction nor encouragement to plunge her tongue into Sandra's hot, wet slit and begin an energetic gamahuching with her teeth scraping against Sandra's erect clitty.

With this arrangement to her satisfaction, Sandra watched as the double broomsticks fucked and buggered the squirming wet holes of their victim, and then she leaned across to replace Julie's masturbating fingers with her own tongue. At the same time, she slipped her hand under Miss Crisp's pubic mound and began to tweak her nubbin hard.

Now it was Miss Crisp who lost control. She moaned in pleasure and shame, the vibrations of her voice thrilling Sandra's tingling cunt, as her own hot flow of piss drenched Sandra's masturbating fingers. The mistress's stockings were completely sodden and underneath her, the linoleum sparkled with her steaming pond.

When Miss Crisp's pee had finished, she continued to moan at Sandra's rubbing fingers, and now her moans were in the ecstasy of orgasm. Her tongue flickered more and more furiously on Sandra's own nubbin and Sandra too gave way to her pleasure, while Julie's squeals of joy signalled her own climax. All three females were soaked in pee and quim-juice, and sated with pleasure, when suddenly there was a knock at the door.

'Miss Crisp? Are you all right? I heard cries.'

Sandra waved a warning finger at the mistress.

'Oh, it's all right,' gasped Miss Crisp. 'I am in the middle of administering discipline.'

'Well, you won't forget the boxing panel meeting. It is just starting.'

'Please tell them I'll be there in a few minutes,' answered Miss Crisp, 'so they may start without me. Oh, and be sure that two extra names are added, Misses Down and Shanks. They are to be given the highest rating at the top of the list.'

8

Twangs

Thwack!

The short brown cane slapped hard against the skin on the side of the girl's left buttock, and directly on the strap of her sussie belt. The girl's bum shivered and a further welt was added to the blotchy mass that discoloured both her left and right fesses. The blow jolted the girl's upended bare bum and a hiss escaped her gritted teeth.

Thwack!

The cane striped the right haunch now, adding a red streak to the numerous weals already laid, and which were darkening to purple. The girl groaned, almost sobbing, and her naked bottom twitched with little flutters like the wings of a trapped butterfly. Apart from the sounds of the caning, there was dead silence in the classroom.

Thwack!

The cane fell again on the defenceless bare skin of the buttocks. The girl's arms and legs were splayed, the ankles fully apart, with her panties quivering tight between her thighs and her knuckles white on the edges of the mistress's high school desk. Each stripe landed on the haunch, only grazing the soft centre buttock, but slamming hard against the sussie strap, alternating from left to right bum-cheek.

'How many is that, Miss Bond?' snapped the mistress, Miss Pottinger.

Her words were accompanied by the whistle of the cane and a further stripe to the left fesse, which made the girl's long, coltish legs shudder and her feet teeter on her heels which were unwisely high for such a severe caning.

'Mm! Mm! Oh! It must be twenty at least, Miss!' she gasped.

'Liar,' said Miss Pottinger coolly, 'and I'll repeat that stripe for lying. It was only eighteen.'

Sandra watched the slim, tall body of Sharon Bond shiver, and the full breasts wobble under the tight, white blouse and flimsy bra-cups. Her long brown mane was rumpled and the ripe melons of her bare bum clenched in anticipation of the stripe. Although Sharon was her chum, she enjoyed seeing her bottom squirm. Sharon had been overly enthusiastic, in her dildo's attention to Sandra's own wriggling bumhole that first night in dorm.

The mistress was as good as her word and laid an extra stripe, now full across the central bum-cheeks. She smiled at the harsh echo of the slap on Sharon's naked flesh. Miss Pottinger stood as tall as her victim, but her full bosom, jutting like majestic cannon-shells over an uplift bra, and her black, pointed boots over navy stockings, gave her the aspect of a destroyer. She brushed a blonde hair from her brow and raised her cane to the full length of her arm. Thwack!

'Nineteen!'

Both sussie straps twanged at the impact of the stripe and the girl groaned. Sandra watched with thumping heart and increasingly wet knickers. She felt sorry for Sharon, but did not want her beating to stop. Glancing at Audrey and Julie, it was evident from their flushed faces that the naked caning excited them just as much. Sandra's fingers were under her skirt, brushing the increasingly moist cotton of her tight, white panties where they encased the hillock of her pubic mound and

101

the tingling cunt-lips wedged with oily, wet knicker cloth.

Thwack!

'Twenty,' said Miss Pottinger as she striped Sharon's bare so hard that her feet jumped out of her shoes.

Again, she aimed left, with a backhand stroke like a tennis player's, which seemed to slither horridly across the bare buttock and leave a glancing blow from the cane's tip to the tight, brown pucker of the anus bud. The shaft struck the sussie strap, removing a hank of threads which flew up to leave the left stocking only half supported.

Miss Pottinger noted this and directed the twenty-first, twenty-second and twenty-third stripes to the livid, dark weals of the girl's right haunch. Sharon Bond's sobbing was now audible as her arse squirmed and clenched under this most pitiless of bare-bottom canings. Sandra's fingers crept from the outside of her wet panties over the elastic waistband, to the damp curls of her pubic forest.

Thwack!

'Twenty-four,' said Miss Pottinger, only slightly panting, as if to mock the squirming girl's gasps.

The twenty-fourth stripe released a knot of thread from the right sussie strap. Sandra's forefinger touched her clitoris and she stifled her own gasp as a tingle of pleasure surged in her belly. She began to rub the distended clitty, focussing on the quivering melons of the whipped girl's bare bum.

'Oh, Miss.' gasped Sharon Bond. 'Oh . . '

'What is it, girl?' snapped Miss Pottinger. 'You asked for it.'

'But not so many,' gasped Sharon, tears streaming down her reddened face.' I didn't know –'

Her handsome features were twisted in pain, but a tell-tale trickle of cunt-juice shone on her bare thighs below her pussy and made her thick bush gleam where the tufts of hair dangled below her gash and anus.

Thwack!

'Ouch! Oh, Miss! Miss Pottinger! Oh, please . . .'

'You know now, Sharon,' said Miss Pottinger pleasantly. 'That was twenty-five. Shouldn't be long now; your straps are quite well frayed.'

Thwack!

'Twenty-six!'

'Oh! Oh! Oh!'

Sharon's striped buttocks twitched madly as her legs stiffened rigid in her agony. Yet the flow of juices from her cunt was plainly visible, wetting her stockings and dripping into the stretched bowl of her panties.

The left stocking was now held to the thigh-flesh by only a couple of trembling threads. The whiteness of her straining thigh muscles threw the awful dark welts of the haunches, and the stripes on the fleshy central buttocks, into stark relief. Sandra's fingers worked fast on her stiff clitty, as she felt her panties gush with wetness. She knew her friends – the whole class, for all she cared! – must be pleasuring themselves too, but didn't care. She wanted her own orgasm to come before the caning ended. She got two, then three, fingers inside the wet velvet of her gash and stabbed at her cunt with eager pokes while her thumb tweaked her stiffened nubbin.

Thwack!

There was a sharp twang as Sharon's left sussie strap broke completely and her stocking sagged.

'Twenty-seven and twangs,' said Miss Pottinger with satisfaction.

'Oh! Gosh, Miss!' cried Sharon, her left hand springing to rub her inflamed bare bum.

Thwack!

The cane whistled again and the class of girls gasped, the noise hiding Sandra's own gasps as her flurried fingers brought her belly and her wet cunt to a heaving come.

Miss Pottinger's unexpected twenty-eighth stripe took

Sharon beneath her fingers, directly on the thigh flesh bared by the drooped stocking, and Sharon squealed.

'Oh! Oh! Miss! That hurt. Oh!' she sobbed, but love-oil dropped copiously from her swollen gash.

'Of course it hurt, and you'd be disappointed otherwise, wouldn't you, Miss?' said the mistress drily, her cane tapping Sharon's panties which were soaked in her cunt's fluid. 'That was for moving before my order. Your stripes are complete now, however, and you may resume your seat. And the class may resume the lesson.'

It was dreary handwriting practice. Sandra's wet fingers slipped on her copy paper as she recommenced the italic script. She glanced at Audrey three desks away, and they exchanged smiles. She knew Audrey had also wanked at the girl's bare-bum caning.

The punishment known as 'twangs' was a fearsome gamble, but a welcome diversion for those witnessing the stripes. By the unwritten rules of Quirke's, a girl sentenced to nine stripes in class could opt for 'twangs'. This meant that her punishment was over when one or both of her sussie straps broke under cane or 'twanged'. Thus, an artful girl could limit a 'niner' to five stripes or even fewer.

A girl who intended to take this gamble would position her straps well back, to the full centre flesh of her arse, although sussie straps had an awkward habit of slipping round to the side, where the cane stung far more. Mistresses or prefects, by the same unwritten rule, had to respect the position of the straps when the bottom was bared and their condition, too. A daring girl would try and fray her straps as much as possible, like a schoolboy wadding his pants with paper before a thrashing.

But the dorm prefects were under orders to watch out for frayed straps at morning inspection and order new suspender belts if necessary. Sharon's punishment had been decreed by Miss Pottinger at the very end of the previous day's class, so she had to wait till next day's lesson for her twangs. She had been caught by Boulter that very morning and ordered into a shiny, new suspender belt.

'Hard luck, Sharon,' said Sandra at breaktime. 'A whole twenty-seven! You took it awfully well.'

They were in the bog, as the WC was jocularly known, and Sharon had her knickers down to inspect her wealed bottom rather proudly in the mirror. She allowed her eager chums to run their fingers over the purple ridges of her fesses.

'Oh!' she said teasingly, 'not so hard. And it was twenty-nine, counting repeaters.'

Audrey's and Sandra's fingers met in the crack of Sharon's bum and they began to tickle the lush brown hairs that fringed her anus pucker, so that she giggled.

'That's quite nice, actually,' she said. 'I bet you chaps were having a jolly good wank while I was being striped. Were you?'

She looked in mock accusation at Sandra, who nodded shyly. Audrey and Julie nodded too.

'I wanted to wank when I was being beaten,' she pouted. 'I was all wet and hot and gushy and I bet you could see my wetness and thought I'd peed. But I didn't pee; I was just thrill-wet. You probably think me a frightful perve.'

'Hmmph!' said Julie. 'You deserve a spanking for cheek. You aren't the only one who gets off on a bum-warming, miss prim and proper. Just wait till dorm tonight.'

'You wouldn't sneak to the Bolt?' said Sharon, feigning alarm.

'Yes, we would!' chorussed Audrey, Julie and Sandra.

It was scarcely a week since Sandra's painful introduction to the disciplined world of Quirke's and the doctrine of 'all girls together'. But she seemed to have been here an age. The obstacle of the preliminary exam no longer seemed so awesome. Many girls were permanent freshers and those that passed got the cane just as much as those that didn't. And no day had passed without Sandra being obliged to take position and 'bare up behind'. The offences were so trifling that the rights and wrongs were never discussed, only the fairness, or attitude of the chastiser. Some stripings were awarded out of pure spite.

Sharon's offence had been chewing gum, a most unladylike practice worth three stripes at the best of times, and an awful no-no in class. But she was really beaten for not saying where she had got the gum. Or, more accurately, in whose pussy the gum had been moistened.

It was a favourite practice, for girls who were best chums, to put sticks of gum in their slits and masturbate till their cunts were wet, then slip the gum to their friend, under the eyes of a mistress, for double-daring. That was known as 'pussy-gum'; For extra super daring, or a very special friend, there was 'bum-gum'.

Sandra had swapped pussy-gum with Julie three times and twice with Audrey. The night before, Audrey had shyly slipped her a morsel of spearmint which had nestled at the root of her anus for two whole hours. Sandra chewed with delight and, as soon as she could, returned the favour. Audrey blushed and swore she would chew it forever. It was to be their secret.

That night, in her bed, Sandra had removed her wedding ring. It left a white stripe on her suntanned fingers but many of the girls had marks where a ring had been removed.

Now, amid the splashes of girls peeing in the gurgling WC, there were more urgent matters. Sandra and Julie touched Sharon on her big, thick cunt-bush and Sharon simpered. Audrey joined in, coolly reaching into her slit.

'So a bare-bum flogging turns you on,' said Sandra.

'Yes! I'm a Quirkean like you. All girls together,' said Sharon.

106

'Would you like us to wank you off, then?' Sandra asked, thrilled to be accepted as a Quirkean.

'Mmm,' said Sharon. 'Yes, please, but hurry.'

The three friends began to masturbate the whipped girl, stroking her wealed bare bum.

'I think Potty was jolly unfair to pick on you,' said Julie as she tweaked Sharon's stiffened and extruded clit.

'And such rotten luck for the Bolt to nab you at inspection,' said Sandra.

'Oh, well,' gasped Sharon, as cunt-oil flowed copiously from her gash, 'I took the chance, you know . . .'

'I think it was more than chance,' said Audrey. 'I think Potty and the Bolt ganged up on you. There is an awful lot of that goes on that girls don't realise. Like poor Tolliver, or Devine, always getting picked on.'

'Mmm! Oh! Yes . . .' Sharon gasped, as Sandra poked her bumhole. 'Oh, a girl needs to be wanked off when her bum's all smarting. Oh, oh! Yes!'

'What about your own case, Audrey?' Sandra reminded her. 'You get picked on something rotten.'

'That's different,' Audrey murmured. 'I'm a sort of martinet. I like to be flogged, not because I like the pain, which is horrid, but because it makes me feel cleansed and righteous. Especially when the stripes are jolly well unfair. But I agree that what we need –' she pinched Sharon's big, plum nipples to crimson stiffness '– is a sort of vigilante group, to police the bullies.'

'Oh! Yes . . .' moaned Sharon. Whether this was in agreement or ecstasy was unclear. 'Poke my slit! I'm so wet for it.'

Julie had four fingers inside her glistening cunt and was poking vigorously, while Sandra churned the whole length of her index finger inside the girl's anus.

'You mean like a gang?' said Sandra. 'In all the school stories, the very best girls had a gang.'

'Yes!' Sharon cried. 'Diddle me hard!'

'The Avengers,' said Julie, as she rammed her fist into the gaping wet maw of Sharon's swollen gash. Sandra's fingers began to flick the pulsing clitty.

Sharon's own fingers joined in the fevered masturbation of her nubbin aleady stiffened by her bare-bum caning.

'The Enforcers,' said Audrey, scratching the girl's bare breasts and nipples with sharp nails, and drawing moans.

Sharon's belly heaved in the plateau of orgasm. Her juices drenched Sandra's fingers, busy at the clitty, while Sharon's buttocks clenched firmly on her churning finger in the anal hole, as though her bare bum squirmed under a new caning.

'Yes, I'm coming,' shrieked Sharon. 'don't stop, don't stop diddling. Oh, you're the best diddlers in school. Oh!'

The girls masturbated with deft eagerness. Now, it did not take long for her to reach orgasm as the cunt-oil gushed from her swollen slit-lips. Sharon yelped seven or eight times as her belly heaved and gasped:

'Diddle me, diddle my clit, Oh, oh, I'm coming. Oh, diddle my cunt! Poke my bum hard! Oh! Ah! Mmm . . .'

The girls squatting to pee applauded. The girls diddling their friend all had stocking-tops drenched in their own juices. Julie, Audrey and Sandra looked at each other, and at Sharon's flushed face, and giggled.

'That's it,' said Sandra. 'We'll call ourselves "The Diddlers".'

The bell rang for next lesson: Miss Swain's. The WC emptied rapidly as the girls rushed for class and left just the four of them.

'Just the four of us,' said Julie.

'The four diddlers,' gasped Sharon, pulling up her stained panties. 'How lovely.'

'We'll need a secret hiding place,' said Sandra gravely.

'A cave, where we can plan our vengeance on . . . on rotters.'

'And wank each other,' Sharon insisted. 'As much as we like. Bumming, too . . .'

Sandra and Julie eagerly agreed. Sandra looked at Julie and they exchanged grins. Sharon would want bumming to be on the agenda.

'I think "Diddlers" is a great name,' said Julie. 'After all, it is the choicest pastime at Quirke's.'

She looked at her watch.

'You bitch, Sharon,' she said playfully. 'You've got me all hot. I can't sit through la Swain's drone without coming first. And I need to pee.'

Audrey and Sandra expressed their feminine solidarity and all three girls squatted on the toilet trough.

'Self-service for speed,' said Julie succinctly, placing an eager finger on her stiff nubbin and then beginning to rub as her jet of pee hissed.

'It'll be stripes if we're late,' said Audrey as she began to tinkle and at the same time began a hearty frigging of her own clit.

Sandra felt waves of pleasure course through her belly as she masturbated beside her friends and sighed with pleasure and relief as her own jet of piss joined theirs in a golden river. It was not long before all three girls gasped loudly in orgasm as the last globes of pee dripped from their quim-lips.

'Girls have always wanked each other at school,' said Sharon as she adjusted her dress for maximum comfort over her striped bottom and hitched up her stockings with a curious arrangement of elastic. 'I know, because a girl called Margaret Betts told me. She said her mum was here, and her mum too, and they said all the girls had pashes on each other and wanked each other off and bummed, ever since the founder, the first Miss Quirke. The title Isobel Quirke is passed on by appointment, you know.'

'So Margaret sort of recruited you?' said Sandra. 'All girls together, eh?'

'You know Margaret?' said Sharon.

'Why,' exclaimed Julie, 'I know her too. She is a busy lady.'

They pulled up wet knickers and petticoats and hurried in some dishevelment towards Miss Swain's classroom.

'We are going to be late. Drat!' said Julie. 'Up for more stripes, Sharon?'

'As long as we're caned together,' said Sharon breathlessly. 'The four diddlers, baring up together. But we'll need a secret password.'

' "Baring up together" sounds fine,' giggled Sandra, and the others agreed.

They knocked timidly on Miss Swain's door, heard a menacing cane swish the air, and were bade enter.

'I say, I think I know where we can find a secret cave,' whispered Audrey.

9

Baring Up Below

The mistresses were a funny lot. Miss Pottinger was starchy and prim, but with a lithe, athletic body, like Miss Crisp. And who would guess that the stern boxing mistress should turn out to crave the birch on her own bare bum! Miss Tate was petite and her schoolmistress's uniform shimmered with a sylph's elegance, yet her caning arm packed unexpected power, and Sandra's bum bore three welts ('for slacking') to prove it.

Miss Swain was actually prettier than Miss Tate, but seemed doomed to eternal dowdiness. A sumptuous figure – pert conical titties with big plum nips visible under her blouse where her cardie left her top uncovered, firm English countrywoman's bum and long, sturdy legs – was camouflaged by stockings, skirt and blouse that seemed forever doomed to be rumpled, as was her generous mane of chestnut hair, apparently comb-resistant. The frayed grey woollie did nothing to help. Sandra would have called her 'oopsy' had she not worn the majesty of a mistress's gown.

Yet this lady greeted the 'Four Diddlers' with a menacing eye behind her thick horn-rimmed glasses and there was nothing dowdy about the way she tapped her cane against her outstretched palm.

'Well! Look at the time,' she murmured, glancing at the clock. 'Four minutes late. A stripe for each minute.'

The rest of the class shivered with a repressed titter

including all the school prefects: Misses Gordon, Long, Cream and Bustard. Miss Swain's class was grammar and spelling, and for this essential instruction, all ranks were mixed. Even the Bolt was there, radiantly chewing gum and sneering from the back of the class.

Sandra and her friends curtsied, then Julie asked slyly if Miss Swain would care to stripe them all together, in order to save valuable classroom time.

'Why, yes,' she said uncertainly. 'I suppose that would be in order.'

She glanced at Stephanie Long, then at Miss Gordon, who nodded, both leering at the four miscreants.

'Shall we bare up behind, Miss?' said Julie innocently.

'All four of you? Yes, I suppose you had better take position. Bums facing the class, isn't that the best way?'

Again, Miss Swain looked at Stephanie Long as though for guidance. Meanwhile the four girls obediently stood in line and, as one, bent over, raised skirts and lowered panties. Audrey gaily pulled down her panties to reveal her taut, bare bum still well-blotched from the previous night's attentions of Miss Boulter, and with tell-tale stretchmarks around her anal cavity where Miss Boulter's dildo had been particularly active. It was tacitly assumed by the gang that the Bolt was the first among rotters to be dealt with.

'Ah, Miss Larch,' said the mistress, almost reverently. 'I'd know that bottom anywhere. Why are you so wicked?'

'Just unlucky, I suppose, Miss,' Audrey sighed.

'I should be so unlucky!' blurted Miss Swain. 'I mean – oh, I don't know what I mean.'

She and the class gasped as they saw the stripes on Sharon Bond's bruised bare haunches. Miss Swain's mouth gaped in awe and her caning arm trembled. She reached out and touched Sharon's naked bottom, drawing breath sharply.

112

'Oh, you poor dear,' she said, steadying herself on her desk. 'Who did this?'

'Miss Pottinger, Miss,' chirped Sharon. 'I took twangs, and it went to twenty-nine.'

'Yes,' gulped Miss Swain. 'Miss Pottinger does cane very hard, I believe.'

And she blushed deeply.

'Well, I have decreed punishment. I suppose you can take another four, Miss Bond. My, such a lot of caning.'

Stephanie Long's hand shot up.

'Please, Miss.'

'Yes, Miss Long?'

'As school prefect, may I volunteer my services, if the mistress would like to be spared the trouble?'

'You mean, Miss Long, that you would administer the stripes?' said Miss Swain, with some relief.

Gordon, Bustard and Cream glowered. Stephanie had beaten them to it.

'Gladly, Miss,' said Stephanie, in a businesslike tone. 'I promise I'll do the four of them quite quickly.'

'Oh, well then ...' said Miss Swain, as if disappointed.

Stephanie rose from her desk as if the matter was decided, and plucked the cane from Miss Swain's hand. Miss Swain sat behind her high desk and looked out at the class.

'Four beauties each for you four sluts,' said Stephanie Long, swishing the cane in the air. 'Short and sharp, eh? But the usual applies: any whingeing gets a repeater.'

Sandra was first in line, nearest Miss Swain's desk. Without warning, the cane whistled and striped her upturned bare, rocking her, and she clutched her ankles as the pain suffused her naked arse-globes, but she was careful not to make any sound. Then she heard the stripe on Julie's bum beside her, then on Audrey's, and then Sharon received the first stroke of her cruel new beating. She too remained silent.

113

'That's the first,' said Stephanie as she walked slowly back to Sandra's 'baring up behind'.

Sandra glanced up. Miss Swain's hands were clenched tightly at her belly and she wore a faraway expression as though the exercise of discipline pained her or fascinated her too much. Sandra shuddered as the second stripe took her right at the soft, top flesh of her bum, but though her legs went rigid, she did not cry. She heard the vip! vip! vip! of the cane on the bare bums of her comrades and suddenly the glow of her caning was a badge of honour. Baring up together.

There was an eager hush in the classroom as the girls took their third stripe, and now Miss Swain had forced herself to observe the four quivering peaches whose striping she had decreed. Her skirt and cardie seemed more dishevelled than usual and her hands were hidden.

Suddenly, Miss Long addressed the mistress.

'Miss Swain, I am sure some girl is chewing gum.'

Sure enough, the hush was broken only by the slurping sounds of mastication. Sandra looked round and saw Boulter's jaws moving in an insolent rhythm.

'Oh!' cried Miss Swain, as though jolted from her reverie, and blushed deep red. 'That's very serious. It would mean nine stripes and an entry in the discipline book. Is any girl chewing gum? Own up.'

Nothing moved except Boulter's jaws.

'I respectfully suggest that the mistress address that question to Dorm Prefect Boulter,' said Stephanie acidly, drawing attention to her own superior rank.

'Oh,' said Miss Swain. 'Well, Miss Boulter?'

'I can see no chewing, Miss,' said Boulter, her mouth gaping innocently to show clearly a wad of pink gum.

'Oh,' stammered Miss Swain. 'False alarm, Miss Long. Let the punishment continue.'

Now her thighs were pressed firmly together, and her hands were clenched between them under the skirt.

'They are remarkable girls, Miss Long,' she faltered.

'Even though you cane hard, not one cause for repetition.'

'No, Miss,' said Stephanie, solemnly lifting the cane for the final stripe.

This time Sandra squealed and tears sprang to her eyes, for Stephanie laid the stripe not across her bare bum, but vertically, taking her on the furrow, so that the stroke fell squarely on the dark raisin of her anus bud.

'Oh! Oh! Oh! Ah . . .' Sandra squealed, then sobbed aloud.

'Hold position, Miss!' ordered the mistress, flushed and breathing heavily.

Hidden from all but Sandra's eyes, her skirt and petticoats were up, revealing white panties already stained dark with juices, and her hands were working vigorously between her thighs. Miss Swain, apparently too timid to administer the cane herself, or to confront the insolent Boulter, was masturbating at the sight of the girls' flogged and squirming bare bums.

Sandra's scalded fesses wriggled in her agony and she sobbed bitterly as her tender bumhole smarted.

'Any complaints, Miss?' said Miss Swain, continuing to diddle her own cunt, though more slowly.

'N-no, Miss,' Sandra sobbed, not sure whether to be dismayed or delighted that Miss Swain was so blatantly 'one of the girls'. Sneaking was the worst offence, even on a hated school pre who had delivered an unfair stripe.

'Then go ahead, Miss Long.'

Julie, Audrey and Sharon received their final stripes in silence and were dismissed to take their places in class. Sandra was to remain in position.

'I – I think Miss Shanks's stroke must be repeated,' gasped Miss Swain, wanking herself less and less discreetly and rubbing her wet gash with surprising new vigour.

Her glasses were steamed up and she paused in her

115

masturbation to remove them, rubbing them on her petticoat. When she replaced them, they steamed up again at once, and she placed them on her desk.

Stephanie Long agreed, and took Sandra again in the stretched and exposed crack of her buttocks, causing new squeals and making her hop as she clutched her ankles. Sandra's knickers slipped down at the furious twitching of her bum and thighs. Her arse felt on fire, a searing lance of white-hot pain suffusing her bumhole and her cunt-lips and the tender perineum between. She grimaced. It was clear Miss Swain would let the caning continue until she had wanked herself to come.

The sixth stripe sliced the flesh of her arse-globes, and Sandra howled, knowing she had nothing to lose. That stripe too was to be repeated, and again, and again . . .

'It seems you are to box, Miss,' sneered Stephanie, 'and I am surprised you are such a cissy under cane.'

'Boxing . . .' murmured Miss Swain, her hands now visibly rubbing the hairy gash-lips rather prettily swathed in their bouquet of dampened panties. 'I am not sure it isn't rather a cruel pastime. To think of a young girl's body punched and hurt. Yes, Miss Long, you may continue the repetition, I mean, repetitions.'

Miss Swain took her glasses from her desk as though to try and clean them again, but instead thrust them inside her wet panties, and directly on the clitty which poked up from the swollen gash. Sandra saw that her pubic forest was wild and unkempt, the curls almost as luxuriant as Sandra's own and glistening with cunt-juice.

Stephanie Long had carte blanche to flog her to exhaustion! Sandra realised that her only hope lay in making Miss Swain come as fast as possible and thus lose interest in further punishment. The strokes mounted. Fifteen, sixteen, seventeen. Still Miss Swain masturbated without coming, as though teasing herself as well as her victim.

116

Now Sandra found that she rode the pain. As always in a caning, she reached the plateau of agony, after which each stripe seemed natural and even welcome, a necessary part of her bare bottom's whole, and her own cunt began to drip juice. Miss Swain's horn-rims danced inside her panties, peeping up for air occasionally, but with the earpieces expertly wanking the mistress's clitty.

Every stripe repeated. Sandra squealed and squirmed and exaggerated the clenching of her scalded bare buttocks, hoping to make Miss Swain gasp in come. At the nineteenth stripe she shuddered violently and bleated;

'Oh! Miss! It is too cruel! Miss Long has a grudge – why, if I had her in the boxing ring, I'd . . .'

She deliberatly stopped, then shrieked as the 20th stripe seared her naked bum. But now she was in control, both of her bum's clenching and of her words, as though the flow of fluid from her pussy, staining her thighs and stockings, and dripping into her stretched white panties, suddenly empowered her with a submissive's authority. A flogged girl – in extremis – was free to speak out.

'What would you do, Miss?' said Miss Swain, masturbating ever more rapidly with her glasses.

The twenty-first stroke lashed Sandra low, just on the soft tops of her thighs, and seemed the most vicious yet.

'I'd pummel her breasts till they were black and blue, Miss. I'd tweak her nips raw, and scratch her and bite her. I'd slam my fist into that slut's pussy of hers –' there were delighted gasps from the audience '– big as a bloody railway tunnel from all the cocks she's had up her! I'd head-butt her, and spank her bare bum till she screamed, and then I'd get her down . . .'

'Yes? Yes?'

Skirts up and her movements quite visible, the mistress's fingers were a blur as she masturbated her extruded pink clitty with her glistening specs. Her petticoat and panties were sodden with cunt-juice.

The cane slashed Sandra three times in rapid succession, knocking her almost off balance, and she moaned. All pretence of 'repetition' was forgotten. She looked through her spread legs and saw that Stephanie Long was openly rubbing her own crotch under her schoolgirl's skirt.

'I'd finger-frig her – you know, down there – Miss, till she screamed for mercy. I'd knock her specs off and get my toes in her bumhole and wriggle and scratch and kick her till it hurt so much she couldn't see for tears.'

The cane lashed Sandra's bare bum like a fury and she must have taken at least thirty. She did not care but she did feel the urge to pee again, so soon after the WC.

'I'd take a birch to her, Miss, to her bare bum, and I'd give her ten times the stripes she's giving me. Yes, I'd make her ugly, white bum purple with the birch, so she'd have the welts for the rest of her life, and every time she sat down she'd remember my birching her naked buttocks . . .'

'Horrid! And with her glasses knocked off! Go on!'

'. . . I'd do it to any rotter, Miss, who picked on me.'

'Surely not to a mistress?'

'Yes, Miss Swain,' Sandra gasped.

She now looked the mistress in the eye as though Stephanie's cane were too far away to hurt her, though the smarting of her bare wealed bum was still awful. Miss Swain's belly was heaving, and her hand soaked with her juices as she masturbated. She seemed almost desperate for come, as though just one thing would bring her off.

'I'd do that to you, Miss!' Sandra cried, and at that moment Miss Swain closed her eyes and gasped harshly. Her hand clamped her cunt-lips and she writhed on her chair in her long-awaited come.

'Perhaps I should acquaint myself with boxing,' she murmured faintly, her face flushed, and she signalled that the beating might cease. 'It seems to toughen a girl . . .'

Stephanie sneaked one last stripe, again to the furrow and arse-bud. Sandra squealed louder than before and released a hot jet of hissing pee that splashed over Stephanie's stockings and shoes. Sandra waited, still in position, until the steaming golden stream had abated, and she stood in a puddle on the classroom floor.

Miss Swain replaced her glasses which were now glistening with her cunt-oil and thus useless. She ignored, or did not see, Sandra's piss.

Sandra stretched and rose with painful gasps, and allowed her sobbing to continue as she rubbed her bruised nates and fumbled to replace her panties. Paying no attenton to her foulness, she sauntered awkwardly to her desk, which was beside Audrey's. She was aware that her own thighs and stockings were well sodden with piss and victorious juices from her gash.

Her lids were heavy and her face flushed as she sat down beside Audrey, who read the signals. In full view of her awed classmates, including the scowling Stephanie and her school prefect friends, Audrey slipped her hand beneath Sandra's skirt, got her fingers into the wet gash, and with a vigorous thumbing of the clitty, wanked Sandra off.

Sandra swore afterwards that Miss Swain actually winked at her. A wealed bum had its own privileges. A girl flogged to deep submission could get away with things.

After school that day, it was clear Sandra would be leader of the Four Diddlers. It went without saying that the fearsome Bolt had to get her comeuppance in due course – 'buggered senseless with a rolling pin,' said Sharon with relish – but it was plain that Stephanie Long must be the very first rotter for their revenge.

'Or else the Bolt,' Sandra said. 'They hate each other.'

'Perhaps we could teach them together,' Audrey said. 'This afternoon, I'll show you where.'

* * *

Sandra and Julie practised boxing for two hours in the afternoon. They sparred in the nude and their friendship did not prevent them from really hurting each other, under the encouraging gaze of Miss Crisp. Sandra ended up taking some smarting whops to her teats and crotch, as well as some painful slaps to her cheeks, and Julie's rueful glance suggested she gave as good as she got. Both Sandra's lush mink, and Julie's sparse pubic crop, were glistening with more than sweat when they ceased their slaps and punches.

Their previous session was not mentioned, but Miss Crisp admired the welts of Sandra's striping by Miss Long. She became visibly excited by four girls baring up together, and said both Sandra and Julie had bums juicy enough for birching, and the thought of four peaches squirming under the birch made her feel quite giddy. She said that an incentive to excel in the forthcoming boxing tournament was that higher up the ladder, increasingly severe punishments were awarded to the losers.

They were to meet soon for Audrey's expedition and the sparring partners showered quickly.

'What I'd really like,' said Sandra, 'is to jump into the sea, nude. There's nothing like it.'

'I guessed you were a nudist,' said Julie. 'That scrummy all-over tan is so jealous-making.'

'Even the main road is out of bounds,' Sandra said, 'let alone the beach. I mean, sometimes I could just murder a gin and tonic at that Feathers lounge.'

'Oh, yes, the Feathers lounge. And there's the spit and sawdust public bar, if you prefer rough trade. Or so I've heard,' said Julie with an impish giggle.

Audrey and Sharon awaited them at the rendezvous by the shrubbery, and they followed Audrey into the undergrowth, which rapidly became tangled and unkempt. It was evident few people came that way. Suddenly they stopped on hearing faint cries. They approached their source, and in a clearing, gazed on Stephanie Long and Tara Devine.

Tara was nude, and Stephanie clad only in bra, panties and stockings. She held a four-thonged leather whip and applied it to Tara's buttocks. Tara was suspended upside down from a tree branch, but only by one ankle, tied tightly with rope, so that her head hung a foot from the ground, her breasts dangling over her chin and striped with welts. Her other leg was bent inwards so that her toe was wedged right inside her anus and her ankle strapped to her thigh.

The buttocks were bared for flogging just below Stephanie's waist height and her gash was upturned and open. Stephanie's breasts bounced in their cups and her body dripped with sweat as she whipped the helpless girl. Julie whispered that this punishment was called the parrot, for it was meant to make you squawk.

'Where? Where?' shrieked Stephanie as she whipped.

'I don't know where, Miss!' cried Tara, writhing as the thongs lashed the arse-crack an inch from her quim.

Direct whipping of the quim was technically against the rules, like smoking and men. But the ban on cock seemed the only rule faithfully observed.

'How many of them?'

'Oh! Oh! Oh, it hurts, Miss!' she screamed. 'Just the four of them! Oh, please let me go! I don't know any more! I thought you'd reward me for telling you. Oh! Oooh . . .'

'This is the reward for sneaking,' said Stephanie grimly, 'even on sluts like Shanks and her crew.'

The whip cracked across Tara's naked breasts, then she took four quick lashes to the bum-cheeks, and two in the furrow, catching the toe and filled anus-hole, which reduced the writhing nude girl to hysterical squeals.

'Well, she is a sneak,' Audrey said firmly, pulling her chums away, 'and we have our own business.'

'Someone must have blabbed to Tara,' said Sandra mildly.

They proceeded further from Quirke's in the direction of the sea, and came to a clump of bracken, and a rock, which Audrey shoved aside, revealing the mouth of a tunnel about four feet in diameter. She produced an electric camper's lantern from under her skirt and illumined the shaft, which was obviously man-made. The walls and sides of compacted earth were shored up at intervals by wooden beams, like a coal mine. The tunnel sloped sharply downwards.

'Follow me,' Audrey whispered dramatically.

The four half-walked, half-crawled, behind Audrey's flickering lantern. At first, the air in the shaft was dank and mossy, but after a hundred paces or so, there was a breeze and the smell of the sea. Audrey paused.

'This is called a priest's tunnel,' she said, her face lit luridly by the lantern beneath her chin. 'I found it from an old book of local legends. The owner of the great hall where Quirke's now stands was a Catholic, and would harbour fugitive priests, then smuggle them to France, to stop them being boiled alive by King Henry the Eighth.'

'Gosh,' said Sharon.

'Gosh,' said Julie.

As they continued down, the wind got fresher, and a pinprick of light became visible at the end of the tunnel. In five minutes they emerged into a rocky enclave overlooking the beach, which could be seen ten feet below through a chink in the rocks. At the clifftop, visible only from the far corner of the rocky enclave, stood a white building, which Audrey said was the Feathers pub. Otherwise the enclave was completely secluded.

Audrey moved to the farthest corner of the enclave, which was in shadow, and the girls saw that one of the shadows was actually an aperture in the rock face, about the width of a person. Audrey slipped inside.

'It looks like a giant pussy!' said Sharon.

They found themselves inside a dank and very cramped chamber, strewn with boulders and wind-blown grasses. The chamber was very long and tapered to a narrow point like an ice-cream cone sideways. Audrey put the lantern on a ledge.

'Voilà!' she cried. 'The diddlers' hole!'

'We should have a name for it,' said Sharon. 'Since it looks like a pussy, let's call it "The Gash".'

This was solemnly agreed.

'Shouldn't we have an agenda?' Julie said.

'The agenda is pretty clear: we chastise Stephanie Long,' said Sandra, 'or the Bolt, or both at once.'

They squatted in the dim light, accustoming themselves to the snugness and quiet. Sandra mentioned the difficulty of the project: how to get a vigorous female down through the tunnel, and keep her here, and what to do with her when they got here. This caused silent pondering.

'Let's freshen up with a naked swim,' said Audrey, adding shyly that she used to come down the tunnel to the beach, and leave her clothing in The Gash, for secrecy.

Soon four nude females were clambering shrilly down to the shingle beach, where they scampered into the sea in mild, autumn sunshine. Sandra's bottom was compared to Sharon's, and Sandra told the girls about her nudist activities, the 'Miss Nude Sussex' beauty contests and the like. Julie joked that they should organise a Miss Quirke's contest for the best-striped bum, and they all laughed.

'Why not? We could call it the "Miss Nude Flagellant" contest,' Sandra said thoughtfully.

Sharon said she needed to make potty, and went behind a rock. The others, shrieking with laughter, dragged her back to the shingle and made her squat and do her business right under their eyes.

'Baring up together!' they chorussed as Sharon gasped in the relief of her copious evacuation.

This was the signal for everybody to 'go', and they took it in turns, peeing openly with thighs spread wide, and critically appraising the brightness, strength and steaminess of their fluids.

'To properly inaugurate the diddlers,' said Sandra as she wiped the last drops of pee from her vulva, 'shouldn't we, ah, ceremonially wank each other off?'

It seemed the most natural thing in the world to seal the sisterhood with a communal diddle. With only the building of the Feathers far above staring at them like a big, white seagull, they sat cross-legged, each girl's hand on her neighbour's cunt and clitty, and with great blushing solemnity they mutually masturbated to orgasm.

'Baring up together,' each naked girl moaned as she shuddered in her come.

After the satisfaction of mutual masturbation, the girls dived into the sea for a quarter of an hour's vigorous splashing, then returned to The Gash, where their clothing was hung very properly in any available nook or cranny. Sandra's was at the far end, where the cornet shape of The Gash narrowed to a point, and she had to stoop.

'Wait a minute!' she cried. 'Bring the lantern here, Audrey.'

None of the girls had dressed. Audrey pressed her nude body to Sandra's and exclaimed in loud surprise.

'There is another chamber,' said Sandra. 'Look. It's hidden by the shadow, and if we push this rock aside –'

A hole was revealed, just large enough for a single body to wriggle through. Audrey said she was frightened, since these caverns might go on for miles like potholes. Smiling, Sandra began to wriggle through the hole. Moments later, her voice echoed.

'Just look at this!'

Audrey overcame her reluctance and in moments, the girls stood in a chamber the size of their dormitory, but with a much higher ceiling, and cluttered with gloomy boulders.

'I – I never knew,' said Audrey.

'This is where we'll meet,' announced Julie. 'If the first cave is The Gash, then this has to be the bumhole.'

The light did not illumine the bumhole as well as The Gash, and when their eyes had become accustomed to the fainter glow, all gasped at once, for the huge boulders were not rocks at all, but metal machines or devices.

'I can't believe it,' said Sandra. 'An old pillory.'

'Stocks,' said Julie, 'and a rack.'

One by one, they uncovered vices and clamps and branks, irons for the enclosure, restraint and chastisement of every conceivable part of the body. There were metal quirts and whips of leather, with canes of springy metal or wood; a mangle; a device like an iron maiden; various whipping frames complete with cuffs and straps. The machinery was of rough wood and stone, antique cast iron or brass.

'It is a torture chamber,' said Julie. 'A medieval torture chamber. But how, who, why?'

'These things are so old,' said Sharon. 'Look how crusted and nobbly everything is, as though hand-made. And covered with dust. It must have been here for centuries.'

'Henry's daughter Queen Elizabeth the First had lots of spies and secret agents,' said Audrey. 'Maybe they tricked the priests, lured them here and tortured them.'

Sandra picked up a thickly clustered bunch of razor shells wired together.

'A sixteenth century dildo,' she said, 'for a priest?' and they all laughed.

'Now we know where we can bring our – our clients for their correction,' said Audrey thoughtfully. 'But we should see if it's in working order first.'

She scraped some of the dust off a cast-iron flogging-frame, with cuffs, a giant metal double penis and menacing extended pincers which could only have been intended for female breasts and cunt-lips.

'They must have tortured more than priests,' she said. 'Witches, perhaps. They called it "putting to the test".'

Four naked females shuddered.

'Poo! The dust!' said Sharon.

'One of us should be the witch,' said Sandra. 'To test the equipment, and the rest of us her torturers. Just in play, of course, so that we know exactly what we're doing when – when we do it for real. Whipping, branking, racking, the pillory, everything. Or we could take turns.'

While the others digested this, Sandra began to peer upwards towards the vaulted ceiling, where the walls were lined with cracks and fissures. Suddenly she climbed up on the pillory and scanned the top of the chamber.

'What are you doing, Sandra?'

'Looking for cobwebs. You'd expect to find some.'

'Ugh! I hope not.'

Sandra jumped down.

'There aren't any. And you see those ledges up there by the ceiling? There is no dust there, either.'

There was a pause and faces frowned in the dim light.

Sandra brushed a smut from her left nipple.

'It is quite easy to make things dusty,' she said, with a shrug. 'Just scatter a bucket of dust. Men wouldn't notice cobwebs, but no lady would let a nasty yucky spider survive long enough to make a cobweb. Nor might she remember to climb up and scatter dust everywhere.'

'You mean this isn't a centuries-old torture chamber?' said Sharon with disappointment.

'It is a torture chamber, but it's not centuries old,' said Sandra. 'This iron stuff is just repro, and can be easily made to look antique. What we have here is a modern dungeon, probably in frequent use, with dust imported for the unlikely event of discovery. Look! most of it is sawdust, like you get in an old-fashioned pub. And this!'

She held up a Marlboro Light cigarette butt stained with flamboyant red lipstick and everybody giggled.

'I say finders keepers,' said Julie. 'Whoever uses this place is pretty sloppy, but if they, or she, want it to be secret, why, so do we. No reason not to share. And it'll be a game. They don't want to discover us, but we will be quite happy to discover them.'

'What if there are more of them than us?' said Sharon.

'Then,' laughed Sandra, 'we'll have a great party. They even smoke my brand. Meanwhile, there is plenty of time until tea to test our new equipment. Who'll volunteer?'

'I will,' murmured Audrey, her eyes moist. 'Just me.'

'Are you sure, Audrey?' Sandra said.

'I was the one who blabbed to Tara Devine. Oh, I'm sorry!'

'So Stephanie knows about our gang,' said Sandra, 'but not about The Gash and the bumhole.'

'It doesn't matter.' Audrey whispered. 'I'm a blab, and so dreadfully, horribly foolish and wicked. Put me to the test, cleanse me, and please, not in fun.'

Sandra's eyes met hers for a long moment.

'Very well, Audrey,' she said. 'You've asked for it . . .'

10

In The Gash

'We'd better get the place cleaned up,' said Julie.

It was agreed that the miscreant Audrey should be charged with cleaning the devices of her own punishment. When she pointed out that there was no cleaning rag, Julie told her to use her skin. And if she took her punishment well, she would be allowed a dip in the sea afterwards. Sandra, Sharon and Julie watched with hands on hips and sneers on their mouths, as Audrey toiled, twisting her agile young body to use her bare breasts and buttocks as polishing cloths. From time to time, on her hands and knees, she was urged on by a kick between the legs, until Sandra said that they should save that for later.

There was menace in her voice, and contempt in all their eyes, as though their naked intimacy and the menacing presence of the disciplinary engines transformed Audrey from a chum and gang member to an errant slave.

'I think, we should each select an implement,' said Julie.

'Bags I the steel cane!' cried Sharon, grabbing a three-foot twangy rod with a handlebar like a bicycle's.

'I don't mind the heavy cat-o'-nine-tails,' said Sandra.

'Which leaves me with this rattan,' said Julie, although it left her in fact with the juiciest choice. The rattan was the hardest of the wooden canes on offer.

Each girl stroked her nude body with her chosen implement as though caressing a furry little kitten.

'Sets of ten I think,' said Julie briskly. 'Each of us in turn, and I suggest we try her in the pillory first.'

Sandra agreed.

'We can work up to the rack and the pulley should come in useful. Or there are stocks for back work,' she said.

'I like those tweezers,' said Sharon, looking at the curious flogging frame with its clamps for tits and cunt and the massive dildos.

'Take her to a ninety: three sets from each of us, and see how she goes,' said Julie, as though discussing a racehorse or motorbike.

Audrey looked up. Her work was almost finished and every machine of pain glowered with shining menace.

'You won't be too hard on me, will you?' she blurted. 'You did say it was in fun. Oh, please!'

She addressed Sandra, who sneered and spat a gob of saliva on Audrey's breast.

'I believe "not in fun" were your words, Miss,' Sandra replied. 'And why shouldn't we be hard on a . . . a traitor? Your thoughtless blabbing has alerted Long to our game before we've even got started. Now get your ragged little arse to that pillory and prepare for your first set.'

The perfect bruised pears of Audrey's arse were neither ragged, nor little, and her pubic mound was already pressed to the pillory, and her bare bum-globes stuck high like two cats begging for a saucer of milk.

They took Audrey by the hair, making her squeal, and placed her throat on the circular indentation of the pillory, with her upper arms in the wedges actually designed for the forearms. Then the hinged block was snapped shut, imprisoning her. The pillory was of a height that she could just manage to support herself on tiptoe.

There was some debate about whether her legs should remain unstrapped, as she might kick under whip. Eventually it was decided to lock her feet in a pair of lead Spanish boots designed for crushing the shins. These were left unfastened but were so heavy that when Audrey's legs were splayed wide, she was quite unable to shift her feet, whose toecaps just touched the ground.

'Look,' said Sharon.

A wooden trap-door covered an excavation in the earth, revealing a space about six feet by six. The hole brimmed with articles of clothing. There were rubber sheaths, corsages of pins and leather, gauntlets and hoods. Eyes shining, Sharon extracted three black latex pixy hoods. Without a word, the three girls donned the rubber hoods, sheathing their faces except for eyes, nose and mouth.

Sandra took out another hood and, with a sly grin, slipped it over Audrey's head. This sheath clung very tightly and had only one aperture: for the nose. Audrey's body stiffened as the rubber covered her face.

'I'm frightened,' she said, her voice muffled and distorted by the rubber. 'I thought it was only a game.'

As she spoke, the latex mask moved with her lips. Julie said she was a rubber duck and they laughed cruelly.

'Blabbing isn't a game,' said Sandra.

It was decided to warm Audrey with a bare-bum spanking before her sets of ninety stripes, and Sandra spanked first. Not a word was spoken as her palm cracked the taut flesh of Audrey's bare, drawing a nice, pink blush and the merest hint of a quiver from the big, pale arse.

'Mmm,' panted Audrey when the set was over, either in regret, apprehension or excitement for more.

Assuming the latter, Julie made her spanking much harder, and now the bare bum was suffused with a red glow and the cheeks began to clench. Sharon followed with a set of spanks that took the shivering girl on the haunches, the buttock tops and low under her furrow. Audrey's moans were long and softly whining.

'Good!' said Sandra. 'Now, who's first with proper striping? I suggest Julie, then Sharon, then me.'

Julie said slyly that Sandra's spanking was a bit weak and asked why she wanted to go last with the cat.

'Why,' Sandra blurted, 'she'll be nicely warmed up and the cat will be hardest.'

'Not chickening out?' said Julie. 'Not wishing it was you bound and pilloried, and your bum taking the stripes?'

Sandra paled, then just as fast, her cheeks flooded red.

'I'll show you,' she said fiercely, and lifted the cat high, then dealt Audrey a savage lash, not on the buttocks but across her pinioned, bare shoulders.

Audrey squealed in surprise and pain. Sandra, undeterred, striped her back a second time. Her fury took the others by surprise and they watched silently.

Sandra striped the girl's naked back again and again until Audrey's body was jerking like a marionette and her shrieks of agony rent the chamber. Her bottom's glow from the spanking had paled by the time her back and shoulders were a criss-cross of livid welts from the cat-o'-nine-tails. Sandra lowered the whip, panting and sweating, and said that Audrey had taken two dozen on the back, a gift which didn't count as part of her ordained ninety. Audrey sobbed and wailed, and the edges of her rubber hood, tight round her neck, were moist with her tears.

Sandra looked round in grim triumph but neither Sharon nor Julie spoke. Both hooded girls had their hands pressed between their thighs, their eyes eating up the welts on Audrey's striped back as they wanked hard. Sandra touched her own wet quim and began to masturbate.

Julie lifted her rattan, while the other hand was firmly embedded in her gash, which streamed with juice. As the heavy cane lashed Audrey's bare bottom, Julie grunted and began to flick her extruded glistening clitty quite fast. Sandra and Sharon followed her, shamelessly masturbating as the naked girl writhed in the pillory, her squeals muffled by her clinging rubber mask, and the harsh stripes of the rattan growing from red to purple, until Julie counted ten and stopped.

Audrey's bottom continued to squirm and clench and a trickle of love-oil was clearly visible at the lips of her gash, dripping to the floor between her hobbled feet.

'Well!' said Julie. 'The slut likes her punishment!'

'Mm! Mm! Mm!' squealed Audrey beneath her rubber hood, but her protests were belied by the love-juice that glistened on the sodden tendrils of her pubic bush hanging well below her swollen gash-lips.

Now it was Sharon's turn. The slender steel cane made a thin, whistling sound unlike the heavy crack of the rattan and its stripes were both deeper and more livid. She paused between each stroke to rub her clitty, like a cat toying with a mouse, and relished the continued squirms of Audrey's flogged bare bum, accompanied by a furious clanking as her trapped feet twisted in their restraining boots. Each of the three girls masturbated with impish glances at the others' glistening, hard clits.

'First to come gets the cat on her bum,' said Julie, 'for soppiness. Agreed?'

They agreed and Audrey inclined her head.

'Oh, are you wanking off?' she gasped. 'Oh, please wet my bum with your come-juice.'

'Silence, worm!' cried Sandra, over-theatrically, and slapped Audrey's face hard, which jerked her head round.

But her own gash flowed harder as she slapped. Sharon's set was over and now Audrey's peach was a glowing painting of agony, the weals striping every inch of her bare, from the buttock tops to the soft underflesh. The haunches too were marked with deep purple welts.

Sharon and Julie looked at Sandra as she lifted her cat-o'-nine-tails above the buttocks whose welts matched the stripes already laid on the shoulders. Sandra removed her fingers from her gash, and Julie said that was not fair. All of them must continue to wank off throughout Audrey's punishment.

Sandra replaced her fingers gingerly at her throbbing nubbin and brought her whip down hard on Audrey's fesses, covering almost the whole of her bare with the vicious little thongs. Audrey sighed deeply and began to moan. The flow of juice from her cunt became a stream.

'Oh! Oh! Mmm . . .' she sobbed at the second stroke, then recommenced her wail.

Sandra's third stroke made her squeal. At the fourth, her bottom began to shudder frantically, the cleft almost disappearing as she squeezed tight the cheeks of her peach.

'Oh! No! Oh! Sandra! Oh!' Audrey screamed as the flogging continued implacably on the helpless bare arse-cheeks.

The metal boots which hobbled the girl's feet clanged in impotent anguish. At each stroke her legs stiffened rigid, in contrast to the almost sensual clenching of her bum. Vivid streams of love-juice cascaded from her gash down her bare thighs and puddled the ground.

Thwack! Thwack!

'No, no.' Audrey whined. 'Ahhh . . .'

All through her savage striping with the cat, Sandra took her time and planted every stroke in the same ruts on Audrey's naked skin, so that by the eighth, her arse was trenched with deep welts.

'Oh!' Mmm! Oooh!' Audrey sang at each crack as the thongs wrapped around her haunches like lovers' fingers.

Sharon's and Julie's fingers twitched at their distended clitties. They masturbated as slowly but as firmly as possible, both obviously aching to come. Sandra regally tweaked her own stiff nubbin as though the throbbing pleasure-bud had to submit, just like the crinkly eye of Audrey's squirming anus.

At the ninth stroke of the cat, Audrey groaned in anguished embarrassment and peed herself, the hot golden stream hissing from her gash and mingling with her juice in the puddle beneath her swollen cunt-lips. Sandra viciously delivered the tenth and now Audrey screamed six or seven times, her boots rattling and her hooded head banging against the pillory's beam. Sandra had flogged her captive to orgasm.

Seeing this, Julie and Sharon masturbated without shame or restraint, and soon the chamber echoed to their squeals of coming. Sandra, panting, lowered her whip and pressed the handle against her nubbin, then thrust it right inside her own wet slit, while her fingers attended the clitoris, and as the others' cries of come abated, Sandra climaxed louder than any of them.

'Well,' gasped Audrey. 'I came first, so the extra ten is for me.'

Her words were clear; her lips showed between the latex folds, for in her agony she had bitten away the rubber.

'Ready for the rest of your ninety, no, one hundred, now,' said Julie, and Audrey nodded.

'I'm sorry I peed,' she said. 'I couldn't help it.'

'That,' said Sandra smugly, 'is stating the obvious. But we are all girls together.'

'Well, the second thirty stripes shouldn't be so bad,' said Julie, 'and by the third lot you'll be in seventh heaven or oblivion. That's how it works for me. It's funny how your bum gets used to a long beating. Remember how awful your twelve stripes at assembly felt, Sandra?'

'How could you know?' Sandra shot back. 'Anyway, it was only the first few. After that I settled into the rhythm.'

'What about my twenty-nine?' demanded Sharon.

'The point is that in any beating, we reach a plateau, and after that, the pain is pure, sweet loveliness. I think Audrey reaches her plateau faster than any of us,' Julie said slowly and deliberately, 'so we shall have to use the rest of these instruments well, to really punish her.'

'If Miss Long was here, we wouldn't have to worry,' said Sandra acidly. 'One stripe and she'd blub.'

'Or the Bolt,' added Sharon. 'Bullies can't take it! She gave my bumhole some pounding last night. It felt like a real cock, and she did it from behind, with my face hooded, which is unusual for her. It was rather madly thrilling, though. Your turn tonight, Sandra, I'll bet.'

'What must be . . .' murmured Sandra vaguely. 'And anyway, don't tell me you didn't enjoy your bumming, Sharon.'

Sharon said with coy satisfaction that she came twice with the dildo ramming her arse-root. Julie reminded them that Audrey's bum awaited further chastisement, and lifted her rattan once more, then paused.

'We should be careful with the Bolt,' she said. 'Long is no problem, but our Miss Boulter has some kind of strange hold over this place: over the pres, and the beaks, even over Miss Quirke herself.'

'Perhaps because she's lesbian,' said Sharon wittily.

'Not like us, eh?' sneered Julie. 'Fucking bull dyke.'

'Not exactly like us,' said Sandra firmly.

Julie began to beat the wealed buttocks anew, taking her time between stripes and laying each one in a different place on Audrey's writhing arse. When the rattan had delivered its second set, the steel whip took over, and then the cat. It seemed that Audrey had indeed reached a plateau of pain, for the clenching of her bare bum became a sensuous dance. They allowed themselves a five-minute break before the final sets, and all the girls touched the hot welts on the flogged bare buttocks, their eyes wide with awe behind their masks.

The third three sets made Audrey pee herself again, and at one point she seemed to faint, but recovered enough to ask that her forfeit ten with the cat wait until she was strapped to the rack. Her insolence in making this decision for her tormentors went unremarked; she was unfastened from the pillory and stretched face upwards on the rack, an oblong metal frame with a single steel cord stretched from head to foot on which the victim was to rest.

The rack was waist-high, so this nasty steel cord obviously would serve for a girl to ride the rail if need be. At each end was a roller, like a mangle, attached to leather thongs that cuffed to wrists and ankles. In addition, there were smaller stretching devices at one-third intervals on each side of the frame, straps with pincers just at the victim's teats and crotch.

Halfway along the span was a single dildo of knotted braid that looked like grey straw, but was iron. It arched up stiff like an erect penis. There was only one and it was agreed this should fit into Audrey's anus.

'This must have been designed for a male victim,' said Sharon coyly. 'Just think: girls torturing a naked man. I suppose the shaft would go in his poor bumhole.'

'If he was a priest, then his poor bumhole would probably enjoy the experience,' said Julie, 'just like you.'

Audrey was lifted on to the spanning cord and quickly fastened by wrists and ankles, and the rollers were wound tight as they would go, stretching her to the full, for the moment. Then she was roughly bum-plugged, the metal shaft pushed up her anus until it would move no further.

Eagerly, Julie fastened the smaller clamps to each nipple and each cunt-lip. Her sensitive portions were to be stretched on the rack, outwards instead of along.

'What about her ten extra with the cat?' she said.

'Oh,' said Sandra, as coolly as she could, 'she can take them on the tits and thighs when she's nicely stretched.'

Sandra was positioned above Audrey's head, with Julie and Sharon taking the sides. All three began to turn their handles. The device creaked, and Audrey's nude body stiffened in fear as the rack began to stretch.

'Wait,' said Sharon.

Appointing herself wardrobe mistress, she went to the cubby-hole and fetched black executioners' costumes to go with their hoods, explaining it was more sinister if the victim was nude but the torturers clad. In moments, all three were wearing black hold-up hose, rubber gauntlets, spiked steel collars and clinging latex body-stockings open at teats and crotch, as if for unforeseen eventualities. Sandra took off Audrey's hood and the girl blinked in astonishment and fear.

'Don't plead for mercy,' Julie said, 'for you won't get any. We might even leave you here, and someone will come to find you nicely trussed. Just think what she might do.'

'It's not a very powerful rack,' Sharon grumbled.

'Sshh,' warned Julie. 'Audrey doesn't know that.'

Audrey's racking began in earnest. She gasped, but was otherwise silent, as the device pulled her taut, every muscle quivering in the lantern's glow, and her naked body beaded with sweat. Sandra made a dramatic show of muscle as she turned the ratchet. The girls worked gleefully. Soon Audrey's breasts were stretched taut by their pincers, the expanded nipples gleaming white, and the whole flesh of her teats pulled flat like pancakes, distended beyond their normal girth. Audrey squealed and sobbed and her stretched body shivered uncontrollably as the racks and pinions creaked.

She craned to look down at her belly and cunt, and saw the clamped quim-lips pulled out so that her gash seemed the centre of a crater, whose saucer rim was the lips, with the lonely hillock of her stiff clitty standing like a sentinel on its wet, pink plateau. The hole of her gash too was opened far beyond expansion even by the thickest cock or dildo, and when Sharon said they could park a car in her, Audrey groaned.

Her groans were muffled as Sandra let go of the machine and suddenly vaulted on to Audrey's body. The steel cord twanged. She squatted facing Audrey's feet with her cunt over the girl's face and her feet on the shoulders. Slowly she lowered herself until Audrey's face took the full weight of her arse. Then Sandra lifted her whip and stroked it gently on Audrey's stretched belly.

'Ten extra, I think we agreed,' she murmured.

Audrey's mouth trembled in Sandra's cunt-flaps.

'Ten,' she gasped.' 'Please, Miss . . .'

Sandra lashed Audrey not too hard on the left thigh, then gave her a second stroke, somewhat harder, but which lightly flicked her quim-lips as though by mistake.

'Go on, thrash gash,' Julie urged. 'I know it's not the done thing, but I love it, like raindrops on a rose.'

Sandra did whip the naked inner thighs very hard. Audrey's body convulsed and her teeth chewed right on the raisin of Sandra's bumhole. Sandra herself squealed and lashed Audrey's belly, the thongs of the cat painting dark bruises on the quivering navel whorl. Now Audrey's mouth fastened on Sandra's soaking quim-lips and, at her third stroke, the tongue found stiff clitty and began to flicker on the throbbing bud in an eager gamahuche.

The next stroke took Audrey's spread inner thighs, and the next. They too bruised satisfactorily. Then there were two strokes across the tits, making sure to catch the drawn nipples, and finally back to the gaping anus hole in Audrey's distended crack, below the stretched cunt-lips flowing with juice that made her thighs and · belly glisten. Sandra whipped Audrey's belly again, and

Audrey sighed. It was evident that her bare belly had been striped before.

'Ten!' Sandra gasped.

'Mmm! Mmm,' Audrey groaned, as her cunt-lips and bruised nips were pinched wider and tighter. 'More . . .' she wailed.

Both Julie and Sharon had their fingers busily flicking their clits. They masturbated vigorously, urging Sandra to continue the punishment.

'Oh,' said Sandra, and suddenly her pee welled in her belly, and a hot jet of fluid spurted over Audrey's face and into her mouth. She felt Audrey gulp it down.

The piss steamed hot and golden all over the girl's naked breasts, pooled at her navel and dripped down her arched pubis into the fleshy, pink pond of her hair-crusted gash. Sharon and Julie bared their teeth and began to hiss like wolves as they masturbated, almost as though hurting their clits with the rapidity of the flicks. Sandra resumed flogging Audrey's quivering belly.

'Strange,' gasped Julie. 'The more she hurts, the more she wants it. How do you punish her? Or any of us? We dread the lash, yet crave it. And we are not lesbians, but long to be fucked and buggered by a lesbian brute like Boulter.'

'It's not the pain,' replied Sandra, flicking her whip hard on Audrey's stretched nipples, whose excitement was indicated by an army of stiff little goose pimples. 'In the Middle Ages, monks used to flagellate themselves. But it's not the same thing as being in another's power. It is the submission, the joy of being helpless and abused. Audrey had no choice but to swallow my pee and take my whip. Complete shame makes us free of shame.'

She ceased the flogging, sprang down from Audrey's slimy wet face and ratcheted the machine up a notch. The thing refused to budge! Sharon was right, and yet

Audrey's body arched in apparent pain as the thongs twanged uselessly.

'Aahh!' she screamed, and at that moment both Sharon and Julie cried out in orgasm.

Sandra masturbated until her come-juice flowed almost as copiously as her pee, then bent over and bit Audrey full on the lips, her teats and belly shaking in her own climax.

'Oh, please,' Audrey begged. 'One of you, touch me, touch my clitty! She's so awake and stiff and longing to come. Just one touch and I'll explode, please . . .'

The three hooded masturbators glowered at her.

'No, Audrey,' said Julie. 'I think we've found your punishment. You shan't come. Sandra brought you off under the whip, but no more whipping, and no wanking off. It is teatime. We'll leave you alone in the darkness and we may decide to come back and fetch you.'

Audrey wailed as the girls stripped and restored their clothing to the cubby-hole, which Sharon carefully closed.

'No, no,' she begged, as the lantern moved away. 'Not leave me, not alone.'

Naked now, Sandra turned and put her finger an inch from Audrey's stiff, throbbing clitty.

'Just one touch, Sandra,' Audrey begged. 'Please wank me off. Oh please. Feel in my bum. There's gum there, I've been keeping all for you, as my special chum.'

Sandra put her hand underneath Audrey's buttocks and raised them high enough to allow the dildo to slip out. Stuck to the end was a pink wad of gum which she stuffed into Audrey's own mouth. Then she replaced the dildo in the racked girl's anus, making sure it struck her root.

'Now you have something to chew over, Audrey,' she whispered, 'all alone in the dark.'

'You wouldn't leave me, Sandra?' Audrey begged.

'Whoever finds you won't be so merciful,' Sandra said. 'We didn't put you in the tweezers.'

She looked at the flogging-frame with the vice and giant twin dildos.

'Pain is nothing among friends. But when you don't know your torturer or see her face: that is submission beyond submission. Whoever is the mistress of this place won't like your intrusion. I'm sure you'll have more pain than even you can bear, Audrey. You'll be all alone, tortured by someone you won't even know. Won't it be hell?'

Suddenly, Audrey screamed long and loud, but her screams were not in fear. Her whole body arched as her lungs heaved in ecstasy. Come-juice flooded from her gash and her belly quivered as Audrey finally exploded in her own orgasm.

'Oh, oh, oh . . .' she gasped finally, her face radiant. 'Oh, that was lovelier than a wank. You're the best chums a girl could have. The best diddlers.'

Sandra took the gum from her mouth and placed it between her own lips. She said they had time for a swim before tea, and released Audrey from the rack. Soon all four girls were best friends again. They splashed naked in the wavelets and the bright lights of the Feathers glared down at them, even though it was not yet sunset.

11

Purple Stilettos

That night, it was as Sharon had predicted. Miss Boulter summoned Sandra to her curtained boudoir, but not until she had witnessed the shameful submission of two girls to the 'spinning top'.

Audrey's bed was unaccountably empty, but this was unmentioned at lights out. Sandra settled down to sleep and suddenly was awoken by a whoop and a light shining on Tara Devine's bed. Tonight the Bolt was arrayed in girly femininity, her long hair brushed to a sheen and hanging softly over a silver-blue gown of brushed silk which clung and shimmered to the curves of her ripe teats and arse.

The gown was not long but frilly and showered outwards like a tutu, revealing silver stockings in small fishnet with white seams, and white patent leather shoes with fearsome pointed toecaps and very high stilettos, on which Boulter walked as nimbly as a faun. Her panties, shown by the bounce of the frilly skirt, were no more than a thong with a spangled starry crotch. Her fount was almost nude.

'Diddle patrol!' she cried gleefully and ripped the covers from Tara Devine's bed.

She revealed two girls embracing with their nighties up and their hands between each other's glistening thighs.

'Devine and Tolliver, wanking off,' she announced to

the now awakened dormitory. 'We all know what that means.'

'Please, Miss Boulter, we felt lonely,' quavered Tara Devine, which seemed to increase Boulter's rage.

'That' apparently meant the spinning top. Sandra was enlisted to help, along with Julie and Sharon, and, not unwillingly, they stripped the two quivering masturbators and held them beside the eagle. With practised skill, Miss Boulter unlocked two central struts of the flogging machine and positioned them at vertical. Then she applied KY jelly to their ends which were slightly swollen like the bulbs of two penises. The shafts were in fact circular and of the same dimension as rather large cocks. Two separate pulleys were drawn down from the ceiling, each with thonged cuffs at their ends.

Sandra, Julie and Sharon were required to bodily lift Tara Devine on top of one protruding shaft, while Miss Boulter deftly fastened her wrists above her head in the pulley's cuff. She took a roll of adhesive tape from beneath the flogging-frame and, as Sandra and her friends held Tara, Tara's thighs were forced up against her teats and wrapped in adhesive cling-film seven or eight times, immobilising her in a silvery cocoon, with her legs stuck grotesquely in the air and cupping her skull.

At the Bolt's signal, Tara was lowered on to the gleaming greased shaft so that the bulb entered her gash. The girls let go and Tara sank right on to the pole so that it was embedded to the root of her cunt, taking her weight as she dangled helplessly. Now it was Tolliver's turn.

'Please, Miss, no . . .' she whined. 'I was only playing Tara's game. She insisted. It was her fault . . .'

Tolliver should have known better than to sneak. She received the same treatment, but when she was wrapped securely in cling-film and dangling over the pole, Miss Boulter directed the girls to insert the prong not in cunt but in anus. Tolliver was abruptly released to fall on the shaft and emitted a shrill cry of pain as the hard bulb penetrated her bumhole and pierced straight to her root.

The girls were ordered back to bed and watched as the prefect went back to her boudoir and emerged with a long, rattan cane which she flexed menacingly.

'Two spinning tops!' she crowed, and suddenly deliverd a vicious stripe to the exposed bare bum of Tolliver, who was indeed sent spinning around helplessly like a top.

Her croup striped lividly and, as she whirled, the stripe of her welt from the cane flashed past, alternating with the livid gash of her exposed cunt. The backs of her thighs, trapped by the cling film, were naked for the cane.

As Tolliver spun, Tara Devine received her first stripe, and the blow was so hard that she too spun around. Then it was Tolliver's turn again. The Bolt caned her on the bare thigh-backs, making her shriek in pain.

Now Miss Boulter began the caning in earnest. She flogged each girl alternately, striping in turn the buttocks and the thighs with teasing strokes a hair's breadth from on the wet, hairy cunt-lips, causing the miscreant girls to shriek and shudder. And all the time, the force of the cane-strokes made their trussed bodies spin faster and faster on their greased, embedded poles.

Sandra looked across at Julie and Sharon and saw the soft movements of their bedclothes at their crotches, and their knees and thighs undulating like desert dunes. They were masturbating as they watched the chastisement. Then Sandra saw that every girl in the dorm was wanking off.

Sandra's own fingers slipped beneath her nightie, yanking it up so that her loins and bum were bare, and began a slow, luxurious masturbation, tweaking her clitty and getting three fingers inside her wet, pulsing slit, as she thrilled guiltily at the spectacle of the naked girls, bound, whipped, spun and poled. They had been caught wanking each other off, and now, with the grim logic of punishment, every girl in dorm was masturbating.

Soon after Tara Devine had taken her twentieth or twenty-first stripe, she groaned that it was too much. It should only be nine, Miss Boulter was acting improperly . . .

It was as though Tara craved extra punishment, for the enraged lesbian declared loudly that nobody could touch her, that she could do anything and get away with anything. Not even Miss Quirke would threaten her and if anyone was to be expelled – not that the dread word expulsion had been mentioned – it was the two diddlers now spinning with their bums and cunts black and blue.

Though it was Tara who complained, it seemed that Tolliver was getting the worst of it, since she had the shaft in her anus and, despite the KY jelly, the wood was knotted and unpolished, and very thick and wide. As she spun, the distended anus was painfully visible even in the dim light, as if the shaft would crack her bumhole.

But it was also clear that as the beating continued, both victims were dripping juice fom their exposed cunts, and Tolliver's flow was more copious than Tara's, as though the pain in her bumhole thrilled her the more. Both girls now moaned instead of screaming and they panted as though each stripe was the penetration of a male cock.

As Boulter's frilled skirt bounced up at each cane-stroke, her spangled thong panties were clearly shown, as well as the white sussies and straps. The crotch-piece and the bare skin beside were gleaming wet with cunt-oil and she seemed to be muttering to herself.

'Well, Stephanie? How do you like that? Want some chewing gum, Miss Long? I'll oblige . . .'

And as she muttered, her caning became almost superhumanly vicious, and the thrashed bodies of the

145

spinning girls the object of some revenge. At various stages of the flogging, muffled grunts and gasps were heard around the dorm, as the girls writhing under their bedclothes masturbated themselves to come. Sandra diddled also, but, too consumed with curiosity, pleasured herself to a warm glow while holding back from orgasm.

Miss Boulter ended the flogging at about fifty stripes. She was panting, and pouring with sweat, and her stockings and crotch were visibly sopping with come-juice.

'You can dangle for the rest of the night, you filthy masturbators,' she growled, her hand unconsciously rubbing her own bulging cunt-lips. 'Like your friend Larch. She's been whipped naked and well caged in the refectory, and tomorrow you can all pelt her with your breakfast.'

Her eyes fastened on Sandra who was pretending to be asleep. Brusquely, Miss Boulter beckoned her.

'You didn't think you'd escape your turn, slut?' she sneered, as Sandra docilely slipped off her nightie and padded nude into Boulter's cubicle.

There was no preamble. Sandra's face was forced down on Boulter's scented pillow and her buttocks raised high, and spread. She heard the rustle of Boulter's dress and the slither of the strap-on dildo. Peeking, she saw that the dildo was a twin-pronger, and that Boulter's end went smoothly not into her cunt, but into her anus. This dildo was flesh-coloured and looked just like a huge, male cock, even down to the simulated tattoo of a rosebud halfway down the massive nobbly shaft. Both prongs were identical.

Sandra stifled a gasp as the first cane-stroke bit her bare cheeks. She took a full twenty stripes without crying or making any other sound than a hoarse gasping. From time to time Boulter thrust her hand between Sandra's legs and felt her gash, already sopping from her own masturbation, and now flowing wetter at the searing agony of the cane.

Boulter gasped and the sound of her rustling, silk frilly gave away the fact that she was herself wanking off. Every few strokes she would pause to straddle Sandra's bare bum with her naked cunt and rub her clitty in the crack of Sandra's arse, wetting her with her slimy, copious love-juice.

'Turns you on, slut,' grunted Boulter. 'Turns you all on. If only I could really hurt you.'

'It hurts awfully, Miss,' whimpered Sandra, not sure if she spoke the truth or was only playing her ordained role.

'A girl is never quite sure when she really feels pleasure,' murmured the lesbian, 'or when she's just pretending. Maybe the pretence of pleasure is pleasure.'

As though to compensate for her sudden sincerity, she delivered a flurry of stripes in quickfire succession right on Sandra's crack and anus bud, and it was all she could do to stop from screaming as her tears flooded the pillow, and her come-juice coursed uncontrollably on to Boulter's rubber bedspread, in unfeigned humiliance.

'Bah!' exclaimed Boulter, 'all power is pretence – only the cane is real – and this . . .'

'This' was the fleshy, hard dildo of knobbled rubber that now thrust brutally into Sandra's bruised anus without benefit of lubrication. Sandra squealed and strove to relax her sphincter to admit the massive engine, but it took Miss Boulter three stabs before the shaft sank fully to Sandra's root to begin a vigorous, rhythmic bum-fucking.

'You're wet, you filthy little slut,' gasped Boulter as she buggered Sandra. 'You like it best in bum, don't you? You're one of us. Confess it.'

'Yes, Miss,' whimpered Sandra as the heavy dildo pounded her anal shaft and the cunt-juice flowed from her gash.

'Wank off, then, slut, as I bum you,' hissed Boulter.

Sandra obeyed, sighing with gratitude as her fingers found her throbbing clitty and began to tweak vigorously. It only took a few moments before she squirmed and yelped in a strong orgasm and Boulter cried in satisfaction that Sandra was a true Quirkean.

'You take your prelims tomorrow – I suppose you'd forgotten – but don't worry, I'll make sure you fail. You'll be hooped, of course, as punishment for failure, but you'll be in my dorm forever, and you'll like that, won't you, girly?'

Sandra heard herself sob, 'Yes, Miss.'

As she gasped in the warm afterglow of her orgasm, the buggery increased in fervour, as though Boulter had sensed truth in her words. It was Boulter's fingers that now probed Sandra's gash and diddled the still-erect clitty, sending shocks of pleasure pulsing up Sandra's spine. She sank on to the bed in total submission and thrust her bum up to receive the anal punishment of the dildo.

'I can make anything I want happen at Quirke's,' Boulter hissed, her fingers pummelling deep inside Sandra's cunt as she bum-fucked her squirming arse.

And once again, so soon, the flashes of pleasure quickened in Sandra's belly and she cried out as a second spasm flooded her.

'Yes,' said Boulter, rubbing her own clit on Sandra's arse-crack, her fingers stroking the ridges laid by her cane. 'I have real power, a hold over Quirke's . . .'

The lesbian's cunt-juice cascaded over Sandra's welted buttocks as the buggery relaxed to a trembling, twitching caress, and the dorm prefect wanked herself off on Sandra's behind. She sealed their union by peeing copiously down the crack of Sandra's arse, making her dangling pubic bush a golden jungle sodden with pee and slimy cunt-juice.

The dildo withdrew with a plopping sound and a tickling so delicious that Sandra clutched her clitoris again. Her luxuriant forest hung down well below her gash. Suddenly, Boulter knelt and plunged her nose between Sandra's quim-lips, then took the soaking, hairy tangle into her mouth and sucked it dry, swallowing the mingled piss and cunt-oil.

She did not look Sandra in the face, but smacked her bare buttocks once and told her to go away. Before Sandra had even parted the curtains of the cubicle, Miss Boulter was curled asleep on her rubber coverlet which glistened with fluids, sucking a thumb stuck firmly in her mouth.

Sandra found herself unable to sleep. After a restless half hour of tossing and turning, as the dorm snored, she crept from her bed and, clad only in her nightie, crept barefoot through the deserted passages and down to the refectory. There, suspended three feet above the dining-tables, was a cage about four foot square. This was the punishment device in which Audrey had been confined, large enough to hold a body but small enough to oblige the occupant to squat crouching. At breakfast time Audrey's naked body would be pelted with gobs of porridge or rotten eggs and tomatoes. But the cage was empty.

Sandra padded outside, shivering in the cold air. The half-moon showed her the way to the tunnel's entrance and gingerly she entered its darkness. She had no light, but negotiated her way by hand-holds, until suddenly she saw a light flickering at the end of the tunnel. She hurried to catch up. The holder of the light was Audrey, shivering and nude. She gaped at Sandra in surprise, which turned to pleasure.

'How –?'

'I guessed you'd head for The Gash,' said Sandra. 'You'd want to try the tweezers on yourself, and I ... Well, I remember Julie's sneer, that my heart wasn't really in punishing you and I'd rather be the submissive myself.'

'Would you?' said Audrey.

Sandra thought a moment.

'Yes,' she said. 'I was going to flagellate myself – like the monks – to see if I could bear to inflict my own pain.' She described briefly the events with Miss Boulter.

'If I could whip myself to agony,' she said, rather lamely, 'then I wouldn't need Boulter, you see.'

She tried not to look at Audrey's bare bum and cold-stiffened nipples, and the bulging forest of her pubis.

'Or me!' said Audrey. 'So I don't know if I want you to succeed. You're right. I was going to put myself in complete bondage, in the tweezers, with one arm free to loose myself. I've heard of time-locks, that you can bondage yourself completely and can't get out until the clock releases you. I'm quite good with locks and things. Getting out of the cage is child's play, in fact usually the pre doesn't even bother to lock it. You have to stay on your honour and that makes the suffering more exquisite.'

'I suppose we both want the same elusive pleasure,' said Sandra. 'We can only try.'

'Everybody at Quirke's tries,' said Audrey, as they emerged from the tunnel. 'That is what's so frustrating. We are here to submit to cane, but how does a mistress inflict pain when pain is precisely what gives the subject pleasure? Even the humiliation of service in a frilly maid's uniform is so delicious! For example, I knew that silly rack didn't work, but I didn't want to spoil your fun. So I acted up.'

'But you came, Audrey, unless that was acting too.'

'No,' said Audrey gravely, 'my come wasn't acting. I convinced myself that it hurt. Same as we convince ourselves that we are lesbian, when in truth, we are just enjoying the freedom of naked friendship that is latent in all women. Boulter and . . . and some others, are truly

150

lesbian. But we get to the same problem: How do you punish a lesbian who wants to be whipped and bummed by other girls?'

'Don't tell me your whipping didn't hurt!'

'Oh, yes,' said Audrey, rubbing her bare bottom. 'That hurt a lot. The Bolt's right: the whip at least is real.'

Sandra took her nightie off and rubbed her bare breasts, feeling the gooseflesh. She murmured that afer no sleep, she was bound to fail her prelims exam, and Audrey laughed.

Both nude, the girls came to the entrance of The Gash, and suddenly froze. The Gash itself was in darkness, but beyond, a sliver of light peeped from the crevice of the bumhole, from their dungeon. There was the unmistakable crack of a cane and the night was pierced by a scream of anguish. There was another stroke, followed by a louder scream, then another, and then a series of cracks which made the voice one long, unbroken wail. The voice was female. And then another female voice was heard.

'Not ready to confess?' it said.

Under the warm, silky tone was coldness. Audrey and Sandra looked at each other uneasily: this was not a game. The domina made sounds of impatience, as though doing her best to enjoy a tiresome job. There was the flick of a cigarette lighter, a breath and exhalation.

'N-no, please,' whispered the unseen victim.

There was a sudden crack of the cane and a squeal.

'I'm getting tired of your girly stupidity,' said the caner. 'You do want it, you know you do, and you know you're going to get it. So why not admit it and hurry up?'

'I – I don't know. Oh! I'm so confused . . .'

The cane whistled and cracked again on naked skin.

'Ouch! Oh, Miss! Oh . . .'

Thwack!

'Oh!'

Thwack! Thwack! Thwack!

'Oh! Ahhh . . .'

'No ashtray here. I suppose I'll have to use your filthy wet gash instead. That should make a nice sizzle.'

'No! Oh, this has gone too far! Let me go, please.'

There was a laugh.

'Why ever did you come, then, Miss? You want to go? Then just order the prefect to release you and fuck off home.'

Both Audrey and Sandra crept forward and pressed their eyes to the crevice. The narrow gap afforded only a partial vision of the dungeon. Both girls saw the subject of the torment and the lower quarters of two dominas.

The smoker wore high leather boots, with steel pointed toecaps and hold-up black latex stockings. Her arms were visible in clinging, rubber gauntlets. The female who had not spoken wore a shimmering, short frock of silvery, pink silk, flounced and frilly, revealing spangled panties, fine pink fishnet stockings and purple stiletto heels.

The caned female was naked and strapped in the 'tweezers'. Her buttocks were raised and stretched very high on a hard iron rest, with legs splayed wide, revealing the wide, swollen cunt – shaven clean – and the bud of her anus. The feet were shackled at the legs of the punishment device and her arms were stretched straight up over her head, the wrists fast in cuffs at the end of metal struts, as though she were a fly caught in an iron web of a spider.

An iron vice held her up so that her back was arched like a bow, with her teats squashed by its slabs, the nipples protruding stiff as apples. Her cunt-lips were pegged and stretched as Audrey's had been on the ineffectual rack. Above her titties and her spread arse-crack stood two candlesticks from which hot wax dripped on to the upthrust nipples and down her open perineum on to her cunt-lips.

The woman's buttocks and shoulders were wealed with numerous cane-stripes, extending well into her spread bum-crack and all down her bare haunches. Her caned anus bud glowed with welts. Now, however, the anus and cunt were stopped with the giant double dildo built on to the central strut of the machine, the rail on which this victim helplessly rested. She was not hooded and her hair hung matted and dishevelled over her striped shoulders.

'No . . .' begged the victim. 'I didn't mean that. Oh, I don't know what I mean.'

She squirmed uncomfortably on the massive dildos that stretched her cunt and bumhole to drumskins.

Thwack!

The cane, a heavy rattan, lashed her bare bum hard.

'Oh, for pity's sake!' she howled.

'For pity's sake, then, I propose to give you a formal set of exactly twenty stripes, Miss,' said her domina.

She patted the squashed bulbs of her victim's nipples, then pinched them hard and scratched off some of the congealed candle-wax. The naked female groaned. The domina pushed the wax in her mouth and made her swallow.

'After the twenty, you shall make up your mind. To take what you came for or free us of your miserable presence. Any more whining and you shall be gagged. If you take your set and make no more comment, then your requested treatment shall be continued without further discussion. Agreed?'

'Oh! You are cruel!'

'Your answer.'

'Yes, Miss,' sobbed the naked woman.

Sandra and Audrey looked at each other in shock. There was no doubt: the naked woman was Miss Isobel Quirke.

The decreed set of twenty stripes began, very hard, and assumed a savage crashing rhythm. Miss Quirke's bare buttocks shuddered helplessly at each stripe, but the cheeks were stretched so wide that clenching was almost impossible; and there was no escape from the cane, nor the drip of the hot wax on nipples and cunt.

The third female remained in shadow; Sandra found that by wedging her face right in the dirt and peering upwards through the crevice, she could identify the female administering the flogging. She saw bright blonde hair, a gash of flamboyant lipstick and a cigarette dangling insolently from the mouth as the rubber gauntlet rose and fell. It was Angela, the landlady of the Feathers.

Both girls withdrew and, in whispers, discussed this new situation. It was clear that Miss Quirke had come here of her own volition. Sandra said there must be a path down to the beach from the Feathers from which Angela had approached. But how to explain the mysterious third party, referred to as a prefect? If she was a prefect of Quirke's then she and Miss Quirke must have been here a long time, for no one had passed Audrey in the tunnel, where she had lingered for quite a while after releasing herself from the cage. So, either the headmistress and prefect knew of the tunnel and had passed through much earlier, or, all three ladies had come straight from the Feathers via the beach.

'Seventeen, eighteen . . .' Angela murmured, as the cane lashed Miss Quirke's dancing bare bum.

'Nineteen, and twenty!'

Miss Quirke gasped and sobbed. Her bare wealed buttocks did not stop their frantic writhing, but she said nothing, except to groan as Angela lifted her and freed her cunt and anus from the twin prongs. Without a word, Angela turned and strapped on to herself a larger dildo with a single prong. She rolled a lurid strawberry-coloured condom over its tip.

Then she changed places with the third female, who emerged into the dim candlelight and pushed aside her spangled thong to reveal that she too wore a dildo, a massive flesh-coloured device with a rose tattoo clearly visible on the erect shaft. Audrey and Sandra found that by crouching with their teats pressed painfully into the dirt, each of them could observe one end of the proceedings as well as the central figure of Miss Quirke.

The headmistress took Angela's strap-on between her lips and began to suck as Angela thrust her haunches and fucked her in the mouth. Drops of strawberry-coloured dribble trickled down Miss Quirke's chin and she moaned in deep shuddering gasps. Standing between her thighs, the frilly female plunged her dildo deep into her cunt and began to fuck. She reached down and scraped the mound of candle-wax from the clitoris, then fucked and wanked off Miss Quirke so vigorously that her bobbed hair flounced up and down.

'Miss Boulter!' Sandra blurted. 'But it can't be . . .'

The cunt-fucking continued for some minutes, during which time Miss Quirke was insistently masturbated on the clit and brought to climax. When this happened, and she had ceased shuddering in pleasure, the flesh-coloured cock was transferred to her gaping anus. 'Miss Boulter' pinched the anus lips aside quite roughly before thrusting the cock inside the bum-shaft, so that the balls slapped against Miss Quirke's arse as a vigorous buggery began.

There was no ceasing in the masturbation of Miss Quirke's nubbin, and after a few minutes, still sucking and biting on the strawberry-coloured dildo, she shook in another climax, her cunt-juice generously puddling the floor beneath her.

Now there was another swap. 'Miss Boulter' – Sandra could not believe it was really the prefect – returned to Miss Quirke's head, while Angela applied herself to the bum-fucking. Now Miss Quirke's eager lips embraced the bulb of the giant flesh-coloured cock naked and took it right to her throat, sucking eagerly.

'Miss Boulter' fucked her just as vigorously in the mouth as she had in the cunt and bumhole, while Angela's muscular buggery was just as fierce and her masturbation of the clitty just as intense. The fleshy cock pulled right out of Miss Quirke's clinging lips before plunging back inside, and the prefect tossed her head, fully revealing her face.

Sandra swallowed hard: it was Miss Boulter!

The prefect's breath became laboured and her fucking more insistent, as though she were going to come. Sandra surmised that a twin prong of the dildo was embedded in her cunt. Meanhile Miss Quirke's quivering, nude body glowed with need for new come and her loins writhed in response to Angela's continued masturbation of her clit. Angela too was masturbating, breathing heavily, with her skirt up and her own gash revealed, the glistening swollen quim-lips wreathed in a jungle of black pubic hairs.

'Say you want it!' hissed Angela.

'Oh! I want it! I need it!' cried Miss Quirke.

Angela grunted in satisfaction.

'Not like your friend Long, that fucking lesbo . . .'

Miss Boulter's dildo thrust further and further out from Miss Quirke's lips, revealing the whole bulb and glistening shaft before plunging back. All three females seemed to be nearing climax together, as if this was what Miss Quirke had wanted, or not wanted, or was confused about wanting.

'Now you'll get what you came for,' Angela hissed, masturbating quickly and on the brink of her own climax.

The giant, fleshy dildo slammed into Miss Quirke's throat, withdrew and poised at her lips, and suddenly Miss Boulter groaned and a jet of white slimy cream spurted from the dildo's peehole right into Miss Quirke's mouth.

The bulb of the dildo was not the same pale pink as before and had darkened to swollen purple. The shaft too seemed engorged. The massive organ thrust again, not deep this time, but at the tongue, and further fierce spurts of cream bubbled over Miss Quirke's lips, as she made little slurping noises and licked her lips to swallow every drop of juice. Suddenly, at Angela's continued masturbation of her swollen nubbin, she shook and shrieked in a third come.

All three orgiasts now cried in climax. The cock's spurting continued for seven or eight thrusts, after which Miss Quirke held the still-hard organ in her teeth and licked it clean of sperm with smacks of delight.

'Ooh . . .' she moaned. 'Thank you. Damn you!' And she looked up at the red, blinking eye of a video camera.

Angela removed the condom from her dildo and thrust it into Miss Quirke's mouth and she sucked contentedly. The two chums made their furtive exit.

Once more in the tunnel, Sandra explained to Audrey that she had been buggered with the very same fleshy dildo only an hour before, that it was not a 'squirter' and had certainly not spurted and she had left Miss Boulter sound asleep. Unless she had overtaken them, using another secret tunnel.

Noiselessly they returned to the refectory, where Audrey resumed her caged naked confinement and Sandra donned her nightie. Audrey said her own question had been answered. That was how a lesbian was punished: by making her submit to cunt-fucking, making her swallow spunk, and admit she craved it. Even by some strange androgyny, that was Miss Boulter's secret.

Sandra, in disbelief, rushed back to the dorm, where she ripped back the curtains of Miss Boulter's boudoir, an insolence which would certainly merit a public striping, except that she knew the bed would be unoccupied.

The Bolt's bed was not unoccupied. Miss Boulter lay there, curled up in her frilly blue skirts and still wearing her white stilettos. She was sucking her thumb exactly as when Sandra had left her. Her skirts were up, revealing her spangled thong and the fleshy quim between her thighs.

12

Wedged

By the time Sandra took her place for breakfast, Audrey's cage and her naked body were covered with gobs of porridge, and bits of egg and tomato. She was wet from tea and water thrown over her by the laughing girls. There were livid, fresh stripes on her bum, and her ankles, though not her wrists, were shackled to the cage roof, so that her gash was spread bare for any missile accurate enough to strike her there. The lips of her cunt were a mess of egg and rhubarb jam. At the high table, Miss Quirke and the mistresses solemnly took breakfast. Only Miss Quirke glanced occasionally at the caged girl.

After the meal, Sandra joined Audrey in the WC and squatted to pee as Audrey showered.

'I don't mind the cage,' said Audrey, 'because I get more for breakfast that way.'

She rubbed her bottom.

'The Bolt came down beforehand and gave me a sixer with her riding crop. Can you see the welts?'

Sandra said that she could. The bum was criss-crossed with six expert crimson stripes.

'And she wanked off, too, bouncing in her lovely little blue frilly like a ballerina on heat. Such energy! After whopping Miss Quirke last night, and . . . and all that.'

'All that is what I wanted to talk to you about, Audrey,' said Sandra, and related what she had seen on

159

returning to dorm: Boulter asleep in her blue frilly, whereas before she had been in pink.

'She could not possibly have got back to dorm before me and had time to change,' said Sandra firmly. 'And what we saw Miss Quirke swallow last night, well, I am sure it was real spunk and that was a real male cock she was sucking.'

'So the Bolt is a man in disguise! How intriguing!'

Sandra said primly that she had observed Miss Boulter's quim as she slept and she was truly female.

'Don't you see?' she said. 'We are a proper gang now, because we have a secret hideaway, and a mystery to solve.'

'The bumhole is anything but a secret, Sandra. As for the Bolt suddenly growing a cock: I'm not sure I don't rather like it. Oh! What an unQuirkean thing to say. You must promise me a bare spanking for it. But for now, why not join me in the shower. We've time for a quick wank before the exam.'

'Audrey, you are insatiable,' groaned Sandra, as she rose from the lavatory and joined Audrey in the cold shower, where the girl wiped her anus clean with eager fingers. 'We'll be striped if we are late for the exams.'

'But a good wank helps you sleep through it,' said Audrey. 'And you must spank me later, for mentioning cock, the C word.'

'What about Miss Quirke, though? She liked cock.'

'This is Quirke's school. Miss Quirke is above question.'

The fingers at Sandra's anus made her giggle, and when her bum was clean, Audrey began to rub her cunt, now beginning to seep oil, while the clit stiffened in excitement. Sandra let her palm brush the ridged welts of Audrey's bottom and said it was a work of art. So many stripes seemed the perfect maquillage for such a luscious, firm peach.

'Not a work of art,' Audrey said gravely as she fingered Sandra's cunt. 'More a work of nature . . .'

'We'll be late,' said Sandra faintly as Audrey smoothly wanked her. 'And I forgot my essay; the delights of being a lady and all that. I'm sure I'll get a striping.'

'Who cares?' said Audrey, sighing with pleasure as Sandra's fingers moved to caress her own stiff clit. 'I'm always late for prelims. And I always fail, as you will. The Bolt sees to that. Then we'll be hooped. It's awful.'

'How many times have you taken the exam, Audrey?' said Sandra, gasping with pleasure from her masturbated clitty.

'Oh, oodles of times.'

'Then how long have you been a Quirkean?' Sandra said. 'Oh, don't stop, that's lovely. Put your fingers in my gash, Audrey. I'm all wet. Yes, like that . . . Oh! Oh!'

Sandra began to come, erupting in delighted little yelps of orgasm, as her own fingers probed Audrey's wet gash and throbbing nubbin, and soon made her friend come too.

'Don't ask,' said Audrey. 'Time spent outside Quirke's is not real time, Sandra. And don't worry about your fresher's essay. The mistress simply reads out the winning essay – but it's a set one, always the same and very naughty – then picks a name at random, pretends to be angry and the unlucky winner is striped very hard, no matter what she actually did write. Everybody wanks off whether she squeals or takes her unfair stripes like a lady. It's tradition. So, to save you the trouble, I've already handed yours in.'

The exam classroom hummed with boredom and glum agitation. Three whole hours of scratching and scribbling, when there was nice, crisp autumn day outside! Gum was furtively passed and chewed. Girls stifled yawns under the gaze of the school prefects Long, Bustard, Cream and Gordon, who patrolled the aisles with canes in hands. The Bolt sat in her customary seat at the back, head lolling in undisguised slumber. No one tried – or dared – to wake her.

The girls all rose at the entrance of Miss Tate, a svelte and sensuous woman in her mid-twenties, in tight dark skirt and blouse, who walked with a bobbing pigeon's gait to the lectern. She carried a bag of papers and a long rattan cane was affixed to the belt of her pretty, pleated skirt. Her blue stockings shone immaculately, and her conical, pointed breasts thrust pertly against the tight fabric of her perfectly starched blouse. Her hair was straw-blonde and bobbed like Miss Boulter's, though a little longer. Her legs were long and coltish, slightly out of balance with her slender torso, as were her fesses, like two melons barely constrained by tight, navy-blue skirt-pleats.

Miss Tate laid her cane across her desk, then bade the class be seated and took a document from her case. The front row of desks were unoccupied and a single desk stood on its own between the mistress's desk and the class. At the back of the room stood four girls in frilly French maid costumes, each solemnly bearing a china chamberpot.

'Your examination paper is on the desk in front of you, ladies,' she said. 'You will open it when I give the signal, and stop writing when I say "stop". You have two hours to complete the examination, and the remaining half hour shall be devoted to reading out the prize-winning fresher's essay from those I have in front of me. There will, of course, be no permissions to leave the room for the WC. I know that girls frequently need to evacuate in the stress of an important event, so put your hand up and a chambermaid will attend you for your business. The exam results will be published after lunch, as well as the list of those girls sentenced to be hooped for slacking.'

Miss Tate permitted herself a thin smile, not bothering to explain how exam papers could be marked so quickly. Then very carefully and, with much fussing of skirt and petticoat, she settled into a small rocking-chair and swayed back and forth, surveying the girls.

'You may begin,' she said.

Gloomily, Sandra opened her paper and scanned the questions, then looked round at her friends. All the diddlers were there, and Tolliver and Tara Devine, and there were faces whose names Sandra had first known from the discipline book: Jennifer Reid; Susan Fanshawe; Zena Lambton; and Cerise Purley among others. All yawned, as Sandra did, and giggled, for the questions seemed too easy to be true. No writing was required, as all the questions were multiple choice – even those on spelling and grammar – and needed only one out of three boxes to be ticked. Suddenly, Miss Tate barked:

'Stop writing! One girl is picking her nose. Come forward, Miss Fanshawe, for punishment.'

Sheepishly, Susan Fanshawe edged forward and stood with her head bowed before Miss Tate's desk. She was a big girl, taller than Sandra, but with the same lush mane of hair which now dangled forlornly over her jutting teats and straggled on her back, as though itself an accomplice in disgrace. The mistress shifted in her chair but did not rise and her cane pointed to the solitary desk before her.

'Four stripes for foulness,' she snapped. 'Bare up below, Miss Fanshawe. Miss Cream, please oblige.'

The school prefect advanced, a skinny whippet of a girl with long, muscular legs rippling under her blue stockings and a skirt short enough to show a peep of sussies and stocking-tops. Susan bent over the solitary desk and lifted her own pleated skirt, then rolled down her panties to reveal a bare bum, shining white and scarcely blemished. Sandra recalled that her last listed punishment had not been stripes, but a lengthy

163

spanking. Miss Tate ordered her to splay her legs with panties stretched on her thighs.

'You see, girls,' said Miss Tate, tapping the desk with her rattan, 'a bad girl is the enemy of you all, for your examination time is wasted while you witness punishment, according to the rules.'

She squirmed a little in her rocking-chair, then smiled and nodded. Miss Cream raised her cane, bringing it down hard across the girl's bare buttocks, leaving a vivid, pink stripe. Susan moaned and gripped the corners of the desk, her legs swaying. Miss Tate ordered the stripe to be repeated for the unruliness of making a noise under cane.

Miss Cream lashed the bare buttocks again and now Susan's eyes were wet with tears, and she gasped, but made no sound otherwise. Her panties twanged at the violent trembling of her parted legs. Sandra's hand unconsciously brushed the crotch of her own panties under the desk. She pretended to scratch and saw that many other girls were itchy too. Her panties were beginning to moisten at the spectacle of the almost virgin flesh of a naked bottom taking cane. Even the mistress seemed agitated as her chair quickened its rocking.

'Now the second stripe,' intoned Miss Tate. 'Take your time, Miss Cream, until the beastly girl stops wriggling.'

In truth, Susan Fanshawe's bum was clenching repeatedly as the two weals darkened to red and it was only when she was perfectly still that Miss Cream got the nod to deliver the official second stripe. It took Susan at the top of her bare, just below her spine, and the girl jumped and shuddered quite violently, strangling a sob. Again, she had to become still before the next stripe was delivered.

The third took her on the left haunch and the squirming of the bare buttocks became frantic. Sandra's fingers rubbed her stiff clit and she panted as she masturbated.

The fourth and last stripe came rapidly, before Sandra – and, she suspected, most of the diddling girls – had time to bring herself off. Miss Tate smiled thinly at the class as if well aware that girls were masturbating. She ordered Susan to remove her knickers and place them in front of her on her desk, for shame, then sit with her skirts pinned up, so that her bare bum would press directly on the rough-hewn wood of her stool as an extra punishment.

Her rocking-chair slowed its pace slightly and the girls were ordered to recommence their exam papers. Sandra ticked a few boxes, more or less at random, and wondered how she was going to fill the hours that remained for this easy-peasy test which she knew she was bound to fail, and which didn't matter anyway.

'Stop writing!' Miss Tate barked again.

Now it was Zena Lambton's turn for a four-striper, 'for fidgeting', which seemed to be Quirke's code for unproven masturbation. Her face flushed, Zena slouched to the front of the class and, without further instruction, bared up below, almost carelessly continuing to chew gum. Her big, pear-shaped buttocks were well mottled with previous stripes and she took her four with scarcely a squirm, even though Miss Tate, rocking in some agitation, ordered a repeater for dumb insolence.

This time it was Miss Bustard who delivered the stripes. She was a sturdy and no-nonsense figure, rather similar to Miss Swain, only with her firm, military physique presented to proud advantage, unlike the oopsy mistress. She was unsparing of Zena's thigh-backs and the fourth stripe caught her well in the bum-crack, but though Zena made a face as the cane lashed her soft thigh-skin, she was careful to make no sound.

As she walked back to her desk, panties in hand – and well soiled by the sluttish look of her – she made no attempt to wipe away or even conceal the trickle of come-juice that seeped from the swollen, red lips of her cunt. Her panties were also placed before her on the desk and, without a care, she continued to 'fidget', grinning.

Sandra blushed. Her own cunt was very wet as she had masturbated continuously throughout Zena's striping and was on the brink of coming. Drops of sweat moistened her exam paper. She put her hand up and a frilly maid came to her side to extend the chamberpot. Sandra rose, then squatted and lowered her wet panties to pee, hoping her stiff clitty was not too obvious to the gawping girls. Her heavy jet sprinkled wide and splashed the fingers of the maid, who remained expressionless. However, the relief of her copious pissing merely delayed Sandra's desire to come.

The agitation of Miss Tate's rocking-chair always seemed to signal a discovered miscreant. It was not long before the command to stop writing came yet again, and this time it was Cerise Purley, who was sentenced to six stripes. Cerise was a real, unvarnished slut, with long, unkempt hair, teeth discoloured from smoking and hooded eyes which, with her thin, sneering lips, gave her a harlot's jaded expression. Her offence was too blatant to be called fidgeting and Miss Tate swallowed hard before pronouncing the dread syllables 'diddling in class'.

Cerise swaggered to the front and bared her magnificent bum almost contemptuously, removing her knickers entirely and placing them in mock-solemnity on the desk before Miss Tate, who blushed, then paled in anger. Her rocking-chair quivered. The knickers were sodden with cunt-juice and generously soiled.

'When ... when did you last change your undergarments, Miss Purley?' she blurted.

Cerise pretended to think.

'It must have been recently, Miss,' she said innocently. 'Before the last fresher's exam, I'm almost sure.'

At this insolence, Miss Tate ordered Cerise to strip off her blouse and bra. The white bra too was soiled and stained, and Miss Tate wrinkled her nose in disgust. Clad only in black laddered stockings and tattered sussies, whose colour disguised their unseemliness, Cerise Purley was ordered a further four stripes. She was to take a tenner and Miss Long was chosen for the job.

Grinning, Stephanie Long flexed her cane, and at Miss Tate's direction, gagged Cerise by stuffing her fouled panties into her mouth. Her wrists were then knotted together with her bra, whose end straps were tethered to the desk legs, as though she were a horse. Now Cerise's insolent eyes began to show a flicker of uncertainty and her holed stockings beat the floor nervously.

Stephanie lifted her own cane, a rattan three-and-a-half feet long and half an inch thick, therefore whippier and more painful at close quarters than any rattan Sandra had taken. Miss Tate nodded in approval, signified also by the vigorous motion of her chair, and she craned slightly to look at Cerise's soiled bare arse, with the unkempt dirty tangle of pubic hairs beneath her bum-crack.

Sandra's fingers crept inside her panties and into her wet gash. Her thumb found the pulsing bud of her clitty. She swallowed hard so as not to gasp aloud at the surge of pleasure when her thumb tweaked the throbbing nubbin. Her panties were soaked, and her stockings and skirt too, and the electric thrill from her gushing cunt threatened to blossom to a come at any moment.

There was a shocked gasp from the class as Miss Long delivered the first stripe lengthways, straight up

167

the crack of Cerise's big, mottled bum, and catching her squarely on the prune of her bumhole. It was not clear whether the cane had illegally caught her on the cunt-lips, but the agonised bouncing of Cerise's naked fesses suggested so.

The second stripe fell in exactly the same place, and for all her sluttish toughness, the frantic clenchings of Cerise's bare buttocks told their own story. Her breath came in short, clutching gasps and, when the third stripe took her on the soft left haunch, followed almost at once by the fourth on the right haunch, she sobbed loudly through her panty gag, her legs rigid behind her and her naked buttocks threshing in pain as her wrists slammed against the bra that bound her to the punishment desk.

Sandra masturbated with firm rapid flicks to her throbbing clitty, and now had two fingers embedded in her wet gash. She knew she would come before the end of Cerise's awful, enthralling stripes. Miss Tate rocked quite energetically on her chair and licked her lips at every twitch of Cerise's flogged bare.

'I heard a noise, Cerise, so the fourth will be repeated,' she said mildly. 'Woudn't it be ironic if your essay won the fresher's prize and then you'd have reward instead of punishment.'

Those in the know tittered, puzzling the fledges who did not know that the reward was a severe thrashing and the whole essay prize a 'traditional' Quirkean joke. Sandra assured herself that her chances of 'winning' were slight, or at least one in nineteen.

The stretched crack of Cerise's squirming, bare arse glowed crimson as the rattan cane striped her lengthways again for the repeater. Sandra saw the anus bud twitch in agony as the bare buttocks clenched.

Cerise's feet actually left the floor at the fifth stripe, which took her mid-arse, as did the sixth and seventh. Then she moaned in a long, broken sob, and the seventh was repeated, Miss Tate becoming sterner and more excited as each weal bloomed on the writhing girl's bare bottom and thighs.

Sandra's fingers flicked faster and faster on her clitoris. Her cunt was gushing with come-juice and her panties were sopping the chair beneath her, but she did not care as the eighth and ninth stripes to the soft underside of Cerise's taut, bare bum brought her to the brink of come.

Then the tenth repeated the vertical stroke of the first, and this time Sandra was sure Stephanie's cane tip had caught Cerise right in the open gash, and she shuddered as the ecstasy of her come coursed through her body.

'Very well. Enough,' gasped Miss Tate, wiping her flushed face, as though she had taken the stripes herself.

Weeping, Cerise tottered bare-bum back to her stool, clutching her panties clawed by teethmarks, and her tattered bra. Yet there was a river of come-juice on both of her thighs and her tangle of mink-hair was as soaking as her swollen gash. And when she had stopped sobbing, she sighed, and her hand pressed between her thighs, the arm moving up and down in the evident motions of vigorous masturbation.

'Back to your exam, girls,' rasped Miss Tate, after Cerise Purley, shyly stroking her welted bare arse, wanked herself off with unconcealed moans of joy.

There were no further beatings for twenty or so minutes, although the time was taken up by an almost uninterrupted succession of girls who needed to pee, so that the exam room was a symphony of tinkles and hisses and gasps of relief. Hands shot up and their owners were assuaged by the efficient delivery of chamberpots to unsheathed peeholes, waiting impatiently above variously stained panties.

When the girls had peed, the frilly maids wiped them clean on both quim and anus with pink tissue paper, although some girls insisted on performing the operation themselves. Audrey made her evacuation and refused the tissue paper, wiping herself clean with her own fingers, with which she casually brushed her nose and lips, smiling.

At last the inevitable happened: Tara Devine couldn't wait, and peed herself, staring aghast with her face crumpled in embarrassment as a big golden pool steamed below her piss-drenched panties, skirt and stockings.

It was with satisfaction rather than anger that Miss Tate ordered her to bare up below.

'Mayn't I wipe myself clean, Miss?' quavered the unfortunate Tara.

'No, you may not,' said Miss Tate pleasantly. 'You'll take your stripes wet-bum, Miss, for extra discomfort. Six stripes on the bare for foulness. Miss Gordon?'

And again, her rocking-chair began to waggle energetically as the muscular prefect lifted her cane and lashed the quivering jellies of Tara's naked buttocks. Stephanie Long watched avidly. The welts she had raised in Tara's 'parrot' were still livid, especially in the arse-crack and around the anus pucker.

Tara took her six with an admirable show of restraint, squealing only once when Miss Gordon quite blatantly caught her square on the bumhole but flicked up a little to brush the quim-lips which were sopping from pee and from a glistening, oily fluid.

Sandra found herself stroking her still-wet panties and the stirring clitty, and wondered whether to exhaust herself with another come. But after the repetition of Tara's stripe, the decreed welts were soon complete, and no sooner had she obediently placed her panties on her desk than Miss Tate called that exam was over and they must stop writing.

Dumbfounded, Sandra looked at Audrey, who shrugged. None of the girls had finished their papers, which were now perfunctorily collected by the prefects, who handed certain girls, including Sandra, a single document in return. Miss Tate explained that these were bank drafts to be signed for the purser by those girls who elected to progress for a further week's tuition. Sandra gasped. The fee for her second week was eight hundred guineas, a whopping increase. Without leaving her rocking chair, Miss Tate made a show of searching her bag and retrieving a sheaf of papers.

'I shall now read parts of the prize-winning essay. The winner shall guess her reward, as my reading progresses.'

The newer fledges looked expectant, but Sandra shuddered, mindful of Audrey's warning.

The Bolt was asleep and Audrey's eyes were shut as though she daydreamed. Her fingers were under her skirt, and as Miss Tate began to read, Audrey slowly began to masturbate.

' "The Delights of Being a Lady",' Miss Tate intoned. ' "One of the best things about being a lady, or a grown-up girl, is looking at yourself in the mirror and running your fingers over a silky bra and up and down seams of fishnet stockings, and pulling up your knickers so that they are as tight as possible in your crevice. Also fun is making sure your skirt is very tight across the bum so the panties scarcely show. It is yummy to wear a frilly bra to match your knickers and suspender belt and, if possible, a corset, too, very tight and laced up as much as it will go, with whalebone stays that leave marks on your skin. Perfume is lovely to dab on your ears and nips and between the lips of your fount, though it stings a bit in the gash." '

' "Another yummy thing about being a grown-up girl is when you have been naughty and have to take your knickers right down for a bare-bottom spanking. It is awfully thrill-making as a mistress watches you unclip your garters and roll your stockings down so she can get good whacks at your bare thighs, and then you roll the knicker-cloth over your bare bum, ever so slowly, and bend over to take position, touching toes with knickers twanging between your knees." '

Miss Tate paused.

'A promising beginning,' she said, and continued. ' "The air is all cool as it blows through the lips of your bare crevice and you can feel your pink getting a bit moist with excitement. Because it is so yummy and warm to be spanked bare bum! And it makes your nubbin all stiff and tingly, just like when you are snogging with a –" '

Miss Tate paused again and frowned.

'I think we can skip a few paragraphs,' she said tersely, then recommenced. ' "A bottom warmed up by a good bare spanking of fifty or sixty slaps is now ready for the greater delight of the cane. Only cissies tremble at a bare-bum caning and proper girls welcome proper correction, which helps them to be ladylike in all things. 'Six of the best' is a lot of rot. A sound girl can take dozens and dozens of stripes on the bare, no matter how painful and squirm-making, as long as they are delivered by an expert." '

Miss Tate said she was well pleased and the lucky author could expect a nice reward. Then her brow darkened as her eyes scanned ahead.

' "Six or seven or even eight dozen with a stout whippy rattan is not unheard of and can make the naughtiest bum blush all purple with horrid deep welts. But a true lady will take her punishment and if she is a real girl her crevice will be dripping with juice by the end of her striping and she will want to diddle herself to a lovely big come. A good mistress will let her, and won't mind if she pees herself as her bum squirms under the cane, even if she soaks her panties and stockings." '

Miss Tate frowned openly, and said she was going to read on, although the tone of the essay changed decidedly for the worst, in order to make the prize-

172

wi nner know just what of reward such disgrace could expect. Some of the fledges might wish to cover their ears.

No one did and even the Bolt was awake and bright-eyed. Audrey's masturbation was steady and rhythmic and she was joined surreptitiously by several of the older girls including Sharon and Julie who began to finger their clits beneath damp panties. Sandra herself could not help masturbating again, her nervous fingers caressing her nubbin now stiff in her moistening cunt as the mistress read primly:

' "Best of all is to have your bare bum whipped to the bone by an absolutely fearful, top-hole caning, and your fount dripping with come-juice, and then a gorgeous hairy man takes you from behind, and pokes his huge, throbbing willy right between the lips of your gash, which are sopping wet just for him. Then he pokes you as hard as can be, right to the root of your gash and tickles your throbbing clitty while he squeezes and pinches your bare stiff nips, and you can feel his hairy belly slapping against the welts on your bare buttocks as he pokes harder and harder, and then you hear him groan and squeal and feel a lovely, hot spurt of cream inside your gash, and that is when a well-disciplined girl gives way to the throbs of pleasure in her clitty and just comes and comes and comes." '

Miss Tate was squirming vigorously in her rocking chair and her face was bright red.

'Well!' she said. 'Obviously, the appropriate reward for this disgraceful and malicious obscenity is flogging. Are the prefects ready?'

The four prefects stood to attention and Miss Tate peered at the document.

'The winner,' said Miss Tate, her voice dripping with eager scorn, 'is Miss Sandra Shanks.'

Before Sandra could speak, the prefects flew on to her, as though forewarned. She was grabbed by the wrists and ankles and carried over heads to the punishment desk at the front of the classroom. There, she felt rough hands rip her clothing from her, leaving her nude, save for her stockings and sussies. Finally there was the indignity of feeling her bra twanged against her back before Stephanie Long contemptuously ripped it from her, hurting her teats and leaving them to wobble bare over the floor.

Her belly rested on the desk and she was helpless, with each wrist and ankle clasped. Then her wet panties were pulled over her head as a mask. There were eager gasps, then sly cheers. Sandra could peep out of one thigh-hole of the panties and saw Audrey serenely masturbating, staring straight at her bared bum.

It was not long before the first stroke landed, a vicious stinger that knocked the breath from Sandra and had her squirming at once. It had to be the rattan. Then a thinner cane took her right on the bum-bud, and she squealed. There was no formality in a flogging, and no repeaters. Every stroke was a repeater.

A third cane swept up and lashed her hanging, bare titties squarely across the nipples, and at the same time two strokes came in rapid succession on each of her tender haunches. Sandra howled, the wet panties now moist with her tears and only slightly muffling her cries. At each deep inhalation of breath, the knicker-cloth was sucked into her mouth, filling her with the taste of her own pee and come-juice.

'Naughty, naughty, girl!' Miss Tate gasped.

Now the drubbing assumed a harsh and relentless rhythm: a stroke to each bare fesse, from different canes, then strokes to the haunches, the top bum, the undersides and inside thighs where it hurt most, and the left and right titties in turn. There was scarcely any pause between strokes and no matter how much her naked body wriggled and shuddered, the hard hands held her helpless by her extremities, her legs wide apart so that the cane could touch her innermost crevices.

'Oh! Oh! Oh, no, please . . .' Sandra heard herself gasp.

The pain was frightful. There were no rules in flogging, and neither the clenching snake of her arse-crack nor her open, naked bumhole were spared wealing. The cane-tips flicked deftly right on the lips of her cunt in defiance of Quirke's rules. Sandra saw a figure slip through the door and dimly recognised Miss Quirke herself.

'Aaah!' she screamed, as she felt the entire width of the rattan thud between her cunt-lips and touch her throbbing clitty, and then fingers scooped her opened gash. She realised that her humiliance had her flowing with come-juices, and that Miss Quirke was licking her fingers.

Through one tear-blurred eye Sandra looked pleading at her chums. Many girls had their skirts up and knickers down and were masturbating quite openly. Even the frilly chambermaids had put down their brimming pots and were frigging each other's clits under their ruched, frilly skirtlets, their shaven founts gleaming with love-oil.

Sandra's belly rubbed against the rough desk as her naked body threshed under her caning like a fish. Her squirms inched her forward on the desk until her cunt was on the wooden surface and slightly protected from blows. But the cane continued to rain on her naked bum and titties, and her wriggling now put pressure on her clitoris which was as hard and distended as in her own masturbation.

Suddenly Sandra wailed as a great flood of pee emerged from her pussy, soaking the desk and the feet and stockings of the prefects. This indignity increased the frequency of their lashes and Sandra now squirmed like an eel, her cunt slippery in a bath of her own piss, and her clitty jolting pleasure up her spine as each stroke lashed her bare bum.

Her flogging was a treat for all the girls! Sandra groaned. She sensed that Miss Quirke too was masturbating at the helpless writhing of her flogged, bare buttocks and titties and cunt. And beneath her groan was pride in giving pleasure. After nearly one hundred strokes of the cane on the bare, Sandra screamed again, but this time in release, and frantically wriggled her loins against the schoolgirl desktop as she exploded in a glorious come. As she shuddered in her pleasure she saw that Audrey was coming too, wanking off in time with Sandra.

The bell rang for luncheon and the caning abruptly came to an end. Sandra was left draped and panting on her belly over the desk. Sobbing, she managed to free her head of her panties and looked round. Only Miss Tate was left in the classroom, still sitting in her rocking chair, her face red with pleasure or embarrassment.

'You have not yet signed your banker's order, Miss Shanks,' she said in a strangled voice. 'Eight hundred guineas . . .'

Sandra's hand flew to her lips and she signed at once.

'I am dreadfully sorry, Miss,' she said.

'Well, you were being flogged. I dare say it escaped your mind,' said Miss Tate tolerantly. 'But I must request your aid. I seem to have become stuck in my chair.'

Still nude, Sandra went to help Miss Tate, but the chair's arms seemed quite wide enough for the woman's lithe body. If she was wedged, there must be some other reason. Sandra clasped her under the arms and tried to pull her up, but she remained locked fast to the chair seat.

'Go and fetch Matron,' said Miss Tate helplessly. 'She knows what to do.'

'Better than that, Miss,' said Sandra mischievously, 'I'll take you there myself.'

She pulled on just her panties and draped the rest of her clothing, along with Miss Tate's briefcase, across the squirming woman's lap, then pushed the rocking chair out of the classroom and slid it along the corridor, like a wheelchair, with her bare breasts bouncing on Miss Tate's head. They passed the queue for luncheon on their way to Matron's surgery and the girls whistled admiringly at Sandra's striped body, her bare teats criss-crossed with welts and her purpled buttocks well revealed by her panties which she had pulled high on purpose. Miss Tate was crimson with embarrassment by the time Sandra knocked on Matron's door.

'Enter,' said Matron's steely voice, and Sandra pushed the door open with Miss Tate's feet.

'You'll have your money's worth, girl,' spat Miss Tate.

Sandra glanced at the open briefcase and the pile of 'essays' which were now scattered apart. Each one bore the name 'Sandra Shanks'.

13

Tube Girl

'And what seems to be the trouble?' drawled Matron, her lips curling in a knowing grin, 'as if I can't guess.'

Miss Tate blushed fiery red.

'I think we may dismiss the schoolgirl,' she stammered.

'And I think not,' said Matron. 'Miss Timmins has gone for luncheon and I'll need a witness, I mean, an assistant.'

She looked at a piece of paper and then coolly appraised Sandra, who was clad only in panties. Feeling foolish, Sandra tried to cover her naked breasts which made Matron laugh, a low, silky and somewhat sinister chuckle.

'This one is Shanks. She's on the hooping list, so I have to examine her anyway to certify her fit for punishment. Though it seems she has taken quite a lot already. That must be what has excited you so, Miss.'

Matron was a tall, slender figure with prominent breasts and bum, her legs and croup rather accentuated like Miss Tate's. An unlit Marlboro Light dangled from her flamboyantly rouged lips. Her surgery was gleaming and antiseptic, and she wore a hygienic nursing costume of expected severity: blue, of course, but not the usual sombre, navy blue, rather a baby-blue of garish brightness. It was a tight, one-piece shirt-dress which ended a few inches below her pubis, revealing the long, tan legs sheathed in white hold-up stockings, and a generous portion of bare, brown thigh between the mini-skirt's hem and the stocking tops. A packet of Marlboro Lights and a book of matches were wedged into her flowery stocking tops.

The neck was fastened by a white zipper, or rather unfastened, for the garment was open to below her large brown teats, holding them squashed together like a scalloped bra – she was braless – and just covering half of each big, dark nipple. Around her waist was a ceinture that widened into a little square of white apron, just enough to cover her pubis.

White flashes adorned her shoulders and she wore a cylindrical white bonnet with a blue stripe, like a squashed-down chef's toque. A surgical mask was hanging around her neck. Auburn hair was piled up inside the toque and there was no way to estimate its length, though the bulging of the toque suggested an abundance of tresses. For footwear, she wore white shoes with perilously high stilettos, and Sandra realised with surprise that the entire costume, including stockings and shoes, was made of clinging rubber that showed every crevice of her superb fount and bottom to stunning advantage.

'Stuck again Miss Tate?' said Matron brightly. 'The usual remedy should suffice.'

She motioned to Sandra that her assistance would be required to ease Miss Tate from her chair, as and when this mysterious remedy took effect. Sandra looked nervous.

'Nothing to be squeamish about, girl,' said Matron, making no mention of the livid marks of flogging on Sandra's teats and exposed bum-cheeks. 'A muscle relaxant is all we need. I don't like hypodermics. The best way is a little gentle hypnosis, aided by mother's ruin.'

She opened her cabinet and retrieved a tumbler and a

bottle, and filled the glass with a clear, oily liquid which she handed to Miss Tate. The mistress made a face and gulped down some of the liquid, which made her splutter.

'Easy does it,' said Matron. 'Just sip, while I put you into light hypnosis.'

She unzipped her tunic to her navel, baring a pair of stunning, large teats which sprang free of the constricting rubber to reveal their melon dimensions: a 44D cup at least, Sandra at once thought, or even 46. The breasts were tanned a uniform brown without bikini marks and Matron smiled at her.

'I sense we are sister nudists, Miss Shanks,' she said.

Sandra, emboldened, asked what the medicine was.

'Export strength Tanqueray's dry gin,' said Matron. 'In fact, as it is lunchtime, I think we may offer ourselves an aperitif, only I suggest adding tonic water.'

Sandra agreed and wondered if it was too much to ask for a cigarette as well. Matron, divining her thought, threw her the packet and matchbook after flicking a match with her long, red thumbnail to light her own. On the matchbook was a design of a girl nude, except for riding boots and crop, and the legend: THE FEATHERS.

Then Matron squatted in front of Miss Tate so that her rubber skirt rode up and Sandra saw her naked cunt between her thighs, shaven and with a small butterfly tattoo right in the bare swelling cunt-hill. Matron began to undulate her torso so that her massive breasts swung back and forth like pendulums. She pinched the huge, brown nipples to make them erect. Each nipple was pierced with a golden ring, and the movements of her swinging teats were indeed hypnotic.

'Just relax, Miss Tate,' said Matron, as the mistress, less nervous now, sipped her 'medicine', 'and think of something happy. Your problem will be solved in no time.'

180

Sandra mixed two stiff gin-and-tonics. Everything was there in the refrigerated medicine cabinet, down to ice and freshly cut lemon. She watched Matron's back sway, the ripe melons of her buttocks and the arse-crack, clearly moulded by the clinging rubber, which moved in the rhythm of her swinging, bare titties.

The glass was a third empty and Miss Tate clutched it with both hands, a smile now playing on her flushed face. The ringed nipples flashed in her wide, dilated eyes.

'Just tell us about something nice that you remember, Miss Tate,' said Matron. 'Something that would make you feel all relaxed.'

'Oh . . .' whispered Miss Tate, in a girlish treble. 'I remember when I was a new fledge and I got my first public striping from Miss Quirke – nine on the bare for smoking in the bog – and after my striping I went to the bog and wanked myself off while all the other girls stroked my bare bottom and ran their fingers up and down my welts and I felt awfully nice.'

Sandra lit a match and ignited her cigarette. The book matches were quaintly shaped like school canes.

'Anything else?'

'I remember when – when Miss J was head pre in the old days, and a gel was tarred and feathered after a striping of fifty, Gloria Harness I think it was. How she howled and wriggled under the cane! Her bum was all red and striped like strawberry ripple ice cream. I was sitting with Miss Boulter and we wanked each other, and went on wanking as the gel was tarred and feathered. Her howling turned to an most awful sobbing and our quims were quite wet just watching, and Miss Boulter's fingers brought me to a lovely come. I think every girl in school was wanking off as she was painted with hot tar then rolled in the feathers. It made me come and come! Then Gloria had to remain nude for a week until all the feathers had been flogged from her titties and bum, and only then was she allowed to scrub with turpentine, and the frilly maids had to lick her pussy and anus clean. Pooh! But I don't know why tar and feathers are so awful, nor why Miss J was expelled.'

'I think it was for extreme enthusiasm,' said Matron. 'Miss Quirke disapproves of extremes.'

She puffed on her cigarette and took a sip of her drink. Sandra swallowed smoke, exhaling luxuriously.

'Well, you are feeling very relaxed, now, Miss Tate, aren't you?' said Matron. 'There is no one here but you and me, is there?'

'No, Matron,' cried Miss Tate. 'Oh, you are a good egg. Will I get an enema afterwards?'

'If you are a very good girl and relax all your muscles for me,' said Matron.

Suddenly there was a hiss and a flood of golden pee spurted from the seat of the rocking chair and soaked Miss Tate's skirt and knickers, puddling on the linoleum floor.

'That's a good girl,' said Matron. 'But we had better get those wet things off you. Miss Shanks, if you would oblige.'

Gingerly, Sandra tried to extricate Miss Tate from her piss-soaked skirt and frillies. She managed to lift her up a few inches and pulled at the sodden panty-cloth, then her eyes widened in astonishment. The knickers were split-crotch, but that was not cause for wonder. Embedded in Miss Tate's cunt and anus were twin flesh-coloured dildos, exactly like Miss Boulter's, which were hinged into the seat of the rocking chair. Miss Tate had not been wedged in her chair, but her cunt and anus had somehow constricted to clamp on the dildos and trap her. Matron laughed.

'It is quite common,' she said. 'A case of rigor vaginalis and also rigor analis. Miss Tate is a greedy girl! The sphincter muscles lock in a spasm, caused by too much pleasure or fear of pleasure. You see it in farm animals and women. The cause is purely psychological.

Your flogging, Miss Shanks, must have excited her beyond endurance. Ready to relax now, Miss Tate?'

Miss Tate drained her glass of gin and nodded woozy agreement. Together, Matron and Sandra pulled her up, and the dildos emerged wet and oily from her holes with a loud plop. Matron's bare breasts brushed Sandra's face, and Sandra smelled a fragrant, slightly medicinal perfume. The ringed nipples were hard as bricks, and she felt a tingle of desire and moistness between her thighs. Matron swigged at her drink and puffed on the cigarette as Miss Tate rose unsteadily and attempted to adjust her dress.

'The dress can come off altogether, Miss,' said Matron, as though addressing a mere schoolgirl. 'And the panties too. I want you bare bum.'

She took from her cabinet a long quirt of six thick thongs, four feet long and made of stiff, black latex.

'There is the question of my fee,' she smiled. 'And my rather irritating jealousy. So you used to wank off with your lesbic chum Miss Boulter?'

Sandra was reminded of Audrey's hesitant remark about lesbians: Miss Boulter, and others.

'You have no monopoly on her affections, Matron,' stammered Miss Tate, 'and it was a long time ago.'

But she dropped her wet skirt and panties completely so that she stood bare bum, wearing only her sopping stockings and her blouse, which under Matron's stern gaze she knotted up below her pert, stiff-nippled teats.

'I can order medical treatments as required,' retorted Matron, 'and in this case, a hygienic application of the rubber quirt is necessary to ensure complete relaxation of the vaginal and anal areas, and to prevent a recurrence of this distressing condition. At the same time my assistant will administer a thorough cleansing of the anal cavity.'

'If you deem it medically necessary,' murmured Miss Tate, her naked gash already beginning to seep with the moisture that betrayed her excitement.

Matron lit two cigarettes and passed one to Sandra, asking her to freshen their gin and tonics. From the distance came the sound of baying schoolgirls as some unfortunate fledge was baited or punished in refectory. Matron smiled and said that if Sandra felt hungry, she could take some smoked salmon and salady bits from the fridge. Sandra nodded and then received her instruction as 'tube girl' for Miss Tate's enema.

The mistress was bent over an operating table with her arms and legs outstretched. Her buttocks were supported by a rubber pillow wedged at her cunt, and were higher than her head. The linoleum floor sloped towards a drainage hole in the corner. Sandra held a long, thin tube while Matron greased the mistress's bumhole with KY jelly, clawing the lips of the anus bud apart with her long, red fingernails and working the grease deep into the anal cavity. Sandra's pulse quickened at this casual humiliation and Matron noticed her blush.

'You next,' she said simply.

Sandra took a deep breath as her cunt seeped faster.

'But not with the quirt?' she said, trying to be jaunty.

'Only if you want,' said Matron. 'You are to be hooped later, you know.'

She pinched Sandra's bare, right nipple between two red talons and Sandra grimaced as the nipple hardened.

'I think you want,' said Matron.

Sandra pushed the nozzle into Miss Tate's anus until it struck the root and would go no further. The bumhole was distended quite wide, well over three times its normal girth, and presented no entry problem. Miss Tate's anus was evidently used to the frequent invasion of even larger devices. The tube was attached to a large, glass jar filled with green liquid. There was a plunger, and all Sandra had to do was depress it to squirt the cleansing fluid into the anus. She stood back as Matron positioned herself beside the bared, upturned buttocks and raised her quirt.

184

'Depress,' she ordered, and Sandra pushed the plunger.

The liquid gurgled and filled the tube, and Miss Tate groaned as the pressure drove it into her anal shaft. One plunge, and the glass jar had emptied by a fifth, and the tube's contents had emptied into Miss Tate.

'Hold,' said Matron to the groaning mistress.

She brought the heavy, rubber whip smartly across Miss Tate's bare bum and Miss Tate groaned louder. Six pink stripes appeared at once across the big, pale buttocks which clenched and trembled.

'Oooh . . .' gasped Miss Tate. 'It smarts terribly, Matron. You are a hard whipper. Oh! How long must I hold?'

'Set of ten,' said Matron, her cigarette waggling in the corner of her mouth as she spoke. 'Refills between.'

The second and third strokes of the quirt were delivered with rapid force, darkening the welts to red, and Miss Tate's bum began to squirm. The clenching of her arse-crack became continuous and her long legs trembled then shot out straight behind her as the whip lashed the naked skin.

'Oh! Oh! Oh!' she shrilled, like a canary.

Matron paused to tap ash from her cigarette on the cleft of her buttocks, then delivered a flurry of strokes till Miss Tate's arse was deeply bruised with crimson welts.

'Sting a bit?' said Matron laconically.

'Oh! Oh! Oh!' wailed Miss Tate, wriggling. 'Oh, yes . . .'

Matron ripped the tube from her anus and ordered her to release. A jet of green fluid spurted from her anus like a geyser and dribbled away down the sinkhole. Sandra reinserted the tube and pressed the plunger. Matron said the green came from extract of seaweed and algae which she gathered herself from the beach.

When Miss Tate's bumhole was refilled, she took her

second set from the rubber whip, much faster now that her bottom was 'warmed up'. Matron had not bothered to zip up her shirt dress, and at each furious lash of the rubber whip, her naked, brown breasts bounced energetically and the big nipple rings clashed like tiny cymbals. The rings were wide enough to admit and squeeze an erect male penis.

Miss Tate's wails subsided to a gasping sob as the thongs of the rubber quirt snaked into her bum-crack or even tickled her quim-lips. At each set, the green liquid was lowered by a fifth, and Miss Tate's belly swelled alarmingly. Finally, after fifty strokes with the quirt, her bare bottom was a mass of black and blue welts prettily streaked with purple at haunches and top bum.

Sandra watched as her gash seeped oil. It was easy for her to brush her quim-lips, outlined clearly under the sopping tightness of her panties, and she made little hopping motions as her thumb tweaked her stiffened nubbin, alternately gazing at the mistress's striped bum and distended belly, and Matron's bouncing, brown titties. The glass jar had a capacity of two-and-a-half litres.

Groaning, Miss Tate rose from the rubber cushion and handed it to Matron. It had an open nozzle just where it had been wedged in her gash. Carefully, Matron upended it and poured out a clear liquid through a funnel into a glass bottle, which she labelled, stoppered and placed in her cabinet on a shelf beside dozens of similar bottles. Miss Tate's was half-full of come-juice. Matron took ten of the bottles and refilled the enema jar, adding a phial of green liquid until the fluid clouded green.

'There!' she said brightly. 'Ready for you, Miss Shanks. Drat Miss Timmins! Miss Tate, if you would be so kind . . .'

Sandra nervously rubbed her bum.

'Still sore?' said Matron sympathetically.

Sandra nodded, and Matron clamped the crotch of her panties, feeling the slimy wetness. Her eyes gleamed.

'Too bad,' said Matron. 'Panties off, girl.'

As Sandra slipped out of her moist panties, Matron pinched her bare nipples very hard between her fingernails and smiled as the nipples tweaked to hardness. Then suddenly she placed the rubber quirt in Sandra's hand.

'You can do yourself, Miss Shanks. Just like the flagellant monks. Go on, kneel and whip yourself.'

Embarrassed, Sandra knelt and lifted the whip, then brought it down across her own shoulders. Matron pushed her head down and ordered her to lick clean her white rubber shoes. Sandra did, her lips and tongue eagerly tasting the acrid rubber as she scourged her own back wth increasing vigour, the pain flooding through her somehow sacred, as it was self-inflicted.

Matron stuck each shoe right to the back of Sandra's throat, making her gag, but neither her self-scourging nor her licking of the rubber ceased. Miss Tate's hand was now at her split-crotch panties and the mistress was firmly frigging her clit. Matron took Sandra by the hair and raised her head. She lifted her rubber skirt and pushed Sandra's head inside, enveloping her in rubber and pressing her face against Matron's bare, streaming cunt-lips.

Sandra took the stiff nubbin between her teeth and bit gently, making Matron sigh in a shudder of pleasure. The cunt-lips beneath the shaven fount hung very low, like stretched rubber pillows, and Sandra began to chew and lick them, swallowing the copious come-juice which flooded in response to her gamahuching. She continued to rain searing whipstrokes on her own bare back, and breathed the heady fragrance of the lesbian's cunt-perfume as it mingled with the pungent rubber.

Suddenly Matron raised her skirt and Sandra gulped fresh air. Her back smarted awfully, but she glowed with pride as Miss Tate held up twin mirrors for her inspection.

'The monks had a dungeon in the cliffs nearby,' said Matron, looking deeply at Sandra. 'They had all sorts of thrilling torture devices. But you wouldn't know, would you? Out of bounds, eh? You'd be severely hooped.'

'Gosh, Miss,' said Sandra, 'I try to be a good girl.'

'The hoop,' said Matron, 'is jolly good fun. As long as you don't roll away and into the sea.'

She gestured that Sandra should lie on her back on the operating table, thighs spread and knees pressed to her teats. Miss Tate placed a new rubber cushion under her bum with a very wide aperture that encased her whole crevice. Matron now took a stiff, double birch, like a sweeping-broom with the centre removed, so that the flogging tongues formed a vee at the end of a short handle.

She greased Sandra's bumhole, her painted claws delving deep into the anal shaft and making Sandra squirm in pain. Then Miss Tate inserted the nozzle into her arsebud and pushed hard. Sandra winced as the tube penetrated to her root. It seemed much larger than the largest cock and her quim dripped copiously with shameful come-juice.

Suddenly Matron vaulted on to the operating table and squatted over Sandra's face. She saw the lesbian's open cunt, the heavy flaps of her quim-lips and the little butterfly tattoo right above the nubbin. The clitoris seemed like the butterfly's body. The cunt-lips were studded with tiny rings and there were rings right along the perineum and in the anus bud.

Matron sank her cunt on top of Sandra's face so that Sandra's mouth was pressed to the swollen lips and her nose in the ringed bumhole. She gasped for air as Matron began to writhe on her with her full weight. Matron was masturbating herself, using Sandra's chin to diddle her throbbing clit, while Sandra tongued and chewed the cunt. Her nose burrowed at the taut button of Matron's anus, pushing inside so that Matron wriggled and cried out.

Sandra's anal cleansing began. She felt the warm liquid spule her anal cavity, the pain filling her until she thought she would burst. Her belly swelled in horrible distension and Matron ordered her to hold the fluid inside her for the first set of birch-strokes.

As Sandra lapped Matron's cunt and swallowed the juices, each tongue of the vee-shaped birch lashed Sandra on one buttock and thigh simultaneously. Sandra jerked in agony and was unable to cry out while Matron sat on her face, stifling her, so she bit the cunt-lips quite hard. Now Matron jerked in pain and delivered frantic angry lashes, without pause, to Sandra's bare buttocks and thigh-backs. By the tenth stroke, Sandra's mouth felt as swollen with come-juice as her bloated anus and belly.

'Release,' Matron panted, and with a muffled groan, Sandra felt her anus drain and the pressure in her belly subside as she squirted the anal contents over the masturbating Miss Tate's hand, crotch and thighs.

A whole half-litre! There was a pause and all three women panted until their breath subsided and the birching enema was resumed.

'The birch is a bitch,' said Matron cheerfully. 'Bearing up all right, Sandra?'

'Mm . . . mm . . .' murmured Sandra.

'Good! Your bum looks awfully pretty,' Matron continued. 'I think I'll take up that idea of Boulter's for a Miss Flagellant contest. Miss Nude Flagellant. You'd like that, wouldn't you, Sandra?'

'Mm! Mm! Mm!' Sandra squealed in protest, as further birch-strokes seared her scalded bum-flesh.

The Miss Nude Flagellant contest was her idea. Where had the Bolt got it? One of the four diddlers was a sneak.

'We are both nudists. I dare say you are familiar with the Goldensands club near Sedgedean. Nudism is perfect cover for lesbian encounters. The butterfly tattoo is the signal. I knew you were one of us, Sandra, in every sense. The butterfly means not just a lesbian, but a lesbian flagellant, the flutter of her wings like the shivering of the bare buttocks under chastisement. But you know . . .'

'Mm! Mm!' Sandra protested, but without conviction.

The next set with the vee-shaped birch commenced and Matron wriggled her wet vulva to place the clitty directly at Sandra's tongue. Matron yelped in pleasure as Sandra licked the throbbing nubbin, and her birch-strokes did not falter, taking Sandra again and again on the same burning welts of her naked, unprotected bum.

She groaned in agony as the green enema liquid filled her anal shaft once more, and now she felt a pressure on her own throbbing clitty and a finger poking inside her sopping, wet slit. Miss Tate began to masturbate Sandra with deft flicks to the clit, and added a second, third and a fourth finger inside her pulsing gash. She finger-fucked Sandra's cunt, her nails sharp at her womb's mouth.

'It is ironic that we lesbians still need our cunts filled, isn't it?' said Matron, squirming heavily on Sandra's face. 'If only nature had evolved a female cock.'

Sandra moaned in protest, or agreement, her head spinning with pain and submissive joy. Matron's cunt-juices poured into her throat and nose, and Miss Tate's insistent thumbing of her clitty made her flutter in the plateau of coming. The birching sets continued. As the fourth enema swelled Sandra's belly, she gurgled and cried out and electric pleasure pulsed in her spine. She howled, gasping at the power of her come, as the birch lashed her bare buttocks.

Matron continued to birch her, not talking now, but

squirming hard and faster until she too cried out very deep and loud in her come. The fifth enema and birch set were so thrillingly impersonal that Sandra felt herself coming again. Matron threw aside the birch and buried her own lips and nose in Sandra's pulsing, wet pussy. Sandra evacuated her fluid, kissed and licked Matron's gash, and both she and the lesbian climaxed again, while Miss Tate's own moans of masturbation to coming filled the room.

'I think you would enjoy Saturday entertainment at the Feathers,' said Matron, gasping slightly. 'We are all girls together and Angela Jones would see you well served, or well served up. I am sure you have made her acquaintance.'

'In brief, Matron,' Sandra replied. 'I remember she wears bright lipstick and smokes Marlboro Lights.'

Matron took three cigarettes from her pack and inserted them in her cunt. Then she lit a match, her belly fluttered, and she put the flame to each cigarette. They ignited promptly and she handed them round.

'Miss J is an adept at that trick,' said Matron. 'Her cunt can light a whole pack.'

'Miss J?'

'Angela Jones, of course. Sandra, now I know you are one of us, tell me the truth. You came here to become submissive for your man, didn't you?'

'Yes,' said Sandra.

'It was Margaret Betts who recruited you?'

'Why, yes.'

'She is one of our best recruiters,' said Matron, thoughtfully blowing smoke through her nose. 'And now you are here, is that still your reason for submitting to strict discipline? Look at your bare bum, girl.'

Sandra turned to look in the mirror and gasped in horror, delight and pride. Her bare buttocks were a rich, livid quilt of welts.

'I'm . . . I'm not sure,' she said.

Matron lifted her rubber bum-pillow and carefully decanted its contents into the glass specimen bottles. Sandra's come-juice filled three whole bottles.

'I think I'll press you into my service as a frilly maid. You would be at my submission, though you'll continue your normal routine, except you'll be dressed in submissive costume instead of school uniform. You'd like that, wouldn't you? There are certain benefits. A frilly maid may drink and smoke, and wear blue stockings, at my discretion.'

Blue stockings! Eagerly, Sandra nodded.

'Sign here, then,' said Matron, presenting a form headed AGREEMENT TO INDENTURED BONDAGE.

Sandra did so. Blue stockings . . .

'Now, you are my bound servant,' said Matron thoughtfully. 'At my beck and call, which overrides that of Miss Boulter or any school prefect. I have considerable authority here, so I may set Matron's bounds, which may include crossing the clifftop road . . .'

'To go to The Feathers?'

'And you are privileged to address me as Mistress, instead of Matron,' said the lesbian with a smile.

Suddenly the door opened and a tall girl entered. She wore a frilly maid's outfit: short ruched skirt and apron, heels even higher than Matron's, a blouse of white lace open to below the frilly scalloped bra and seamed fishnet stockings of the yummiest royal blue! Sandra recognised her as one of the chambermaids from the examination room.

Regally nude, Matron's breasts quivered in anger.

'Miss Timmins, you are late from your trough.'

'Miss Gordon perched and caned me six, Mistress,' bleated Miss Timmins, rubbing an evidently sore bottom.

'Well, now I am going to give you more. You will please strip and hand your uniform to Miss Shanks. She is to be my new slave, as I have no further use for your sloppiness.'

Crying and pleading for another chance, Miss Timmins stripped, her firm body like Sandra's, but with smaller titties and bum. Her pubis was shaven and there was a ring through her left cunt-flap, and one on the perineum below her anus cleft. Trembling, Sandra put on the frilly maid's uniform very slowly, while its nude former tenant bent over and touched her toes to await her bare-bottom punishment for unpunctuality.

Slowly, Sandra pulled up the royal blue stockings over her wealed thighs, and played with the straps as she fastened them, the elastic twanging on her welted, bare bum. Then came the panties, wet from pee or come-juice. Everything was a size too small, including the delicious waspie corset or cincher which she hooked very carefully until her belly strained under its vicious clamp, and her big teats jutted up like melons. The scalloped bra felt three sizes too small. However, she squeezed into everything and Matron nodded her approval. Timmins trembled, naked.

'How many, please, Mistress?' she whimpered.

'Oh, just a few dozen, with rattan,' said Matron airily, tipping tobacco ash in the crack of the girl's arse.

'Thank you, Mistress,' said Miss Timmins.

Sandra looked at herself in the mirror and preened, then turned to curtsy to her new mistress. As she did so, she noticed the red winking light of a video camera. Matron – her Mistress – saw her glance.

'All my proceedings are videoed, maid,' she said, 'for my medical records. Not, well, not like Miss Boulter's. But I'm forgetting, I have to certify you for hooping.'

Matron lifted Sandra's skirt and twanged her panties, revealing her fesses covered in purple welts.

'Certified fit for punishment,' drawled Matron.

Sandra grimaced at the touch of her Mistress's fingers on her raw bottom. Then Matron laughed, not unkindly.

193

'But your bum's taken enough for one day,' she said, 'so you can take your hooping tomorrow, along with Miss Larch. If you survive in one piece, I might let you attend me on a little outing.'

The door closed behind Sandra.

Thwack!

'Ouch! Ooh! Oh, Mistress!'

Thwack!

'Oh! Please no!'

Thwack! Thwack! Thwack!

'Ahhh . . .'

Sandra shuddered at the implacable sound of her new Mistress's cane on the bare bum of a miscreant bonded maid.

14

The Hoop

Sandra was allowed only a short respite. There was little free time for a bonded maid. Shortly after her dismissal by Matron, she was visited by a sullen Miss Timmins, who rubbed her bottom and said sulkily that Matron wished to see her at the double. Sandra rushed to surgery, where Matron greeted her as though she had not seen her for ages.

'Where have you been, maid?' she snapped. 'Skulking, I suppose. I should give you a sixer for laziness, but there are plenty of jobs for an idle bondsmaid.'

At Quirke's, time was diluted. Yesterday's stripes were unmentioned, as though a girl began every day, or every hour, with a fresh, bare bottom. Matron addressed her as a familiar, annoying pest, and when Sandra ventured to admire Matron's rubber uniform, and said she would love to have one like it, Matron greeted this daring impertinence by reaching under Sandra's skirt and tweaking her tight thong panties just at her clit, then twanging her sussie straps with a sardonic smile. Then Sandra was sent scurrying with messages and summonses from Matron to prefects, fledges and beaks – the mistresses – and a frilly maid always curtsied, even to a fledge.

At teatime, the frilly maids ate before the rest of school, standing up and not looking at each other. They were a sullen lot, Sandra decided, most of them on temporary punishment rather than full bondage, so that they looked jealously at Sandra's blue stockings. Their uniforms were less sumptuous than Sandra's and they were less careful of smuts and splashes as they trundled the food trolleys through the refectory. It was hot work and Sandra's sweat made her clothes stick to her, and her stockings and blouse moisten. Her corset, yummy to look at, was now unbearably tight. Two girls were caned that time, with their faces thrust into Sandra's soup tureen, both by Miss Gordon, and one peed herself at her seventh stripe. Sandra had to get down on her knees to wipe up the mess, enduring a bum-pelting with lumps of stale bread.

She also had to serve coffee at high table, where Miss Quirke said casually that she had an unexpected striping for a very serious offence and it was bound to end messily. Would Matron mind lending her a new maid? Matron agreed, and Miss Quirke looked at Sandra as if noticing her for the first time, and sniffed that this one would do.

After tea, Sandra arrived at Miss Quirke's study, recalling her 'civilian' visit of an age before. Now she was a drudge, skimpily and shamefully attired in the briefest and most uncomfortable costume, and she curtsied low as she was bade enter. Sandra carried sponges and cloths and an ornate chamberpot, shining clean. Miss Quirke did not look up, but waved her to a corner like a domestic animal.

Shortly afterwards, there was another knock, and Cerise Purley entered, looking scarcely less sluttish than during her tenner in the exam room. Now Miss Quirke looked up. The girl did not curtsy, but Miss Quirke glared stonily at her until she did. There was a dirty look from Cerise to Sandra, for witnessing her small submission. Miss Quirke coldly ordered Cerise to stand in front of her desk.

'Miss Long has sent you for a headmistress's striping,

Miss Purley,' she said. 'I have the details, of course, but perhaps you would care to explain yourself.'

She glanced briefly at Sandra, who stared at the floor. Cerise grinned nastily before arranging her face in an innocent expression.

'I'm sure Miss Long has got her knickers in a twist about nothing,' Cerise said.

Miss Quirke flushed and said that was not part of a lady's vocabulary.

'Well,' Cerise continued, 'me and some girls just . . . just found some videos in the WC. We were going to hand them in, Miss! I don't see why that got up Longy's nose.'

Miss Quirke winced.

'There is the subject matter of the videos found in your possession.'

Cerise's eyes widened.

'Well, I wouldn't know, Miss. I have no TV or video. I'm a good Quirke's girl.'

'I understand from Miss Long that the labels contained graphic description.'

'I couldn't understand any of it, Miss,' said Cerise, her eyes even wider. 'All those big words and stuff, like, medical words, you know?'

Miss Quirke winced again, but now her frown was sombre.

'I think you know very well what was in those videos,' she said coolly, 'and are less innocent than you pretend, Miss Purley. Normally this would merit a naked public striping, but due to the embarrassing nature of the offence, I shall administer your punishment in private. I am aware that you took ten stripes this morning, for fidgeting during exam. You shall now take fifteen stripes on the bare.'

Cerise gulped and paled slightly.

'Unless,' said Miss Quirke acidly, 'you have any objection. Nine of your stripes are fixed punishment,

Miss, the other six being suspended, in case you recover some of your memory during your niner. Agreed?'

'Y-yes, Miss,' said Cerise sullenly, with a glance of resentment at Sandra, as though she was responsible for her plight.

'Good!' said Miss Quirke briskly, and lifted a yellow cane with a traditional crook handle, which was very long and whippy.

It made a loud whistle as she slashed the air. Cerise shuddered and bit her lip.

'I'll take you over the chair,' Miss Quirke said, 'unless you'd rather touch toes.'

'The chair will be fine, thank you, Miss, if that is your pleasure,' said Cerise, with sudden timidity which Miss Quirke noticed.

'Funny how the prospect of beating is somehow worse than the beating itself, isn't it, Cerise?' she said brightly. 'A girl's bottom can absorb literally dozens of stripes, delivered with care, but a mere fifteen? Well, just thinking about it gives even me a little shiver. Bend over now, please, with legs apart. You know the drill, but I think I'll have your panties right off and you may remove your blouse and skirt as well, for your own comfort. It is quite humid today. Please place the garments on my desk.'

Cerise rolled down her skimpy knickers, whose narrow thong was well soiled and crusted; her admission that she did not change her underthings frequently had been the truth. Then she unbuttoned her blouse, looking at Sandra, who looked back at her. Cerise's big, floppy titties were scarcely contained by her soiled, little bra, which was a size too small. Miss Quirke made a pained face, but to Sandra's surprise, did not remark further on this unQuirkean sluttishness. Then, slowly, clad only in bra, stockings, shoes and sussies, Cerise bent over the back of the chair, and raised her bare bum high, with thighs spread, the wide, full buttocks still mottled with her morning's stripes.

Sandra felt a tingle as she scanned the girl's wealed bare and the tangled rug of the pubic bush that hung unkempt between her thighs, and covered the big, fleshy cunt-lips like a swathe of jungle. Some hairs even clung to the bum-crack and crept up as though to ensnare the big prune of the anus, like clematis or ivy. Cerise's knuckles whitened as she gripped the arms of the chair.

'Repeaters as usual, for undue squealing or squirming,' said Miss Quirke pleasantly. 'However, in a suspended sentence, repeaters can be for squealing or not squealing.'

Thwack!

The first stripe slashed Cerise's bare fesses without warning and made Sandra jump as well as the flogged girl, whose legs jerked rigid in the sudden pain. A nice pink stripe glowed across the centre of her naked bum. Cerise swallowed and gasped.

Miss Quirke beamed and glanced at Sandra. Then, as though to herself, she said:

'Let us see what this naughty maid knows about the murky world of secret videos.'

Sandra had the impression that Miss Quirke was addressing her.

Thwack!

The cane whipped again, landing aslant on the naked bum-flesh, and now Cerise began to clench her cheeks and the big, bare arse quivered like a jelly.

Thwack!

The third stroke made her squirm deliciously, and Sandra felt her own pussy moisten at the sight of the bare-bum caning.

Thwack!

'I wonder if you have nothing to tell us about what was in those videos, Cerise,' said Miss Quirke thoughtfully, as she delivered the fourth stripe to her top bum, and Cerise shuddered and gasped. 'What you saw in those wicked, obscene films.'

Cerise's welts were now darkening to crimson.

'I . . . I'm sure I don't know what you mean, Miss,' she gasped, her voice cracking in a sob, without asking how the headmistress knew they were obscene.

Thwack! Thwack!

Sandra felt a gush of come-juice in her pussy, as two stingers landed in quick brutal succession right at the underside of the girl's straining, bare buttocks. Now Cerise jumped, her legs stayed rigid and quivering and the crack of her arse was a maddened clench, disclosing then hiding the big prune of her bum pucker.

'Are you sure?' said Miss Quirke angrily.

Thwack! Thwack! Thwack!

'Ahh! Ohh!' Cerise cried out as her body convulsed, and one teat flopped loose from its cup. 'Oh! Oh! Oh, Miss!'

Miss Quirke paused to let the naked girl squirm and sob, before coolly informing her that the last three stripes would be repeated for blubbing.

'And that does not count the six remaining, which I don't think I shall suspend after all. Unless you confess what you saw and from whom you obtained the videos.'

With the tip of her cane, she prodded Cerise's exposed, bare teat back into its cup.

'You see, Miss Purley, a lady knows when to remain silent –'

Thwack!

'Ahhh!'

'And when –'

Thwack!

'Oh! Oh! Miss!'

'– she should have the sense to answer a civil question.'

Thwack! Thwack! Thwack! Thwack!

'Oh! Oh! Ahh . . .'

Cerise's bare bottom was a maddened squirming mass of livid welts.

200

'You have taken twelve, Miss, but I can order repeaters for this disgraceful whingeing. We could be here until bedtime. Three more repeaters, Cerise. Why not speak up?'

Thwack! Thwack! Thwack!

The last three strokes were upenders, vertical strokes right in the cleft of the buttocks, and lashing squarely on the writhing anus pucker. Sandra's cunt was dripping with come-oil and her panties and stocking tops were sopping. Cerise groaned in a long, drawn-out wail, her scorched, bare buttocks pulsing in agony.

'Mmm! Oh! We got them from Miss Boulter! They were harmless fun, she said.'

Thwack!

'Ahh! I mean, they showed ladies diddling, taking cane bare-arse, being bummed with dildos, and . . . sucking. Sucking a man's cock and swallowing spunk and being fucked in the bum and pussy by the man. Only he was dressed like a lady.'

'Where were these disgraceful scenes?'

'In some kind of cave, Miss.'

'And whom did you recognise in this cave? Not a Quirke's girl, for that would be out of bounds.'

'Miss Boulter herself, with a huge cock, I mean a dildo that spurted cream –'

Thwack! Thwack! Thwack!

Cerise's tear-stained face turned defiantly towards her whipper.

'And you, Miss! Fucked and buggered and sucking cock like the rest!'

Miss Quirke paled.

Thwack! Thwack! Thwack! Thwack! Thwack! Thwack!

'Ahhhh . . .' Cerise screamed as her bare bum took a whole sixer in as many seconds.

Her welted buttocks squirmed madly, and suddenly a stream of steaming, golden pee hissed fom her matted cunt-hairs as she pissed copiously on the shiny linoleum floor. Both her titties shook free of their bra-cups but Miss Quirke did not replace them.

'Your eyes must have deceived you, Cerise, mustn't they?' she hissed.

It was not a question. She pressed the cane's tip to Cerise's lips.

'Miss Boulter and me, and ... and a male person! You were dreaming or delusional.'

She touched Cerise's bum-flans with the cane and stroked her very gently, then put the tip of the cane inside the girl's anus, and tweaked till she wriggled.

'Yes, Miss, I suppose you are right.'

Thwack! Thwack! Thwack!

'Oh! Oh! Oh ... Miss, you are right! I never saw you, or Boulter, or anybody that even looked like you! I didn't see nothing! Never!'

Miss Quirke sighed in satisfaction and said that Cerise had taken her punishment satisfactorily. She looked, now, at Sandra, straight in the eyes.

'A Quirke's girl knows not to go where she shouldn't, and see things she shouldn't, and imagine things that could not possibly have happened,' she said. 'Maid, you will attend to your cleaning duties after Miss Purley has received three stripes of the cane for her appalling solecism of a triple negative. "Didn't see nothing, never", indeed! And for due humiliance, Miss, you shall take your stripes from the maid.'

She handed Sandra the cane and, with trembling fingers, Sandra lifted it over Cerise's bare fesses. She swallowed, knowing that Miss Quirke's eyes were on her stocking-tops sodden with come-juice.

'Hard,' said Miss Quirke.

Sandra obeyed, laying three hard stripes right in the centre of the quivering buttocks, and at each crack of the cane on bare, she felt an electric jolt in her throbbing clitty.

Cerise was allowed to wipe her tears, while Sandra, as maid, attended to the cleansing of her piss-soaked cunt, then set about mopping the floor clean, squeezing Cerise's pee from sponge to chamberpot. Cerise left with a baleful stare, and Miss Quirke dangled her black-stockinged legs and black shoes in front of Sandra's face as she knelt. When the mopping was over, the pressure of her foot in Sandra's cleft prevented her from rising. Miss Quirke observed that her shoes and stockings were spattered with pee and the maid must lick them clean.

Sandra obeyed, applying her tongue to the head-mistress's shoes and stockinged ankles, dimly aware of Miss Quirke's hand moving jerkily under her skirt at her cunt. Her free foot now had the toe wedged between Sandra's raised cheeks into her anus bud.

'There is no place for obscenity at Quirke's,' said the headmistress. 'It leads to fidgeting in class. Any lady who comes into contact with such filth will forget –'

Thwack!

'She ever –'

Thwack!

'Saw it!'

Thwack!

Sandra's panties were scalded with three hard stingers as Miss Quirke's toecap wriggled in her mouth, until Miss Quirke gasped very harshly six or seven times and then Sandra was released. She rose, wiping tears from her eyes.

'I do hope you didn't mind striping Cerise's bottom,' said Miss Quirke, panting slightly. 'I fear you may have made an enemy, but that will help you remember who your friends are, eh, maid?'

'Message understood, Miss,' Sandra said, curtsying with a bitter smile.

She left the study, bum smarting and cunt sopping with come-juice, and went straight to the bog, where, ignoring the throng of squatting girls, she raised her skirt, lowered her panties and inspected her bare, striped buttocks in the mirror. She looked defiantly round at the walls and ceiling.

'I hope you are getting me on video, Miss Boulter!' Sandra cried, as she wanked herself off to a noisy, juicy, glorious come.

There were several candidates for hooping and Miss Quirke decreed that these punishments should take place at the same time as the early heats of the boxing tournament. Miss Crisp had ordered a boxing ring to be erected in the middle of the sports field and the miscreant fledges whose exam results had disappointed were to be hooped round the ring as the combatant girls sparred. Hooping, of course, had nothing to do with exam failure, but was Miss Boulter's mysteriously powerful whim. The selection seemed quite at random: Susan Fanshawe got the hoop, but the insolent slut Cerise Purley escaped. Audrey and Sandra were of course on the list, and, ominously, their punishments were to be last of all.

Miss Crisp, who was referee, had offered Sandra a postponement of her own boxing match, in view of her impending chastisement, but Sandra firmly declined. She wanted to box, especially since she was drawn against the cocky Cerise, for whom she had conceived a dislike. Julie was to fight Zena Lambton, and the tournament was opened by a friendly bout between Miss Boulter – who was seeded straight to the semi-finals – and, surprisingly, the timid Miss Swain, even though she was a mistress. Miss Crisp had a strange gleam in her eye.

Matron attended Miss Swain's corner – ominously, perhaps – and was resplendent in her shiny, blue rubber surgical kit, whose tight latex showed off her unsheathed teats and ripe, knickerless bum to full advantage. She had her shirt dress unzipped, but rather more decorously than in surgery, so that only the tops of her squeezed, brown melons gleamed naked in the warm, autumn air.

While the hoops were made ready, Miss Boulter and Miss Swain entered the makeshift roped ring, both wearing dressing gowns. The Bolt pranced and punched the air, as though she had already won. Miss Swain stood shyly in her corner, as though bemused at the honour. Meanwhile, an ashen-faced Susan Fanshawe was strapped into her hoop.

Almost the whole school had turned out to watch. Sandra was the only boxer, and the only candidate for hooping, to wear a frilly maid's uniform, and she permitted herself to preen, allowing her little skirtlet to flutter up in the breeze and show off her lovely, blue stockings and sussies, and the half-moons of her bare bum, uncovered by her high, skimpy knickers. An abashed and sullen Miss Timmins was back in her normal black stockings and pleated skirt with white blouse, and seemed distinctly miffed at her liberation from Matron's bondage.

The hooping was supervised by the four school pres, under the direction of Stephanie Long. Susan Fanshawe was the first candidate and she shivered as she stripped off her uniform, neatly folding the clothes and placing them on a tarpaulin on the grass, to stand naked, and have her wrists and ankles fastened in tight, leather cuffs. Then she was lifted up by the pres and stretched nude inside the hoop.

The hoop was just what the name suggested: a circle of wood and metal like the frame of a bass drum, about six feet in diameter. The body of the miscreant girl was fitted inside so that her back and thighs were pressed to the frame and her toes plugged into her mouth. There was an aperture in the frame which allowed the bare buttocks to extrude, held in place by a steel loop, which both pushed the buttocks out and up and gripped the belly. The protruding, bare bum of Susan Fanshawe was the only imperfection on the smooth hoop's surface. The hoop was placed so that Susan Fanshawe's face and feet were next to the ground. Her bare bum quivered, in the light breeze, covered in gooseflesh.

Meanwhile, the two combatants dropped their dressing gowns to stand nude for battle: Miss Boulter with a flourish and Miss Swain timidly, and almost in shame, though the big, firm plums of her naked bottom rivalled Boulter's, her teats and belly were quite firm, and her arms and legs lithely muscled.

Both women squatted and were oiled by their seconds, who rubbed grease all over the nude bodies, especially at the founts. Both women had shaven pubic mounds, as did Sandra. Miss Crisp had advised that the rules of boxing permitted hair-pulling, and thus no head-cover was allowed, but a wise girl made sure her mound was bare, even though this exposed the lips of her gash. Miss Swain's mane of hair billowed over her naked breasts to her disadvantage.

Miss Boulter's second wadded a thick tube of chewing gum inside the lips of her gash and another in her anus. Miss Swain eyed this procedure somewhat nervously and was persuaded by Matron to submit to the same indignity. The chewing gum was to prevent stray fingers from scratching painfully at the inside of these orifices during a punch to cunt or bum, as though it was tacitly admitted that Quirke's rules of fair play might be ignored in the heat of boxing.

Stephanie Long raised her foot and delivered a mighty kick to Susan Fanshawe's hoop. This started the smooth drum rolling across the hard, flat grass. Abruptly, Stephanie's arm flashed and a stinging, loud blow from her cane cracked across the pinioned girl's exposed buttocks. Susan shrieked in pain and a livid welt appeared at once on her naked bum. The force of

206

the blow had the effect of increasing the hoop's speed, and propelled it to Miss Bustard, who added three fast stripes with her own rattan, driving the tumbling cylinder to roll still faster.

The pres were skilled, the strokes of their canes directing the hoop in a circle, so that Susan was flogged around the boxing ring, and whenever her hoop slowed, eager feet from the jostle of schoolgirls kicked it into motion again. This was rarely necessary. The stripes were so hard and accurate that the hoop built up speed, with Susan's reddened face peering in bewildered agony, as though from the window of a tumble-dryer.

The glee of the whippers and the watchers was the glee of little girls making a top spin, except that many of these grown-up girls had their hands blatantly beneath their skirts whose pleats moved up and down in the motions of masturbation.

Suddenly, the crowd's attention was distracted by a sharp flurry of whacks from the boxing ring and a scream from Miss Swain. Miss Crisp, as referee, wore a white gym skirt with fluffy socks, tennis shoes and bare legs, with a singlet like a man's string vest tight across her bosom, so that her big nipples showed faintly. Her face was red. She was supposed to start the bout with a whistle, yet Miss Boulter had pounced on her opponent even before the oopsy Miss Swain had got her guard up. In the Bolt's corner, Tara Devine had charge of a whirring video camera.

'What is Miss Swain doing in a boxing ring?' Sandra murmured to Audrey.

'Can't you guess?' said Audrey mysteriously.

Miss Swain was doubled up in pain; the Bolt had landed a hard set of blows to her bare nipples and followed that with two contemptuous punches to her cunt, which spun the mistress round, only to receive a ferocious kick, which landed Miss Boulter's toe squarely in her gummed anus-hole. The lesbian prefect held the mistress with her toes between the buttocks, as though playing a hooked fish, and when she kicked Miss Swain to the ground, the gum was on the end of her big toe.

Groggily, Miss Swain rose, remembering to raise her fists to guard her bruised teats. But the Bolt swooped low with a punishing flurry of punches to the belly, then a vicious kick right to the cunt, which made Miss Swain stagger. The Bolt held back, not letting her opponent fall, and as Miss Swain swung wildly at the Bolt's own breasts, she side-stepped and kicked Miss Swain's groin again, following up with a single right hook that lingered in the crevice for a second, until the Bolt removed her unclenched fist to show she had taken out Miss Swain's protective gash-gum. Miss Swain's face streamed with tears and she aimed a single ineffectual kick with her toes to Miss Boulter's shin.

This left her gash wide open, and the prefect slammed right into the open lips of Miss Swain's cunt, letting her fist rest inside, gouging, while she tugged at her hair, until Miss Crisp angrily blew her whistle and forced the mismatched fighters apart. Miss Swain writhed in agony, rubbing her fearfully bruised teats and pussy.

Now, above the cheering of the schoolgirls, Susan Fanshawe's own howls of pain could be heard, as she was hooped round and round the brutal enclosure. The air was electric. Sandra looked down and saw that Audrey was masturbating. Her own pussy was sopping wet and she knew that her precious royal blue stockings and sussie straps were stained and soaking with come-juice, but she kept her fingers from her clitty, to reserve her energy for her own contest and her hooping.

Audrey seemed to have no such inhibition and was eagerly masturbating with her skirt up and her well-stained panties visible. Her fingers were energetically frotting her glistening, stiff nubbin. Her free hand crept to caress Sandra's bum, first through the frilly skirt, then under it on the panties, then, as Audrey sensed Sandra's own excitement from her wet knickers, she moved her hand under the panties, and on to the bare skin of Sandra's unconsciously.clenching buttocks.

Audrey worked the tight bum-cheeks apart and got her thumb into Sandra's anus bud. Sandra parted her thighs and buttocks and let Audrey work her way into the anus. It was all she could do to restrain herself from wanking off with her lustful friend, and she was glad to grant Audrey's plea that Sandra wank her off. Sandra's fingers slid beneath Audrey's panties and grasped the swollen, wet lips of her gash, playfully tweaking and pinching them, until her thumb rested firmly on Audrey's distended, stiff clitty, and she began to wank off her chum with hard, frotting strokes.

Miss Quirke's eyes met hers, and Sandra returned her gaze, wide-eyed and unblushing in the knowledge that their bodies were hidden amid the other girls. She held Miss Quirke's stare and licked her lips, as though fellating a cock – a strawberry-flavoured one, she thought mischievously – until it was Miss Quirke who blushed and looked away with a smile of quiet enjoyment.

'Oh . . . Ooooh,' squealed Audrey softly. 'What a lovely frig. You wank beautifully, Sandra, and this will make up for the horrid hoop. I know Longy is going be very brutal today. The Bolt told me when she was fucking my bumhole last night.'

Sandra murmured in surprise.

'You kept me awake,' she said. 'I thought the bed was going to give way.'

'I got a really hard pounding,' said Audrey. 'But I came and came with that dildo in my bum, and I peed her bed twice. I don't think the Bolt came at all.'

'Oh, Audrey,' said Sandra, continuing to masturbate the girl's sopping, wet cunt. 'How do you put up with so much? It is always you that gets picked on.'

'Don't stop wanking me off,' Audrey gasped. 'Oh,

yes, frig my clitty. She is always so stiff for you, Sandra, wank me harder, please. It is a question of money, you see. I'm not rich. You could say I'm a poor scholarship girl . . .'

Miss Swain was flopped, trembling and bruised, in her corner, and had to be pushed to her feet as the whistle sounded the beginning of the second round. Miss Boulter did not wait for her opponent to approach, but leaped forward, and began to hammer the mistress's nipples, sending her staggering back to crash into Matron's teats, earning the Bolt a glare of distaste. But Miss Boulter pressed her advantage: she had Miss Swain on the ropes and was battering her hard in cunt and teats, until Miss Crisp vainly tried to separate them. When the Bolt would not yield, she blew her whistle and declared she was stopping the bout. Miss Swain opened her tear-stained eyes.

'No!' she gasped. 'Please! I've had no real punishment!'

Miss Crisp drew back, as though shocked. Miss Boulter paused for breath, her massive, bare breasts pumping for air and the nipples as stiff as new plums. Streams of gash-oil flowed from the swollen lips of her cunt as she raised her hands again, one fisted, and the other with open fingers.

She raked Miss Swain's skin savagely with her nails, right from teats to belly, and dug into her cunt. Miss Swain screamed, as Miss Boulter clawed her gash and, with the balled fist, punched her on the bare, bruised nipples, which nevertheless stood as stiff as Boulter's own. There was a shiny rivulet of juice gushing from the bruised, swollen lips of her exposed quim.

She staggered to her feet, cannoned backwards against the ropes, and bounced forwards, as though eager for further punishment. The naked lesbian grabbed her thick mane of hair and pulled it right to the roots, making Miss Swain squeal in despair, then let the trapped woman have it in the belly and titties, scratching and gouging at her cunt and inner thighs, until Miss Swain swayed and could hardly stand.

Suddenly, Boulter dropped to her knees, leering at the crowd of cheering, grown-up girls, now reduced to a mass of primitives at the spectacle, their enjoyment revealed by the shuffling motions of girls' blouses, as their owners delved with eager fingers into their knickers to wank off at the sight of Miss Swain's welted, naked body.

Susan Fanshawe's hooping had come to an end. She was released, sobbing, from her confinement, and her place taken by Tolliver, who trembled as she stripped naked, while Susan put on her uniform, crying in her shame.

Sandra glanced at Susan's bare bum before the bruised orbs slipped under the white, cotton panties. Each fesse was stained from the grass and criss-crossed with black and blue welts. The pres yoked the next fledge, and sent her spinning around the boxing ring, accompanying their cane-strokes with whoops of merriment, as though trying to distract attention from Miss Swain's ordeal. But as the Bolt battered her naked opponent into a bruised pulp, all eyes were on the boxing arena, including those of Miss Quirke, accompanied by Misses Tate and Pottinger, gazing benignly as though inspecting a game of lacrosse. Helplessly, Miss Crisp tried to halt the 'friendly' contest and at each attempt, Miss Swain begged for her punishment to continue.

Occasionally, when Miss Boulter's ardour seemed to slacken, Miss Swain would actually land a feeble punch on the lesbian's quivering, bare titties, which had the effect, desired or not, of inflaming the Bolt, so that her drubbing continued. Julie and Zena Lambton were impatient for their bout to begin, but they had to wait until Sandra had fought Cerise Purley.

Suddenly, Miss Swain doubled up and sank to her knees, after a particularly vicious, clawing crotch-kick. As she squatted, the Bolt knelt, grabbed Miss Swain roughly by the waist and forced her down across her bare thigh. At once she began a ferocious spanking of the mistress's bare buttocks. She wedged her fingers in Miss Swain's cunt, with her thumb on her pubic bone, and held her in a tight clamp, while she relentlessly spanked the bare, squirming fesses.

Miss Swain groaned and wriggled, seemingly more humiliated by her bare-bum spanking than by all the punishment of the boxing ring and, as her bruised buttocks flailed in the lesbian's grip, she sobbed, and a stream of golden piss steamed from her swollen cunt-lips. Bum wriggling, Miss Swain peed all over the Bolt's thighs.

'Oh! Oh! Oooh . . . ah, what a lovely come!'

Beside Sandra, Audrey groaned, as Sandra's fingers wanked her off to a wet, clit-shuddering orgasm. And then it was Audrey's turn for the hoop.

As Miss Swain's bare-bum spanking continued, Audrey smiled at Sandra and allowed herself to be shackled inside the hoop, her toes stuck firmly in her mouth and her well-scarred buttocks protruding for her flogging. Miss Long dealt the first lash. The norm for a hooping seemed about thirty or forty, but Audrey took well over one hundred lashes on the bare bum, and Sandra could see that at each spin, a glistening stream of cunt-juice flowed on her belly and breasts and into Audrey's mouth.

Over the thwack of cane-strokes, Miss Swain's voice was raised in an anguished wail, as the Bolt's palm cracked on her wriggling, bare buttocks for well over the one hundredth spank. Miss Swain was crying, not in pain, but as she shuddered in a deep-throated come. The Bolt ceased the spanking and helped the piss-soaked mistress to her feet, and then raised Miss Swain's hand to declare her the winner.

'Thank you, Miss Boulter,' the mistress sobbed, her face as red as her spanked bottom, 'for such a lovely introduction to boxing.'

It was now time for Sandra to meet Cerise Purley. Both girls took their corners, Sandra beside Matron, who took charge of her frilly maid's uniform, and folded it lovingly, piece by piece, as Sandra stripped naked, very slowly, taunting Cerise with her nudity and the perfection of her striped, bare peach. Matron complimented her on the gleaming, freshly shaved swelling of her pubic mound. She felt Matron's supple fingers oiling her, with especially loving attention to her anus and pussy, and exciting her with a firm frottage, before wadding her holes with gum.

Despite her contempt for Cerise, the hard, sensuous body excited Sandra. To drub or be drubbed? Her clitty tingled as she thought of Miss Swain's submission and orgasm. Either way, she would come in combat with the naked slut Cerise, whose shaven gash already gleamed with the juice of masturbation.

'You won't notice your hooping, slut,' hissed Cerise Purley, 'because I'm going to kick your fucking cunt unconscious.'

15

Drubbing

Sandra looked at her opponent, particularly her eyes, which smouldered for revenge. Cerise had had her punishment by Miss Quirke witnessed and, to complete her abasement, had taken three final stripes from Sandra herself. Cerise glowered as the audience of schoolgirls giggled, mocking her.

Sandra had nothing against the girl apart from a vague distaste, mixed with curious envy that she could be so sensuous, and carelessly sluttish: clothed, she seemed nude, yet her nudity suggested the most blatant whore's attire.

She looked closely at Cerise's features. They were sinewy, sensual, almost oriental. She thought of Ray out east, doing it with one of his little brown fucking machines, except that Cerise was European in size. Still, the image lodged uncomfortably in her mind. She decided that she had her own vengeance to take, and that the best way of defence was attack, à la Boulter.

Cerise obviously figured that the best way of attack was attack. No sooner had Miss Crisp blown the starting whistle than the naked slut leaped for Sandra, and Sandra reeled as an agonising kick landed right between her thighs, followed by a flurry of jabs to the points of her titties. She squealed in dismay and lashed out with her foot, catching Cerise on the thigh, then managed to land a return kick to her pussy. They

214

wrapped arms, slamming with thighs and teats. Miss Crisp parted them, and both girls backed off, panting and sullenly furious.

Now Sandra leaped in assault, dodging Cerise's powerful legs, and concentrating on punches to the teats and belly, which winded Cerise, and took the force out of her kicks. Cerise staggered and hooked a foot behind Sandra's left calf, accompanying it with an uppercut to the quim, that caught Sandra agonisingly on her exposed clitty. She stumbled and went down.

She lay on the grass, struggling to rise, and suddenly Cerise was straddling her, facing her feet, and her big, taut bum was inches from Sandra's lips as Cerise began to punch rapidly and with painful accuracy, alternating between belly and cunt-lips. Sandra tightened her belly muscles to ward off the force of the punches, but could do nothing to protect her cunt, except jam her thighs tightly together. Still, her mound was unprotected and was fiercely pummelled.

Miss Crisp blew her whistle and had to push Cerise off Sandra, excessive enthusiasm apparently deemed unladylike. The mistress blew her whistle again to end the first round.

'Go for the titties,' Matron urged as she sponged Sandra down. 'She's top-heavy and will go over easily.'

Sandra breathed in Matron's rubbery scent and smiled.

The second round was announced and Sandra advanced. At that moment, the purser came up and whispered to Matron, who nodded gravely. The brief distraction meant that Sandra's guard was down, and Cerise was able to launch herself, hitting with full force so that Sandra went down under her weight. Cerise's bare buttocks sat on her throat. Sandra twisted and sank her teeth into Cerise's cunt-lips, biting hard until Cerise howled, after flailing with couple of punches to Sandra's groin. Cerise toppled off, rolling on the grass in fetal crouch with whimpers of agony as she shielded her bruised quim.

'Put the boot in!' chanted the seething schoolgirls, hopefully.

Sandra began to kick savagely at Cerise's exposed arse, getting her toes hard into the bum-crack, where she felt the sticky, protective gum. Cerise howled, but as she tried to rise, Sandra wedged her foot in her anus and propelled her forwards, so that her face was pressed to the grass with her bare bum wriggling on the end of Sandra's foot. Sandra heard Julie cry: 'Do her, Sandra!'

Filled with wild elation, she crouched over the pinioned slut, and, from close quarters, rained jabs on her shoulders as Cerise protected her teats with her arms. Then, with her toes still poking in Cerise's gummy anus shaft, she pulled her head up savagely by the hair, exposing the big, bruised teats.

She kicked the titties, then grabbed Cerise's right nipple and began to pinch it with sharp, clawing rakes that had the girl screaming. Tears streamed down Cerise's cheeks, but her squirming gash shone wet with come-oil.

Sandra succeeded in extracting her bum-gum, and stuffed it into Cerise's mouth, covering her lips with her foot until she swallowed it. Then her toes entered Cerise's cunt. She kicked hard, seven or eight times, until Cerise groaned and her body sagged. Sandra had her whole foot wedged inside the wet gash, and she poked out the cunt-gum, this time depositing it in a dirty smear across Cerise's titties. Her foot stabbed again in the cunt, while she pulled fiercely on Cerise's hair, which seemed to hurt the slut more than anything else.

Contemptuously, she sat down cross-legged. She pushed Cerise's face in the turf with her bruised buttocks upthrust on Sandra's thighs, and then began a ferocious bare-bottom spanking, with the toes of her left foot firmly inserted in the girl's slippery cunt. At each smack, she thrust inside, viciously foot-fucking the girl, and Cerise's cunt gushed come-juice all over her toes as she spanked.

Cerise's moans of pain turned to sobs, then gasps, then sighs, and Sandra felt her clitty stiffen as she hurt the wriggler, pulling her back and forth by her hair as the bare bum went crimson under her palm. Then Cerise wailed and groaned again, louder, and began to yelp. Sandra's foot was awash in cunt-oil; her bare-bottom spanks had brought Cerise to come.

Suddenly, Sandra stopped. Her own pussy was swimming in juice and, as Cerise quivered in her come, the girl reached out to stroke Sandra's haunch, touching her intimately, as the orgasm coursed through her newly submissive body. Sandra flashed the thought that she was the pinioned, drubbed girl, brought to orgasm by pain and submission. In that moment, she wanted to be Cerise.

As if to punish the girl for this impudence, she transferred her toes to the now unprotected bumhole, and sank her big toe inside, painfully churning the elastic anus until she could follow it with another and the anal cavity was stretched like a drumskin. As she recommenced her spanking, she buggered Cerise with her sharp toenails until her moans of coming became sobs of distress.

Smack! Smack! Smack!

The spanks from Sandra's palm rang out above the crowd's cheers.

'Submit,' Sandra hissed. 'Submit, you filthy slag.'

'Fuck you!' Cerise gasped, her bare bottom wriggling in anguish.

Smack! Smack! Smack! Smack! Smack! Smack!

The girl's naked fesses were turning from crimson to purple and, as Sandra's body poured with sweat, her own gash dripped come-juice. She took the spanking to well over one hundred; behind her, schoolgirls gazed, enchanted, many of them openly wanking off at the spectacle of Cerise's naked, bruised humiliance. Matron's hand was under her rubber skirt and moving softly in masturbation; Julie and Sharon each had her hand in the other's panties.

Suddenly, Sandra removed her toes from Cerise's anus, making a squelchy noise, and wrenched Cerise by the hair, turning her over so that her buttocks wriggled on Sandra's knee. The spanking continued, but now Sandra's palm descended on the open, swollen lips of Cerise's bare cunt. The clitty stood hard and inviting as Sandra spanked the naked gash.

Smack! Smack!

'Oh! Oh!'

'Submit!'

'Fuck you, cow!'

Smack! Smack! Smack! Smack!

'Ah! Shit! Oh! Oh! Ah! You bitch!'

'Give in, Cerise.'

'Piss up you!' the girl whimpered.

Smack! Smack! Smack! Smack!

'Oh! Oh! Ahhh!'

Cerise's eyes rolled. Far away, Miss Crisp's whistle blew, but Sandra paid no heed and the crowd drowned the referee's whistle with boos.

Smack! Smack!

'Oh! Oh, don't . . .'

Sandra's open palm rained spanks on Cerise's unprotected gash, until suddenly Sandra doubled up, pressed her face to the hot, wet cunt, and began to chew on the stiff, slippery clit. Cerise's body went rigid, then quivered like the wings of a butterfly. Sandra bit harder and then Cerise screamed:

'I submit! Stop, stop, no, don't stop . . . Oh, you bitch, I submit . . . Ahhh . . .'

But Sandra did stop. Panting, she rose and

acknowledged the cheers. She looked down at her vanquished opponent and saw a writhing, bare body, covered in sweat and come-juice and bruises: a girl shamed and truly naked. Yet Cerise's hand was at her crotch and she was vigorously masturbating.

Panting hard, Sandra turned away, her own thighs slippery with come-juice. Too late, she saw the alarm in Matron's eyes and her mouth open in warning.

Sandra's face hit the grass with a heavy thud, as Cerise rammed her. She saw a black thong fly through the air from a grinning Miss Boulter, and suddenly Cerise held a heavy, studded man's belt, like a biker's, and she was pulling Sandra's hair till she screamed, and rolling her over to raise her bum.

Leather whistled and the buckle end of the belt cracked on her exposed croup, jolting Sandra as the pain seared her bare buttocks. The studs were of heavy, sharpened steel and their lash striped Sandra's buttocks with white-hot weals. She tried to rise, but Cerise's weight was full on her shoulders, then suddenly she relaxed, as the grass tickled her clitty, and she felt a tingle of sudden joy at the humiliating pain of a bare-bum leathering. She groaned and whimpered, chewing turf as she felt Cerise's toes wriggling excruciatingly in her cunt and catching her nubbin, sending shocks of pleasure up Sandra's spine.

All girls together.

The noise of the crowd was far way. There was only Cerise's nude body atop hers; the juices flowing from her whipper's cunt down her bum-cleft; the steady thwack of the leather biker's belt striping her wriggling arse. She dimly heard Cerise call for her own submission and groaned a refusal. Yet she did not resist, letting her body flop on the grass as the belt lashed her bare bum.

Sandra closed her eyes and imagined herself sunbathing nude amid the scents of her own lawn in Sedgedean, so far away and so long ago. Her body was bathed in Cerise's fluids and the grass beneath her quim was soggy with her own come-juice. The pleasure of her submission welled in her like cream, and she cried out, rubbing her stiffened nubbin hard against Cerise's foot as her belly fluttered. Her nipples and clitty were hard, tingling crystals and the whistling leather smacked her burning, bare bottom again and again.

She fantasised about her husband whipping her, then his hard, meaty cock slamming in and out of his little brown fucking machines; in Cerise's slippery wet cunt; then Sandra's own furry, warm hole welcoming the onslaught of cock after cock, Ray's cock among them, a legion of heavy male bodies using her, spurting their cream till her cunt brimmed, Sandra Shanks's squirming body no more than a thing, a submissive tool of pleasure.

Sandra cried out loud and long as the waves of her come pulsed through her spine and belly, soaking the grass with her copious flow of cunt-juice.

'Oh! Yes!' she squealed. 'Whip me to the bone, flog me raw, crush me . . .'

Her whipping continued for a minute or so after her climax, until Miss Crisp finally decreed the contest over and Cerise the winner. Cerise rose, and Sandra kissed her toes and the leather of her flogging. Then Stephanie Long grasped her arm and took her for her hooping, saying her bum was nicely warmed.

'All girls together,' Sandra gasped, radiantly.

Sandra's hoop was smaller than normal and she was wedged in a ball, with her bum stuck awkwardly over the belly-bar and her toes in her mouth. She could only gurgle her outraged reply when Matron came up and conveyed the purser's message to her. The bank had telephoned to advise the purser that Sandra's signed draft was unacceptable. Her joint account held insufficient funds.

'But I've got over two hundred thousand pounds in there!' she gasped in horror, except that her words came out as 'Urrgh! Mmm!'

A sharp crack of Miss Long's rattan in her arse-cleft brought tears to her eyes and the hoop started rolling.

'Mm! Mm!' she cried to Matron, meaning that she had to get to a telephone.

Then she screamed as her buttocks were striped not with the rattan, but with the ferocious crackling birch, which smarted like fire.

'Ahh!' Sandra wailed, hearing Miss Bustard laugh.

The hoop rolled round and round the boxing ring where Julie Down was slugging it out in more traditonal style with Zena Lambton. The spectators were distracted by the nude boxers, and Sandra felt the hoop veer away from the arena and into the woods. She gagged on her muddy toes stuffed in her mouth, and her eyes were blurred with tears. Her head spun, and at each revolution of the hoop, the grass and nettles stung her bare bum, enhanced by the rattan, or Miss Bustard's birch. Miss Gordon followed, wielding a flail of three-foot rubber thongs studded with winkle shells, and Miss Cream used a thin ashplant, generally more suited for classroom work, but just as painful in the open air.

The prefects whipped Sandra further and further away from school. She heard them mutter about a safe place to interrogate her. Her head spun and her toes were covered in mud and drool. She had no idea where she was. Yet the relentless whipping of her exposed nates was shamefully exciting, as was the dreadful prospect of 'interrogation'. Would she crack?

Suddenly, the ground seemed to give way and Sandra's hoop spun faster and faster out of control.

'She's going down the scarp!' cried Stephanie Long.

'You've lost her, you bloody fool!' shouted Miss Gordon.

Footsteps threshed the undergrowth as the hoop ran

away, and now Sandra's bare bum was prickled not by canes, but by thistles and thorns. She rolled so fast, she seemed to be falling in the direction of the beach. Her pursuers' voices were far behind.

Gradually the slope levelled, and the thorns gave way to moss and grass, shadowed by high foliage. The hoop suddenly came to a jarring halt, and Sandra looked out, dazed, to find herself wedged in the garden gate of a pretty little cottage, garlanded with honeysuckle. She smelt flowers and sea air. The door of the cottage opened, and a young woman of Sandra's age, with a mane of long blonde hair stepped out to greet her visitor with a smile.

'Well!' she said, as she freed Sandra, 'you are in a state! I expect you'd like a nice cup of tea.'

Groggily, Sandra accepted, and followed the woman into her dinky cottage. Sandra was entranced by her long legs and graceful tallness, the sway of her ripe body and big teats, and the perfect brown pears of her bottom. The woman was nude and had an all-over suntan, with a very lush pubic forest. She reminded Sandra of herself, before her cunt was shaved for boxing.

'It is so nice to have visitors,' the woman said.

'I – I was hooped,' said Sandra, somewhat superfluously.

'Jolly painful, isn't it?' said the woman, as she led Sandra into a cosy salon. 'And so shame-making! Come into surgery and I'll put some salve on your welts. My, you seem to have been in the wars. Sandra Shanks, the new fledge, isn't it? You boxed Cerise Purley; she's a tough little slut.'

'I don't really feel new,' said Sandra. 'Rather used, if anything.'

'How thrill-making!' said the nude woman. 'Gosh, you do have a nice suntan. I expect you are nudist, like me. That's partly why I live alone. The owner is rather kind to me; I do her small favours. I used to be Matron, you see, and I keep a small, rather specialised surgery for my own needs and those of guests. I call it the rubber room. Isn't that a conceit? But school found my methods a bit unorthodox. Nudism, for example, as therapy, not punishment. There has always been a sort of nudist faction at Quirke's, ever since the 1930s, and for a while Quirke's was actually completely nudist. Then things went the other way and the board of governesses insisted on full and proper schoolgirl uniforms, since how would nude girls know they were adult schoolgirls? I think it was all those yummy underthings – seamed stockings and bras and sussies and everything – that the American soldiers gave out during the Second World War. Don't you find the 1940s just too sinfully tempting? The rationing, then Dior's new look, and those hats and veils? Mmm . . .'

'The owner?' said Sandra. 'You mean the head-mistress, Miss Quirke?'

The nude woman laughed and her jutting, bare breasts jiggled pleasingly.

'Heaven, no. You are still a new fledge, aren't you? You and your gang: the four diddlers? How quaint! Well, come on, and I'll see to your welts.'

Sandra followed her into a room lit only by pale-blue fluorescence, with a pungent pleasing odour of rubber. The surgery contained the usual equipment, all of it appearing battleship grey, and Sandra touched the operating table, a chair and a medicine cabinet. Almost everything in the room was made of rubber, including the ceiling and floor and the padded walls, which were adorned with curious restraining harnesses, straps and cuffs. In the corner hung an array of instruments for flogging.

There were whips, quirts, canes and tawses, and every item was gleaming grey rubber. The only things not of rubber lay in a display cabinet: bottles and jars of coloured fluids; an assortment of rings, pincers, tweezers and needles; all of steel, like a tattooist's equipment. There were two other things: the baleful purple lens of a video camera and a giant TV wall screen.

Sandra obeyed the nude woman and lay belly down on the operating table. She felt soothing fingers rub unguents into her weals, then she turned over and the woman massaged her whipped breasts. Her own titties swayed elegantly as she worked and the tips of her big, plum nipples had hardened like thimbles.

'There isn't much I don't know about Quirke's school, Miss Shanks. My great-grandmother studied here in the 1930s! The thing is –' she sighed '– I was awfully good at being Matron, really I was, and sacking me was jolly unfair. But then, in a way, I suppose it wasn't. I . . . I used to put my own needs in front of the patients' needs. I admit it! I am a submissive, you see, Sandra: an extreme submissive. I wanted the girls – in the nude, of course – to whip my bum and bondage me with splints and gauze and plaster ! Now I have my own surgery, and like-minded girls visit, or . . . or I can do myself. That's what we call bondage, doing someone. I have time locks and safety releases, and things, and I can do myself for hours and hours, in the heaviest bondage – naked in rubber! – knowing I shall only be released after a certain time lapse. Of course, sometimes it is more fun with two to play. You may know my name: it is Gloria Harness. I would like it awfully if you would play, Sandra.'

Her finger rested in the lips of Sandra's shaven cunt, and brushed her clitty.

'You are very lovely,' she whispered. 'I saw you in uniform. From afar, I thought you my twin. Your stripes say you are truly submissive, Sandra.'

'I . . . I want to be,' Sandra blurted, as Gloria stroked her wealed breasts.

'If we play, you must switch, and crush me totally, as you did Cerise.'

How did Gloria Harness know so soon?

'I'll do my best, Matron,' murmured Sandra. 'But first, I need a phone.'

Sandra felt quite at ease being naked with a sister nudist, but nervous as she dialled the 24-hour number of the offshore bank. Gloria, also easily nude, made tea, and the two women smiled in anticipation of the session to come.

'Perhaps Quirke's should go nudist again,' said Sandra.

'The Miss Nude Flagellant Contest will be a start,' Gloria answered. 'Such a wonderful idea of Boulter's! I'm sure you'll win, dear.'

'Miss Harness – Gloria.' Sandra blurted. 'It's not fair to credit Miss Boulter, that was my idea! I told only a few girls. One of them has blabbed.'

Just as Tara Devine blabbed to Miss Long, after Audrey blabbed to Tara, Sandra thought.

The phone connection was made, and Sandra gave her secret password ('Exhibitionist') then listened aghast as the bank official informed her that a large cheque had been written by Mr Shanks, leaving their joint account in the red by 5,509 pounds and seventeen pence and that she had not responded to letters or telephone calls, so no one knew where she was. Mr Shanks had assured them by e-mail from Singapore that there would be ample funds arriving soon, but in the meantime the bank was unable to extend further overdraft facilities. As to how the purser knew so fast of this embarrassment, the purser of Quirke's was apparently an old friend, due to certain common interests. Caning grown-up schoolgirls on the bare bottom, no doubt Sandra thought. He suggested Sandra use her credit cards.

'But Quirke's won't take credit cards!' she cried. 'Only blasted guineas!'

'Never mind, dear,' said Gloria. 'Here's your tea, and before you do me in the rubber room, I'll tell you a few little secrets about Quirke's . . .'

'A little tighter, dear,' gasped Gloria Harness. 'In fact, a lot tighter.'

Sandra did her best to wrap the hideously constricting rubber cincher further around Gloria Harness's pinched, bare belly. She got it into the second last buckle hole, then, as Gloria complained, knotted her muscles and wrenched the garment as tight as it would go. Gloria's bare bum and big, jutting teats were bunched out like wax fruits, the swollen nipples like grapes.

'Are all extreme submissives so fussy?' Sandra panted, only half in jest.

'Yes,' said Gloria. 'We can be bitches if we are not made to suffer properly. But if we are, we can come without even wanking off.'

Sandra, in her role as dominant, was somehow made to feel the submissive as she obeyed Gloria's friendly, but terse commands, especially as she worked in the nude, while her companion's body would be enfolded in bondage.

The rubber cincher was the first thing. Then Gloria produced a roll of brown adhesive packing tape, and instructed Sandra to bind her legs and arms, rolling the tape skin-tight, then telling her to tape her back and belly right up to her neck. Sandra sheathed her entire body, including her feet, except for her titties and cunt-lips. The bottom, too, was to be left bare.

'You'll notice I haven't shaved my legs for a couple of days, nor trimmed my mink,' she said casually, 'so it will hurt awfully, as the tape is pulled off.'

Then Sandra laid Gloria on her belly on a rubber bar suspended from the ceiling by thongs, like a playground swing. She had to insert Gloria into a ferociously clinging, one-piece, rubber body-stocking, wriggling the thin, smelly latex up, until it fitted her skin-tight, right to her neck. Gloria did not help much, explaining that she was just meat to be treated. There was a hood and, before her face was covered, Gloria gave her final instructions.

After listening intently, Sandra pulled the black latex hood over Gloria's head, carefully pushing her golden mane down her back. The rubber sheath resembled a body-bag; it had holes for the nipples and cunt and for the buttocks, and the hood had holes for the eyes and mouth. Gloria lay there face down on the rubber swing. From the ceiling, Sandra drew two separate pulleys of knotted, rubber thongs and fastened each on a wrist, then winched them up, until Gloria's arms were distended and stretched up behind her back, and quivering like harp-strings. At each tightening of the winch she gasped, until her back arched up off the rubber saddle.

Hanging on the saddle were two flaps of thick rubber, like coal-heavers' aprons, with three buckled straps. These were drawn like a corset over the small of Gloria's back and Sandra, straining, fastened them right to the last buckle-hole. Gloria's waist was squeezed to a peapod.

Now her wrapped legs and feet were bent all the way underneath the saddle of the swing, so that her body was pressed like a rubber paperclip, with her feet against her collar-bone. Her bound feet were then fastened with a buckle which looped round her nape, leaving the titties jutting, swollen and bare.

Two outsize safety pins were clamped to each nipple, each pin threaded through existing pierced holes in the nipple grapes and fastened to a bolt on the floor by tight, rubber cord, which stretched the nipples to pale white balloons. Any movement of Gloria's body would be agony to the teats. The nipples were pulled so tight that they seemed ready to pop at any moment.

Gloria winced at the breast-pinning and her face was flushed. She sighed in satisfaction as Sandra performed the same operation with her cunt, pinning the pierced lips and fastening them with cords from the same floor-bolt. Gloria resembled a dangling string puppet, stretched by her nipples, head and cunt, with the big, bare bum upthrust for caning.

Then Sandra wadded Gloria's gash and anus with a slimy, malleable substance, which Gloria said was orthodontic gel, the kind used to make impressions for dental plates. She pushed the rubbery substance in until the anus hole and cunt were completely filled.

'It is solid, but flowing as well,' said Gloria, 'and when I squirt it out, it will keep an exact mould of my twat and bumhole. I keep them as souvenirs.'

The final touch was the insertion of Gloria's latex head into a Second World War gasmask, an eerie contraption of rubber, canvas and stained glass which had the date '1940' engraved on the mouthpiece and stank foully, even though freshly polished. The rubber straps were fastened behind her neck to maximum tightness.

'Ahhh, that's better,' Gloria sighed, her voice hollow and distorted in the gasmask. 'I'm ready, Sandra, once you've turned the video camera on. One of my great pleasures is watching myself being done on video and then wanking off.'

Sandra obeyed. The camera whirred and suddenly the giant TV screen was filled with the scene: Sandra nude, a domina, and her tethered submissive in rubber. Sandra gazed, fascinated, and her cunt began to moisten.

She positioned herself at Gloria's rear and began a slow and methodical hand-spanking of Gloria's bare bottom, gently at first, and in sets of ten, with pauses of a minute, rising to a furiously hard spanking by the hundredth smack. Every third set of spanks were delivered not to the buttocks, but to the jutting, swollen bubbies, with Sandra centring her smacks on the strained nipple-flesh. Gloria's bottom and teats pinked nicely, then the flush deepened to a lovely crimson. Each smack made her tethered body shudder, and the cords that fastened her nipples and cunt twanged loudly.

'That must be awfully sore on your nips and pussy,' Sandra said.

'It is,' rasped Gloria from her gasmask. 'But look at my twat.'

The stretched cunt-flaps glistened with come-oil.

Next was the quirt: a vicious flail of thirteen rubber thongs, three feet in length, and the rubber taut and stiff.

Thwack!

Sandra's first stroke to the croup made Gloria's bare arse clench violently. Her whole body shuddered as her suspending thongs twanged like enormous sussie straps. Gloria groaned in evident pain and evident pleasure. The quirt, too, was applied in sets of ten, alternating on bare bum and wealed, naked breasts, leading to one hundred. Sandra flogged hard, sweat dripping from her own bare breasts and her shaven cunt, but mingled now with the seepings of her quim-juice, as the whipping excited her. Gloria, too, was wet with come-oil, which was dripping copiously from her wide-open gash-flaps, and forming a sparkling pool on the floor.

Thwack! Thwack! Thwack!

Sandra's body writhed like a ballerina's as she moved sensuously to the rhythm of a bare-bum striping, efficiently altering her angle of delivery from left to right, and up and down, so that no part of Gloria's bum, teats and crevice was spared the lash's impact.

She concentrated particularly on the naked, open wrinkle of the anus bud, which bruised sweetly as the tips of the quirt caught her there, and made her buttocks and her whole body quiver violently, like her twanging, rubber bonds.

Thwack! Thwack! Thwack!

'Oh! Yes! Yes!' moaned Gloria. 'Don't worry about missing roll-call and tea; I'll give you a chitty. Oh, please stay, Sandra, and whip me raw.'

Sandra thanked her. She had been a bit worried. Now she was radiant in her role as naked dominatrix, except that Gloria still seemed subtly in charge.

'All that rubber, Gloria,' Sandra gasped as her seventy-seventh whopped the squirming bare bum-cheeks. 'It looks so yummy . . .'

Gloria laughed raucously within her gasmask.

'Just wait, Sandra,' she said. 'All girls together, even though my introduction to spanking and bondage was via beastly males.'

Her crimsoned bare breasts shivered as she spoke. At one hundred, Sandra replaced the quirt with a wide tawse, its three tongues studded with simple office staples which, Gloria assured her, caused exquisite pain. The tawse was much heavier than the quirt, but Sandra applied it to the purple welts of the naked fesses with as much vigour. Also, it made more noise. She glanced more and more at the TV monitor; she touched her wet cunt-lips, and felt her clitty throb. Gloria could see it too and gloated at her own naked humiliation.

'I'd love you to wank off, Sandra,' she said. 'Though as domina you don't need to be invited. Open wide, dear, for the video, and do a good lusty wank.'

Sandra began to masturbate vigorously as she flogged the writhing bare buttocks, which seemed to shimmer like moons before her. Gloria's voice was disembodied as she described her introduction to chastisement.

'I was assistant matron at Cardew's Sixth Form College for Boys near Rottingdean. I'm sure you know all about corporal punishment in boarding schools, now outlawed by the nanny state. At Rottingdean, there wasn't the cane, as such, but rather an unspoken code. Boys were sent to surgery, for treatment, and were honour bound to tell you what for: smoking and the like. I actually began the system, but I got carried away. A well-known skiver – Timmy, his name was – came in on some pretext, but reeking of tobacco and beer. I told him to get his trousers down for proper treatment, then I put him over my knee and spanked him on the bare, till his bum was lovely and red and wriggling, as hard as I could, but only about thirty whops. And my twat got all wet when I was spanking the boy's bare bum, all clenching and sore and red, and I saw he had an enormous bone on. His meat was the biggest whopper! But anyway.

'Word got round and, after a discreet suggestion by the head, I received a steady stream of young miscreants for treatment. Oh, how I loved making those lusty bums squirm! I had no cane, but graduated to using a knotted stethoscope, which is extremely painful and effective. I used to shame them by putting them in unnecessary splints and bandages, or hobbling them as I whopped their bare bums, or making them wear my skirts and sussies and stockings. Too, too shame-making! My cunt would be so wet, I got into the habit of wanking off after I had serviced them, but increasingly, I longed for it to be my bum that was whipped and, as I masturbated, I would beat myself on the bare with the rubber stethoscope, flogging myself really hard and wanking my clitty to come. Sometimes I peed myself in my excitement. Eventually I used to wank off as I was actually administering the beating.

'My downfall was when I asked a boy – that wretched Tim again – if he would do me the favour, and he agreed. I took eight dozen glorious, tight stingers with the knotted stethoscope. I needn't tell you what the beastly boy was doing as he beat me! I was on my seventy-fifth whop and my bum was black and blue – I had the mirror rigged to look – and I was wanking myself senseless, almost ready to come, and I told him

231

to put his bone in the right place, and the beast sank it into my bumhole! It was huge! I gushed with come-juice. I'd never had it in the arse before and I was so shocked, I pissed myself, and my pee soaked my nurse's uniform, and my lowered knickers and stockings, and my white nurse's shoes. And just as he was buggering me to a lovely come, Matron herself walked in . . .

'Outraged! Well, you can imagine! She sent Tim away – he was expelled, of course – and then she continued my punishment and flogged me until I did come! I was dismissed, and Quirke's were glad to have me, now that I had done the "boy" thing, and realised a lady's bum is best whipped by another lady . . .'

'Ahhh . . .' cried Sandra, as a flurry of stripes made Gloria jerk and cry out, and Sandra wanked herself off to a noisy, quivering come, almost slipping in the pool of come-juice below her dripping gash.

'Hurry – the cane!' Gloria said. 'Hard on bare, tight as you can! Oh . . .'

'I'm going to depart from instructions, Miss Harness,' said Sandra in pretend fury. From the cabinet, she retrieved a stethoscope, and knotted the rubber tubes, then lifted it over Gloria's bare bum.

'One hundred stingers with the stethoscope, you naughty boy!' she thundered.

'Oh, no, please, Miss, anything but that!' wailed Gloria.

Suddenly, Sandra's thighs and quim were drenched in a fine spray as Gloria pissed herself, the pee squirting like water from a sprinkler round the wad of gel that filled her gash. As she pissed, she moaned in orgasm. Her frantic cries mingled with the throaty roar of a distant motorbike engine, reminding Sandra how near they were to the coast road.

'Thanks awfully, Miss,' panted the flogged woman through her gasmask.

'Gloria . . .' said Sandra timidly.

'Yes, dear?'

'Could I have a go? I mean, would you do me?'

She smiled impishly.

'I'm rather an exhibitionist, and I fancy being a video star.'

'All girls together!' Gloria replied. 'I hoped I wouldn't have to ask.'

16

The Bottom Line

Gloria Harness had indeed whimpered in pain, as Sandra unwrapped the strong adhesive tape. The tape came away with difficulty, flecked with downy, little hairs from Gloria's arms and legs and a thick tuft which had been wrenched from her pubis.

'All part of the fun,' Gloria gasped.

The two nude females ate a light salad supper, giggling whenever a dab of salad cream spilled on their breasts.

'I still can't believe all those things you told me,' said Sandra as they returned to the rubber room.

'Schooling is a business like any other,' said Gloria. 'No pay, no play. I only told you what you need to know. There's a lot you don't, and shouldn't.'

'All this worry about money,' said Sandra doubtfully, as she prepared for her own bondage. 'And men, damn them!'

'That's the Quirke's spirit,' said Gloria, looking up at the gloating purple video lens. 'You want to stay, don't you?'

'And be a video star . . .' said Sandra.

Sandra was fastened in a white rubber waist cincher like a corselet, and panted for breath as each eyelet was tightened with its metal clip. Gloria's powerful muscles were knotted as she fastened the constrainer. The top of the cincher jutted under Sandra's teats, pushing them up and out. Her nipples were already erect and her quim moist.

'You've taken quite a pounding today, Sandra, so I'll lay off your bottom and concentrate on your bondage.'

'No!' Sandra cried fiercely. 'I want everything. Goodness, Gloria, I've been at Quirke's long enough. My bum's leather by now.'

'Perhaps a light spanking, then, and just a few stripes,' Gloria bantered. 'The important thing is to get you well trussed.'

She switched on the video camera and Sandra watched every detail of her binding in the monitor. First, she slid on a pair of white, rubber stockings, awfully tight, which were affixed to the sussie straps on her corselet. The rubber swing swayed ominously in front of her, with the restraining cords dangling from the ceiling like fronds. Gloria adjusted the height of the swing so that the bar was uncomfortably higher than Sandra's waist. Then she gave Sandra a pair of white, rubber shoes with daring spike stilettos, at least six inches high, and the fit much too small. Gasping with discomfort, she squeezed her feet inside the shoes.

Too late, she saw that there were little, steel rings at the toecap and heel, and deftly, Gloria stooped to thread a cord through these rings, fastening it tightly to the floor bolt, and thus immobilising Sandra within a radius of a foot or so like a puppy on a leash. She further shod Sandra's feet with heavy lead Spanish boots, or hobblers, which clanged shut on their hinges with a menacing thud. Sandra was completely hobbled and, within the narrow arc, could only move her feet with the greatest effort.

'Are you sure I should be able to move at all?' she snapped and Gloria smiled.

She was bent over the bar of the swing and her wrists clamped in thick rubber cuffs, then fastened to the ceiling pulleys with her arms splayed wide, so that her body was now stretched in a taut x shape. Gloria winched her up to the maximum, and Sandra's body was strained to the full with her tightly cased feet pulled uncomfortably on tiptoe within the lead boots.

'A bit like the rack,' said Gloria casually.

'I imagine the rack is far more painful,' retorted Sandra, but shivering a little. 'Come on, Gloria, do me properly. You are going to mask me, aren't you? I want to see myself done on the screen.'

'Maybe,' said Gloria, and Sandra made an exclamation of impatience.

Her thighs were stretched very wide and she felt the air cool the flushed, moist lips of her cunt. The bar of the raised swing bit into her navel, and she was inclined at an angle, as though for a seaman's flogging. Gloria now took a coil of rubber rope – about two inches thick and flat, like a fireman's hose – and began a methodical binding of Sandra's legs. She wrapped the rubber rope very tightly from her ankles right up to the lips of her pussy, doing first the left, then the right leg.

'Matron and Miss Boulter are going to be in charge of the Miss Nude Flagellant contest,' she said brightly. 'All the contestants are to receive a bare-bum caning of thirty stripes, a day before – which means tomorrow morning – and then wear a special chastity belt for the next twenty-four hours so they can't cheat by giving themselves extra stripes. Not a skimpy little cub like Margaret Betts's but thick, rubber knickers with a proper padlock and evacuation holes. Like this.'

She held up the garment: heavy panties, like old-fashioned bloomers, of grey rubber an inch thick. It was not waist-banded to size, but was a single, adjustable wrapper which fastened with a zip, with only the smallest apertures at anus and peehole.

She prised open Sandra's anus and fingered her hole with three sharp talons, making Sandra wince. Then she took a knob of gel and thrust it to the root of Sandra's bumhole, not filling the anal cavity, but nonetheless leaving her with an itchy discomfort where the gel clung to her fundament.

236

She fiddled in Sandra's arse-cleft for a moment – Sandra could not see clearly – and fastened the rubber legging sheath, binding it with superglue just under Sandra's quim-lips and furrow.

Then she wrapped her belly, neck and shoulders, and arms until Sandra was completely swathed in rubber, with only her head, loins and teats naked. The rubber binding, below and above the titties, pushed them out like balloons ready to burst. Her entire bondage was connected by filaments to the system of rubber suspension thongs.

The thought scared her that there was some electric device embedded in the rubber cords. She shuddered, not seeing that as part of her submission, though she had been told of subs who played 'sparky games'. Gloria pinched each of her nipples between her thumb and forefinger, making Sandra squeak suddenly, and Gloria expressed approval that the nips were brick-stiff. She proceeded to fasten them with severe clamps like clothes-pegs, and winched up the suspension cords till Sandra's nipples were stretched like pale, pink gussets on a level with her mouth. The pain was searing. Gloria clasped Sandra's shorn pussy and held up her palm, now glistening with come-oil.

'I do the piercings and tattooings here at Quirke's,' she said, 'not the current matron, as she is not ... sympathetic enough.'

Gloria gestured proudly at her own nude body and, focussing in the dim light, Sandra made out innumerable tiny pinpricks in nipples, cunt-lips, belly and cleft.

'For formal occasions,' she said rather coyly. 'If you are a good girl, Sandra, I'll pierce you everywhere: nips and twat-flaps and bumhole and belly-button. Even your face, and maybe a tattoo on the clitty to go with that sweet butterfly on your bum. Would you like that?'

'Of course I would!' Sandra blurted. 'Now, I expect you to hood and mask me, and if that is so, please hurry up, Miss Gloria. And I'll want a hand-spanking, then I want to squirm properly under tawse and ditto under cane. And surely you must have a birch? My bum's positively begging to be birched bare.'

Gloria smiled broadly and fetched the rubber hood.

'The present matron and I get on very well, you know,' she remarked. 'Sometimes she is my guest, and does me quite beautifully. But sometimes I fear that she is too much the lesbian, like Stephanie Long, and does not like her subs to make their wishes known or give orders, as true subs always do, Sandra. They are right bitches, sometimes.'

She paused to let the import of her words sink in.

'What about Miss Boulter and Miss Long?' asked Sandra. 'And Miss Quirke?'

'The current Isobel Quirke has never been able to overcome her craving for cock or even conceal it from herself,' said Gloria, matter-of-factly. 'Few women can. Miss Long is one. As for Boulter, she is perfect, because a happy fate has enabled her to transcend lesbianism; that is, flourish as a lesbian, without being deprived.'

Sandra frowned, puzzled, and Gloria told her to wait and see.

'Now, Sandra, I told you that true submissives can be bitches,' she said, 'and you have been bossing me like a bitch. Draw your own conclusions.'

Gloria held up a rubber pixy hood. This garment had an aperture at the crown, the size of a fifty pence coin. Through it, Gloria painfully pulled Sandra's thick mane, then knotted it in a pony-tail. She fitted the rubber hood snugly on Sandra's head, then lashed the knot of her pony-tail to a dangling rubber frond which she winched up tight. Sandra's head was jerked back and up by the tugging of her hair, and she winced in the pleasure of this small humiliation.

Then the gasmask was strapped on to Sandra's head and the smoky glass eyepiece misted with her panting breath. The thing stank, and was stifling, and her breath echoed close and laboured in her ears. Gloria's voice came from far away through the thick apparatus of canvas and rubber. With her hair pulled tightly up, Sandra had to crane to see herself in the monitor screen: self-inspection meant further pain.

What she saw made her cunt seep deliciously with quivering drops of come-juice. She was completely helpless and immobile, with her bottom and teats shining like big bare moons ready to be lashed by cane or whip. Sandra's bound body could do no more than quiver. Her thighs were spread so wide that she doubted that her bottom, if caned, could even clench satisfactorily to lessen her pain.

'That girl's luscious bum deserves the birch,' she insisted through the gasmask.

Gloria lifted her hand and brought it down with a sharp smack, across the bare buttocks. Then with a firm, fast rhythm, she spanked Sandra to one hundred, without saying a word. Sandra gazed at her quivering, bare bum in the monitor, and at the graceful motion of Gloria spanking her, and the naked chastiser's fesses and titties swaying like rushes in the breeze. She could see her spanked arse shiver at each smack and her cheeks vainly trying to clench. The pain flooded her, but watching herself on the big screen was like watching another woman spanked in bondage. Gloria's blonde mane tossed in the rhythm of spanking, and Sandra imagined she herself spanked that big, bare bum.

When the spanking was over, Gloria solemnly took the heavy, rubber tawse and beat Sandra's naked buttocks one hundred times, very hard but very slowly, giving her bottom full time for the squirming of each stripe to ebb, before the next one struck.

There was no sense of time. Sandra watched herself – her two selves – on the screen in the dance of chastisement, and her cunt gushed with come-juice. A bare-bum striping was thrill enough, but to watch your own likeness making your bum wriggle!

Her clitty throbbed and she knew that one touch would make her come. She also knew that Gloria would not accord her that precious touch and she loved her shame of wanting. Over the roar of her breath, in the smelly canvas and rubber of the gasmask, she heard a motor-cycle engine like the cruel cawing of a distant seagull.

'Hurts much?' panted Gloria. 'I've quite lost track of time.'

'Oh, how it hurts,' Sandra moaned.

'Your cunt is very wet,' said Gloria as if observing a scientific fact. 'Mine too.'

'Won't you wank me off?' Sanda begged. 'Oh! My clit's ready to explode.'

'You know better than to ask. But when I cane you, I'll wank myself off.'

She allowed Sandra a moment's rest. The searing pain of the tawse gradually ebbed, but Sandra's bruised fesses still quivered, as though begging for more. Gloria said that she enjoyed switching roles occasionally, but still, it was supremely strange and lovely to be a sub. Most people, the unenlightened, would balk at the application of even a dozen stripes, clothed, let alone a full caning on the bare.

'A naked caning, without limits – to bare up below, and take it without a whimper – that is the ideal,' she said, lifting the four-foot thong of thick rubber, that was her cane.

'This will hurt more than spanking and the tawse together,' she said mildly. 'Are you sure you want it?'

'I am yours to command, Matron,' panted Sandra, proudly, then screamed as the first cane-stroke striped her bare bum.

Vip!

'Ouch!'

Vip!

'Ah!'

Vip! Vip! Vip!

'Ahhh! Ahhh! Oooh . . .'

Sandra sobbed and her scalded, bare buttocks squirmed helplessly.

'A full hundred?' she stammered, panting in her gasmask.

'Whatever you like, Sandra. You're the sub: you're in control,' said Gloria smugly.

'Yes, cane me a full hundred then.'

Vip! Vip! Vip! Vip!

'Oh! Oh! Ahh!'

The cane seemed to lacerate Sandra's bruised flesh to ribbons, with Gloria timing the stripes so that she was carried to a plateau of smarting agony, but never quite tipped over into a swoon. In the monitor, Sandra watched through her tears as Gloria masturbated, her practised fingers flicking her stiffened clitty which peeped above the lush, blonde pubic forest and the swollen gleam of the gash-lips. Sandra's own cunt flowed with copious come-juice. The caning proceeded in sets of ten, with long pauses now, but right to one hundred. Suddenly, Sandra felt unbearable pressure in her belly.

Without a word, Sandra released her pent-up flood of steaming pee, and watched Gloria suddenly kneel between her spread thighs to let the piss stream over her naked breasts and belly, soaking her pubic bush. Squatting, Gloria then followed suit, and the room was silent but for the whirring of the video and the hiss of women's pee. Gloria caught her fluid in a rubber cup and emptied it over Sandra's arse.

'Time for the birch,' she said.

She took a long, crackly birch, thicker and stiffer than Miss Crisp's, and wiped it gently on Sandra's bum and gash, till the rods were soaked in pee and come-juice.

Then she delivered the first birch-stroke and Sandra's whole body jerked.

Thwack!

'No!'

Thwack! Thwack!

'Oh! Oh!' Sandra began to whimper.

The strokes of the birch, on bare bottom, followed each other briskly.

'Ahhh!' Sandra screamed.

'Much worse than cane?' said Gloria.

'Oh! Gloria! Oh!'

Sanda's cunt flowed with copious come-oil.

Thwack! Thwack! Thwack!

'Oh! How it smarts! Ahhh . . .'

She saw Gloria's fingers kneading her clitty, masturbating closer to come.

'Oh, wank me off, please,' Sandra heard herself beg.

Thwack! Thwack! Thwack!

The birch was merciless and terrifying. Sandra felt her bladder open, and another, shorter, flow of pee burst from her convulsed, wet pussy. Gloria now knelt, so that her open mouth was under Sandra's flowing peehole, and she swallowed noisily as the golden piss bathed her face, and her fingers masturbated vigorously.

Thwack! Thwack! Thwack! – It felt as though it were punishing her for the shameful piss.

'Oh! Oh! Oh!'

Sandra screamed and sobbed, and her body writhed frantically in her bondage, until she had taken thirty with the birch on the bare and her croup felt opened to the bone.

'I don't think you can take any more, ' said Gloria.

'I want . . .' Sandra sobbed.

Gloria lifted the birch again and, placing her own bare within the view of Sandra's gasmask, dealt her own buttocks six savage stripes with the birch. Her croup soon mottled to red, then was streaked to purple as she flagellated herself. In the distance, the telephone rang and an answering machine clicked on. Gloria paused in her self-flagellation, tears streaming down her own cheeks and her bare fesses squirming hard. She began to birch Sandra's buttocks, as well as her own, with alternate strokes. Both the bare croups wriggled in unison, with Gloria masturbating and Sandra's cunt gushing with come-oil while her clitty tingled in frustration.

At last, Gloria groaned, then gasped. Her masturbation slowed to powerful, deliberate flicks on the nubbin and she began to shriek in her come. As she convulsed in orgasm, she knelt and buried her face at Sandra's soaking cunt, her teeth biting on Sandra's clitty, and Sandra yelped with joy as her own orgasm pulsed through her.

Gloria padded to her sitting-room, and Sandra heard her click her answering machine, then lift the telephone. She spoke, listened and returned to the rubber room, a Marlboro Light smoking between her lips.

'I have some business outside, Sandra,' she said, 'so I'm going to leave you here in bondage. I may have use for you again.'

'Suddenly, you don't sound very like a sub, Gloria, or should I say, Miss Harness,' Sandra groaned through the gasmask.

'I told you, we can be right bitches,' Gloria drawled, blowing smoke at Sandra's gash.

Briskly, she zipped the rubber knickers of the chastity belt over Sandra's bruised loins and buttocks, pressing them hard against her bum-crack, and then fastened her with the rubber padlock.

'There! Your bum's protected from further chastisement should anyone else intrude.'

A shiver went up Sandra's spine. Gloria spoke as if intrusion were to be expected.

'I told you about a timer switch I use to play games with myself. It is electronically operated and I've set it to open all your clamps, the chastity belt, boots and fasteners simultaneously. But I shan't tell you when, or how long it will be. And I could be away for hours, or days. Just think, Sandra! All alone with nothing to do but watch yourself in the screen, trembling in delicious terror. And nobody knows you're here. That, Miss, is what true submission is all about.'

Sandra let out a long moan and began to sob as Gloria closed the door of the rubber room. The front door opened and closed, and Sandra was left alone. She looked at her buttocks in the monitor, padlocked in the big, rubber knickers of the chastity belt, and the sight of her discomfort mesmerised her into a dreamy, submissive satisfaction. She had what she wanted: to be completely in the power of a woman who could be her twin, alone, uncertain and in helpless, painful bondage.

Her cunt began to gush with fluid, her nipples stiffened in excitement and her clit tingled. Sandra gazed at her bondage and smiled. Suddenly she froze, as she heard the roar of a motorbike engine stopping outside the house. The front door opened and heavy footsteps entered.

'Gloria? Gloria?' said a man's voice, mellow and oddly familiar, like a girl's voice lowered several octaves. 'It's me, Timmy, and I'm in a mood to whip your bum raw, before I bugger your big, meaty arse. I've got hold of Sandra's frilly maid outfit. You'd like me to dress as her, wouldn't you?'

Sandra was silent.

'Oh,' said the male Timmy, 'you're in the rubber room, are you, doing yourself with the time lock. I'll bet you're belted and sheathed so I can't whop you properly. But I'll bugger you all the harder till you squeak, Miss.'

There was a pause and a rustle of clothing.

'I'd like to bugger Sandra Shanks,' declared Timmy.

'She's gagging for it. Miss B says so, and she's bummed her a lot. But you'll do for the moment. There! Sandra's coming, Gloria, she's going to bum you and spunk in your dirty, little girly's bumhole.'

The door of the rubber room slid open, and Sandra saw a figure enter, dressed in her own maid's uniform, right down to the blue stockings, sussies, stilettos and apron. The figure had shiny, black hair, swept back Elvis-style. With a shake, Timmy released his coiffure and, after a few casual flicks, it hung bobbed below his ears like a girl's. He held a heavy studded biker's belt, the same belt that Cerise had used on Sandra in the boxing ring, supplied by Miss Boulter. Timmy tossed his head disdainfully.

'The chastity belt, eh, Gloria? You know how mad that makes me. Looks like you're in for a tit-flogging before I bugger you. Don't tell me about your time lock; I know you always set it for two hours.'

Sandra yelped as the belt lashed her naked teats, making her nipple clamps jangle. Her wail was of intense pain, fear – and sudden enlightenment. No, Gloria certainly had not told her everything.

Timmy's frilly skirt rode up to reveal the bobbing shaft of the biggest cock Sandra had ever seen: a bulging, striated monster which throbbed and swelled with livid veins as though ready to bite her.

The belt savagely striped her bare titties, but the pain seemed a distant whisper. She had seen that giant cock before, with Audrey, when they eavesdropped on Isobel Quirke's chastisement by Angela Jones, and the third person they thought was Miss Boulter. Timmy was the third person. Timmy was Miss Boulter's twin.

He flogged Sandra disdainfully on the bare breasts, catching the stiffened points of her nipples with his belt buckle. He seemed satisfied that her reaction was muted terror. Then he stepped back and lifted the maid's skirt fully.

He put on a falsetto voice, imitating a woman: it was Miss Boulter's voice. Now he threw back his black hair and told 'Gloria' that if a tit-flogging didn't make her squeal, then buggery certainly would.

'I haven't fucked a wench for an awfully long time,' he trilled in the prefect's voice. 'Miss B doesn't count, of course. That isn't fucking, that is being ourself. My balls are just crammed with spunk to shoot into that tender, elastic hole of yours, Gloria. Then when your timer goes, I'll unlock those knickers and do your bare bum with one hundred stripes of the stethoscope. Remember all those years ago, how you liked that? And we shall make a lovely video for the punters. Let's do a browse, shall we?'

He clicked a switch and the monitor began to scan from one video clip to the next. She saw familiar faces and bottoms, filmed in the cave Sandra knew as the bumhole, or else in this rubber room: Miss Quirke, Miss Swain, Miss Crisp, the pres – except for Longy – and Audrey. All dripped with come-juice or tears, taking and giving cane, twisted in bondage, stretched on the rack, whipped to the bone on raw black-and-blue bumskin and all pounded by Timmy's fearful fleshy shaft in squirming anus or cunt.

Audrey was in almost every frame, abused, flogged and buggered, sucking and cunt-fucked. If anyone was a star of the screen, it was Audrey Larch. And Sandra suddenly flashed with the idea: that is how impoverished Audrey gets the guineas for her tuition.

Sandra groaned and her gash flowed with juice, as the bulb of the penis wriggled inside the hole in her rubber knickers and brushed the stretched lips of her anus bud. Timmy entered her, waggling his cock teasingly. The stretching of her hole made her gasp and squirm, then inch by inch, the huge organ penetrated her bum-shaft.

'Oh, you can take it, Gloria,' grunted Timmy, as he plunged right to Sandra's root with a cobra's thrust, and

Sandra screamed in pain. 'You've taken it so many times before, and from so many cocks. But that's the beauty of bumming: every time is the first time.'

Timmy began to fuck Sandra vigorously in the stretched elastic of her anal shaft, and she howled, thinking the massive cock would split her bumhole. Timmy grunted in satisfaction at her cry. But as she adapted to the savage pulse of her buggery, her cunt moistened and her anus began to suck and embrace the giant cock.

Her clitty throbbed and she knew she was filling the rubber knickers with come-juice, which she felt dripping from her gash. And she knew she would come in the giddiness of her humiliation by a powerful and irresistible cock.

'I'm not Gloria,' she groaned. 'I am Sandra! Oh, don't stop fucking me, please.'

Timmy merely grunted in surprise, slamming his massive cock again and again at the root of her anus. He gasped harshly; as her bumhole filled with his hot spurting spunk. There was a hum and a click, and Sandra felt herself, softly and suddenly, released from all her restraints. Sobbing, she sank to her knees, tore off her gasmask and took the cock in her mouth, licking every last drop of the slimy spunk.

She worked her sphincter muscle and excreted the knob of gel which Gloria had inserted. Instead of the gel, out popped a node attached to a microscopic filament: Gloria's time lock. The gel was designed to melt in the heat of buggery.

She looked up at the proud features above her. The hair, the face, the eyes, were Miss Boulter. The male body was poised like its female twin's. Sandra saw the Boulter twins as as two halves of one being, or rather, two faces of one being.

'Oh, Miss!' she sobbed. 'Why did you wait so long to fuck me with your real cock?'

The door of the rubber room slid open and Gloria Harness entered, still nude, and with the gleam of stripes on her raw, bare buttocks. She went straight to the video and played back the scenes just recorded, smacking her lips.

Sandra's eyes widened in surprise that Gloria was still nude and, with a charming blush, Gloria admitted that she had not gone far away.

'Welcome properly to Quirke's school, Sandra,' she said. 'Now let's ensure you win the Miss Nude Flagellant contest. There's a lot of money riding on that bum of yours.'

'The bottom line is always money, isn't it?' said Sandra coquettishly. 'Audrey is a superstar. Now I understand how she can afford the fees at Quirke's.'

Timmy Boulter looked at her in amazement.

'How wrong you are,' he said. 'The only payments are made by the punters worldwide who hit us on the Internet. Don't you know how many people are exhibitionists? Check out the raunchy magazines in the newsagents, full of photos of readers' wives, and their stories of being convoy-fucked, while their hubbies video the action. People beg to be filmed, especially in humiliance.'

Gloria Harness smiled shyly.

'Quirke's videos keep my sister Timothea at school and the whole school out of the red, if only they knew! Superstar she may be, but the girl you know as Audrey Larch gets nothing.'

17

Feathers

'Two roll-calls missed,' snarled Stephanie Long. 'And tea, of course. Where were you, Miss? Breaking bounds? Meeting some boy at The Feathers?'

She swished her cane, a thin yew rod about a quarter of an inch thick, and glared at Sandra, who stood by her bed in her nightie. Her frilly maid's costume was hung neatly in her cabinet.

'May the fledge Audrey Larch ask what the school prefect Miss Long is doing in the dormitory of Miss Boulter?' Audrey asked sweetly.

Stephanie whirled and cracked the palm of her hand across Audrey's mouth, then again across her cheek with a backhander. She slapped Audrey's face over a dozen times until the girl's cheeks glowed red.

'No, the little bitch Audrey Larch may not,' Stephanie snapped.

'I was dazed from my hooping,' stammered Sandra. 'I wandered around until my head cleared. Then I found my way back to school.'

This was not strictly untrue. Gloria Harness had furnished her with a note of excuse, but Sandra witheld it, fearing further embroilment.

'Naked in the woods? For so long? Further disgrace.'

'A – a kind lady gave me tea and a blanket,' Sandra said. 'Miss Harness . . .'

'Miss Gloria Harness –' spat the prefect, '– has no

official position at Quirke's. She was once Matron, but had to relinquish her post, for impropriety. The whore was consorting with men in the vilest and most promiscuous ways. I need not sully girls' ears with the filthy details, but rumour has it she appeared in obscene films. If I find there is substance to this rumour, then anyone consorting with her will be expelled.'

Stephanie had a nasty gleam in her eye.

'The punishment for missing teatime roll-call is a sixer, Miss Shanks, and a further six stripes for missing dorm roll-call.'

'But I got here in time for lights out,' Sandra protested. 'And a dorm offence is for Miss Boulter. Missing tea is a school offence, and I am presently in Matron's bondage for punishment in that matter.'

'Only while you are wearing your uniform of servitude,' said Stephanie, glancing at the folded maid's uniform. 'The dorm matter may be left to Boulter, as and when she deigns to arrive, but I will deal with the school matter, here and now, unless you care to get the whole twelve stripes over and done with. I don't think Miss Boulter will be too pleased to hear you have been consorting with Miss Gloria Harness.'

Indeed, Sandra did not know if the Bolt would take kindly to one of her own dorm being buggered by her twin, without her presence or authority. She looked at Audrey for guidance in this diplomatic impasse, and Audrey nodded her assent. Better take the twelve, and placate the vicious Stephanie Long.

'I'll take your twelve, Miss,' said Sandra.

'Very well. Miss Sandra Shanks,' said Stephanie formally, 'you have agreed to accept just chastisement. You will bend over your bed, and lift your nightie for twelve stripes on the bare.'

Glumly, Sandra obeyed, and felt her head pressed down, while her nightie was lifted high over her bottom and Stephanie's hands caressed her bare buttocks.

'Well! Quite a patchwork, Miss, so I dare say another dozen won't make much difference,'

'No, Miss Long,' said Sandra, po-faced, 'I dare say it won't.'

'What! You cheeky – right, you little slut, you've got it coming!'

Sandra's arse clenched and she gasped as the first stripe bit her bare bum. Stephanie lifted her caning arm to its full height, and there was silence in the dorm, as Sandra took the twelve stripes in hard, rapid succession. Her only sound was a stifled wail at the seventh – which was duly repeated – and a groaning sob when she had completed the set. Her fesses, raw with weals, continued to clench as she muffled her sobs in her pillow.

'Don't be too sure of the Miss Nude Flagellant Contest and your thirty stripes tomorrow morning,' sneered Miss Long. 'Matron may pronounce you unfit for chastisement, and hence disqualified. No cheating, girls, and no mischief, or dorm spankings. I've had a good look at your bums and I'll know. In the unaccountable absence of Miss Boulter, I'll call lights out now and stand guard outside, until she honours us with her presence. Miss Tara Devine, you will please attend me. I wish to discuss your candidature for Miss Nude Flagellant.'

The lights dimmed and Stephanie stalked from the dorm. Audrey whispered that they should wait until Miss Long went to pee, which should be soon. Sure enough, after a few minutes, they heard Stephanie's feet pad towards the WC and her groans of satisfaction as she evacuated with a loud tinkling. As Stephanie was peeing, there were muffled gasps and the noise of cane on bare flesh, and Tara Devine squealed.

Noiselessly, the four diddlers crept from the dorm, still in their nighties – to change in dorm would be noticed by Miss Long – and headed for the gym.

'It's Saturday night at The Feathers,' said Julie. 'Why else is the Bolt away?'

Quickly, the four girls changed into gym kit: white pleated tutus, blue knickers and skin-tight cotton blouses, with no bra, but not forgetting sussies and stockings to add a touch of formality to the escapade. Sandra's blue stockings were in the dorm, so she wore black ones like the others.

'I don't trust Longy,' Julie said as they went out into the cool night air. 'She and Tara are cooking up something. She's made the girl her slave, and I bet between now and the contest, she'll find ways to whop her raw, chastity belt or no chastity belt.'

Sandra gave them an edited version of her rescue from hooping by Gloria Harness. She made no mention of the rubber room, or her buggery by the Bolt's twin brother, but pointed out that Matron and Miss Boulter were the only ones who would have keys to the padlocked chastity belts.

'I'm sure we can trust the Bolt,' said Sharon, 'for she's a good egg in her way, and hates Longy. But can we trust Matron? Eh, Sandra? You are her bondsmaid.'

'I'm not sure,' said Sandra. 'I'm not sure of anything . . .'

Before going to The Feathers, they decided to freshen up with a moonlight skinny-dip. They used the secret tunnel, passed the entrance of The Gash, and could not resist the temptation to crawl in and inspect the disciplinary appliances in the cave of the bumhole. A dim nightlight was on in the deserted chamber and everything had been polished, as though awaiting use.

'Miss J may have plans,' said Julie. 'Let's have our bathe and then go up the cliff path to The Feathers. Last one in's a cissy!'

Eagerly, the four girls stripped naked and laid their folded gym kit neatly in the cave. There was something thrilling about running to the sea completely nude and thus defenceless. Sandra thought of the giddy, exhibitionist pleasure of dogging: fucking, naked, in a conspicuous car, ready to be surprised by a copper.

They romped naked in the gentle surf, under a bright half moon. It was cold and they shrieked in their excitement. Audrey scanned the clifftop as they began to shiver.

'There's plenty of time,' she said. 'A good diddle will warm us up.'

It took little argument to persuade the girls to wank off in a circle, each girl with a hand in her neighbour's quim, so that the four did a little ring-a-roses as they writhed in two-handed masturbation. First Audrey, then each of them, peed, not ceasing to frot as the steaming fluid hissed over their hands and thighs and joined the pattern of their come-oil in the sand. Sharon came first, after Audrey poked a finger in her anus, and Sandra and Julie spanked her bum. Each claimed to be juicing more than the others, and soon they all trilled and gasped in climax, their bare titties fluttering as their swollen cunts gushed with copious come-oil. Suddenly a voice barked:

'What's this? As if I can't guess. Wanking off, and in public? Disgraceful!'

It was Miss Timothea Boulter.

The lesbian wore a leotard of shiny, black rubber, teetering high heels on thigh-boots that revealed inches of fishnet, and garish, frilly stocking tops with the sussie straps affixed to the metallic hem of the leotard. The garment had breastplates of conical steel with sharp, shiny points which stuck out grotesquely, but left the big, plum nipples quite bare, as was the knickerless mound of her cunt. At her neck was a metal collar, with two-inch spikes. Her waist was looped in a chain, which constricted her tightly, and then criss-crossed her torso like armour.

She carried a crook school cane lodged at her waist-chain and, coiled in her hand, a long stockwhip. Her teeth gleamed in the moonlight as she smiled at the four nudists, who were shivering again now, and her hand allowed the stockwhip to uncoil. It was a heavy oiled leather thong, a good six feet in length, and she cracked it on Audrey's back.

'We were just having a naked swim, Miss,' said Audrey, wincing. 'No harm meant.'

'Breaking bounds, and wanking off, and no harm meant!' said the Bolt. 'If you are to play frotting games, you shouldn't shriek so much.'

Sandra wondered how the Bolt had clambered down the path so quickly on those yummy spiked heels. The prefect slowly unwound the chain from her waist and torso, and jangled it in the still, night air. There were four spiked collars, like her own, set into the chain and she ordered the four naked girls to form a line facing her and raise their heads. They did so meekly and, one by one, they were snapped into the metal collars, not constricting, but with the spikes tilted upward to keep their heads raised. Miss Boulter cracked her whip across their bare bums, then ordered them about face towards the cliff path. Above them, the lights of The Feathers shimmered in the faint sea mist.

'Quick march!' she rapped, pointing up the cliff, and the girls went, obedient and barefoot, in front of her, towards The Feathers. The naked girls hobbled painfully, urged on by frequent cracks of Miss Boulter's whip to their bare shoulderblades, and when they lagged, she would cane each naked bum with a single, sharp swish from the crook. They were scratched and sweating and bruised by the time they arrived at the back door of the pub. The front door, Miss Boulter explained, was locked.

Inside the dimly lit lounge, the arrival of the naked cortége was greeted with polite applause, all the more menacing for its mildness. This was no whooping Saturday night crowd. Drinks were sipped, and cigarettes and cigars were smoked, with the quiet decorum of a gentleman's club, except that no gentlemen were present. Behind the bar, Angela Jones presided, her hair peroxided and a Marlboro Light dangling at the corner of her lips.

She wore a pair of spiked black stilettos in patent leather, fishnets and sussie belt, a pair of black rubber gauntlets, and a black rubber carnival mask with apertures for eyes, nose and mouth. Otherwise, she was nude: clusters of golden rings festooned the nipples of her massive, bare breasts and the pierced clips of her cunt, with its hillock freshly shaven. Strapped at her pubis was a huge, black dildo of gleaming rubber.

Her customers – or guests – were draped in languid poses, although some sat at the bar. They were in two groups: femmes and dominas. The femmes were dressed in schoolgirl uniform, or frilly, frothy civvies, short skirts and flouncy petticoats, knickers and stockings in pastel hues. Some femmes, however, were nude, their necks on dog leashes held by smiling dominas. These femmes were attired either on the Boulter or Angela Jones model or in flowing gowns of black, clinging latex, or bra and panties bristling with studs and spikes. Some dominas wore simple prefects' uniforms and blue stockings, even though they were not current Quirkeans.

High spike heels were de rigueur for most, though some of the nude femmes perched at the bar were hobbled in heavy leaden boots attached to shackles which bound their waists and held their wrists behind their backs. Others crouched on all fours. Many had clamps fastened or pierced on their cunt-lips, with chains attached.

One nude femme was intricately spangled in piercings to nipples, cunt-lips, navel and arse-bud, all connected by interlinked chains. Her hair was cut in a shaggy gamine style and her bare bum was livid with welts. Sandra recognised her as Miss Swain, quivering under casual cane-strokes from the rubber-clad Miss Tate.

The kneeling femmes were fed drinks by their

dominas, like kittens, their bare buttocks being rewarded with cane-smacks if they dribbled or spilled. Sandra thought Miss Swain dribbled on purpose. Some of the dominas in bra and panties wore strap-on dildos of black rubber, the shafts sculpted in the erect position. The largest dildo belonged to the gum-chewing Cerise Purley, who leered, and flexed a riding-crop, as the gang hobbled into the lounge, especially at Sandra.

There was no music save the lazy crack of whip on bare skin, and some of the antique decorations, which Sandra had admired on her previous visit, had come alive. A nude girl shivered in stocks at the foot of a gibbet, from which her hair was pulled and suspended while a whip lashed her shoulders. The whip was wielded by Miss Gordon. The bare shoulders belonged to the hapless Tolliver. Susan Fanshawe's flogged buttocks bounced luridly in a dim corner.

Zena Lambton, nude save for heavy clamps on nipples and quim, was riding a rail, the sharp, iron bar wedged between her bruised cunt-lips, while Miss Crisp, attired in a bridal gown of flowing white rubber, birched her bare buttocks. The girl groaned and balanced precariously, her feet anchored to the floor in heavy lead hobblers. Otherwise her cunt took the whole weight of her body on the rail.

Sandra recognised others, but not Tara Devine, or Miss Long. Many females were masked like Angela. One submissive was completely sheathed in a rubber catsuit, with an opening only for her nose and the buttocks and teats left bare. Her bum-cheeks were forced apart by a grappling-hook, and a lighted candle was poked in her anus, the wax dripping on her exposed bumhole. The cleft of her arse was a solid river of wax.

Her nipples were pierced and clamped with heavy safety pins. She was wrapped and chained to a pole like a roasting spit, with her arms pinioned in a strait-jacket, also of rubber, beneath which her clamped breasts jutted. Stripes were laid at whim by a masked woman in a spiked, rubber bikini, either on the quivering buttocks, or on the breasts, with sharp undercuts from a short scourge of three canes bound specifically for that purpose. Both her buttocks and breasts were deeply wealed and crimson.

There was little small-talk, other than terse instructions – 'Bare up, girl!' – as though all were participants in a masquerade. Most of the illumination was reflected light from the nude girls' bodies. There was a TV monitor, showing silent clips of previous videos, as Sandra had seen in the rubber room, these with Angela as a nude, studded vixen.

Angela watched enthusiastically as her filmed self wielded cane or whip, and, over the bar, the video camera whirred quietly, its red eye twinkling. Miss Boulter invited her gang to perch on bar-stools, still chained. Angela served them gin and tonics, offering her pack of Marlboro Lights. Sandra helped herself with a shy smile.

Sitting chained and nude with a gin and tonic and a cigarette soon seemed the most natural thing in the world, and The Feathers the most natural location. Predators – female ones – lustfully eyed her nude body as though she were on the meat rack. All in all, The Feathers seemed like any other south coast pub on Saturday night, and Sandra began to play up to the ogling women, preening and pouting and crossing her legs as she would do in a pub full of blokes. Miss Boulter strutted as though in charge and even Angela deferred to her. The cash register was not in operation.

'When you have finished your drinkies,' she said pleasantly, 'you'll be prepared for the Miss Nude Flagellant contest. It has been decided that Sandra Shanks is to win, for the good of the school, but there must be a show of competition. Cerise Purley has generously agreed to take a dive, as we say in boxing, in

257

return for the pleasure of taking part in Sandra's preparation.'

Sandra looked uneasily at Cerise's riding-crop.

'I say!' cried Sharon, 'That's hardly fair, Miss –'

She was silenced by a hard slap across the face from Angela Jones's gauntlet.

'Look,' said Audrey.' Sandra's bum has had enough. Take me instead; I don't mind.'

Her head was rocked by four slaps to the face from Angela.

'You are a foolish tease, Audrey,' said Angela. 'You know very well that for a true flagellant, there is no "enough". To the uninitiated, even a dozen stripes is horror, but to a proper girl – a Quirke's girl – a dozen times a dozen is not enough. The human bottom is very resilient, once the mind and nerves accept the necessary joy of chastisement. It is a question of pausing: a set of ten on the bare in quick pace is terrible, but one hundred stripes, with intervals of, say, four, or even eight minutes between sets, is a crescendo of sensuous pleasure. The extras – the restraint and bondage, even the supreme humiliance of tar and feathers – are icing on the cake. Stripes are its sugar.'

Like Gloria Harness, 'Miss J' seemed proud to recite the Quirkean creed.

'The board of governors is to adjudicate,' said Miss Boulter, 'and Miss Nude Flagellant will not be just the best-striped bum, but the juiciest all-round bum. There will be a preliminary striping of thirty, then a day in a chastity belt, then an inspection for the first award of points. After that, the contest will be one of endurance to see whose bum shows to best advantage under new stripes. Points will be given for beauty, endurance, poise and elasticity.'

She patted Sandra's pertly perched buttocks.

'The slut Shanks is, in my opinion, the front runner on all counts. We want a good contest, albeit one where

258

the outcome is certain. Ladies from the discerning and specialised media will be there, and the huge profits from video sales will –'

Sandra put her hand up.

'Permission to speak, Miss?'

'Permission granted.'

'Have you considered Matron's interest. She is your co-sponsor, isn't she?'

Miss Boulter laughed and pointed to the rubber-sheathed woman in the strait-jacket, who was moaning as her naked parts were caned by the domina in the rubber bikini.

'Matron has come round to my way of thinking,' she replied.

Suddenly, Angela touched a switch, and a spotlight played on the little stage at the far end of the lounge, illuminating the sobbing figure of Zena Lambton riding rail. Her flogging ceased, and she was pushed to all fours, to be led, nude, back into the lounge, rubbing her sore bottom and pussy and whimpering.

Miss Boulter handed Angela her stockwhip and was given a thin, rattan cane in exchange, under half an inch wide, but over three feet in length: a 'stinger'. Into the spotlight, a frilly French maid escorted a schoolgirl in full uniform with white, tight blouse unbuttoned to show her bra cups, black stockings and a pleated skirt, short enough to show the sussies and knickers. The schoolgirl's head was fully sheathed in a pixy hood of black latex, from which only her eyes and nose peeped. Over her hood was strapped the same gasmask that Sandra had worn in Gloria's rubber room.

Under the smoky glass, the eyes were wide and scared, yet lustfully curious. Miss Boulter stepped into the spotlight and the frilly maid bent the masked schoolgirl over the rail still gleaming wet from Zena's come-juice. The schoolgirl was obliged to touch her toes, with the bar biting into her pubis, forcing her to

259

tiptoe. Her frilly knickers of white but well-soiled cotton were unceremoniously pulled down to reveal the bare globes of her arse.

Then she had to step out of her stained, damp panties, and her ankles were splayed to be cuffed by the French maid to the base of the rail. The buttocks and thighs were stretched apart until they quivered with the strain, and exposed the dripping lips of her cunt, as well as her bright, wrinkled anus pucker. Her hands now hung straight in front of and below her, touching the floor.

'You are guilty of extremely bad behaviour,' intoned Miss Boulter, 'and I sentence you to a public striping of twelve with the rattan cane. The slightest quiver or squeal earns a repeat of the stripe. The only exclamation you are permitted is assent to the propositions I put to you. And there will be extra punishment for fouling yourself with fluids, whatever their source. Understood?'

'Yes, Miss,' the girl replied, her whisper muffled by her pixy hood and gasmask.

The big, pale buttocks were pure, mottled with the merest flush. Any previous stripings were long past. The Bolt's teats quivered as she lifted her cane, then, with a sharp exhalation, brought the wood down on the girl's raised, bare fesses.

Thwack!

The girl's bum shivered slightly, but she made no sound.

'You are a worm, aren't you? Unworthy to wear Quirke's uniform.'

'Y-yes, Miss Boulter.'

Thwack!

Again, the schoolgirl took the stripe in silence, but her breath was harsh, amplified by the gasmask.

'You are a filthy slut who likes to suck cock,' observed Miss Boulter.

'Yes, Miss.'

Thwack!

At the third stripe, her buttocks clenched, and she began to shake her head from side to side, but still without sound. Angela touched a switch, controlling the lens of the video camera, which zoomed in on her striped, bare bum-cheeks.

'You wank off, thinking of all the cocks you've sucked, don't you?'

The schoolgirl hesitated, before agreeing to this monstrous slur, and she was too late. As she began to speak, the cane lashed her hard in centre bum.

Thwack!

'Repeater of the third, for hesitation! Answer truthfully: you wank off, don't you, imagining all the big, stiff cocks you've sucked and all the spunk you've swallowed.'

'Yes, yes, Miss,' stammered the schoolgirl.

A rivulet of come-juice glistened, dripping from the spread lips of her cooze, and her clit was visibly stiffening. At the whistle of the cane, her fesses clenched in anticipation of the stripe.

Thwack! Thwack! Thwack!

Three stripes came in rapid succession, the last one an upender taking her in the arse-crack, the cane's tip striking the anus bud. The girl's head flew from side to side and up and down and her buttocks, at last, began a helpless squirming.

'Repeater of the sixth, for fidgeting,' said Miss Boulter.

Thwack!

The cane lashed her arse-cleft again and the nates clenched furiously. She stifled a sob and did not cry out.

'How often do you wank off, Miss?' the Bolt asked.

'Oh, all the time, Miss.'

Thwack!

'Repeater of the sixth, for vagueness.'

261

'Oh! Mm, I think, mmm . . . Oooh . . .'

The girl was trying to disguise her gasps of pain as part of her reply.

'Oh! Mm! Every day, Miss, I masturbate at least once a day!'

Thwack!

'Seven! Where do you masturbate, Miss? What chamber do you soil?

'Ahh . . . in the bog, I mean the WC, Miss Boulter.'

'In the presence of other girls? Details, please.'

Thwack!

'Oh! Yes, Miss, I love to show them my gash and frot my clitty while they watch and let them spank me on the bare as I wank off, Miss, and I tell them what a slut I am and how many cocks I've sucked,' the schoolgirl wailed, in a broken sob.

The buttocks were well and cruelly striped now, with the whole skin of the bum deeply mottled and streaked in purple. The fesses quivered, as though about to weep.

Thwack!

'Tell us what you tell the girls, as you wank off in the bog . . .'

'I tell them about all the big, stiff cocks I've licked and sucked, and how I love to be buggered and fucked by two different blokes, and take a third in my mouth, and squeeze the cocks with my bum and cunt till I milk all the hot cream, and suck and suck till the come spurts from his knob, and I swallow every drop as the blokes spurt in my holes.'

Thwack!

'Repeater of the ninth, for using slang.'

Sandra's own cunt was awash with come-oil at this juicy beating and she saw that Angela, and most of the dominas, were eagerly masturbating, while the tethered, nude femmes had gleams of fluid on their thighs and gash-flaps. The naked fesses of the schoolgirl writhed in an eerie dance, despite her efforts to stifle their squirming.

Thwack!

'Do you wank off other girls, too, and listen to their smut?'

'Yes, Miss. Oh! Oh! Yes! Oh . . .'

The schoolgirl screamed, then sighed in her distress, and at last the flogged bare buttocks leapt into a furious wriggling.

'Repeater of the tenth, for blubbing and squirming without permission.'

Thwack!

The repeater took her full in the arse-cleft, and the girl's body jerked rigid, her head arched back in a silent scream.

'Which girls?'

Thwack!

'Oh, all the girls, Miss. We all love to wank each other off and spank each other's bums, and taste our come-juice dripping from our twats.'

Thwack!

'Repeater of the eleventh, for vagueness. Which girls, exactly?'

'Oh . . . Oh . . . All of them, I swear!'

Thwack!

'Repeater of the eleventh, for dissembling. Which is your favourite girl? The one you wank off when no one else is looking?'

'Oh! Oh! Oh!'

The schoolgirl's striped fesses shuddered as the sobs choked within her gasmask. The lens of the video craned greedily forward like a heron to catch every wriggle of her bare buttocks in sensuous close-up. And suddenly, the girl moaned aloud and peed herself, a golden stream hissing from her cunt and sprinkling her feet and thighs.

Thwack!

'Repeater of the eleventh, again, for foulness,' Miss Boulter said severely. 'Whom do you diddle the most?

Who is your favourite for wanking off, you slut? Stephanie Long?'

'I . . . I mean. Oh, Miss . . .'

The girl's feet trembled in her lake of pee. Miss Boulter handed the cane to the frilly maid and received a strap-on dildo, which she fastened around her waist. She stood over the flogged girl's spead arse-cheeks and thrust the rubber appliance into her anus, making the schoolgirl jerk violently.

'Oh! Ouch! That hurts, Miss!'

Angela pressed a switch and the video screen showed a tall, buxom young lady in prefect's blouse, stockings and skirt, supervising the disrobing of a nervous fledge. Behind her in scholar's gown stood the headmistress, a younger Miss Isobel Quirke, her arms folded as she supervised the chastisement. The tall prefect had a lush mane of jet, black hair and wore a striped school prefect's tie, pushed up by her jutting titties under her tight, white blouse. She held a cane in her left hand, a thin 'stinger'. In her right hand she held a smouldering cigarette.

She proceeded to cane the fledge on the bare with the girl bent over in position. They seemed to be in a chamber equipped with sanitary facilities. The fledge took over twenty stripes with the prefect's cane and her bare bum was whipped raw and red.

Miss Boulter jerked her hips and, with a savage thrust, sank the dildo right to the root the schoolgirl's anus to begin a vigorous buggery. The lounge of the Feathers echoed to coos and sighs as the dominas masturbated more and more lustfully and the Bolt slammed her dildo harder into the girl's squirming, raw bum. Come-oil flowed from the buggered girl's cunt and the Bolt reached below her and began to wank her off, kneading the stiffened clitty with her fingers.

In the video monitor, a naked male entered the picture, his giant cock already fully erect. Without ceremony, the prefect ordered the flogged girl to kneel on all fours, and directed him to straddle her, and he did so. The huge, fleshy shaft of his penis slid smoothly into her gaping bumhole and he began to bugger her vigorously. The headmistress's hand slid under her skirt and she rubbed her cunt in blatant frottage.

'You don't just wank off, do you? She buggers you too.'

'Yes, Miss. Oh, yes! Oh, I didn't know you would ask so much ...'

'But you prefer a man's cock? Even to my *obispos*?'

'Yes, Miss,' the schoolgirl sobbed, as her buttocks quivered under the fierce anal fucking and the ridges of her welts writhed like purple worms on her skin.

The scene on the TV screen had changed. Now the naked male had moved to the junior girl's head, and she was sucking the cock which had buggered her, while the prefect, resuming caning her wealed arse-globes, had her skirts up, revealing herself knickerless and wanking off. The headmistress masturbated vigorously and came, as the male jerked in spasm and his cream spurted all over the kneeling girl's lips and chin, while her throat made swallowing motions. The filmed prefect delivered her final stripe, but did not yet masturbate to her own climax.

The Bolt's hand tweaked the buggered schoolgirl's clitoris with contemptuous ease, and suddenly the girl howled and shuddered in a come. Then the Bolt withdrew the dildo from her anus with a loud plop and unfastened it. She herself began to masturbate, teasing her clit with the dildo's bulb and fucking herself in the cunt, all the while twisting her loins for the video camera's telephoto lens.

Miss Boulter's cunt was wide open as she fucked herself, and her clitty was stiff and glistening as her cooze dripped with come-oil. The vigour of her masturbation matched the vigour of her buggery of the

265

schoolgirl, and the dripping dildo clearly had an extra prong for clitoral stimulation of the wearer. It took only a few flicks of thumb to nubbin before she gasped in her own climax, her cunt a lake of come-oil.

'Ahhh . . .' Miss Boulter moaned in her satisfaction, then retrieved her cane.

Thwack!

'That's your dozen. Who bums you and wanks you off? Stephanie Long?'

'Oh! Oh! Ahhh . . . yes, Miss, yes! It is Stephanie!'

Thwack! Thwack! Thwack!

The girl cried aloud, and her buttocks now squirmed uncontrollably.

'Three repeaters of the twelfth, for . . . for sneaking!' said the Bolt. 'Punishment over.'

The flogged schoolgirl, sobbing, was freed from her ankle cuffs and helped to rise. Her thighs glistened with her copious streams of pee and come-oil. She was made to wipe up her piss before being allowed to put on her sopping panties again.

On the video monitor, the naked, whipped fledge was now manhandled by the prefect and the naked male. Adhesive tape was applied to her nose, lips and eyes, and the headmistress shaved her head completely bald with barber's electric shears. A rubber tube was inserted in her mouth, and she was immersed in a large bathtub full of black, oily liquid, until only the breathing tube was visible. The liquid frothed as she squirmed in her tar bath, then she emerged, steaming, and was rolled on the floor of the chamber, now strewn with tiny, white goose feathers, until she was fully covered.

In the video, the adhesive tape was removed from the tarred and feathered girl's face. She curtsied, and her chastisers saluted her, with the school prefect lifting her skirt to expose her naked loins, and finally masturbating herself to come as, sucking on a cigarette, she gloated over the girl's feathered nudity. The school prefect was clearly recognisable as Angela Jones; the naked male bugger was Timmy Boulter. The tarred and feathered fledge was Miss Timothea Boulter herself.

At that moment, the front door of The Feathers opened at the turn of a key, and a male figure, clad in black biker's leathers, entered the lounge. He smoothed back his Elvis hair-lick and smiled, then began to unfasten his heavy, studded belt.

'Thank you, Miss Boulter, for my just striping, and my just buggery,' whimpered the freed schoolgirl as she curtsied, and her eyes, moist behind her mask, met Sandra's, as though begging her not to tell. The eyes were Miss Isobel Quirke's.

18

Beauty Queen

Vip!

Cerise's vicious riding-crop made Sandra clench her bum-cheeks rather more than she had intended.

'Ouch! That hurt!' cried Sandra.

'It was meant to,' said Cerise.

Vip! Vip! Vip!

'Did those hurt?'

'Oh! Bitch! You know they did,' Sandra gasped.

'Just wait till you feel my *obispos* in your hole,' said Cerise smugly.

'That comes later,' Angela Jones interrupted. 'Striping first – a tenner on the bare from one and all, with nice long pauses – then we'll test her bum for elasticity . . .'

Sandra was helpless. She wore only stockings, sussie belt and her spiked collar to hold her head up. Her belly was secured to the bar by a thick, leather corset. Her legs were splayed wide – and her ankles secured – by cuffs at the skirting-board; her feet were hobbled in Spanish boots, and her wrists pinioned to the bar in clamps, which looked like bottle-openers. Whips and other instruments of her agreed chastisement were arrayed on the bar, for her eyes. Audrey had seen to Sandra's bondage.

'It is jolly decent of you to take all our stripings for us,' she said, 'even though I know it's to win Miss Nude Flagellant.'

Cerise's tenner was over, and Sandra was given a rest of eight minutes for her smarting to subside. Then it was Miss Crisp's turn. She used a small, crackly birch which made Sandra's bare buttocks shudder at each stroke. Her flushed face dripped sweat, and Angela mopped her brow with a Carlsberg beer mat. Angela was right: a beating could be prolonged, and endured indefinitely, by a determined flagellant, given proper pauses.

Over the next two hours, Sandra took one hundred and ninety strokes on the bare, with cane, birch, tawse and four-thonged quirt. She cried out only at strokes to her exposed anus bud, which were frequent. Her welted bare bottom was a lake of molten pain.

After each set, she was allowed a smoke and a gulp of strong gin and tonic. The spotlight played on Sandra's nudity, and she felt all alone in her pain, but oddly comforted. It did not matter that her flogged bottom writhed in anguish or that she bit her rubber mouthpiece to shreds, just as the whips shredded her bum-flesh. They knew she would blub and wriggle and pee herself, which she did three times. They wanted her to. She had been offered the choice, later, of cunt-fucking, but insisted on bumming, to achieve optimum elasticity for the beauty contest. Complete shame is no shame, she thought.

One of the dominas dressed as a prefect was the first to bugger her, using Miss Boulter's strap-on, and fucking her anus over one hundred times. Sandra's cunt was gushing with come-oil from her beating and, as the hard rubber penetrated her bumhole, she flowed in a torrent. Then it was Angela's turn.

Her buggery was fiercer, and Sandra writhed and sobbed, yet the hard bummng made her clitty throb and her soaking cunt pulsate. After that, she was arse-fucked by a succession of dildos, all of them ecstatically painful, and all of them bringing her nearer to orgasm, as the come-juice of her buggers trickled down her thighs and stockings. When it was Cerise's turn, Sandra was granted permission to be wanked off, as it was cruel to excite her otherwise. Audrey masturbated her efficiently, as Cerise arse-fucked and spanked Sandra's raw bottom. Sandra came with a shriek of pleasure.

At last, she felt hard, male hands caress her buttocks, and knew that Timmy Boulter was straddling her. She gasped as his huge knob plunged ruthlessly into her anal shaft, feeling suffocated by his size, the throbbing male flesh far bigger in her bumhole than the toughest dildo. Timmy began to bugger her, and her sphincter reacted, squeezing and milking his cock, but he laughed.

'I am programmed not to come without Miss B's permission,' he said, as Sandra's belly writhed on the bar, wet with her pee and come-juice.

He smelled of leather and engines; Sandra worried that her stockings might stain. Suddenly, Timmy withdrew and moved behind the bar, placing his glans at Sandra's head. Eagerly, she took the bulb between her lips, then the engorged shaft, sucking it deep inside her, while her tongue licked the glans and peehole. Timmy's cock was replaced in her anus by his twin's dildo, worn by Miss Boulter herself.

Her bumming was Sandra's hardest yet, making her bum jerk as she sucked the huge cock and felt the kneeling Audrey's tongue flicking on her throbbing clitty. At this gamahuching, she came again almost at once, clamping Timmy's cock between her lips until he grunted and a jet of cream spurted at the back of her throat. The massive engine bucked like a stallion in her mouth as she swallowed every drop of the creamy come.

Suddenly, the lounge door was unlocked, and a woman in the uniform of an auxiliary police constable, complete with truncheon and handcuffs, shone a torch inside. It was Miss Pottinger, and beside her, smirking righteously, stood Stephanie Long.

'Grounds for arrest, I think, Miss Pottinger?' she said. 'Keeping a bawdy house . . .'

'This is a party on private premises,' retorted Angela, 'and you are trespassing.'

'Lewd and immoral purposes,' said Miss Long. 'Grounds for foreclosure of your mortgage, I think, Miss Jones.'

'What –?'

'The entire Quirke's estate, as if you didn't know, is mortgaged to English Channel Properties Ltd, of Guernsey,' said Miss Long. 'Which happens to be a wholly owned subsidiary of Long Investments SA, of Aruba, Netherlands Antilles, holder of the title deeds. There are no grounds for foreclosure on the school, as long as the mortgage payments are made. Licensed premises are a different matter. Depraved usage justifies repossession.'

She gazed at Sandra and the hulking nudity of Timmy Boulter. She turned her eyes from his cock, blushing.

'However,' she gulped, 'I would be satisfied with a *nolle prosequi,* if the principal miscreant is delivered up to the authorities for chastisement. I mean Miss Sandra Shanks. It is plain from the state of her posterior and orifices, that she has been the instigator of moral turpitude and deserves the ultimate chastisement.'

'Tell me, Miss Long,' said Angela, 'how long is it since your bum tasted the cane?'

'Really!'

'Or cock?'

'My tastes are seemly, Miss. When I become headmistress, I shall cleanse the school of all impurity.'

Timmy Boulter rose, as did his cock, and now Stephanie was presented with his shaft fully stiff and glistening with Sandra's saliva. She gazed, transfixed.

'Isn't this what you really want?' murmured Timmy.

'Enough!' Stephanie screamed, her face livid. 'Deliver me the miscreant Shanks, and the rest of you may continue to wallow in filth.'

'Miss Long wishes to tar and feather me, don't you, Miss?' Sandra said.

'That is the ultimate chastisement,' hissed the prefect. 'The tar takes a month to disperse and the feathers a month to shed from the skin's natural accretion. During that time, the featheree must submit to stripes at whim, until her bottom is lashed clean.'

'Then, if that will settle the matter, I gladly consent to my punishment,' declared Sandra. 'Release me, please, Audrey, and I shall accompany Miss Long.'

Miss Boulter was pale with rage. She grasped her twin's cock and pointed it at Stephanie, as though the peehole's eye would hypnotise her. Stephanie gasped.

'No!' she cried, turning her head. 'Miss Shanks will accompany me, and Miss Pottinger as witness. No beauty contest for this slut . . .'

Sandra was obliged to remain hobbled and nude, save for her soaked stockings, as Stephanie took her leash.

'My thanks, Audrey,' Stephanie said mischievously, and Audrey looked away.

Sandra was led through the pre-dawn mist, down the path to the beach. They climbed to The Gash. The opening was now sealed by a heavy metal door, which Stephanie unlocked and swung open. They entered the cave and squeezed through into the bumhole, where the oiled machines of chastisement lay awaiting their victims.

Long and Pottinger manhandled a large boulder, and a third cavern was revealed, also dimly lit, and stinking of tar. A metal door was set into the rock and Stephanie unfastened the padlock. Sandra was led inside and saw a cavity in the floor the size of a bathtub, full of black, steaming tar.

'It was brought to the boil some hours ago,' said Stephanie, 'so it should be warm now, Sandra. How lucky I am to have such a loyal, informative slave as Audrey.'

Sandra said nothing as Miss Pottinger ripped off her underthings, and released Sandra's feet from their hobblers. Her neckchain stayed. Miss Pottinger briskly sheared Sandra's tresses with a cut-throat razor, then took a battery shaver and shaved her stubble. She applied the razor to her armpits, legs and pubis until Sandra gleamed like an eggshell. Both her captors donned strawberry-coloured rubber gloves.

A rubber tube was placed in her mouth and sealed with vinyl tape, then her nose and eyes were taped too, and her cunt and anus filled with orthodontic gel. They lifted her by the armpits, and Sandra felt her toes dip into the warm, reeking tar. Then she was speedily lowered in up to her neck. A lead weight was clipped to her neckchain and she sank immediately under the surface.

She lay, unable to move, immersed in the treacly, hot liquid. She could no longer smell, and it felt both sticky and oily at once. Her wealed bottom smarted abominably. Sandra imagined herself to be a worm, cosily floating in the primeval soup of evolution.

At length, she was hauled up by her leash, the lead weight requiring two lifters. She stood, steaming and dripping tar, on a carpet of goose feathers.

'She'll give no trouble now,' said Pottinger as Sandra was released to stand with her head bowed, completely naked, her vinyl tapes and gel fillings still in place.

The rubber gloves eased her to the floor, and she was rolled back and forth until her sticky body was sheathed in feathers. At last, she was allowed to rise, and her bum and cunt plugs were removed, then the tape. She felt her shaven, feathered skull, then looked down at her body, and cried out in astonished delight, which her captors took to be distress. They returned to the bumhole, and her captors laid Sandra on the rack, to which she was tightly and uncomplainingly strapped. Stephanie began to turn the winch.

'You'll be glad to hear I've had this fixed,' she said. 'I'll come and release you after the Miss Nude Flagellant contest. Do try not to mess your feathers.'

273

Sandra's eyes moistened, and she whimpered as the rack stretched her.

'Enough,' said Miss Pottinger in a concerned voice and, with a growl of displeasure, Stephanie desisted.

'Don't expect your smutty friends to rescue you,' she snarled. 'I'm locking you in.'

'I'm only worried about stripes for missing roll-call, Miss Long,' Sandra said.

She heard the doors slam shut, and the locks click, and, though her limbs shrieked in agony, she fell into an exhausted faint. After a while, she heard fumbling noises from the tar-room, then hammers, and Angela Jones's naked breasts entered the cave, followed by Angela herself.

'Have you out in a jiffy,' she said, releasing Sandra from the rack.

Behind her came Audrey, Sharon and Julie, with blankets and soup. Sandra stood up and rubbed her feathered muscles.

'That is my secret passage,' said Angela, gesturing to an aperture in the roof of the tar-room. 'What a bitch that Miss Long is!'

Sandra preened and rubbed her feathers, enjoying her friends' awe.

'Thank you for sneaking, Audrey,' she said. 'It was always you, eh?'

Audrey nodded guiltily.

'I knew about the title deeds and mortgage and everything,' she said. 'Miss Long found out and said that unless I became her slave, and sneaked for her, she would have me expelled. She's always wanted to be head, and make Quirke's unbearably lesbian. I suppose I deserve a horrid striping, don't I, Sandra?'

Sandra hugged her and promised her the whopping of her life.

'Except she is not as lesbian as she thinks,' said Angela tartly. 'Did you see her gawp at Timmy's cock?

Never mind, have some hot soup, dear, and cover yourself.'

'Are you crazy?' said Sandra, ruffling her feathers like a swan. 'Never mind soup and blankets. Why didn't you bring me a mirror?'

Sandra watched from the bushes as fourteen flogging-stools were set up beside the boxing ring on the hockey pitch. Each stool enabled the chastisee to kneel, with her ankles fastened in cuffs – built into the stool's base – and the thighs separated by a bar to keep them, and the buttocks, wide apart for caning. The miscreant's belly was supported by a cushion, and the stool curved upwards in an arc, also cushioned, with breast-cups. Her arms were shackled to the sides, so that she had the choice of holding her unsupported head high, or letting it droop. If a girl fainted, the stool and bondage would keep her safe in her inert position, as it kept her secure for her flogging. Directly under the pubis, the cushion narrowed in a rubber groove.

The Miss Nude Flagellant Contest was to coincide with the boxing final and to take place while the judges retired to deliberate. The bout was between Miss Timothea Boulter and Miss Stephanie Long. The girls had the day off classes, and were dressed in best uniforms, as the fourteen flagellants were led out to their flogging-stools. Miss Quirke, splendid in gown, mortar-board and black stockings, read the roll, imperiously noting the absence of Miss Sandra Shanks.

'Ready, Sandra?' said Gloria Harness.

'Yes,' said Sandra. 'I'll know the right moment. And thanks for putting me up and seeing to me. It feels funny to be bare bum, when all the rest of me is downy.'

Sandra preened and blushed as her feathers rustled.

The fourteen contestants were ordered to shed their skirts and knot their cardigans and blouses up high under their bras, on this bright, chill autumn day. They obediently stripped, and showed fourteen croups encased in thick, rubber chastity belts. These were ceremonially unlocked by Matron and Miss Boulter. Matron was attired in her prettiest white rubber uniform, and Miss Boulter resplendent in prefect's blazer, striped tie and a skirt whose short pleats left her sussie belt and stocking-tops – and the narrow thong of knickers – well on view. Despite the evacuation holes, the two sponsors wrinkled their noses at the stained garments, which they carried to a laundry basket, to be wheeled away by a smiling French maid: Miss Timmins, apparently reinstated in Matron's affections.

The ladies of the press clustered with cameras and tape recorders, and were clad scarcely less dramatically than Angela Jones at the Feathers ladies' night. Gloria whispered that they represented specialised papers like *Spanking Review* and the *Lesbian Times*.

Bottoms bared, the contestants knelt at the flogging stools, and the school prefects strapped them down for punishment. The cushion of each stool touched the pubic bone, raising and spreading the buttocks, so that the anal and vaginal regions were open to view and defenceless against a cunning 'upender' cane-stroke.

The board of governors were introduced as judges. First was a sprightly lady in her mid-fifties, impeccable of dress and stature. She wore a long, black gown, hat and veil in the Dior New Look of the 1940s, and was applauded on being introduced as Miss Isobel Quirke. Gloria whispered that she was the grand-niece of the original Miss Quirke, the founder, and had flown from her villa on Mykonos. She got more applause when a breeze flounced her dress: between her blue, silk sussie belt and stockings, she sported a knickerless silver-grey bush, and a firm croup, delicately striped with pink.

Next was Angela Jones, her hair dazzling peroxide, wearing a clinging strapless tube frock, with a total absence of underthings. Gloria whispered that, as a condition for 'going quietly' as head prefect, Angela had accepted a governorship and the lease of the Feathers.

The third governor was the current Miss Quirke, the headmistress, and the fourth was Margaret Betts, dressed as a Quirke's schoolgirl, her blazer, pleated skirt and shiny blue stockings impeccable, and her white blouse stiffly starched over jutting breasts.

'The cheeky cow!' Sandra exclaimed. 'She tricked me into enrolling at Quirke's . . .'

'Are you sorry?' asked Gloria, and received a blush in reply.

The judges inspected the bare bottoms which were striped from their thirty the previous morning. Sandra recognised Sharon's, Julie's and Tara's bottoms, but Audrey's was not on view. Neither she, nor Gloria, remarked on this.

After their first bare bottom inspection, the judges wrote in their notebooks, and then the four school prefects stepped forward with three-foot rattan stingers. The headmistress explained that each contestant would take sets of six, the time elapsing, as the prefect passed along the line, giving the bottoms time to settle for the next striping. Miss Long took the first caning, efficiently delivering a sixer to each naked bottom, and making its owner strain against her bonds at each stripe after the third. Tara strained in her bonds from the very first cut.

As soon as Miss Long had finished, Miss Cream repeated the canings, then Miss Gordon, and finally Miss Bustard. All the contestants were squirming vigorously and sobbing, and the headmistress reminded them they were free to abandon the contest at any time. No one did. There was a pause for coffee, served by the French maids, while the chastisees sobbed uneasily, lapping from saucers. The ladies of the press buzzed with excitement, and Sandra overheard requests to sample 'baring up below'.

Each girl had taken twenty-four stripes with the

whippy stinger. Now it was time for the thicker and longer rattan. The pres caned in the same order as before, and the purpose of the runnels in the flogging-cushions became apparent, as Tara all of a sudden peed, her stream of golden fluid hissing safely down the rubber channel into the grass. As if on cue, each squirming girl had pissed by her beating's completion.

Elevenses with cream buns were now served, as the contestants were left to ruminate on their forty-eight stripes. The judges inspected the flogged bums, with fingers probing bumholes and encouraging remarks spoken into the sobbing girls' ears. The founder's relative showed her lips and chin to be enthusiastically smeared with cream, and applied a playful gobbet to Tara Devine's bum-crack. Sandra said this was favouritism: Julie should by rights be the favourite, and indeed, her welts were almost as fine as Sandra's own.

The morning continued, the flogged girls' increasingly frisky bottoms darkening with criss-cross stripes. By lunchtime, each girl had taken twenty-four stripes with stinger, twenty-four with heavy rattan, twenty-four with the cat of studded thongs one-and-a-half feet long, and twenty-four cuts of the birch, fresh birches being provided for each set, a mere six hard stripes denuding the instrument completely. As her naked bottom squirmed under the birch, each girl pissed herself long and copiously. Sandra looked at Gloria. They both blushed and the two voyeurs silently wanked each other off to gasping comes.

After ninety-six stripes, the flagellants were inspected for elasticity: each judge donned strawberry-coloured rubber gloves and thrust her forefinger into the girl's anus.

'Been buggered a lot: a bit much slack.'

'Nice springy bumhole, juicy welts.'

'Stripes vividly, good rubbery anus.'

278

'Grips well . . .'

Sandra noticed that she and Gloria were not the only masturbators.

The atmosphere for the boxing final was tense. The flagellants were released and led away for robing by Matron. They returned in scanty, silky corselets, complete with stunningly high heels, fishnet stockings and tight sussie belts. The merest whisper of a thong covered the crotch, so that the buttocks and mounds were almost bare, save for the tight string in the arse-cleft. They were to be judged for poise and deportment.

Miss Boulter and Stephanie entered the ring, not nude, but clad for modesty before the cameras in spangled leotards, which left most of their bums and teats bare. Both girls had their hair down. The spectators leaped into the air, and even climbed piggy-back to crane, thus obscuring Sandra's view. There were whoops and cheers, groans and thwacks, and the sound of a belt on bare bum. It seemed from the cheers that Miss Boulter was getting the worst of it. Momentarily, the throng parted, and Sandra saw her, slumped and battered in the grass, her hands clutching her crotch. Stephanie stood triumphant over her wielding Timmy's studded belt, with which she had thrashed her rival's buttocks.

'Learned your lesson, slut?' she hissed.

Suddenly, Boulter leaped nimbly up and, disdainfully flicking her hair, rubbed her wealed, crimson buttocks. The crowd gasped as she peeled off her leotard, and stood with naked chest: not the Bolt's big teats, but a male's bulging pectorals. The leotard came off and Timmy Boulter threw away the steel crotch-guard to stand nude before the outraged Stephanie, who paled as she saw Timmy's cock stiffen completely. The elder Miss Quirke watched on tiptoe, licking her lips. The air was magic.

'No, you fucking dyke,' said Timmy, 'it is time for your lesson. On your knees!'

'No . . . no . . .' moaned Stephanie, unable to take her eyes from the huge male organ.

Gradually, she approached, stripped off her leotard and, nude, sank moaning to her knees. She gave up her belt and, as Timmy began a vicious striping of her naked buttocks, Miss Long wailed in despair and plunged the bulb of the cock into her mouth.

She began to suck furiously as the belt rained weals on her squirming bare and, as Timmy increased the vigour of his beating, the lesbian took the full shaft of his cock into the back of her throat and began to masturbate her clitty, her gash open between spread thighs. Timmy waited until she had wanked herself off to a come, and after a good sixty lashes with his belt, he discarded her, moaning and sobbing, to lie in a crumpled heap on the grass, while the real Miss Boulter, nude herself, entered the ring and ceremoniously pissed on her rival's face, then sprinkled her naked teats and cunt. The crowd was entranced.

Miss Boulter knelt and sucked Timmy's cock in obeisance, then turned to crouch with her buttocks spread. His cock entered her anal passage; after six rapid thrusts, the cock slamming the anus right to his balls, Timmy came with a jet of spunk so powerful that it spurted from Timothea's hole and gleamed like pearls on her thighs.

Timmy held up his twin's arm and pronounced her champion. At that moment, Miss Timmins sounded the gong to indicate judgement time. Timmy seemed to disappear, and everyone crowded round Miss Boulter to celebrate her astounding victory, some, including the reporter from the *Lesbian Times*, rubbing their eyes in disbelief. Meanwhile, the fourteen contestants lined up in a row, bums facing the judges. Sandra prepared to rise, but Gloria restrained her. The headmistress was flustered.

'It seems we have a tie,' she said, 'with equal points

between Julie Down and Tara Devine. The contest shall therefore be decided by a stripe-off, that is, a flogging continued until one of the two contestants withdraws.'

Both girls defiantly regained their stools.

'Now!' hissed Gloria.

Sandra stood up and walked right up to the headmistress, to whom she curtsied. The crowd hushed.

'Sandra Shanks, reporting for roll-call,' she declared.

'I believe,' she addressed the elder Miss Quirke, 'that a featheree enjoys certain school privileges, such as lateness for roll-call.'

'Why, yes,' said the mature lady, with an impish smile. 'And another thing; in my great-aunt's day, a featheree was exempt from all tuition fees for the period of her adornment. And if she chose to submit to regular feathering, why, she could enjoy free tuition indefinitely, and save a fortune in hair spray. I know I did. So that is why you have discontinued the practice, Head-mistress: stinginess!'

The current Miss Quirke had the decency to blush, and stammered that there was no one to confirm such information, to which only the head prefect would be privy.

'But,' Sandra said, 'the head prefect is present.'

The crowd parted as Sandra marched to Audrey Larch and held her arm.

'Here is the head prefect of Quirke's,' she declared. 'True or not, Audrey?'

'True, Sandra,' said Audrey, blushing. 'Gosh, and I was having such a lovely time!'

Suddenly the nude Stephanie Long burst forward and, with one jerk, ripped open Audrey's blouse and bra, exposing her naked breasts.

'Liar!' she cried. 'Where is the head prefect's brooch?'

Sheepishly, Audrey lifted her skirt and reached inside her panties, lifting her left leg as she poked inside her bumhole. She emerged with a glistening, strawberry-

281

coloured condom, and removed a golden brooch in the shape of a school cane, which she shyly pinned through her pierced right nipple. Stephanie Long wailed and sank to her knees, sobbing and clutching Audrey's shoes, and saying she was sorry.

'Pardon is up to the headmistress,' said Audrey, also addressing the elder Miss Quirke. 'Though who the headmistress will be tomorrow is uncertain. In Quirke's tradition, once the identity of the head prefect becomes public, there must be a general assembly to appoint new ranks. Am I right, Miss?'

'Quite right,' chortled the elder Miss Quirke, evidently enjoying herself.

Gloria Harness now stepped forward and said that Miss Nude Flagellant had yet to be declared, and that she proposed the fledge Miss Sandra Shanks.

'Very well, but most irregular, Gloria,' said the headmistress, with a rueful grin.

Sandra's well-striped buttocks were minutely scrutinised – and her anal passage probed to the root – by each judge, and then Sandra meekly suggested that it would be no fair contest unless she, also, took her ninety-six stripes. This was agreed. Miss Timmins was sent to organise a buffet luncheon, and some ladies of the press were heard exclaiming they were sure to pee themselves, watching such a lovely bum squirm. Miss Crisp went in search of fresh birches.

The feathered, nude body of Sandra Shanks was strapped to a flogging-stool, and, as he afternoon wore on, her buttocks jerked and wealed. Her stripes mounted, Miss Boulter having replaced Miss Long among the caners. Sandra sweated, and pissed herself three times, as her flogged, bare bottom writhed under cane, cat and birch. When her ninety-sixer was complete, Sandra was cheered and unanimously declared Miss Nude Flagellant.

She heard a click and the noise of a video camera

packed in its case, and then the thrum of a motor-bike engine receding into the distance. The ladies of the specialised press clustered round her, firing cameras and questions.

'How do you feel?' asked the bespectacled lady from the bi-monthly *Flagella*.

'Sore,' replied Sandra, 'and proud to be a Quirkean. Now, if you don't mind, I have to go. I mustn't be late for tea or I'll earn a striping.'

19

Shanks

Three fledges of Quirke's school waited nervously outside the new headmistress's study, attended by a French maid in uniform.

'I'm not used to stripes,' said one. 'I'm awfully nervous.'

'I'm nervous too,' said the second, 'but I know I deserve them.'

'Six, perhaps?'

'Or maybe a niner?'

The French maid clutched her bottom and made a face, mocking them.

'Well, let's bare up below,' said Audrey Larch. 'All girls together, eh?'

The trio was bade enter. A long sofa stood where, before, had been an armchair. The headmistress greeted them warmly and said they should get straight down to business. She said there were some changes in the caning rules: sixers and niners were replaced by dozens, eighteeners or two dozens.

'Quirkeans are a hardier breed nowadays,' she said, 'as my own nates can testify. A triple private striping is also new, and you fledges should feel honoured. Now, you will please assume the position.'

The girls bent over the sofa, necessitating their standing on tiptoe, and raised their pleated skirts. The French maid in rubber, instead of the usual satin, solemnly lowered their knickers to expose the bare croups. The headmistress studied the naked globes, flexing her whippy rattan stinger.

'You two for eighteen,' she said, 'and you, Miss Larch, for twenty-four. I rely on you to set a good example, Miss Larch, and show the new fledges how a Quirkean takes stripes. I promised you the whopping of a lifetime for sneaking – after your two dozen – but for these two worms, in view of their inexperience, I have limited their stripes to eighteen.'

'Please, Miss, I am frightened of the cane,' begged the first girl, her bare bum already shivering over her lowered knickers. 'I am awfully afraid I might pee myself.'

'A normal reaction,' said the headmistress, 'although it earns an extra six.'

The headmistress extended her forefinger to examine each anus for gum. She spent a long time probing the elastic holes, and said that on the advice of the former matron – the French maid nodded coyly – the girls of Quirke's would henceforth undergo regular anal and vaginal inspections to determine their fitness for more intriguing punishments than the cane. Public stripings would also be grouped in threes and the subjects flogged standing, naval style, and completely nude, save for shackles and restraints. Stripes would be taken on bare back as well as buttocks, with a minimum of twenty-four. This would increase the pain, and the deterrent effect of the spectacle, and the new regime of nudist days, for all staff and girls, would ensure that no stripes went unnoticed.

'Ooooh . . .' moaned the first fledge. 'I don't know if I could take it, Miss.'

'Then let's find out, shall we?' said the new headmistress brightly, as her cane lashed Stephanie Long's bare buttocks.

Vip! Vip! Vip!

She whopped the three bare bums in smart succession.

Vip! Vip! Vip!

'Oh! Oh! ' cried the two new fledges.

'Repeaters for you both, of the second stripe, for blubbing,' said the new headmistress.

Vip! Vip!

The two bare bums clenched as thin crimson welts streaked their pale nudity and the girls gasped. Audrey's bare shivered too.

Vip! Vip! Vip!

The striping continued, broken only by muffled sobs or the vocal advice of repeaters. The French maid watched avidly and her fingers crept to the split crotch of her panties. She began to masturbate at the sight of squirming girls' bottoms. Both the new fledges peed themselves at the thirteenth and fifteenth stripes respectively. By the end of the lengthy caning, Stephanie Long had taken thirty-three, Audrey twenty-nine, and the other fledge thirty-five, counting repeaters. The new fledges were ordered to clean up their pee with their own panties before donning the wet garments, while Audrey was not permitted to rise.

'You bared up awfully well, girls,' said the headmistress as the girls shifted in their sopping knickers. 'I trust, Miss Cardew, that the introduction to the cane on your fesses has been suitably chastening.'

'Y-yes, Miss Shank – I mean, Miss Quirke,' stammered the former headmistress. 'When I was matron of Cardew's, my father's school, I always knew I wanted to be headmistress and disciplinarian. Then, when Gloria Harness was sacked for her beastliness with Timmy Boulter, I wondered if I shouldn't follow her . . .'

'And as for you, Miss Long, have you learned your lesson?'

'I needed bare-bottom caning to take me down a peg,' said Stephanie, blushing.

'You two are further sentenced to five days' frilly maid service for fouling your knickers,' said the headmistress. 'You may not change or remove your knickers in that time, except for major evacuation, and all visits to WC must be supervised by a prefect. Report to Matron, Miss Boulter, for a preliminary anal examination.'

The new headmistress of Quirke's school, formerly the fledge Miss Sandra Shanks, was left alone with Audrey Larch in position for caning.

'Stand up, Audrey. I promised you the whopping of a lifetime,' she said, 'for your beastly sneaking, without which I shouldn't be here today.'

'Yes, Sandra.'

'You address me as headmistress! Even if it's only till tomorrow,' said Sandra.

'Oh! So soon! But who shall be headmistress then, Headmistress?'

'You shall find out, Audrey, tomorrow. My husband Ray is coming home. I've been dreaming of that big, hot cock of his. I don't care how many little fucking machines he's serviced, I want him in my furry, brown holes. You are the lucky one, Audrey. How long have you been Mrs Timmy Boulter?'

'Oh, ages, ever since I was a biker's bitch. I used to like convoy-fucking, but Timmy was special. He knew I needed regular caning. So here I am, a Quirke's lifer . . .'

'And now it is the whopping of a lifetime for you. Please assume position.'

Gravely, Sandra handed her the rattan stinger, still hot from the girls' bums, then raised her scholar's gown and her pleated skirt to reveal her knickerless bottom and a pair of hold-up black stockings clinging to her thighs, without sussies.

'Before I resign as headmistress, Audrey, I order you to give my bum the whopping of a lifetime. I choose "twangs".'

'But you are not wearing any sussies to twang.'

'How remiss of me! I dare say the only thing to do is cane my bare bottom until that twangs . . .'

Audrey raised her cane as, above them, the video camera whirred.

Thwack!

Sandra Shanks gasped, then sighed blissfully as her naked bottom clenched at the first stripe of her farewell caning by the future headmistress of Quirke's school.

It was a bright autumnal day, warm enough to swim, as Sandra Shanks returned home. She took a taxi to Sedgedean, then walked along the clifftop path, happily acknowledging the ogling at her frilly French maid's costume in delicate latex, her teetering stilettos and sheer, cropped head dazzling with white feathers. Through the peephole in her hedge, she saw two bodies on the grass by her patio, the male naked, and the female in dishevelled schoolgirl's uniform with skirts up.

The male upended the female and gave her a strong, bare-bum spanking, of well over one hundred, and then, as she squealed and wriggled in delight, he entered her cunt from behind and began to fuck her vigorously. Before them, a TV set flickered with a video. Sandra silently climbed through the hedge and made her way to her house.

'Hello, Ray,' she said shyly, hands clasped at her crotch, and carrying her small case.

Ray looked surprised, then leered. He did not stop fucking Margaret.

'And you, Margaret,' said Sandra, as Margaret Betts writhed in her fucking. 'I'm afraid I'm interrupting and I suppose I'll get a bare-bum caning for it.'

'That is for your master to decide,' Margaret gasped, masturbating her clitty as Ray's huge cock slammed in her wet cunt. 'Although I would decree three dozen, or more, if he deems your intrusion shameful. Not to mention your conduct in his absence.'

On the video, Sandra's bare croup writhed over the bar of The Feathers.

'Shall I prepare myself for punishment, Master?' she said to Ray.

'Yes, slut.'

'Very good, Master.'

Sandra went indoors and stripped naked, except for her stockings and sussies and her perilous stilettos. Then she collared herself, clamping her nipples and quim-lips to the chain, and returned on all fours to hand the leash, and a rattan stinger to her husband. From her case, she took a heavy, rubber chastity belt, ready for his next absence. Continuing to fuck Margaret's cunt, Ray began to cane Sandra on the bare.

'You'll be whopped regularly, Sandra, now I know what a slut you are,' Ray said as he striped her squirming, bare fesses. 'You'll be my caged bird, naked and chained, while I whip obedience into that slut's bum of yours . . .'

'At your command, Master,' gasped Sandra as the cane bit her bare fesses.

He looked lustfully at the rings on her pierced nipples, cunt-lips and arse-cleft, and the little butterfly tattoo above her clitoris.

'I'm rich, Sandra: I bought a Thai rubber factory. I can afford a slave.'

He gave her a packet, brightly labelled SHANKS. Inside was a row of transparent wrappers containing strawberry-coloured condoms.

'Thank you, Master,' gasped Sandra, as her bare bum smarted, making her cunt and nipple rings jangle. Her gash was flowing with come-juice, wetting her stocking tops.

'Your arse is gnarled like teak,' Ray said approvingly.

'Thank you, Master. The cane has taught me to obey.'

Ray fucked the masturbating Margaret Betts to a

289

noisy come, then withdrew and ordered Sandra to roll a condom over his throbbing cock with her mouth. Then he ordered her to spread her cheeks for an arse-fucking.

'Yes, Master,' said Sandra, and obeyed. She opened her anal passage and retrieved the strawberry condom containing her head prefect's brooch, which she proudly pinned through her pierced and clamped right nipple. Sandra grinned shyly at Margaret Betts, and then gasped as her husband's cock sank to the root of her furry brown bumhole. Her lips and tongue began to gamahuche Margaret's gaping, wet cunt and throbbing clitty.

'All girls together,' murmured Sandra Shanks joyfully.

NEW BOOKS

Coming up from Nexus, Sapphire and Black Lace

Discipline of the Private House by Esme Ombreux
January 2000   £5.99   ISBN: 0 352 33459 2
Jem Darke, Mistress of the secretive organisation known as the
Private House, is bored – and rashly accepts a challenge to submit to
the harsh disciplinary regime at the Chateau, where the Chatelaine
and her depraved minions will delight in administering torments and
humiliations designed to make Jem abandon the wager and relinquish
her supreme authority.

The Order by Nadine Somers
January 2000   £5.99   ISBN: 0 352 33460 6
The Comtessa di Diablo is head of the Order, an organisation
devoted to Mádrofh, demonic Mistress of Lust. Tamara Knight and
Max Creed are agents for Omega, a secret government body charged
with investigating the occult. As they enter the twilight world of
depraved practices and unspeakable rituals, the race is on to prevent
the onset of the Final Chaos, the return of Mádrofh and the ushering
in of a slave society over which the Comtessa and her
debauched acolytes will reign supreme.

A Matter of Possession by G.C. Scott
January 2000   £5.99   ISBN: 0 352 33468 1
Under normal circumstances, no woman as stunning as Barbara
Hilson would have trouble finding a man. But Barbara's
requirements are far from the normal. She needs someone who will
take complete control; someone who will impose himself so strongly
upon her that her will dissolves into his. Fortunately, if she can't find
a man to give her what she wants, Barbara has other options: an
extensive collection of bondage equipment, an imagination that
knows no bounds, and, in Sarah, an obliging and very debauched
friend.

The Bond by Lindsay Gordon
February 2000   £5.99   ISBN: 0 352 33480 0
Hank and Missy are not the same as the rest of us. They're on a ride
that never ends, together forever, joined as much by their increasingly
perverse sexual tastes as by their need to satisfy their special needs.
But they're not alone on their journey. The Preacher's after Hank,
and he'll do anything to Missy to get him. The long-awaited third
novel by the author of *Rites of Obedience* and *The Submission
Gallery*.

The Slave Auction by Lisette Ashton
February 2000   £5.99   ISBN: 0 352 33481 9
Austere, masterful and ruthless, dominatrix Frankie has learnt to
enjoy her new life as mistress of the castle. Her days are a paradise
of endless punishments and her nights are filled with cruel retribution.
But with the return of her arch-enemy McGivern, Frankie's haven is
about to be shattered. He is organising a slave auction in which lives
will be altered forever, and his ultimate plan is to regain control of
the castle. As the dominatrix becomes the dominated, Frankie is left
wondering whether things will ever be the same again.

The Pleasure Principle by Maria del Rey
February 2000   £5.99   ISBN: 0 352 33482 7
Sex is deviant. Disgusting. Depraved. Sex is banned. And yet despite
the law, and the Moral Guardians who police it, a sexual underworld
exists which recognises no rule but that of desire. Into this dark world
of the flesh enters Detective Rey Coover, a man who must struggle
with his own instincts to uncover the truth about those who recognise
no limits. Erotica, science fiction and crime collide in one of Maria
del Rey's most imaginative and explicit novels. A Nexus Classic.

A new imprint of lesbian fiction

Getaway by Suzanne Blaylock

October 1999   Price £6.99   ISBN: 0 352 33443 6

Brilliantly talented Polly Sayers had made two big life shifts concurrently. She's had her first affair with a woman, and she's also stolen the code of an important new piece of software and made her break, doing a runner all the way to a seemingly peaceful coastal community. But things aren't as tranquil as they appear in the haven, as Polly becomes immersed in an insular group of mysterious but very attractive women.

No Angel by Marian Malone

November 1999   £6.99   ISBN 0 352 33462 2

Sally longs to test her limits and sample forbidden pleasures, yet she's frightened by the depth of her yearnings. Her journey of self-discovery begins in the fetish clubs of Brighton and ultimately leads to an encounter with an enigmatic female stranger. And now that she's tasted freedom, there's no way she's going back.

BLACK
lace

Doctor's Orders by Deanna Ashford
January 2000   £5.99   ISBN: 0 352 33453 3
When Dr Helen Dawson loses her job at a state-run hospital, she is delighted to be offered a position at a private clinic. The staff at the clinic do far more than simply care for the medical needs of their clients, though – they also cater for their sexual needs. Helen soon discovers that this isn't the only secret – there are other, far darker occurrences.

Shameless by Stella Black
January 2000   £5.99   ISBN: 0 352 33467 3
When Stella Black decides to take a holiday in Arizona she doesn't bargain on having to deal with such a dark and weird crowd: Jim, the master who likes his SM hard; Mel, the professional dominatrix with a background in sleazy movies; Rick, the gun-toting cowboy with cold blue eyes; and his psychotic sidekick Bernie. They're not the safest individuals, but that's not what Stella wants. That's not what she's come for.

Cruel Enchantment by Janine Ashbless
February 2000   £5.99   ISBN: 0 352 33483 5
Here are eleven tales of temptation and desire, of longing and fear and consummation; tales which will carry you to other times and other worlds. Worlds of the imagination where you will encounter men and monsters, women and gods. Worlds in which hermits are visited by succubi and angels; in which dragons steal maidens to sate special hungers; in which deadly duels of magic are fought on the battlefield of the naked body and even the dead do not like to sleep alone.

Tongue in Cheek by Tabitha Flyte
February 2000   £5.99   ISBN: 0 352 33484 3
When Sally's relationship ends everything seems to go wrong for her – she can't meet a new man, she's having a bad time at work and she can't seem to make anything work at all. That is, until she starts hanging out around the local sixth-form college, where she finds the boys more than happy to help out – in every way.

Nexus

NEXUS BACKLIST

All books are priced £5.99 unless another price is given. If a date is supplied, the book in question will not be available until that month in 1999.

CONTEMPORARY EROTICA

THE ACADEMY	Arabella Knight	
AMANDA IN THE PRIVATE HOUSE	Esme Ombreux	
BAD PENNY	Penny Birch	
THE BLACK MASQUE	Lisette Ashton	
THE BLACK WIDOW	Lisette Ashton	
BOUND TO OBEY	Amanda Ware	
BRAT	Penny Birch	
DANCE OF SUBMISSION	Lisette Ashton	Nov
DARK DELIGHTS	Maria del Rey	
DARK DESIRES	Maria del Rey	
DARLINE DOMINANT	Tania d'Alanis	
DISCIPLES OF SHAME	Stephanie Calvin	
THE DISCIPLINE OF NURSE RIDING	Yolanda Celbridge	
DISPLAYS OF INNOCENTS	Lucy Golden	
EMMA'S SECRET DOMINATION	Hilary James	
EXPOSING LOUISA	Jean Aveline	
FAIRGROUND ATTRACTIONS	Lisette Ashton	
GISELLE	Jean Aveline	Oct
HEART OF DESIRE	Maria del Rey	
HOUSE RULES	G.C. Scott	Oct
IN FOR A PENNY	Penny Birch	Nov
JULIE AT THE REFORMATORY	Angela Elgar	
LINGERING LESSONS	Sarah Veitch	

THE GOVERNESS AT ST AGATHA'S	Yolanda Celbridge		
THE MASTER OF CASTLELEIGH	Jacqueline Bellevois		Aug
PRIVATE MEMOIRS OF A KENTISH HEADMISTRESS	Yolanda Celbridge	£4.99	
THE RAKE	Aishling Morgan		Sep
THE TRAINING OF AN ENGLISH GENTLEMAN	Yolanda Celbridge		

SAMPLERS & COLLECTIONS

EROTICON 4	Various		
THE FIESTA LETTERS	ed. Chris Lloyd	£4.99	
NEW EROTICA 3			
NEW EROTICA 4	Various		
A DOZEN STROKES	Various		Aug

NEXUS CLASSICS
A new imprint dedicated to putting the finest works of erotic fiction back in print

THE IMAGE	Jean de Berg	
CHOOSING LOVERS FOR JUSTINE	Aran Ashe	
THE INSTITUTE	Maria del Rey	
AGONY AUNT	G. C. Scott	
THE HANDMAIDENS	Aran Ashe	
OBSESSION	Maria del Rey	
HIS MASTER'S VOICE	G.C. Scott	Aug
CITADEL OF SERVITUDE	Aran Ashe	Sep
BOUND TO SERVE	Amanda Ware	Oct
BOUND TO SUBMIT	Amanda Ware	Nov
SISTERHOOD OF THE INSTITUTE	Maria del Rey	Dec

Please send me the books I have ticked above.

Name   ....

Address   ....

              ....

              ....

              .... Post code.........................

Send to: **Cash Sales, Nexus Books, Thames Wharf Studios, Rainville Road, London W6 9HT**

US customers: for prices and details of how to order books for delivery by mail, call 1-800-805-1083.

Please enclose a cheque or postal order, made payable to **Nexus Books**, to the value of the books you have ordered plus postage and packing costs as follows:

UK and BFPO – £1.00 for the first book, 50p for the second book and 30p for each subsequent book to a maximum of £3.00;

Overseas (including Republic of Ireland) – £2.00 for the first book, £1.00 for the second book and 50p for each subsequent book.

We accept all major credit cards, including VISA, ACCESS/ MASTERCARD, AMEX, DINERS CLUB, SWITCH, SOLO, and DELTA. Please write your card number and expiry date here:

....

Please allow up to 28 days for delivery.

Signature ....